The Kixing

Frank Graves

Author - Frank Graves

THE KIXING

Published by Frajil Publishing

Website: www.theancestraltrail.com

Copyright Frank Graves 2000

ISBN 978-1-873133-08-8

The characters and situations in this work are entirely imaginary and bear no relation or any real person or actual happening

Book Kindly Edited by Ray Rohrbach

"THE KIXING"

by

FRANK GRAVES

CHAPTER ONE

The group of five watched the lights of Christine's vehicle reach the corner at the top of the road, turn left and disappear, the man built like the proverbial privy brick wall turned to his companions.

"About a half an hour for her to get home before we move, you guys check around to see if there's any way these mothers can possibly get past us." The leader said softly in his slight Italian accented voice.

The shadowy cover of darkness soon engulfed the two moving quickly away along the pavement to the far side of the of the property, one man in his late fifties was short, balding and had a chilling clown-like infectious smile that seemed to stretch from ear to ear, he looked a very unlikely sort of person to be heavy handed. The other, seemed more to fit the part, he was tall, his thickly-set bared arms covered completely from wrists to elbows with an assortment of weird and wonderful tattoos, The group leader together with the two remaining companions returned to their parked Land Cruiser to await their given moment. It was only once all five had again checked the tools of their unsavoury trade, did Antonio give the signal that it was time to move. He always felt most comfortable with his trusty revolver neatly tucked into a shoulder holster, the other two sported sawn-off shotguns while the short man following a little way behind, carried a spiked jemmy metal bar that now rested on his shoulder.

"You cover the back of the house, watch for any dogs, we know he has at least one and we don't need any slip-ups so, get them first." Antonio ordered.

Two men moved cautiously around the house until they reached the kitchen window, one carefully ducked low moving on all fours below the windowsill to cross to the other side. He straightened up and cautiously peered into the well lit kitchen, standing at the stove across the room with her back to the window was what he thought was a young servant or cook, beckoning to his companion they continued slipping past each window in similar fashion making certain that there were no further signs of movement from within the rest of the downstairs rooms. Having circled the house they then met up with the tall man circling from the opposite direction.

"Servant girl in the kitchen."

"There's one female and a child watching television in the front room."

"Pity… Where's the man?"

"Don't know, he's definitely in there somewhere."

"He's upstairs maybe, so if we move quickly we will quickly gain his attention, no matter where he might be hiding right now." They made their way towards the front door, the tall man laughed quietly and cruelly.

When all were in their appointed places the short man carefully inserted the metal bar between the framework of the front door, the tattooed man propped his double barrel shotgun against the wall and grabbed hold of the end of the bar with both hands. The two looked towards Antonio for the signal to move, he withdrew his revolver and nodded. Both men heaved simultaneously at the metal bar, a loud ripping crunch split the silence as the heavy wooden door at first resisted giving way then with another wrenching effort, the rock-solid looking door splintered and gave way, springing loose from its unyielding timber door frame. The door flew back and reaching the end of its travel, crashed solidly into a table, something fell and smashed to the floor as the tattooed man grabbed at his sawn-off shotgun and hastily followed the others straight into the house. Beyond the timber panelled entrance hall, the leader momentarily paused, looking to his right he could see the wide-eyed youngster turning to face him. He nodded his head, the tall man sped up the stairway to the floor above while the stocky man moved quickly into the lounge to attend to the wide-eyed occupants. The woman remained frozen to the spot, the man tried reassuring them with a smile yet placing a finger before his mouth.

"Shoosh."

He moved straight to the woman and firmly placed his hand across her mouth and threateningly lifted the metal bar above his head to demonstrate he meant business. He had done this several times before and by now knew the signs well, she was more likely to be the type that would remain quiet before suddenly letting out a frantic scream once full realisation had struck home and what was happening to them. He certainly didn't want, or need that distraction right at this moment.

"Where's your father?" He hissed, the words spitting from his mouth venomously. He raised the bar higher to indicate that he would have no qualms in striking the boy's wide-eyed mother.

"C'mon, otherwise she gets it."

"I-In the s-study," blurted the boy.

"What the fuck…" Suddenly all hell broke loose, the door at the far end of the hall opened, two black and brown dogs streamed into the passageway straight towards Antonio who was the closest target to their line of attack and quite unprepared for this sudden intrusion.

"Kill!" Antonio spun, hastily letting off a shot that missed its mark; the leading Doberman went straight for his gun arm and sank its teeth firmly into its mark. The larger dog, a huge German Rottweiler leapt forward going for Antonio's unguarded back. Peter Edwards filled the doorway of his study, baseball bat in hand and ready to strike. The short man grabbed the boy, pulled him towards his powerful frame and lifted the jemmy as if to strike.

"Stop!" His shout was to attract Peter's attention, the Doberman immediately turned and baring its fangs, step by step started moving menacingly towards its young master in mortal danger from this short trespasser. It snarled softly, its fangs drooled showing that it meant to use them to protect its owner. Antonio in the meantime was face down trying to protect himself being shaken like a soft toy puppet by the huge Rottweiler that had embedded its teeth deep into the man's shoulder.

"Call them off, or else the boy's skull will be transformed!" The short man didn't need, or even like dogs, especially the vicious looking Doberman now stalking him.

"Attack! Kill!" Peter Edwards screamed. The dog immediately responded to the command, the short Italian pushed the youngster straight forward into the path of furious canine. The two collided, it momentarily threw the dog off balance and out of its stride, this momentary confusion lasted just long enough for the short man to react, this allowed him that split second to bring the iron bar down on the narrow head of the Doberman. It was not a clean strike but instead, glanced off the side of the beast's head.

"Shit!"

The Doberman yelped as it half fell, half slithered sideways onto the highly polished floor, rolling to one side but then, quickly got to its feet and rigorously shook its head in a manner indicated desperately trying to regain its senses.

"Attack!" Peter Edwards screamed again and the dog instinctively turned, the short man was bearing down, arm raised for the final coup d' grace. Moving intuitively from a standing start, the dog wheeled left springing straight towards its assailant's throat. The short man swung the iron bar in a wide arc, catching the incoming beast against its shoulder and sending it tumbling into and over a low table, the animal immediately came out of its battered position and turned to attack once again. This time the dumpy man was prepared for the next expected onslaught, he couldn't easily reach the dog because it now had the table between them as a barrier, this was sufficient time to weigh up its opponent and was even possibly considering its next move, the two carefully eyed each other. Unexpectedly, the boy flew from the floor where he had landed and straight into the short man.

"Please don't kill him!" The boy screamed, it broke that instant tension between man and beast and was just enough for the dog because the man having been slightly distracted, the Doberman seized its opportunity to react, almost flying through the air and taking the man's arm in its mouth, the combined weight of the beast carried forward by the momentum meant man, boy and dog, were all thrown off balance to the ground. The dog wasn't about to give the man a second chance, it was trained to kill as it bit hard and deep into the soft fleshy arm, the iron bar clattered to the floor.

"Call them off!" He couldn't have seen what was taking place in the lounge at that moment, the one who had been upstairs, hearing the commotion had come racing down the stairway stopping when halfway down. He only had a clear view of the entrance hall and was now aiming his shotgun straight at the small of Peter Edward's back.

The man could only partially make out what was happening beyond Peter and instantly realised that if he had tried to shoot either animal attacking his companions, he would probably injure or kill his prone accomplices.

"C'mon, call them off; otherwise you're going to end up being turned to fucking mincemeat!" Peter turned and faced the unexpected villain and very quickly became conscious that he was defeated, there were just too many bodies around his house to contend with on his own, they were also heavily armed.

"Rex! Down!" The Rottweiler reacted immediately; it came to the big man very pleased with itself for the protective work that had been put in to help the family. Antonio's right shoulder, thigh and cheek of his backside a mass of red where the dog's powerful jaws had torn at the intruder. He rolled over, pain and thunder etched his features.

"Kill that fucking thing." Peter moved forward slightly in an almost pathetic motion to protect his canine companion. It worked, suddenly the two that had been at the back of the house arrived in the hallway, the nervous young cook ahead of them, one immediately rushed to help Antonio while the other armed intruder, moved rapidly into the lounge recognising the short man's plight. The Doberman still frantically tore at the arm rendering it defenceless against this attacker, the second man instantly raced towards them and using the barrel of his sawn-off shotgun stock like a heavy club swung it in a controlled arc. The impact was heard by everyone as he slammed home his strike against the side of the beast's body, the heavy dull thud knocked the wind from the furious animal. He swung the weapon a second time catching the dazed Doberman full square against its head, the crunching blow would do for the beast, it dropped like a sack of potatoes exactly where it stood. In a single movement, he rotated the shotgun placing the barrel against the back of the animal's neck, it was all over for the valiant Doberman as its blood spattered across the carpet.

"Nooo!" The young boy screamed.

"Get in there!" The man on the stairway indicated to Peter and the young cook to move into the lounge, the Rottweiler jumped against his master for any sign of approval for what it had done, it was very pleased with itself. Peter lowered the baseball bat and moved around the still prone Antonio and crossed the lounge to the armchair where his wife was seated, still in frozen terror.

"W-what do they want?" She spoke for the first time.

"Shh." Peter raised a finger to his lips and tried giving her a tenderly reassuring look. His son sobbed uncontrollably.

"What's this all about?" Peter demanded.

"Shut up and sit down. Make sure that dog doesn't move and keep the brat quiet." The man pointing the sawn-off shotgun at the family ordered. Peter knew that if the weirdly tattooed man pulled the trigger now, they would all end up being hit because the shot spray would quickly spread outward from the moment it left the cut down barrel. His mind was furiously racing although inwardly he knew that they were helpless.

"Now Mr Edwards, let's get down to business. You messed with the wrong people and owe some friends of ours nine hundred thousand. They've tried to be reasonable, but you wouldn't listen and now the debt has been passed onto us and we're here to make sure the debt is collected. Either you pay up or we'll use more unsavoury methods on both you or your family ...the choice is yours." The words came from Antonio now propped against the door frame, his companion having used his belt as a tourniquet strapped around Antonio's leg.

"I...I told the party concerned to come and see me in my office tomorrow."

The Kixing

"We are here to collect from you, now. Where is your safe?"

"I don't have one."

Antonio nodded at the short man who had partially recovered from the attack, blood streamed from a massive tear in his arm.

"OK. You're sure that there isn't a safe in the place?"

"I told you there wasn't."

The short man kneeled over the Doberman and with several expert flicks with his knife cut deeply into the dog's head, turning to face the room, he opened his hand and revealed both bloody ears. Even through the suffering pain, a wonderful broad smile crossed his chubby features. Peter's wife screamed and the boy simply closed his eyes.

"Shut up!" The short man moved past them and dropped the dog's ears into the wife's lap, she looked as if she was about to collapse from paralytic fear.

"Now, Mr Edwards, let me ask you again and this time, we want the truth. Where is your safe? If you lie to me this time, it'll be your son who will find himself without ears." Peter's mind raced at a million miles an hour, it was his wife that suddenly changed his thinking, Antonio's statement had suddenly loosened her tongue.

"Peter... Tell them it's in the study, for god's sake, l-l-let them take whatever they've come for."

"Ah! Now we're getting somewhere. C'mon let's go and have a look what's kept there, you lead the way." Peter Edwards knew that he was beaten.

"Rex, Stay!" He felt emptily reassured that if anyone tried to touch his wife or boy, the dog would hopefully also give its life in an attempt to save them. He moved past the still form of the Doberman

10

and on through the doorway past Antonio who hobbled behind him. He went to the beautifully timber-lined study with its assortment of antiquated leather bound books covering two walls and pulled at one of them, a small section of shelving swung back revealing a wall safe.

"Open it up and then stand back," commanded the tattooed man who had followed them to the study. Peter did as requested, he noticed that when turning the tumbler dial of the safe that his fingers were trembling uncontrollably, the reason wasn't fear of the men standing behind him but rather, knowing what they were about to discover. Antonio, showing signs of terrific pain sat at Peter's desk ordered his companion with a nod, to examine the contents of the safe.

"Sit down there Mr Edwards," the tattooed man ordered, immediately taking everything from the safe and spreading the contents on the desk in front of Antonio.

"My, my; what have we here? Preparing for a fast getaway… Passports, traveller's cheques, bank drafts and this." Antonio turned the contents of a small bag onto the desk.

"Whew, that must be worth a fair amount. How much are they worth?"

Peter Edwards felt an icy blast pass through his entire nervous system. On the desk lay an entire fortune which had been filtered out of his failing company to reset up abroad. He knew that there was no way that he now could save his own construction business from folding so had steadily hidden away as much as he could. The contents on the desk were going to be used to start life anew.

"A… about two million," he replied.

"What about these?" Antonio lifted the traveller's cheques and bank drafts.

"Roughly the same."

"Okay. There's more than enough to cover your debt. You owe Johnson's a little over nine hundred thousand, right?"

"Not really but yes, I suppose so."

"Well, let's say nine hundred thousand, plus our collection fee of ten per cent comes to nine hundred and ninety thousand …another ten for the damage your dogs caused to my backside and the other guy makes it a round million. Right?"

"As you say, a round million." Peter's heart skipped a beat; the man was only going to take what was rightfully owed to them. A crook with honour he mused silently to himself.

"Right, sign over a million and for the trouble you caused…" He stared down at the pile of glittering diamonds. Peter felt his elation tumble, this was it, the rub.

"Also, to compensate us for extreme pain and suffering caused today, I'm going to relieve you of these," he picked out five perfect smaller yellow white diamonds and slipped them into his shirt pocket. Peter breathed a sigh of relief, they did have honour. "That all right with you, one for each of us and we were never here?"

"Sure, be my guest."

"Don't get shirty with me my friend, you're extremely fortunate that we are only relieving you of what is properly owed, we believe we are men of honour and not thieves, our payment is the ten percent included in the client's fee. Come on, get signing so that we can get out of here, this must be very distressing for you and your family and fortunately it would seem that you have the funds to cover your debt." Peter signed the necessary bank drafts in favour of Johnson Interiors.

"Thank you Mr Edwards. Now, we're leaving," he stood up and

moved in close, placing the blade of his knife against Peter's throat.

"Please don't kill me, take all the diamonds."

Slowly and deliberately, Antonio cut a thin furrow right along the right side of the man's jaw.

"Jesus!"

"Just a scratch Mr. Edwards. We will be taking the boy with us but …don't worry, that cut will always remind you what will happen if these papers aren't cleared for payment in the morning. It is also a present from me for the way you fucked around and treated one very refined lady."

"B-but…"

"No buts and no police. As security we keep the boy and once everything has been paid then he will be safely returned. But if… anything goes wrong, well, what can I say…" He left the menacing ending hanging loosely in the air like a puff of cigar smoke.

The tattooed man disappeared and they heard the wife's mournful scream.

"She's a real pain in the arse, but then again, most women tend to become far more emotionally upset than men do. You will have to comfort her Mr Edwards, only you know whether the boy will come to any harm or not. I want you to explain what's happening to him, no hysterics please, just the facts."

The tattooed man brought the boy to the study, Peter quickly told his son what was about to take place, the lad didn't cry, he simply seemed to accept the facts without hesitation. Peter thought his boy must still be in a state of shock at what the men had done to his Doberman.

"Until tomorrow Mr Edwards. We'll keep our word and look after the boy if you keep your end of the deal. It's only business you must understand."

They left, Peter watched the attackers and his son make their way down the driveway and heard the vehicle start up then saw the lights move away up the hill. He pulled a face, shook his head and turned back to the hallway.

"Don't panic, they won't harm him, hopefully it will all be over the morning, as soon as he's returned, we're leaving to start that new life abroad."

Silently he thanked his lucky stars, they had at least left him with about three million to achieve this aim, that bitch had warned him that she was not going to take this lying down and he had not heeded her warning.

"You and your bloody crooked schemes. If they as much as harm a hair of his head, you're dead ... I will personally kill you."

He shuddered to think what they would have done if he had harmed either of the twins in any way, so long as the heavies were true to their word and did nothing to his son then, possibly he had had a very lucky escape, it would probably be his own body now staining the lounge carpet. Peter took a large breath as he comforted his grieving wife. It was going to be a very long night to reflect the dismal failure of his business that had led to this evening's events. It was not his fault, the whole sorry episode was down to M H Group Holdings and that sophisticated bitch.

The Kixing

The Kixing

"THE KIXING"

CHAPTER TWO

Life has an insatiable peculiarity to either reward or desert mankind in random stages of our existence, some win, others lose but, always with consequences, especially the relinquished will always feel aggrieved that their role in the divine picture of our universe has been ill-timed.

"...One, and two, and three....." The moment of truth somehow always caused adrenaline to pump by the bucketful, he was still rapidly falling towards the ground when suddenly, the sound that every parachutist wanted to hear broke through loud and clear..."Whoosh!"...the parachute had released from his back pack and with a loud pop, silk material opened like a huge multi-coloured balloon above him. Paul checked upwards seeing attached lines untangling themselves like a spider's web, each led directly from his shoulder straps to the various points on the chute. He instinctively braced for the sudden stop always taken fully in the crotch by downward force into the harness. Completing part of the exercise, he concentrated on the large white marker at the landing point, carefully judging the distance and hoping that the eastern prevailing wind and his calculations were correctly computed. He had to allow for any surprise cross wind effects that would play a very definite part of his arrival, especially once he reached the last few hundred feet. Now, dead on target, feet together, Paul prepared himself for impact, at the last second swinging his body towards the centre disc, he hit the ground with a hefty thump automatically rolling over backwards up onto his feet collapsing the chute before it could drag him along the ground. Swearing, he turned to face his long time coach and friend who rushed in to mark the spot where Paul's foot first touched mother earth.

"Shit! Missed again, everything was right, the wind drifted slightly… It threw me off balance."

Jerry had spent weeks religiously helping Paul with his training, pulled at his cheeks making a face of trying to look totally disgusted.

"How many times must I repeat myself, it's you throwing yourself off balance, it's not the wind that causes it, now, get the gear together and try again."

"No," said Paul firmly "that's it, Let's call it a day, I must have a drink, I'm parched."

They stowed his gear and drove towards the white bricked flying club building in Jerry's beat up, open-topped Landrover which seemingly, was on its last legs and about to depart to that eternal junk-yard in the sky. Paul hated this journey, the vehicle seemingly having a mind of its own while somehow pretending to be a violent bucking bronco bouncing in all directions across the tufted grassy field, both men clung to the roll-bars for dear life.

After ordering his usual ginger beer and milk mixture, Paul found a seat near the large display windows, from here he could observe the comings and goings out on the airfield as well as those inside the club-house. His gaze drifted across the crowded lounge to see whether there were any fresh young things that could be chatted up, he had known most of the younger female club-members intimately at one time or another but, was always on the prowl for new conquests being aware that he was blessed with a certain magnetic attraction, he mentally tallied previous victims. Tracy made her way towards his table, turning to the window he quickly checked his reflection, ran his fingers through his unkempt hair, his handsome boyish look was the key which most females found irresistible. Waiting until the girl reached the table, he playfully kissed his own reflection.

The Kixing

"Hello beautiful lovely."

"Are you talking to me or yourself?"

"Myself of course," he teased. The casual but, smartly sophisticated brunette in her early twenties looked more like a skinny teenage model than a fully fledged woman, pecked him on the forehead.

"You conceited bastard, I wouldn't put anything past you," she remonstrated, this had been one of his latest conquests when they had recently met on the tennis courts alongside the clubhouse and now, her hazel eyes peered over the rim of her glass, she leaned back in her chair to emphasise the full outline of her small breasts as she carefully studied the man.

"Stone mad are the only words that spring to mind, no way would you get me diving out into space like that, the mere thought, scares me shitless, I've been watching you most of this afternoon.

."It's not dangerous."

"Oh no? It's a damn death wish, one slip and it's goodbye, ...gone, ...finito, with you and the only reason that I can think of for this silly sport is your male ego, anyway what made you take up that crazy sport?

"Tracy, Tracy... My darling girl, skydiving is the second best sensation in the world so how can you criticise something you've never tried yourself? You only understand why we do it, when and if you've mustered enough initial courage and then done it yourself." Paul's voice was tinged with suggested sarcasm, also knowing full well in the back of his mind that there was a time when he would have fully agreed with her. Now his thoughts drifted back some years, had it not been for Norman Minter's persistence, he would have probably still be too afraid to have made his very first jump.

The Kixing

"No way, Jose!" Insisted the young companion.

"It's funny... I once told Norman Minter the same thing, except in far more direct language."

Norman Minter was Paul's boss, a tall robust, no nonsense sort of person. Paul's eyes flicked away from his companion across the club lounge, his chairman was busily entertaining several guests at the far side of the room.

"I really don't know how the hell did I let him talk me into these madcap ventures?" He said softly to his companion as he remembered his negative reply all that time ago and how frightened he had been then but, inwardly knew he could never have said no to his single minded boss. His thought pattern was interrupted as Tracy-Anne Cicirelo carefully placed her glass on the table and winked at him, a wicked grin creasing her young face.

"Leave sky diving to the birds, it's their domain and as for me, I get my jollies from a different type of vaulting, that's my motto." she gave out a tantalising giggle "With my type of sportsmanship one can never get hurt by leaving any opening too late... can one?"

"I'll let you into a little secret, I often think that one day I will definitely leave the chute's opening too late, Until then, God, I love this sky-diving lark, you never know what will happen next but, I suspect that one day it will still be the death of me... C'mon let's go, I want to practice your type of exercise, what did you call it the other day?

"I called it chandelier athletics, who knows we could even enter into the Olympics in the future... but first, I think we should put in a lot of practice time before becoming professionals at that sport." They laughed, as he rose from his window seat he quickly glanced across the room, of all the things he had since experienced, that first parachute jump had to be among the most exciting moments of his life, he had been a rather timid individual up until then, now circumstances had changed and the one person he had to thank for his latent capabilities, was his boss and mentor, - mister Norman, …bloody, Minter.

"See you at the office tomorrow Norman." Paul called across the room

Norman Hilton Minter acknowledged Paul's departure with a friendly wave, he was busily holding court with friends around a large table festooned with food and drink. The dominating, dark-haired thirty two year old bachelor was also, chairman and major shareholder of the Minter business empire and fortune. The original company having been founded by John Minter, his grandfather in 1933 trading as a small hardware shop in the Gray's Inn Road in the city of London. The company's real wealth was acquired during the second world war when the store had grown at a fantastic rate due to the continued German bombing, by 1945 the company had outgrown itself and spread its wings to become one of the largest builder's merchants situated around London, due mainly, to the misfortune of others, the company had by then branched into demolition work since very few people had foreseen that wrecked buildings left standing could create tremendous hazards, it also provided Minter with free second-hand building material for use after the chaos. However, John Minter, was then nearing his sixtieth birthday and becoming somewhat frail, he handed the business over to his only son, also named John once he had been demobbed from the army in 1945.

John junior was still in his prime at twenty seven when war had broken out and although happy to do his bit for Britain, was glad to get home to the substantial changes in fortunes made by his father during his long absence. John senior was a wily old bird, his being there at the right time and place meant he was able to charge unrealistic rates for work and materials that very few of his immediate competitors seemed to have readily available. The small shop grew very quickly to become an empire with a fierce dog-eats-dog campaign to envelope most of the similar type firms throughout London. If any of their opposition fell on tough times, had financial problems or in need of capital to purchase materials or; could not get enough credit to handle large projects which had been created by the war, Minter Holdings quickly stepped in and with consummate ease and some clever manoeuvring, found themselves becoming the major shareholders of those unfortunate firms and so, the company grew extremely quickly.

This state of imbalance couldn't exist forever and the younger Minter knew it, both he and his father had suspected that there would be a financial killing to be made on the day that Britain declared war with Germany. He realised that with him being away his strong willed father and partner would be enough to create themselves into wealthy men by the time it was all over and so, he came home to take over the business, realising that even if Germany had won the war, he would have no qualms and would go with his new masters therefore, no matter how badly the political outcome, he was going to end up top dog when it had all ended. When war was finally terminated, the unexpected business results for the Minter family did something to John junior, it somehow gave him a new sense of understanding and the taste of power over his fellow men and moreover, turned him into a particularly greedy person.

John's financial respectability was shrouded by a thin veneer, his two passions being the business and his all encompassing love for the promotion of major fights in the boxing world. With these two strengths being used in tandem, he was now able to acquire anything, or anybody he wanted to, very often using very unconventional methods in achieving his ultimate goals. This particular trait was passed down the family line and inherited by young Norman well before his becoming the conglomerate chairman when his father suffered an untimely heart attack and died. During those early days, Minter Holdings Limited changed its name to become MH Group Holdings and Norman diversified the main investment company by creating a series of smaller satellite companies hidden under a corporate umbrella. Their product ranges expanded into manufacturing and supplying builder's merchants, contractors and the like with all forms of materials used within the construction industry.

Where Minter was very ingenious, was to allow targeted companies to extend credit from thirty days to as much as nine months in some cases and depending on their size, before MH Holdings would then suddenly clamp down on their targeted prey by insisting on instant repayment being made. Their debtors invariably couldn't pay and as a consequence were swallowed up into the conglomerate rather than legally having to shut the struggling company's doors. This sequence of take-overs continued right up to his death and was always carefully planned out and controlled. Norman had been carefully groomed into this world of hostile take-overs in order to eventually succeed his father's position in business, he too had also acquired a similar love for company raiding and boxing promotion as he was always kept informed of exactly how the older man operated and wasn't about to upset the successful system.

Having found a likely target, Minter dispatched young, hand picked business experts that were known as 'his soldiers' to go and investigate the complete structure of the firm without their knowledge that this was being carried out or that they were to become caught up within the MH honey trap. These soldiers would somehow infiltrate the company, talk to its competitors and find out everything from top to bottom about the targeted company. The operation was headed by a commercial lawyer who, in the early days had joined Minter straight from university. In each case, by the time Minter was ready to make his move, the little lawyer knew everything in minute detail. Then and only then, would he work on any obvious weaknesses, finding unreliable points that eventually lead to MH Holding's total control and manipulation of that firm. This practice had been tried and tested, Minter Holdings entered every aspect of the construction field which ranged widely from major property development down to manufacturing shower cubicles.

This is exactly the way that the well known shop-fitting company of Johnson Interiors Limited was now being caught out without even suspecting what sort of precarious position they were in. Their owners, Ernest and Christine Johnson were identical pigeon-pair twins that had pooled their resources almost a decade before. They had inherited a small inheritance sum from a distant relative's will and with that windfall had decided to go into business for themselves. At first, the small business concentrated on doing various carpentry repairs, glazing and general shop-fitting work but, as the years went by and their reputation for excellence spread, they extended the company by venturing into a complete gamut of projects such as furnishing supermarkets, petrol stations and the like and their company was now seriously being considered one of the leading firms of its kind throughout the London area. Nothing ever came easily and the business had a long hard struggle uphill to make the grade, this success had almost cost Christine her first marriage... and, her life. The twins had taken a gamble by continually investing all profits into new machinery which would help to prefabricate components in the workshop rather than on site. It was this calculated gamble that had paved the way and made them highly efficient and profitable, when large supermarkets came into vogue and started springing up around the country, they were all looking for a top company specialising in this type of operation and Johnsons were always geared up to accommodate their orders. This heavy investment also had drawbacks by having placed large financial burdens on their company to repay the banks, the business package was a two pronged fork because as an asset the business was a lot simpler to control than it had been before the machinery had arrived to simplify operations. The down side was that they had a fast growing order book which together with the automation had to somehow be regularly paid for. Johnson Interiors was a very tidy operation with its annual turnover being increased substantially as each year passed by. Unfortunately this growth also made significant demands upon their financial resources at the bank and was taking its toll, most of their suppliers were helpful and allowed them extended credit. Much of their spare liquidity was locked up in retention's, bonds and various other forms of inactive capital usage. Having grown and reinvested capital too quickly, meant literally a hand-to-mouth type existence and now, they were now experiencing a financial pinch. They handled this well and all available funds were used to purchase materials for the blossoming contract orders, but what nobody within Johnson Interiors realised at the time was that the majority of their purchases were being covertly channelled through various subsidiary companies of the MH Holdings Group. Nobody, not even Christine with her sharp mathematical thinking realised that all their credit was carefully being controlled and manipulated for an eventual hostile attack. of her company. Blindness to surrounding events lulled them into a false sense of security and the one thing everybody was aware of, was that without these generous amounts of credit facilities, the company would be struggling to maintain its rapid march forward.

The Kixing

"THE KIXING"

CHAPTER THREE

The whole sordid attack had started when Norman Minter sat at his massive leather bound desk, he pushed down the third button of the combination telephone intercom which was immediately answered by the distinctively precise voice of his personal assistant, Rhona Steel.

"Yes Knuckles?" Rhona was the only person, other than his mother to use this enduring term. His parents had always called him Knuckles or Norm, Rhona had picked up on the name, secretly John Minter had insisted in his will that she and she alone kept this tradition. As a rule, when any of the other employees were about, she always called him 'Sir' or Mr Minter, always maintaining the manner of a proper servant by keeping up a sense of decorum. Norman had never married, his whole life seemed to revolve around business and sport, though on many occasions he thought that Mrs Right had been found but usually, after a few months had passed he became bored because they no longer challenged him. By now, he convinced himself that there was nobody out there for him and that he would forever remain a bachelor therefore, MH Holdings and Rhona Steel were now his surrogate wife and family. Rhona's face, like her body was petite, having become slightly more rounded with increasing age, her mouth always seemed to be smiling which belied the acute business brain developed over the years working for the firm. She loved her boss deeply but, more in a sisterly sort of way, at odd junctures during his reign they had shared both very happy and sad times together, even occasionally having made love under exceptional circumstances. Yet with this closeness between them, there was never enough underlying passion or desire that would ever cause them to form any sort of marital relationship. She was quite happy to remain his friend, lover, consort and business associate and in her mind there was no reason to complicate matters.

"Rhona, could you please get hold of David and tell him that I would like a chat as soon as possible?"

Not waiting for him to complete the sentence, Rhona interrupted his request.

"Would you like him to bring anything specific with him to the meeting?"

"No... I don't think so at this point. Oh, and could you rustle up something to eat, its going to be a lengthy session so we're not going to be able to get away until late this afternoon. "

With that, he leaned back in his swivel chair and once again lifted the thick computerised file which he had already been studying for some time. This particular folder appeared on his desk no later than midday on the eighth day of each month, it contained the accounting heart and soul of all MH Holdings Group and was used as the company bible by only four people who would ever be privy to its entire contents. The heavy file contained condensed computer printouts of every subsidiary within the conglomerate. Religiously, every department of each company within the group were made to submit all details and transactions which were then individually collated by the head office accounting staff. Each manager checking his performance by the end of the month, it was a rule that these accounts were all in by no later than the second day of the following month. Final collation into the mainframe computer formed the master file which Norman now held in his hands, each and every detail carefully mapped out for him. Debtors, creditors, capital expenditure, balance sheets and new investments, Norman leaned back, this was the time of the month to feel well and truly smug with himself.

The Kixing

"Come in David," Norman watched the balding man move in his strangely hunched, unfluid gait across the red carpet from the solid carved door at the far end of his enormous office to one of the large chairs facing a huge desk. He removed his steel rimmed glasses and with an oversized white handkerchief, proceeded to clean them vigorously. Norman wondered why he always did this, suspecting that he was totally unconscious of his annoying habit.

"Rhona said you requested my valuable presence."

"Yes Dave. There's something in here that needs your opinion, have you had something to eat or, will you share something with me now?"

"No and ...yes in turn."

David was not a person to waste words, yet there was something very evil in the way that he portrayed his body language, it was nothing that Norman had ever managed to put his finger on, simply his manner of being hunched like a vulture even when cleaning those dammed glasses. For years he had helped John Minter to build up the empire and now here he was, helping yet another Minter. How apt he was for the job, looking the part that he always played the role to absolute perfection. David Lividsky was short at about five foot five weighed in the region of fifty kilograms and almost completely bald and this, coupled with the small rimless glasses gave him this somewhat evil aura. Norman had seen him in action many times, his smallness did not matter when he went after something for the company, he was merciless and transformed instantly, his peculiar shape seemed to gain in stature, he instantly became a menacing bully with a voice that could change from a gentle whisper one second, to a thunderous roar the next and his total command of several languages, the way he combined these qualities was like a master swordsman with a delicate rapier, able to strip just about anybody's confidence to the bone, leaving them verbally naked. Norman had witnessed this puny runt of a man mentally cripple some of the most brilliant business brains in the country, yet, with assets like these, he had one major weakness, an enormous inferiority complex which he was unable to hide. The bigger his adversary the more he needed to show the world what a powerful man he really was. Norman lifted his company bible and walked to a huge circular main board table designed from beautifully burnished inlaid timbers acquired from all around the world, his father having dubbed it his King Arthur's Table, it was from this table where he would always conduct his campaigns. David followed across the room, seating himself in the high backed red upholstered chair next to his chairman. The only way to indicate which chair represented the head of a round table was that just one of the fourteen around the huge table had a beautifully carved black eagle with spread wings mounted above it, David had always thought it was a bit over-ostentatious. Otherwise, all fourteen black and red high backed seats were identical.

"So, what's on your mind."

"David, what do you know about Johnson Interiors, ...the shop-fitters?"

"Not much, except that they have a good credit rating, pay all accounts at no more than sixty days,"

"Look at this closely," handing him the file, "tell me what you notice I've already highlighted their dealings with us."

David took the file and opened it to the marked index, slowly he ran his finger along the column until it reached the total. The inter-leading door opened and Rhona Steel showed a young girl into this holiest of sanctums.

"Over there." She ordered.

The young girl pushed the trolley to where she was directed and made a quick exit from the room. Like a mother hen, Rhona prepared cold meat and salads onto plates for the two men, she poured two cups of coffee and left without a word. Eating and reading at the same time, David efficiently flipped through the various pages making certain mental additions to the figures, Norman watched without saying anything, allowing the little man to draw his own conclusions. Within minutes David handed back the file and pulled his mouth back showing his crooked line of teeth.

"Whew! That's a lot for just one company, what if they suddenly hit a snag? We could be left holding a rather large ugly baby."

"The surprising thing about their account is registered in the ninety day and over column. Except for one small outstanding amount, which is probably something that is in dispute like a delivery, otherwise everything else seems too good to be true, don't you think? They haven't purchased this much material from us before and what's more unusual, is they are bang up to date with their payments," mused Norman.

"Exactly, that's not normal for today's contractors." reflected David. "Their past payment record shows me that their account has been growing steadily over the last few years and yet, every month a payment arrives before the twenty fifth of the month with all discounts deducted. There has been only one month that their payment arrived late and possibly that outstanding amount is the one small sum in dispute. It could have been due to the postal strike at the time and not even their fault."

David knew exactly what was passing through Norman's mind, sometimes he was so like his father to the well trained eye.

"You want me to find out about them for a killing, ...don't you?"

"Yes I do.. But, I don't think this one is going to be that easy, this tends new territory for us because, any firm with the type of credit record this clean and tidy, it's a well run, fast expanding outfit and so is not going to be your normal pushover. I take it that our usual bet stands, ...okay? I am going to enjoy this one because I don't think you'll find many vices there. Right let's get cracking and check it out."

Like Norman's father, David had a standing bet that he could penetrate any company, find out what made it tick, what its weak points were and get out without anyone realising that they were being investigated. To date he had won every bet.

"I agree, this isn't going to be as easy as others but as usual, our bet stands and I will take your money, yet again."

After lunch, having discussed what tactics would be employed, David rose to leave, the meeting was at end and he was keen to get started.

"How long to put all this together?"

"As soon as you possibly can. I think in this case, you're going to have to dig deep to find what we are looking for."

Norman opened the file to the Johnson account once more as David started towards the door, as if called by some sort of telepathic message, Rhona entered to clear the table. This didn't surprise David, they had all been working for the Minter organisation for so long, that by now, that they could almost guess each others thoughts and actions.

"Thanks for the lunch sugar, I'll return the favour when young Norman here loses his bet. We'll make an afternoon of it."

Rhona was surprised, it was the first time that the little man appeared to be more than a walking computer, a slight smile sprang to her lips.

"That's all right David, you should know after all these years that I don't accept lunch or anything else for that matter from strangers, especially strange company employees."

The Kixing

"That's right Rhona, you pull him down a peg, our legal beagle friend is a little too cock-sure that he's going to win the battle this time, but I'm not certain he will get to first base." All three laughed.

David left, smiling, knowing full well that she served one person only, that's the way it was and that's the way it had always been, well almost always anyway.

Rhona Steel had been with the firm for nearly twenty years, arriving straight from school with limited knowledge, her first job was as a dogs-body to the contracts manager. Times then, were not easy, she desperately needed the money but had unfortunately got herself pregnant, the younger lover having disappeared to leave her to fend for herself. She had a sharp mind and quickly realised that her looks stood her in good stead so, had learnt to use her body language to acquire whatever she needed. This innocence had landed her in trouble with baby and no parental help however, as young as she was, it was her decision to keep the child. After the birth, she went back to work, hating the idea of being anyone's mistress and fearing losing her job if she resisted the contracts manager's continual advances. This led to a disastrous liaison with him, the big man became very demanding with little affection for anybody but himself, she endured the affair simply to protect herself and child while biding her time and carefully put together a damning file on what he and other members of the contracting division were getting up to.

John Minter was exceptionally grateful for her allegiance when he received that comprehensive report and that's when their lifetime affair began, it had always suited her being his secretary, mistress and partner and she would do anything he requested. Years later, at the company's Christmas party, she found herself talking to a young man who seemed to understand her every feeling about loyalty to the company. Uncharacteristically or because of the amount of the cheerful atmosphere of the occasion, Rhona found herself wanting to more than simply talk to this handsome and understanding young man. The two quietly agreed to slip away upstairs with a bottle of champagne, both having had more to drink than usual, Rhona leaned forward, kissing him softly on the cheek whilst mischievously loosening his tie. He was then, barely out of his teens, she was already into her middle thirties having had a beautiful daughter almost his same age as this young boy made this intended liaison very risky and even more exciting. It all worked so naturally, the moment, the alcohol, the surroundings, he quite naturally accepted this mature woman without any resistance. Enticingly, she removed the tie, watching his face for some form of rejection or revulsion but instead, the young man stretched out full length on the thickly carpeted floor to allow his ore mature instructor to proceed slowly, deliberately undoing button by button. At that moment he knew well, that he could stop whenever he wanted, but a warm glow from within made him understand that today was very special, he was being baptised into full manhood. Determining to savour every moment to its limit, like peeling a ripened peach, she skilfully stripped away his outer covering to reach the sweet core of innocence, her gentle hands moved to his belt, he lifted his backside so that she could lever the obstructing grey flannel away from his body. Rhona's fingernails worked their magic, scratching ever so lightly from the fluffy hair on his young chest, moving down and teasingly circulating his belly-button then, even further down, her fingers lingered momentarily around his sacred area, enjoying the pleasure she was giving, at the same time, revelling in the delight she was receiving from not forcing this lovemaking. His breath pattern began altering and his eyes started rolling, opening and shutting in disjointed rapidity, trying to concentrate on a fixed spot on the ceiling, but her experience by now had taken over his very soul, as he found himself unconsciously rocking and moving to heighten the magical moment. The world suddenly shattered around the young man.

Rhona gently cleaned everything he had given in this frenetic moment before straddling the prone figure and slowly descended her warm intromittant body onto his waiting manhood. He hadn't even realised that she had removed her clothes, in slow deliberate circular movements, she then brought them both to a heightened and full conclusion.

"Welcome to MH Holdings Knuckles, now you've finally had a taste of everything this company has to offer."

He momentarily opened his eyes, silhouetted behind her head the spread winged black eagle, seemed to be casting its full approval at their union which, to the young initiate seemed to bode good fortune for his prolonged future. They remained locked together on the red carpeted floor enjoying their new found friendship, this time somehow he somehow knew that it was here way of assuring that their relationship would continue to be long and fruitful and it proved to be the correct assumption. Norman's father had appointed her as his private secretary and personal assistant all those years ago, now she not only his confidant but had been made a director of many of the company's subsidiaries, always there, she continued enjoying a unique relationship with John and occasionally from that day on, with the young heir to the group, Norman Minter.

Rhona cleared the remnants of lunch, passing close to Norman she touched him lightly on the shoulder like a comforting mother.

"Another take-over in mind?"

She understood his moods better than most,. he was not seated in his usual chair, this usually indicated excitement and meant something new was about to break, this change in his day to day action spelt trouble for somebody, ...battle was about to begin.

"God," she thought to herself, "how much this young man was like his father before him all those years back when she had first started working for the Minter organisation, both men from the same stable she had tended to their needs in every sense of the word. Today, his temperament like that of his father, was quiet but, ...very deadly."

"Rhona would you get America on the line? I need to check out some details for that fight in London next month."

"THE KIXING"

CHAPTER FOUR

David thoughtfully picked up his pen and started jotting various phases that this operation would require, he turned to his secretary.

"I need everything you can find in our records about a firm called Johnson Interiors as quickly as possible, please don't disturb me for the rest of the afternoon. Oh, one more thing, call the team together for a conference tomorrow morning at nine o'clock sharp. Tell them no excuses will be accepted for anyone not attending, whatever they're doing, they're to drop it and be here without fail."

Susan simply nodded, she was if anything, more of a control freak than David and was seriously contemplating her retirement. The short grey-haired woman had a slight lisp, she immediately started dialling the first number fully knowing that when David ordered something like this, it usually meant something important was about to take place. By four o'clock that afternoon she had contacted all but one person, after several searching and irate calls to various members of the firm, she finally located Paul Hunter at a country hotel. "Paul, get yourthelf into the office tomorrow, David has called an urgent meeting here at nine o'clock sharp, he told me to tell you there won't be any actheptable excuses, so you had better be here."

Dismayed, he listened to her lisping voice.

"How the hell did you get hold of me here? I'm supposed to be on holiday. What's so important to make me come to London tonight?" Susan mentally gave herself a pat on the back when she heard how she had knocked the usually confident Paul off his confident stride, she didn't really like the man.

"I really can't dithcuss that on the telephone but David inthists that everybody be here tomorrow without exception, of course that also includes you. Now what do I tell David? Are you, or are you not going to be at the meeting?"

Paul clicked his tongue to register his objection, then chuckled.

"Don't worry, I'll be there. But, you two beauties are going to have to explain this one to my girlfriend because she's not going to believe me when I tell her."

Susan replaced the receiver, and smiled to herself.

"Well, that's everybody, wonder what's in thtore for them this time?" The intercom buzzed loudly, it cleared her image of a naked Paul scurrying around his hotel room somewhere in the country.

"Where's that information that I asked you for? Have all the arrangements been made for tomorrow?"

"I was just about to bring it into you and yeth, everybody's been contacted about the meeting."

"Tell Trevor to come to my office, now."

Trevor Reece was unkempt, unshaven and wore the same clothes day after day, he had the looks of a tramp or a potty scientist, nobody liked working with him because of his strange behaviour. Yet, despite this, his mind was sharper than any computer because the man was some sort of mathematical genius, John Minter had managed to gather around him, an exceptional team, all experts in their diverse fields. Trevor carried himself well, like a proud sergeant-major but that was probably the only thing remotely defined anything military about the man, his greying moustache was bedraggled and coloured almost ginger from nicotine staining left by his dirty great big pipe that had always seemed to have taken up permanent station at the right side of his mouth. He whistled loudly at David dwarfed behind his large panelled desk as he lazily strolled into the office.

"Where's the fire?"

"Trevor, Johnson Interiors?"

"Good management, never miss a trick on accounting, pay their bills on time and generally no trouble whatsoever, why?".

"I already know all that from the printout," said David irately, "anything more?"

Trevor thought awhile, lit his pipe yet again, stared out of the window, as if his brain, extracting the information was having trouble collating the information and where to start.

"The founding Johnson twins own eighty per cent of the firm's total share holding consisting of one hundred and forty thousand fully paid up shares at one pound each Not a lot in today's market, considering their present turnover. The balance of the company's shares are held by someone within an investment company called Willis or Willcox Investments. I think that their holding was initially a speculative punt in firm by this venture capitalist company, it would seem that they are nothing but a sleeping partner or else, they could also be acting as some kind of nominee shareholder for someone else. The last check made, revealed that their balance sheet showed an annual turnover of almost twenty five million pounds with a pre-tax profit of just over one million pounds. However, that was sometime ago, if you want me to, I'll get the most recent figures."

"Nice," said David "but I need to know more than that by tomorrow, think you can do something?"

"Don't know, it doesn't give me much time to complete everything although, with a bit of luck, I should be able to get someone to locate their balance sheet and thereby track down the real state of affairs by sometime later today."

"Good man, see what you can do. Oh, by the way, as quietly as possible, we don't want them to know we're looking into their affairs."

Trevor again attempted lighting the pipe then nodded. First thing he did when he reached his office was to call a colleague working at the Inland Revenue office, then rustled among some papers and picked up where he had left off before being summoned to see David. He turned to his computer keyboard and with unusual refinement that belied his scruffiness, started typing, completely lost to the outside world, the large printing machine under the next desk started clattering out the printouts requested. As suddenly as it had started, it stopped and his office was again quiet, Trevor closed down his machine with a brisk tap on the keyboard, he knew that the information was stored in the vaulted depths somewhere, tearing a strip of paper from the printer, he checked it and then slipped it into his jacket pocket and walked back to his desk, picked up the phone and asked the girl that manned the front desk to get a Mr Bailey at the Inland Revenue's office on the line. Minutes later, the telephone sounded, lifting the receiver, he listened for a second while battling with his free hand to light the large pipe.

"Roy? Johnson Interiors, the shop-fitters. Yes that's them, Ernest Clive, and Christine Shirley Johnson. I also need some information about a company called Willis Investments. Top priority, we need this information as soon as possible." The voice at the other rattled off figures.

"Got that, I tell you what... Better email that information through today, try to get the other to me before seven. Thanks for everything so far, I owe you a big drink."

David, in the meantime replaced the receiver, he had been talking to an old university friend, he had helped the man in no certain way in the early days to scale heights within the Trade Union Council. Now, as one of the council's foremost negotiators and legal brains, he regularly helped David when he needed advice also, he now maintained an extremely high standard of living, a lot of which was secretly contributed to by the company. MH Holdings often lined his and other pockets to make life more bearable when agreeing to doing little favours for them on the quiet. This request from David was no different from previous interesting situations, he was well and truly in David's pocket and unable to refuse any demands. He consoled himself to another nice pay-day which was once again, just around the corner.

Next morning at nine o'clock sharp, David entered his office, five colleagues were already seated around the table at the far end all had pads, pencils and tumblers set out in front of them arranged by Susan. As one their babbling stopped, this never failed to impress the short lawyer, it was as if electric shocks had simultaneously passed through them all, this was the respect with which he was held by 'his people', they had become known, some even called them the company's military brigade. He carefully studied them in turn before placing his folder on the table in front on himself, each being well chosen specialists within their fields of expertise, these professionals had helped Minter Holdings gain control of more companies in the last fifteen years, than he cared to think about. This team represented the finest group of industrial espionage experts in the country. David had every right to feel proud, they had all been hand picked and trained by him personally.

"We've again been asked to look at another killing, you all know the drill by now." Nobody said a thing.

"The company this time is called Johnson Interiors Shop-fitters, at this stage we need to know everything that there is about them, who's sleeping with who, where their strengths, their weaknesses, we need everything down to the nails hammered into a shop-front, not one stone left unturned, if there's any dirt, back-hander or anyone playing silly buggers, I want to know about it."

"David is there anything different about this one?"

"No..." mused the lawyer, "although, I can tell you now, it's not going to be easy, let's just call it my hunch. Don't ask me why? It's just a feeling I have. Any more questions?" There were none.

"Harry, get amongst the workers, find out about any uneasiness, latest stories, have any men been unjustly fired, hard done by or the likes. Look for signs of any in fighting, jealousy or discontent, whether anybody's not receiving correct wages. Ask about their employers, general working conditions or any tit-bits of scandal. Right?

Harry was a big rough man whose duty it was to get among the workers by creating jobs within the intended target company. The union normally arranged for him to gain a position within the targeted company where they would become latent sleepers, digging in among the employees to find out everything.

"Next, Alan you do the same with the design and contracting departments, my gut feeling is that at the rate that they're growing, they're going to be needing plenty of good designers, so it should be quite easy for you and Harry to get in among company employees."

"Hewitt, as usual, yours is the hardest task. I must warn you that the way the company seems to be run, you're going to battle to make any headway. If we're lucky, the union could help us get you into their premises, otherwise, we're going to have to steal the information, an inside look won't hurt, I want to know everything about their financial status." Hewitt began scribbling madly on the pad in front of him.

"Julie, seeing you're the newest member to the team, you and Paul Hunter will have to join forces because he knows what's expected, as usual you'll both have an open cheque book for entertainment. Search out the weaknesses of the most likely employees, what they do after hours, make friends, find out about any offbeat external company practices and in particular Ernest Johnson, I want you concentrating all your efforts on the managing director. You will all be issued with the usual update information sheets within the next few hours. Any questions?"

David looked about the table, these were the best, they knew what was expected of them, this was going to be another job to get on with. They had worked as a team like this so many times, each member had their own method of dealing with their part of the operation. For a while they idly exchanged ideas and views about the new killing, though David had hinted to the contrary, for these professionals it was simply another job of work and even if it turned out not to be as easy as so many others before, the expectation was that they would cover all bases within very short period of time.

The meeting being over, they filed out of the office, Paul Hunter paced himself two steps behind his gorgeous working associate, his eyes firmly trained on her tight fitting skirt and the swaying movement of her rear.

"Whew!, Good bones Julie." He turned left into the main telephonist's little office. "Be a honey and do me a favour, will you call Johnson Interiors and ask for the name of their chief designer then let me know, I'm in my office."

He walked to the lift, all the while remaining deep in thought he moved into the small cubicle that he called his office, the switchboard girl told him that the name he wanted was Clive Peters. Paul thanked her and scribbled the name onto his pad before calling up Johnson Interiors and asking to speak to Mr Peters.

"Hello," the clear deep voice was onto the line almost immediately.

"Mr Peters, my name is Paul Hunter and I'm a specialist building consultant. Knowing your company is one of the larger firms in its field, I was wondering whether you could help me with some designs that I am working on for a client in the Middle East."

"Mr Hunter, that's most interesting but I'm afraid that I do not have much spare time available, can I ask one of our representatives to call on you and you could then first show them what's required, we can take it from there."

"No, that's not quite what I had in mind because I'm still at the very early development stage of what is going to be an exceptional building and am toying with various initial design ideas. However, there are many problems and considerations that have to be taken into account including the extreme climatic conditions out there that tend to create rather different design factors from the ones we normally use here."

"Oh, you're right it's expert knowledge that you really require? I'm not terribly certain that I'm the right person to assist you."

"You come highly recommended as a leader in your field, I have an idea, would it be possible that we just have an informal chat somewhere, let me tell you what I have in mind and show you my ideas. Don't worry, we will be quite willing to pay you above the average rate for your services on this project, money is no object and we'll make it well worth your while."

"Well..." Clive was obviously weighing up the thought of moonlighting for just a moment, "meet me at a pub called the Monk's Head at about five-thirty. But a warning, be careful about what you say because most of the staff generally have a drink there after work."

"Just an initial chat, that's all I want. I don't want to compromise your position in any way."

"Oh no you won't, but if you're asking me to do some design work out of the office, I could possibly get into slight bother with the company."

"I definitely won't say anything out of place, let's simply play it from here." Paul reassured Clive.

"OK, I can mix pleasure with business, so to speak. Thanks very much for the call, see you at five-thirty and by the way you can't miss me, I'm wearing a grey suit and a shocking red tie. After all I am a designer."

"Fine, until later then. I look forward to meeting you." Paul replaced the receiver and laughingly punched the air, he dialled three digits, waited a few seconds, Julie answered.

"Julie, …Paul - Listen, several employees from Johnsons get together at a pub called The Monk's Head after work and I'm meeting one of them this evening. Care to tag along or maybe, meet me accidentally on purpose? This fortunate coincidence could turn out to be some sort of superb introduction."

"You have been a busy little body haven't you?" Julie teased. "I know the pub but, my preference is that we should make any meeting look accidental, …a timed signal,. greet me casually or something similar. Give yourself the necessary time to hook your one, bring me in a little later, perhaps we can have a little fun with some of the female staff."

Paul chuckled.

"Right, I'll first relax my target, perhaps then he'll automatically introduce us to everyone straight away, that would work out far better, don't you think?"

"Yes, I'll arrive about five and see what I can do by myself. Great work Paul, see you there."

Paul replaced the instrument in and again punched the air, he ha always loved the hunt, in a few short weeks, Johnson Interiors Shop-Fitters would have nothing to hide, nor would anyone of their employees, employers or anything associated with the firm. Paul checked his folder "I wonder what skeletons you're going to uncover in a month from now."

He always felt elated starting a new project even if this time, it meant him taking new partners through the ropes, job satisfaction was always exciting and dangerous. In fact in his own mind, this was nothing less than spying, the penalty and stakes were high and he knew full well that he would probably be treated like a wartime spy, he always kidded himself that if he ever got caught out he could possibly suffer the same fate. Instant career death, because his cover would more than likely be blown and his face spread across the news, that would most certainly finish his lucrative profession for good.

The Kixing

The Kixing

"THE KIXING"

CHAPTER FIVE

It was nearly eight o'clock when Ernest Johnson walked into his sister's office to find her sitting studying various workload sheets. Without even moving her head, the long necked brunette looked up over the top of her *'Pickwick'* style spectacles. "Ernie, you look tired."

"I'm knackered." His body language radiated dejection as he moved to the front of her desk and she knew that he had had a bitch of a day although she didn't know the reason for it.

"Chrissie, I've just been to Powerbuild's offices to try and find out what the hell they are playing at, the bastard has left for the day. I just hope he's not going to do a runner tonight. Tell me, have you got his home address?" Christine Johnson leaned forward and checked through her records.

"Yes, here it is," she wrote the address onto a slip of paper before tearing it from the pad. "I want you to come with me."

"Look Ernie, I've got to check these production sheets before they go into the factory tomorrow morning. Can't you take someone else with you? Get hold of Sandy Nelson, he's the company secretary after all. Anyway it's not my job to collect money, it's to make sure that the contracts are completed and done properly in order to make your work easier to collect that money."

"Chrissie this is no ordinary case, there's a strong rumour that they're in financial trouble and I think we should try to either persuade them to pay what they can now or, try to stop any payments to them until we have received our money. We're going to be short of nearly nine hundred thousand pounds which we can ill afford at present."

The Kixing

"Christ!" Christine shouted. "How the hell did they manage to build up that kind of capital loan with us? Why didn't you or Sandy say something earlier? You should know by now that these types of problems compound themselves, what the hell have you and Sandy been doing all this time? Trying to build up a bloody charity organization for insolvent builders?"

"No." Ernest underlined the point by banging his fist on the desk. "But, their complaints are about work done to two sites not yet having been fixed is a realistic problem. I asked you to arrange this over three months ago because they've continually refused to pay us until their complaints list was rectified. Now my girl, get off your cute little arse and come with me so that we can try to at least put a value to their snag list. They are not entitled to hold everything and they can bloody well pay us the balance tonight." His sister could see how furious he was, she also knew that this was his means of release for allowing the position to go beyond his control. He wasn't mad at her, he was upset with himself and as always, he had turn to her for a shoulder to lean on. She was, after all twenty minutes older than Ernest. Christine glanced at her watch and saw that it was ten past eight and she had wanted to get away to her daughter who was home from university for the holidays. It was times like these that she cursed being in business for herself, she flicked her head and lifted the receiver.

"Right, let me call home quickly and I'll meet you outside."

"No, I will meet you at his home in forty minutes, bring those costing sheets with you in case we need them to prove our figures to that sonofabitch. Also I need you as a back up to help me scare his pants off, he mustn't be allowed to use us as their scapegoats."

"Don't worry Ernest, that bastard will pay up tonight by the time I'm finished with him." Christine although very slim and attractive, was extremely tough in all business matters. When they had first set out in business she had looked after the accounts while Ernest saw to

50

the contracts. But before long it soon became apparent that the company was losing money because he was being so easily manipulated by the clients and workforce alike. She immediately stepped in and took over his role handling the contractual duties and very quickly things changed dramatically. Although he was seen to be the head of the business it was commonly accepted that Christine was the real driving force behind Johnson Interiors.

"Go on, I've got a couple more calls to make then, I'll be on my way." Smiling, Ernest walked through the office mumbling something to himself as he passed through the front doors on his way to the car park. Climbing into his Porsche he thought back to the telephone call he had received from one of their site foremen last night. Thank God when Christine had been out Jim had had the sense of mind to call and tell him everything and not waited to tell Christine the next morning.

"Must give him a rise in pay because he used his initiative," Ernest said to himself. The telephone call had come while he was having dinner and this type of thing was so unusual that he decided to take the call even if it meant his dinner would have to wait. Jim told him that he had tried contacting Christine but she was out and wouldn't be back until much later and that the information needed to be passed on quickly. Ernest told him to continue with his story, he said that while on their tea break that afternoon together with the building foreman on the site, the man had told him that they had not been paid their wages last Friday and that the men had only been paid four days later. Jim then said that it was common knowledge in the trade that the firm was suffering financial difficulties because of a shortage of material on the site. He also revealed that the site foreman had told him that whenever he tried to order something suppliers said that as soon as they received cash they would supply, but not until. This made the foreman's work almost impossible, the man had then gone on to say that this was not the first time the men had been short changed by the company and somebody had told him that the owner was talking of leaving the country. When he had discussed it with his immediate boss, he had been told that it was only a temporary setback but he was going abroad to arrange the finance either today or tomorrow.

"This is not good." Ernest took all this seriously as he knew from his long experience that the men always talked amongst themselves and that they generally had a sixth sense. This inbuilt instinct was borne from years of being treated as the underdogs, like rats fleeing from a sinking ship, they knew long before anyone else that trouble was brewing. He immediately called a good friend from his club whom he knew to have supplied the ready mixed concrete for this particular site.

"Rory, tell me what your dealings are like with Powerbuild?"Ernest asked.

"Don't touch them with a barge pole," suggested Rory. "Why do you ask anyway?"

"Well, they want us to do some extra work for them." Ernest lied, not wanting to cause any panic.

"We'll never do business with them again, they don't pay up and now we've refused to supply anymore material until they bring our account up to date, and even then, we won't unless it's only on a strictly cash basis. The owner is an absolute pig and a downright hoodlum, pity we didn't find this out earlier. We wouldn't have agreed to supply this contract if we had known beforehand and even when we tried getting heavy with him, he moved in some bully boys to work over several of our drivers. No, I don't think it would be your best move working for those bastards." Ernest thanked him and after promising to get together for some golf sometime, came back to the table promising himself to set this straight in the morning. That night, he could not sleep very well, he knew in his heart of hearts that it was already too late to recover the money. But, he was a fighter and would have a bloody good attempt to at least recover some of it and be first in line when and if there was anything left to recover from the receiver he thought to himself. The first thing he did next morning when he got to his office was to arrange an immediate appointment with his company lawyers. He and Sandy took copies of all outstanding accounts to the lawyer who advised them that it was going to be a long laborious task to recover that sort of money. Ernest called Powerbuild's offices all day trying to find someone to talk to but, It seemed as if everybody except the telephonist had gone on holiday. He left it as late as he could before going to their offices where he was quickly fobbed off with the excuse that the managing director and accountant had already gone home for the day. Now at his wits end and as a last resort, he had decided to try and catch the managing director at his house as he pulled the red Porsche to a halt at the entrance of a long asphalted drive and waited for his sister to arrive. The building was set well away from the road and from what he could see of it from behind the large hedge, it was extremely big. The house was situated in one of the most elite suburbs skirting London and the whole appearance of the place smelt of enormous amounts of money having been spent on it.

"Can't pay your bloody bills but can live like a king," murmured the unhappy Ernest. He watched as Christine parked her Jag across the driveway entrance so that those in the house wouldn't be able to slip away. They had been fooled once before and this fish was too slippery to trust. He looked at his sister, she was still a most beautiful woman thought Ernest as she got out and automatically straightened her skirt after locking her car. Ever since they were children, he had always thought that she was the most beautiful person that it had been his fortune to be connected with. Nobody, not his friends or her belated husband had been able to separate this pigeon pair. Overtly she was a mirror image of himself, but inwardly she had captured enough strength for both of them. The tall brunette had always been the real love of his life, he had often thought that by being inexorably bonded together from the womb was the reason for him not being comfortable with female companionship.

"Well, what are you waiting for, Christmas?" This was the moment he was dreading if what Rory had told him was true, then he didn't really want to face up to this man. He had always been a bit of a coward if the truth be known and Ernest had always hated confrontation of any sort. It was always Christine that had lifted him out of scrapes and now, here he was again relying on her formidable inner strength.

"We would like to talk to Mr Edwards please," Christine told the young boy who had opened the door to them.

"Who are you?" The lad asked. "Just tell him, it's Christine." Ernest hung back so that the boy hadn't seen him. The door was left slightly ajar as the youngster went to fetch his father.

Christine stepped into the hallway.

"C'mon," she hissed at her brother. Peter Edwards was a large man whose good living had allowed him to run to seed. His beer belly almost rounded the corner before the rest of his large frame entered the hallway.

"Yes?"

"Mr Edwards?"

"Yes."

"I'm Christine Johnson and this is Ernest. You've been evading us all day by refusing to take my brother's calls. Your company owes us a lot of money for the shop fitting on the Castle Project and you've left us no choice but to come to your house this way. Now, what's the story?"

"How dare you? Get out before I throw you out."

"I wouldn't try that, I'm a karate black belt and you would come off far worse. All I want is what is rightfully ours and I'm not leaving until you discuss the matter with us." The big man had never been threatened by a woman before and for a moment wasn't quite sure how to react. His face bulged and deepened to an almost purplish shade as he exploded in temper.

"This is an invasion of my privacy. Get out before I call the police."

"Why won't you discuss the matter? You owe us the money and your firm's in trouble. We know that you're thinking of skipping the country."

"Listen you. If you want to talk to me about business then come to my office at the proper time. I refuse to be harassed in my own home like this." Christine pointed to a tea box in the hallway.

"I suppose you're packing this because you're going on holiday. To me, this would indicate that the rumours all over town are correct, you're about to do a runner aren't you. Before you go we want our money, do you understand? If not, I'm going to make sure tonight that you are restrained from moving anything from this house, the office or your banks."

"Shit!" Edwards scowled at Christine. That was the last straw, the man turned his back on the Johnson twins and disappeared into the back of the hall whistling for what Christine presumed was his dog. Within minutes, he reappeared holding a baseball bat in one hand and a growling, snarling black and tan Doberman by the collar with the other.

"Now, fuck off before I really get angry!" Edwards yelled. Christine stood her ground. Outwardly she was calm, but her innards were very quickly turning to jelly in case this madman suddenly went berserk and released the dog.

"So, that's your last word. Okay, we'll leave. You may be able to scare others with your bully-boy tactics, but not me, this time I'm warning you that you've bitten off more than you can chew this." With that, Christine turned on her heel and pushed the petrified Ernest through the door ahead of her.

"Yeah, yeah. Now piss off." Christine didn't look back as she and her brother walked slowly down the driveway.

"Jee-sus. What now?" Ernest asked.

"You go home. I'm going to teach that swine not to mess with me." Ernest didn't like her when she was like this, he had seen her in action before and knew that Peter Edwards was about to regret his hasty actions. Christine had been married to a very wealthy Italian who had very dubious connections but, when he had suddenly died from a heart attack, he had left everything to her. Ernest had seen some of their arguments about her starting the business and continuing to work after their daughter was sent to boarding school. He was a traditionalist and she was a dirty fighter who held onto what was hers, even without the business, she was now an extremely wealthy woman. During all their years together, Ernest knew that when she took on this haughty look, she was livid and invariably someone got badly hurt.

"What are you going to do?"

"You don't want to get involved, so it's better you don't know." They reached the front gate and Ernest kissed her on the cheek as he put his arms around her waist. He really loved her and they had been inseparable since the day they were born. She touched him lightly on the cheek.

"Go home. I'll see you in the morning."

"Be careful Chrissie. From what I've heard and seen this man is a real bastard."

"Don't worry." Ernest got into his Porsche and drove away. Christine got into her Jaguar and made a quick call on her car phone, she didn't move the car from the driveway as she waited for about twenty minutes. Then she saw what she was waiting for, it was a metal grey Landcruiser that pulled to a halt stopped behind her car and one man got out and walked to her car. The man was built like the proverbial brick wall and had a large scar running diagonally across his face.

"We got here as quickly as we could."

"I'm pleased." Christine opened her door and handed the man the file with all the copies of work and invoices done by Johnson Interiors for Peter Edwards.

"Is this everything?"

"Yes."

"Is he in the house now?"

"Oh yes. But be careful, he's one very ugly customer, he's just threatened me with a dog and a baseball bat." The man slowly paged through the file without saying anything, for ten minutes he examined everything until he understood everything.

"Right. Our usual ten per cent, the usual fee."

"Done." The man waved at the Landcruiser and then another four men got out and walked to the leader. Each one in turn nodded and put their hand to their brow in recognition.

"You go home now signora, don't worry, we will take care of this pig for you."

"One last thing, make sure he pays for the way he treated me but no deaths. Okay?"

The Kixing

"Okay. but you undersatand, there are to be no deaths to him or his family. you can go home now and leave the rest to us." Christine started her car and drove homewards, when she got indoors she had a light meal before she and her daughter changed and left for London's theatre land. They were dressed in almost identical outfits and could quite easily have been mistaken for sisters.

"THE KIXING"

CHAPTER SIX

The group at the Monk's Head had been drinking steadily for almost two hours, the initial dulcet tones of the place having now picked up significantly in tempo to a somewhat loud and raucous hubbub atmosphere brought about by a constant flow of alcoholic beverage intake. Julie had carefully nursed her alcoholic intake all evening and was now feeling wonderfully light-headed and cheerful, not through the consumption of drink because she was on an assignment and so having been an almost abstainer during the evening, she was quite aware that the few drinks she had had, hadn't really affected her as much as she now pretended it had to those gathered around her. It was nearly eight o'clock when Chris suddenly decided it was time to leave this happy little band and get on home. Julie was on her first assignment of this nature for MH Holdings and was surprisingly caught somewhat flat footed and unawares of Chris's instant decision to depart the group of now merry drinkers. She thought that she had it all under control because of the way she had skilfully managed to get both Chris and Sandy to dance to her every whim, up until now she had been having tremendous fun, almost playing one against the other with her titillating teasing discussion and encouragement of what she could have in store for the two men whose tongues were by this time almost hanging out in possible anticipation of what the evening might still have in store for them.

"C'mon Chris, don't be a wimp, stay and have another drink," she urged playfully.

"No I can't, as much as I regret breaking up this super little party, I have the type of wife that you can bet will be standing behind the front door armed with a rolling pin if I dared to arrive home late. She would just love me to arrive home late, what a bitch."

"Scared of the wife are you? Man or mouse Chris?" Sandy let out a cackle like a chicken.

"No seriously, it's okay for you single guys to mock but, you don't know what it's like to arrive home and then be confronted by an evilest tank of a woman in curlers wielding some form of malicious weapon. It's really not funny to be married to someone who's insanely jealous, it's a real nightmare."

"You can always come home with me then dump her in the morning if you like?" Julie chided.

"No way, she scares me witless and has on several occasions threatened to kill me if ever she thought I was playing away, anything for a bit of peace, that's me."

"Oh well, that's your bad luck but the offer still stands, if you decide to change your mind." Julie said disappointedly knowing that she had momentarily failed her first test.

He thanked them for the super evening, kissed Julie, and then gave Jean, Ernest's assistant a hug and peck on the cheek before reluctantly staggering away as he made his way through the diminishing crowd towards the door. Paul winked at Julie to indicate that he would've won their bet, during the evening he had insisted on paying for most the drinks, but the others hadn't felt very comfortable with this and all half heartedly objected by buying the occasional round. Knowing that this could be the beginning of the party break-up, Paul rose quickly and collected the glasses.

"Let's have one more drink and then go and put something in our empty stomachs. I know a super little place in Fulham and I think you'll all love the interesting decor." Sandy was the first to agree because he knew full well that this would give him the opportunity to now have Julie to himself tonight had only just started. Jean looked at her watch trying to decide whether to go along with the idea, she confessed that she hadn't got anything planned and that the only thing she had to do was watch television and feed her Siamese cat. She looked hopefully at Paul waiting for his answer and as their eyes met for the umpteenth time, she again felt one of her schoolgirl flushes cross her cheek. Jean had very seldom known anything quite like this, it was akin to being a young teenager all over again, every time she looked into this man's eyes it was somehow, almost like looking into some form of deep hellfire, she inwardly suspected he could be dangerous to her well being but, for the first time in many years she allowed herself the teasing and flirtatious luxury. It had been some years since she had last felt as reckless or had so much fun with the attention being heaped upon her as Paul had rapidly charmed his way into her very soul.

"Why not? Let's be daring, I would love to see this strange place of yours." Jean smiled at these two new found friends, they both seemed to be so much fun and it wasn't often that she immediately felt this relaxed and at ease with stranger she convinced herself.

"Great, it's all settled then, I have this feeling in my bones that we're going to have a terrific evening," Paul said, before turning and making his way to the bar. Inwardly he smiled to himself thinking just how easy it had been, their party was just the right size, he thought to himself because Julie had already got Sandy wound around her little finger while he and Jean could later have a pillow discussion about the affairs of Johnson Interiors. Softly he chuckled wickedly as he ordered yet another of drinks for the umpteenth time that evening.

"Like falling off a log it's so easy." Jean wasn't a bad looking woman either he felt that it was a surprising bonus because some of his previous conquests were terrible dragons and he felt that a few of them were way and above the call of normal duty. His mind drifted as he waited for the barman to complete his order, the worst had been the enormous lady who was a horse riding leather freak and had whipped him to within half an inch of his life before giving up the facts that he needed to know. His thought pattern was interrupted by the barman placing a round of drinks in front of Paul who asked to settle the running tab for the evening.

"You know where the place is, don't you Julie? Jean, you come with me and we'll meet them there." Julie and Sandy made their way across the busy road in the direction of Johnson Interiors. Paul tried to talk to Jean about Johnsons as they walked towards his car but she was more interested in what he did for a living and managed to keep tight lipped about her work before quickly altering his line of questioning by switching from this mundane topic and skilfully switching subject matter to various questions about himself. Paul persisted to bring the subject back to her working environment, without success although having had more than her usual intake of alcohol, which really should have affected her by now, she still somehow retained her sense of loyalty towards her employers by stubbornly refusing mix business with pleasure.

"You are a very deep thinking type of person, I've also noticed that you are not very forthcoming or talk about yourself very much do you? Is it because you're a theorist, you're just shy or is there anything wrong?"

"None of the above, it's just that I don't mix a lot and therefore don't have a lot to say for myself."

"I think I know what you mean, you're more the silent type who enjoys being with people to hear them talk. I also think you're a little afraid of voicing your own opinion for fear of making a fool of yourself. Am I right, or am I right?"

"Yes... you're partly correct, trying to be very social has always seemed a bit difficult to me, so I love listening to people but the same problem always arises."

"Don't tell me, let me guess." Paul interrupted as he hooked his hand into her arm. "You feel people are always getting at you? They would like you to say more but your reserved personality doesn't really allow for that?" Jean simply smiled because somehow, he had managed to measure her up quite precisely, this did not bother her, in fact, it was very comforting and she was now unconsciously falling into the trap and beginning to commit similar mistakes that most of her associates fell into. She was both a little tipsy and being a little reckless, for her this was proving an extremely weird mixture because she had always been reserved and everyone was always seeking to get her to open up and talk freely, just wasn't in her nature.

"I don't think it should worry you because it's us chatterers that are the self conscientious ones, not you. Most people cannot stand having what seems like a quiet or intelligent person in our midst. It tends to unsettle us because we wish you would talk more freely and be like us. That trait of non speaking is such a powerful tool in anybody's vocal armoury."

"Is that a fact?" Jean mocked.

"Yes and I know what I'm talking about because my ex-wife before she unfortunately died, was exactly the same and always said I could do the talking for both of us. I loved her for it, she was always the strong willed one." Paul lied convincingly as they reached his BMW, he opened the door for her and once she was firmly settled he leaned forward and looked straight at her and said words that sent her libido soaring for the umpteenth time that evening.

"Don't worry about your little quirk, I love you just as you are and promise me you'll never change." It was said in slightly joking fashion, however, Jean so wanted to believe him, knowing that this was quite some man and she could very easily fall in love with him.

The Kixing

Not much was said on the way to the Gasworks, each seemed wrapped up with their own thoughts. The restaurant when they reached it was all that it was cracked up to be, aged Turkish, Iranian and Siamese carpets lined the wall and were even stuck to the ceilings in some of the many small compartmentalised rooms that were dotted around in some form of designed maze like fashion. The whole place was filled with the most unusual historic brick-a-brac collected by the owner over many, many years these included pornographic art that abounded the passageways and other such valuables, as an extremely ornate and ancient chess board with all its pieces intact and other items, that filled a waiting room where they were placed to have drinks until Sandy and Julie arrived. Paul in his very charming sort of way, implied what the end of the evening might hold in store and by the end of an exceptionally good meal, Sandy, who was quite drunk agreed to show Paul some new ideas that Johnsons were working on. They had agreed that Clive would spend time during the following evening going over some of their new patented systems and the complete layout of the production department to show him how and where the new system was put together. Sandy wasn't worried about his action, after all this was not going to be a demonstration for a competitor but, it was for his new found friend from the Middle East. He was just doing his job and nobody would ever know that they were intending to show Paul this well kept secret because Johnson Interiors had recently begun testing the Middle Eastern markets and not yet become fully involved with larger exports to the Arab world, this was their opportunity to substantially increase turnover into a new market. Paul spent the evening making Jean feel extremely comfortable while Julie flirted outrageously with Sandy so that by the time they were on the third round of liqueurs, the two of them were just about making love at the table. His hands wandered with aimless intent all over her, making Jean somewhat embarrassed and uncomfortable by her associate's activities.

"There's a time and place for everything, they're like teenagers," she whispered to her new acquaintance, he just laughed and soon afterwards, he suggested that they leave the rampant couple to get on with their business. Paul again took her hand as they walked to the car, he was now certain that they were both on the same wavelength, he drove her to her flat situated just off the Earl's Court Road.

"Would you like to come in for tea or coffee."

"Neither." He had switched off the motor outside her flat which overlooked Bramham Gardens. Paul leaned over and without waiting for permission pulled her head forward and kissed her full on the mouth. For the first time that evening she seemed to relax completely and responded immediately, the build up had been absolutely perfect, the drinks, the pornographic art, as well as Sandy and Julie's reactions had all simply added to the desire that had been beautifully kept in check by both of them all evening. It was as if somebody had suddenly placed a burning torch straight into their very hearts and souls as she melted into him and it was her hand that made the first move by going directly to his crotch. She felt the hardness as slowly and deliberately she moved the palm of her hand hard against the small soldier standing to attention and waiting to be released to do its duty.

"My, that's not very gentleman like behaviour when a lady invites you in for a drink," she teased. "But, I love your answer, c'mon let's get indoors, your car will be safe here tonight." Paul smiled inwardly knowing from experience how he had now set a smouldering ember on fire. As they entered her well furnished flat, he quickly pulled her towards him with one hand, suspecting that Jean had no intention of making a drink just at that moment she simply folded herself into his arms and immediately returned her hand to his trousers and took up the steady rhythmical movement which she had started in the car.

"Let's first get comfortable, I may not say much but you're going to remember tonight for a long time to come." She lead Paul through to the lounge and over to the scatter couch where she sat down and tried to pull him on top of her.

"Whoa, don't rush, we've got all night to enjoy each other." Jean leaned over and switched on a small table lamp before going across to a console where she selected a gentle piece of music to make love to. Slowly and as provocatively as she could, she slowly danced her way across the room towards Paul on the couch. He pulled her gently downwards so that her head rested on his lap.

"Now, you've come into your own, here, you don't even have to try to talk." His hand moved forward into her blouse and slowly started to work the little erect bubbles of her breasts. Without waiting, Jean tried to get her hand around to unzip the place where the protrusion was desperately trying to emerge, she was surprised when Paul lifted her hand away.

"Not yet, I told you not to rush this moment, there's plenty of time." She just wanted to get on with it and become intimately involved, but Paul on the other hand insisted the she relax and let his hands first do all the work, for her this was difficult at first but then as his experienced fingers kept moving across her body they began to feel like tiny electric shocks that were reviving her long dormant erotic cells back to life. Slowly his fingers worked their magic as they quickly removed all but her tiny briefs. Her body was now on fire when he gently lifted her up.

"Where's the bedroom?" She nodded her head and he moved through to her bedroom and placed her under the autumn coloured duvet of her double bed and the gentle touch once again moved over her body and for the first time they passed lightly down between her legs. Her whole body was in flames and she wanted nothing more than for him to get undressed and enter her body.

"Hold that. I'll be back shortly." He went through into the bathroom and suddenly she was surprised by the sound of running water.

"He's having a bloody shower," she disappointedly muttered to herself. "The man's crazy."

The heat within her had almost died down by the time he again emerged with a small towel fastened around his middle and like her, he danced slowly around the bed until he reached to bottom of the bed before temptingly releasing the cloth and revealing his total nudity. Her ardour quickly flared into action when she saw the giant pole extending from the front of his midriff, he moved onto the bed and tenderly took her into his arms, allowing his magical hands to again start their magical work once again. Then slowly his head moved downwards along the bed all the while working his tongue across her entire body. She tried relaxing but it was almost an impossibility, she then decided that she wasn't prepared to just lie back and let him do all the work. Jean couldn't remember when last she so badly wanted anyone like this before, he gently pushed her down so she moved her body into a position where he could gain easier access to the intricate parts of her wanton body. She revelled to his lips that continually played around her ears, eyes and mouth and then she moved her hands between his legs and with her fingers began exploring his solidly pulsating penis. His head dropped to her lower regions and her whole frame suddenly felt an intense explosion rising from within as his masterful licking reciprocated and together with both tongue and his skilful fingers working hard on her clitoris she could not prevent the sensation he then halted the action at the crucial moment, he waited until he had her relax completely before his fingers again moved around her vital bump with the dexterity of a professional card shark. Breathing became difficult as yet another magnificent wave of pleasure swept though her shuddering body, she bit down hard onto his neck when the attack on her senses was at its height. Paul yelped and quickly moved away and then onto her before sending himself deep up into her shaking body. He carefully watched her face as he rammed home his manhood in hard long measured strokes so that the intensity of her orgasm grew like some bedevilled earthquake inside, ripping and tearing at her every being. Each successive volley tripling in intensity from the next, she could do nothing but scream loudly with mixed pain and delight as each muscular spasm attacked her small shuddering frame. She climaxed when the waves all built to become just one mighty combined explosion and Jean could no longer control her actions or thoughts as she moaned and then screamed loudly so much so because that experience had never happened to her before, it was as if she was being shaken like a rag doll being torn apart. Paul held on until the massive fury subsided and then gently stroked her whole body, it was like being relaxed back to normality again. For several hours the two felt extreme warmth with one another and their pillow-talk began to unwind and reveal itself because of the warm feelings and due to fact that they had been totally exposed to each other, any hidden secrets between the two were no longer necessary. Paul skilfully probed for undisclosed business revelations very carefully, realising that even with their current closeness, it would still take several such sessions before he knew everything about Johnson Interiors that he needed to find out. At eight thirty the following morning when his white BMW pulled up in front of Johnsons Interiors, Paul already knew for sure that he had her exactly where he wanted her as he took her hand and placed a kiss softly in her palm.

"Thank you so much that was a really fabulous evening and if you don't object, I would like to see you again tonight that is, if you could possibly bear it. Tell you what, how does a show in the West End sound to you?" Jean was looking a little weary and she leaned forward across the vehicle and planted a kiss on his cheek.

"No, I have a better idea, why don't you come around to my place tonight and let me fix something for us to eat? I really am a great cook, I think you will enjoy my food."

"Fine, I think that would be a lovely idea, you have a super day and I'll see you tonight at about eight." She got out of the car and turned back to him, Jean giggled softly and thought to herself that yesterday, she would never have believed in love at first sight, yet here she was, madly in love having already slept with a man she had only met the evening before, right now it was all too much for this beautifully shy girl to comprehend. She turned into the reception area and saw Lynne already sitting at her desk.

"You're early."

"After yesterday's performance I don't want to be on the wrong side of anybody this morning," replied Lynne. Suddenly as if a giant bubble had been burst about her, Jean's love life was forgotten as she was brought straight down to earth with a bump, remembering the fiasco.

"Is my boss in yet?".

"No, but he phoned about five minutes ago to tell you not to expect him for awhile and to cancel any appointments that he has made for the rest of the day. As well as that, I have to cancel appointments for both Sandy and Christine today as well, do you have any clue what's really going on?"

"Nope," lied Jean as she turned to go to her office, although she subconsciously knew that it had something to do with what Sandy had said to her yesterday afternoon. Jean reached her office and quickly looked at Ernest's appointment book and saw that there were only two appointments, one at eleven o'clock and the other for lunchtime. She hoped that she would not create too much fuss by cancelling both appointments, never the less, they weren't very important meetings so it probably wouldn't matter very much, she thought as she lifted the receiver. After cancelling both appointments and promising to arrange fresh meetings once she had spoken to Ernest Johnson, she sat back and thought of how nice it was to be in love once again.

The Kixing

"THE KIXING"

CHAPTER SEVEN

When the alarm sounded the following morning to awake Ernest, he still felt terrible because it had been the second night running that he had hardly had any sleep whatsoever. For ten minutes he relaxed in the single bed made up in the spare room trying to decide whether it was worth even getting up to face what he suspected was going to be an horrific day at the office. Finally, he dragged himself from the warmth of the bed and moved through to the tiny bathroom to have his usual wake up daily shower. Having been unable to get to sleep for some time, he had tossed and turned for quite some time before going through to the spare bedroom so as not to keep waking his wife. Try as he might, he just couldn't get Peter Edwards and his debt to Johnson Interiors out of his mind. Something had to be done, the thing that he hadn't told Christine was that the business would fold if they didn't manage to at least recover half of the money from Powerbuild. He felt slightly better by the time he arrived for his breakfast, seating himself in the small breakfast nook leading away from the kitchen Ernest could see their plump, but cheerful housekeeper bustling around getting his usual breakfast of two poached eggs on toast eggs and coffee ready. When she finally placed it in front of him he could do nothing but complain about the food set before him. By the time he reached the office he had again worked himself into such a state that he knew it was going to be another day of shouting and screaming at his staff. Nothing that anybody said to him in the first few minutes was correct, Christine hadn't arrived yet, so he couldn't find out whether she had had any joy in managing to get some of her not so savoury friends to take on the debt recovery. Ernest could not ever remember feeling this low as he tried desperately to get his thoughts together. After inspecting the morning mail he called Sandy into his office.

"Sandy, I want a full report on my desk about all outstanding debts, in particular, I want anything and everything you can give me on Powerbuild. Also, I want a quick résumé on how much finance we can lay our hands on if we should get rid of certain redundant assets, where we can cut down on staff and the position if we push our overdraft to the limit and lastly, have a good look at where we can extend our credit facilities. Please don't leave anything unturned, it looks like we've been caught out by that company and we're going to need all of and other resources to survive this fiasco."

"You didn't have any joy with those bastards then." Sandy poked his head into the doorway then eased into the office as Jean passed by she pulled a face that made his stop.

"Listen you idiot, it's possible that Powerbuild may be liquidated at any moment and we're going to need all the backup capital we can lay our hands on just to survive this bloody crisis. Get your bloody staff to earn their keep by going out and collecting as many of the outstanding debts as possible." Ernest's blood count was rising with every word, there was no shouting, but rather an ice cold hiss to his voice.

"Also, if they are closed down, things here are going to be difficult for a long time to come, just remember not to say anything about this to anyone of the staff other than myself or my sister if you can. You and I are going to have to try and get some form of financial semblance out of this if we can right now and until we know what's happening at Powerbuild, we must handle this crisis by ourselves in the meantime. We must not cause a panic, do you understand?"

"Yes Ernest. I understand and I'll try to have a fully detailed financial report prepared before lunch and an asset breakdown for you by later this afternoon."

"Make sure you do and remember, you're to keep this right under your hat, we mustn't let on what's happening to anyone either here or outside the firm, it's imperative that we don't start a panic and words have wings and don't want the construction world rushing to Powerbuild's front door. Let's try to put Powerbuild under the hammer by forcing the issue into the courts also, see if our fat lawyers can obtain some sort of holding injunction against either Powerbuild or any of the Edwards assets."

"There's a thing called a Maraiva Injunction, it has both the power and means of stopping all movement of money through any of their bank accounts. All it may do is force the company into liquidation more quickly though and that way we'll also have to stand in line like their other creditors.

"Find out whether we can apply for it today, if we can, then let's go for it because armed with something like that hanging over them, we can at least threaten to close them down immediately if they don't start paying up.

"Sandy was at the door when Ernest suddenly remembered something.

"Oh, by the way, I would like you to give Jim the foreman a ten per cent raise, by using his head, he may, or may not have helped us catch the Powerbuild debacle in time with his quick thinking."

"You know something Ernest? We've both tried our utmost to get this money from them, we should've done something sooner but they seemed so respectable and always had some clever argument about our work. Next time we'll know better and refuse to continue working for them or anybody else when they first start their nonsense. I never suspected anything because they've never given us any problems with payments before. It just goes to show what can happen."

"What we should have done and what we did do at the time is of bloody little consequence Sandy, right now we're going to be lucky to survive if we at least don't retrieve something out of this mess. Hopefully Christine will be doing something to get us out of this jam. Have you seen her today?"

"No, maybe she's at a site meeting, do you want me to find out?"

"No, you get busy with your work." For most of the day Ernest kept himself busy finding out what information he could about their dealings with Powerbuild. On certain occasions that he left his office, he ended up making life generally unbearable for the whole staff. The bad night did not help to fuel his general ill feeling towards any of his associates, Sandy was as good as his word and by three thirty had all the facts together in every form and type. The lawyer was busily trying to obtain the injunction and Christine was nowhere to be found. He felt ready to face Powerbuild in their offices and would be able to trade better punches than they could give in return. He was damned if he was going to submit to this bully, because they had spent years building up what was now a really good business, and he wasn't going to allow it to be snatched from him by someone who did not know how to run his own business properly.

"Jean, get Sandy in here with all the reports, we're going to the Powerbuild office right now. " Sandy stopped at Jean's desk.

"It's worse than I thought, we could also go under if those bastards don't pay up."

"Really that bad?" Sandy nodded his head as he pushed open the door and entered the large office as Ernest pulled on his jacket, collected all the papers together and made for the door.

"Have you got everything?"

"Yup."

"Meet me at their offices, you better take your car in case we need something more or the meeting goes on longer than expected." On arriving at the impressively decorated offices of Powerbuild, Ernest waited on the stairs for several minutes, before seeing Sandy hurrying in his direction.

"Listen Sandy, I'm going to play the diplomat, because you're bigger than me, I want you to play the part of the heavy. Today you've got to give the performance of your life... okay?" This was a particular ploy that they used in certain circumstances in the past and Sandy had a unwarranted reputation among his construction industry colleagues as being very hard and having a vicious temper. This was not really the case but his large size and looks often gave people the impression that he could be the rough gangster type. Ernest played up to debtors with the old good guy, bad guy routine and in most cases it seemed to work. Ernest entered the main reception area for the second time in twenty four hours. The same pretty bimbo receptionist was seated behind her long marble desk and was busily filing her nails. She recognised Ernest immediately.

"Mr Edwards isn't here at the moment, we're not expecting him in until tomorrow."

"Bullshit," Sandy butted in. "His car is in the basement." The girl was taken aback as she try to stammer her way through some excuse. Sandy moved forward threateningly and leaned over the marble counter.

"Pick up the receiver." There was a loud buzz on the switchboard.

"One moment." She listened to whoever was at the end of the line. Sandy noticed that she was relaxing visibly as she suddenly offered the receiver to Ernest.

"It's Mr Edwards... He must have, er, come into the building through the back way," she lied.

"Hello Mr Edwards. I'm here to sort out this mess." After about a minute he pulled a face.

"Look, I know nothing about it. Okay, I'll come straight up." He handed the instrument to the girl and turned to Sandy. "You head off, something's come up and I'll handle it from here. Don't worry we could be out of trouble soon." Ernest didn't want Sandy to know what Peter Edwards had to reveal. Inwardly he was shocked at what his sister had arranged, Sandy was reluctant to leave because he knew that people like Edwards used Ernest by telling him long sob stories. This was exactly why Christine had taken over from him, finally Ernest persuaded him that Edwards wanted to talk to him alone and that some form of payment would be made. Sandy wasn't happy, he had a gut feeling that the man was about to pull another of his stunts to delay payment, he left the building and instead of heading for the office, decided to call it a day. He swung his car south and headed towards his little cottage where his guest from last night would still be waiting for him. Sandy whistled softly as he wondered whether this evening was going to be as good as the last.

"You look knackered, had a rough day?" Julie asked as Sandy moved into his lounge.

"Sit down I'll pour you a drink."

"It's been a bitch. The company's in a lot of trouble." Silently she smiled to herself, this was exactly the news she wanted to hear. She was wearing his dressing gown and her long hair fell loosely around her shoulders. Sandy moved behind her and slipped both hands around her waist.

"Tell me about it."

"Almost like a married couple this, I could easily get used to being waited on. You're welcome to do this as long as you want to." She turned and kissed him long and hard as she started to loosen his tie.

"Okay then, let's go to the bedroom and you tell me about your day." Julie could see that he was down in the mouth and was equally sure that by the time she was finished with him tonight, he would have told her everything she wanted to know. "Where's my son?"

"What do you mean? How the hell am I supposed to know where your son is?" "You know full well what I'm talking about, your gangsters terrorised my family before taking one million in bank drafts to pay your debt, I held up my side of the bargain, now what have you done with my boy?" Ernest was trying to figure out what the man was talking about as he gazed at the two large TV screens fixed to the wall. That was how he had known about their arrival at reception.

"I really don't know what you're on about, please tell me just what happened, I really don't know of any but, I soon mean to find out what the hell is going on." Edwards explained in undiluted frankness the horror of what the men had put his family through before forcing him to hand over the finance to cover the Johnson's outstanding debt. Ernest listened, his senses reeled in elation at having recovered the finance and in equal disgust at how the men had attacked the family.

"I really don't know anything, my sister might though, I promise you I'll talk to her and find out what's going on." He called the office and spoke to Jean who hadn't seen Christine all day. After a few minutes he finally tracked her down at her house.

"Chrissie, did you arrange for some hoodlums to recover the debt? Mr Edwards says he paid up and those guys still have his son as a hostage?" Christine immediately told him to shut up and not to get involved and that the Edwards boy was already on route home at that very minute. There had been some hitch in cashing the bank drafts but that it had all be sorted out. Ernest replaced the receiver.

"He's on his way home, you should get your call in the next few minutes, apparently he was well looked after and came to no harm."

Ernest could see that his statement was of such relief that Peter Edwards was almost about to break down and cry. He picked up his briefcase and quickly bid the big man farewell, as he walked down the front stairs he did a little hop, their business was safe again thanks to Christine and her dubious friends. He had never really dared ask her about them or her relationship with the many strangers that were always visiting her. He knew that it had something to do with her late husband's connections and that she never spoke about her role, but this time it was too much for him to contemplate just how his twin could be involved with people that cut a family pet to pieces in front of them. This was the first time he realised just how powerfully ruthless she was and decided then, that he would have to have a quiet word with her to find out what her other life was really all about.

"God, you're beautiful Chrissie, we live again."Jean was feeling very weepy as she packed up for the day. It had been a mixture of tiredness and the ensuing panic created by Sandy's ominous words that the firm was in serious trouble. The last straw was her employer's frantic call looking for his sister, everything smelt of disaster today. The only bright light on the horizon was the special food that she now had in the bag for her big evening meal with Paul Hunter.

"Night, night Lynne." She swept out of the office and rushed home and at exactly eight o'clock there was a sharp rap on the door. Paul wore casual clothes and had a massive bunch of flowers in one hand and a bottle of Champagne in the other. Jean was dressed in a long flowing kimono and seeing him again, suddenly forgot all the troubles of her day for a few minutes.

"Come here," he held his arms wide apart. She again melted into the warmth of his embrace and once they moved inside the flat he immediately took up where he had left off this morning.

"Stop for a moment, let's have something to eat first."

"With you, I could live on the fruits of love. Tell you what, let's have a candlelit dinner in bed." Jean laughed loudly because she had never been treated this way before. "All right."

"I'm going to have a quick shower, why don't you join me?"

"Because I've just had a bath, anyway, you go ahead, by the time you're finished, dinner will be ready." Paul had his shower and when he entered the bedroom, Jean was sitting cross-legged on the bed with a large spread of delectable dishes spread out before her. Paul noticed that she still had the kimono on and he immediately moved and relieved her of the garment. The two nude figures sat facing each other on the bed.

"Now, how was your day?" Paul asked.

"Disastrous."

"Why?"

"Well, I shouldn't be saying anything but to you about this, but it looks like the firm may not survive much longer."

"How so?"Jean removed six oysters from an ice bucket and placed them carefully on a plate in front of Paul. She continued to speak as she did so.

"One of the construction companies that we've done work for is about to collapse and it could take us with it." Alarm bells sounded in Paul's head, he had to find out who it was because of Minter's diversification in the construction industry.

"What's the name of the company? I'm entering into contracts with several companies and don't want to be caught out." Jean remembered Ernest's words and knew that if she told him, it could have a knock on effect.

"Only if you promise not to pass the information to anyone."

"I promise." She thought long and hard and Paul could see that she was in two minds about telling him, he moved to her side of the bed and pulled her into a lying down position. Carefully he emptied an oyster from its shell onto her belly button, then slowly squeezed a lemon, Tabasco sauce and pepper onto the oyster. Jean squealed as the concoction was slowly mixed together by Paul's finger.

"Now, don't laugh like that, how do you expect me to eat my meal on this plate when it's shaking like this." He leaned forward and sucked at the mixture, then very slowly and deliberately sucked up the remains.

"There, it's good to hear your laughter again, why let a little thing like money spoil your day?"

"You're right, if you have any dealings with a company called Powerbuild I suggest you stop doing any further business with them." Paul emptied another shell onto his human plate, somehow he had to call in the information to Norman or David as soon as possible. Accidentally, but on purpose he removed the plastic stopper and tipped the bottle of Tabasco sauce all over the place.

"Quickly into the shower before the Tabasco burns into your skin." Jean rushed in one direction, Paul in the other. He pretended to be going to the kitchen, in the lounge he quickly called David Lividsky and gave him the news. He also gave him Jean's telephone number and asked him to call him in ten minutes as well as asking him to understand his gibberish because he needed an excuse to leave Jean's flat. By the time Jean returned, Paul had everything off the bed and was busily cleaning up the mess. The telephone rang on cue and David asked to speak to Paul.

"Okay, I'll catch the first plane out tomorrow," said Paul to the caller and then replaced the receiver, he turned to Jean and spread his arms widely. "Bad news I'm afraid. I'll have to leave earlier than expected because there's trouble on one of our sites in the Middle

East. Don't worry though, I'll be back in a couple of days. Now, let's finish that meal." They returned to the bed with some urgency, but this time it was not to complete their dinner until much later. Paul left the sleeping Jean just after midnight and as he drove away he used his car telephone to speak to David.

The Kixing

"THE KIXING"

CHAPTER EIGHT

David Lividsky entered his office to find his five soldiers already seated at the long table and he immediately sat down and began vigorously cleaning his glasses as he indicated to June to be seated on his right.

"Although we thought Johnson Interiors was going to be a hard nut to crack, certain unforeseen events have come into play and it seems that we could be in for an easy ride on this one. Paul got lucky and called me last night to tell me that Johnson's are in financial difficulty, this will probably make our life a lot easier for hasty takeover and that's why I've decided to call this snap meeting to bring everybody up to date and see whether anybody's possibly got anything further to add to Paul's decidedly lucky bit of fortune. Now that we know what's happening and where to concentrate, let's begin putting all of our energy into finding out exactly how bad things are and find out what's going on. Has anyone got anything else to add before we decide what happens next?" Julie sat forward and cleared her throat, indicating that she had some information to impart.

"Word on the grapevine through a friend of mine is that Johnson Interiors are into a construction company called Powerbuild for over a million and apparently, if the company goes under, it's going to take Johnson's with it."

"Great!" David raised both hands and closed his fists in a gesture of glee.

"That confirms the story that Paul gave me last night, it would appear that now having two separate and independent accounts, the scale of trouble that they seem to be in is quite dire, does anyone else have anything to add." Julie nodded thoughtfully before continuing the good news.

"Also coming from my source, it would seem that Johnson's have landed themselves in this trouble because they've recently installed some very costly automated plant for some newly patented system. Supposedly, this new system was going to radically change the shop fitting industry and it's supposed to be very hush-hush. The Powerbuild saga couldn't have come at a worse time for them. Had it happened a few months ago they could have survived without major difficulties but the investment into this new machinery had cost far more to develop than had been originally estimated. This had placed a heavy burden on their current financial arrangements but then the extra substantial investment that was required, then compounded with Powerbuild's unexpected large default in payment is why the present crisis seems to have kicked off."

"Who's been a busy girl then?" Paul teasingly intervened. Julie just smiled and pulled a playful tongue at him.

"Well, it seems that we're both enjoying our work, doesn't it?"

"As I was saying before being so rudely interrupted. The firm is extremely cash short due to the overspend and this catastrophe coming on top means they're ready to be sucked into MH Holdings at any time soon."

"That's for me to decide," David interjected. "Anything else?" Harry Ronson spoke for the first time. His slightly croaking voice fitted very well with his large muscular frame.

"Just one thing that may or may not be of any relevance to Johnson Interiors, but I was on the main Powerbuild site yesterday and found out that they're not hiring any labour. One of the onsite workers told me that staff are not being paid and so a lot of the crews have been leaving. The man said that he thought that their company was going under and that there was even talk of one of the directors ducking out of the country."

"Shit! They owe our group a lot of money, Jean get Trevor Reece in here quickly. Right people, let's quickly change tack, see what you can all find out about Powerbuild today."

"What about Johnson Interiors?" Paul asked. "I think in view of the circumstances and the amount owed to Powerbuild that we can move in on Johnson's almost immediately. Hewitt, it would seem that our friends from the trade unions won't have to bother making a place for you at Johnson Interiors. Call them and tell them not to worry and that we'll leave this favour for another day. Let's first find out what's really happening to Powerbuild, it's far more important just at this moment." The meeting broke up as the five left David and June alone and now seated at the long table by themselves. The unkempt figure of Trevor Reece complete with unlit pipe in his mouth shuffled his tall frame into the chair beside June.

"Trev, I need everything we have on Powerbuild as quickly as possible. It looks like they're in trouble and we've got to get in before it becomes public knowledge. Depending on what damage they've inflicted on themselves, we may be able to put a rescue package together and end up owning another largish construction company. I want to know what their debts are like, what subsidiaries they have, try to check their order book position and anything else, I need all the information yesterday." The tall man put a match to his pipe and sucked hard.

"What if they're not worth saving? What do we do then? They owe us a lot of money."

"We will need to weigh up all the pros and cons, In a funny way we still may be able to at least lay our hands on a super medium sized business even if we are forced to write off the debt of Powerbuild, if that's the case, it could be cheap at the price. Get the information and we'll have to make some form of decision immediately but by the looks of things, we're going to have to move extremely smartly because if Powerbuild goes, it could take Johnson Interiors under as well, and then we'll have lost both. Time is of essence." Trevor moved quickly. He had been through this type of scenario all before and knew that once rumours started circulating, it was generally too late to react. He knew they had possibly only hours to gain enough information and possibly strike some sort of deal. For now, it was all up to him to gather as much information on Powerbuild's position in the next hour or two. He also knew that Norman Minter and David would want to be inside Powerbuild's offices by no later than mid-afternoon. As he reached his office, he called his two assistants and gave them directions before lifting the receiver to start calling around himself he was working against the clock right now. David in the meantime had entered Norman's office.

"Trouble."

"What?" Norman asked, pointing to the chair in front of his large desk. "Powerbuild are about to take a dive, we have also found out that if they go, they could possibly take Johnson Interiors with them." David sat down and Norman waited for the lawyer to start his usual ritual of spectacle cleaning. Norman reached for his monthly figures without waiting for an answer.

"How much do Powerbuild owe us?"

"In rough terms, about one point six million. It's big."

"Any chance of recovering something from this mess?" David finished polishing his glasses and replaced the large white handkerchief in his pocket.

"I think so, we would have had to pay in the region of six million for

Johnson's if it was clean but against that, we could possibly go as low as one point two if we had obtained them by our usual route. Powerbuild owe Johnson's roughly a million, what we could do in the circumstances, is to write off or buy Powerbuild's bad debt and take over Johnsons with an offer of a rescue package, it could mean that we would be paying slightly above market price for saving them from going under. That's one scenario."

"What's the other?"

"Depending on how bad the situation is for Powerbuild, we could offer a rescue package for their shares and string out the payment for some time to Johnson's, it would have the same affect on them because at the moment, they're extremely cash short, which makes them really vulnerable to an easy takeover."

"How sure are you that Johnson Interiors will fold if Powerbuild goes?"

"Very sure. I have two totally independent reports on the pandemonium within Johnson's, one comes from their accountant and the other from the managing director's secretary. Therefore, the sources are impeccable."

"I don't know how you do it." Norman laughed. "All right, then that sounds like the route we should go. How long before we know the full facts?"

"I've got Trevor Reece and the team working on it at the moment, by midday we should have most of the facts to hand."

"Keep me posted. It sounds as if we're going take instant decisions on this one, you and I are going to have to meet the directors of Powerbuild at some stage, preferably today." By two thirty, Trevor Reece and his assistants had found out everything that they we are likely given such short notice, they had collated all the papers and put them into a folder before presenting them to David.

"If I were you, I wouldn't touch them, that company's in huge trouble."

"How big?"

"If my information's correct, then Peter Edwards, the managing director has been milking the firm for all its worth."

"What are you telling me?"

"That the company doesn't have any real assets to speak of, their managing director is as bent as a paperclip, he's crooked and will probably end up in jail when the shit hits the fan."

"Jesus. How much?"

"My educated guess is that it totals up to several millions, if you add that to what they already owe us, we would be stupid to take it on. In the long run, the shortfall wouldn't be able to be retrieved and we would also end up footing a huge bill to try to save what is now a worthless shell of a company. If I were you, I would cut my losses and concentrate on saving that shop fitting outfit, it's a far better bet and very unfortunate to have been caught out. It at least has enough very good assets to warrant its rescue."

"Thanks for getting this together so quickly Trevor, let me have a look at the report before speaking to Norman. In the end, it's going to be his decision which way we're going to have to jump." Trevor left the office as David started going through the prepared report and by the time he had finished with it, he knew that Trevor was right. He shook his head as he reached for the phone and asked June to get Peter Edwards on the line. He knew that they were going to have to get extremely heavy handed if they even expected to recover even a portion of the outstanding debt. He sat back and took in a deep breath while waiting for the call.

"He's not at work today, apparently he's ill and isn't expected in the office for a few days. Shall I get someone else on the line?"

"Yes. Get me the chief accountant or any of the other directors, there must be someone in authority to talk to." He waited for a few minutes before a woman's voice came on the line.

"Who's that?"

"This is Mary Young, how can I help you?"

"I want a meeting with you, and it must be today, Mary Young."

"I'm afraid that won't be possible."

"Listen young lady..." David paused to gain the maximum effect.

"I am not your normal customer and before you can cough I will be able to shut your company and you'll be out of work. Mr Edwards is away and I have a report in front of me which states your company is trading illegally. Now, you're responsible for the accountancy practice of the firm and therefore, if you leave me no alternative, you'll be arrested before the day's end..." David let the words hang in the air. There was a deafening silence on the other end of the line.

"I...er, I suppose I can fit you in. What time do you intend coming in?"

"Four. It would be in your interest to try and make sure that some of the directors are around, we need to discuss a serious case of fraud and on the other hand, we could even be of help, but... if you mess us around we'll gladly send you and the company down the tube. Do you understand?" Again, the long silence.

"How can you help?"

"That's better, as you know we are the largest company in the construction field and have extremely powerful financial resources. We want to discuss Powerbuild's plight and see if there's a way to avoid the problem now facing you. That's why you must try to get Mr Edwards and the other directors to attend the meeting."

"I'll try." David knew from past experience that the accountant would be the one to take the blame for the company's bad trading, he was also aware that all accountants took their orders from those in power and somehow, he had to get to the person responsible for the mess as quickly as possible. Just perhaps, by offering a possible rescue package often worked and brought the main greedy party to the table. It had occasionally worked in the past, he closed the folder and made his way to Norman Minter's office. Norman and David arrived at Powerbuild's office in Norman's pride and joy, a 1936 Rolls-Royce that had been passed on to him by his father, every week without fail on Wednesday, he would drive this car into town so that it could be professionally washed and polished. If it weren't for the age of the car, he had always preferred driving this older car to his new Rolls. Like his flamboyant lifestyle, he loved fast cars and had a Ferrari and an Aston Martin that he only tended to use on occasional weekends. Parking the valuable car in the basement, he and David took the lift to the first floor reception area. Mary Young turned out to be of average height but had powerfully built shoulders, something like an athlete, reflected Norman in his mind's eye. His gaze quickly assessed the rest of her, she had dark hair, he guessed she was a middle aged women who obviously kept herself in perfect trim by weight training and jogging. Mary showed them to the boardroom and already seated at the table were three men who all introduced themselves as the current directors of the firm. Mary made apologies for Peter Edwards who she said was ill and still unreachable. Without ceremony, David got straight down to the business at hand.

"In this folder is a full report on the state of Powerbuild. The company is still trading even though it's insolvent." The members around the table were all uneasy.

"Furthermore, the firm's funds have flitted away and it would seem that your managing director has been putting his hand into the till in quite a large way. Consequently, your suppliers, sites, men and I strongly suspect, yourselves are not being paid. Everybody here is hanging on in the hope that things are going to change and from experience I can assure you..." He waited a moment. "They won't because this firm is theoretically in liquidation." It was as if all the people sitting at the table had been hit by an earthquake, they all looked quite stunned. David had been through this all before, he knew that they were all unconsciously aware how bad things really were, but somehow were all simply living in hope that the situation would somehow be magically resurrected. It always required someone like David to bring home the full reality that they were about to face for them to readily accept the situation. It was Mary Young that was the first to gain her composure.

"Mr Lividsky, you're right, we are under-capitalised, for weeks now I've been telling Mr Edwards to call in an administrator. However, he's confident that he can raise some extra finance and has on several occasions assured me that he's in serious negotiations with some large bankers who are going to take shares in the company." Both Norman and David had heard it all before, one of the directors spoke up to back her argument.

"Peter is shortly to leave for a final meeting in Germany, when I saw him yesterday he actually showed me an offer from Handelsbank, he had a letter of intent from them that they were already preparing a contract for him to sign." David sat back and thought about this statement for a while.

"You actually saw the original letter from the bank?"

"Well, not exactly. It was a photocopy."

"Did you see who signed the letter?"

"Yes. It was signed by a Herr Manfred Oberman the bank's director in Stuttgart." Norman got up, crossed to the telephone, checked for a number in his address book and called the Handelsbank's head office in Frankfurt. Keeping the line on loudspeaker open so that all could hear what was said, he was put straight through to the bank's president and asked him to check the facts just given them. Within two minutes he was assured that there was no Manfred Oberman working for the bank in Stuttgart.

"Well. it would seem that my facts are correct, your crooked Mr Edwards has been lying to everyone, you included. I would care to venture a guess that some of the major payments made to your suppliers and approved by Mr Edwards have also been filtered straight into his bogus accounts. That my friends is the general pattern of how to denude the company funds." The room was suddenly in total uproar as the truth eventually trickled through the disbelieving minds of the people seated at the table.

"What you've got to do immediately is to call the police and report the theft of funds. Next thing you've got to ascertain is how much is missing, this must be done immediately today you do keep up to date records, I hope?" David posed the question directly at Mary Young.

"Yes of course, the only thing I'm unsure of is which of the payments are to false companies." One of the men who David took to be the technical director knew exactly which clients' had done work for them over the past months offered to help Mary sort out genuine payments.

"Right Mary, do you have a feel for just how much finance the company is going to need to clear its debts."

"Somewhere between three and five million," came the immediate reply.

"Does that include monies due to you?" Norman interrupted.

"I'm afraid so."

"Can you do me a large favour?"

"What's that?"

"Stay on tonight and give me a full balance sheet of the position as of today. And if the situation is retrievable, then perhaps I can convince my board to put together a rescue package." Norman was a hard business man and was skilfully playing on the Powerbuild employees hope of salvation to give up their secrets. Inwardly, he had little intention of bailing out this dead duck, the price was too high but he needed to see exactly what Johnson Interiors' position was like.

"I'll have to stay behind and get a fully detailed statement of affairs ready for you tonight." Norman and David rose to leave but nobody at the table were aware that the Edwards family was at that moment, boarding a British Airways flight bound for Switzerland. Peter had arranged for a Swiss account where he would deposit most of the certificates and diamonds. By tomorrow he expected to be on another aircraft bound for Southern Africa. He could still live comfortably on the funds in his possession.

"Good. I'll have someone collect it first thing tomorrow morning." After being thanked for their intervention, Norman and David travelled back to MH Holdings. Both men said nothing because they knew it was too late to rescue Powerbuild, as Norman turned off the engine he turned to the lawyer.

"If nothing else, we've got Johnson's by the short and curlies, with the amount that they owe us and now this, they're ours. Don't waste time, I want them in the fold as soon as possible."

The Kixing

"THE KIXING"

CHAPTER NINE

"Ladeees and gentlemen! We now reach the highlight of this evening's entertainment!" The compère decked out in a smart dress suit took centre stage in what looked almost like some kind of mixture between boxing ring and cage fighter circle type structure. Norman, accompanied by Rhona Steel could both sense the heightened agitated buzz of crowd expectation now floating across the large banqueting room, the increasingly expectant sounds were drifting across the place, it seemed to move in waves something like the slow rumble of thunder gliding through a deep valley. Norman's ultimate passion was about to unfold in the very elite and extremely secluded surrounds of the 'Pièce de Résistance' Private Club. All patrons *to this particular evening's event* had been very carefully vetted and personally picked out by Norman to share and enjoy the completely illegal sport thought up by him and used for those heavy hitters own entertainment. All invited incumbents were now all seated at finely decorated tables having just indulged themselves with a fantastic six course culinary experience, this audience was not your usual group of fight fans because almost all stemmed from his millionaires row set of associates. Like most major gala premieres there was a broad mixture of high profile associates attending this evening's entertainment. All were sworn to secrecy and consisted of conglomerate chairmen, royalty, bankers and pop stars that now filled this large hall, Rhona took hold of Norman's hand and felt that his palms were sweating profusely.

"Excited?"

"Uh huh." He gave her hand a gentle squeeze, Rhona had seen this type of schoolboy nervousness several times before, it was always the same at his arranged fights, she knew that he became like an expectant child visiting the circus for the first time whenever he arranged these highly private events, the whole upshot was fraught with risk and danger of being caught out because this was not going to be just an ordinary fight night. Tonight was the culmination of weeks of stealthy negotiations coming to a resounding climax that was now reflected in Norman's sweating palms and placing him on some sort of curious adrenalin high that was second to no other sensually elevated feelings that her chairman could ever match or experience.

"Which one's the favourite?" Rhona asked.

"I think that this American has the edge in tonight's fight, he has the better cage fighting pedigree and has already got two Kixing fights under his belt.'"

'Kixing', as tonight's event was commonly referred to among its select band of spectators, it was a highly illegal form of fighting dreamed up by Norman after witnessing Thai kick-boxing sessions and with further development was now used to entertain rich associates as an after dinner entertainment for those with a passion for fighting. The game had taken on sinister proportions after several bouts by moving that extra step further so that by the end of the fight, one of the two contestants would definitely lie critically injured for life or of most occasions would be dead as a result of this new sport called of Kixing, the name was a mixture of kicking and fighting,. It had started slowly but with the thirst for more and more blood it had moved into a very dark area of what could be termed as a sport and for this reason alone, it bore similarities to the classic undertones of wild clandestine bare knuckle fights held during the last century. These bouts were always held behind closed and very secure bolted doors and betting stakes knew no limits on the outcome of a particular bout.

"Would you please welcome the two gladiators into the ring!" The compère announced before a long shrill of trumpet sounded throughout the large hall and that was then immediately followed by flashing lights and loud drumming throughout the hall as both combatants wearing silken dressing gowns, names emblazoned on the backs made their steady way from differing directions and between the tables through the excited crowd towards the central ring. Once they had clambered into the ring and the crowd had roared its approval it then slowly subsided as the assembly quickly settled in to enjoy tonight's spectacle.

"In the red corner, from Britain, we have John ... 'Spikey' McTavish!" The normally reserved and elite, all togged up in tuxedos and long evening dress once again erupted. Their usual niceties and false facades of decorum disappeared in that moment, whistles and shouts echoed right around the room."Also, would you please welcome, ...all the way from America, the undefeated ...Charlie, 'Mean Machine', Brown." The large get-together once again erupted as. both men began divesting themselves of their long dressing gowns to reveal their differing but strange looking attire. Both men now looked for all the world like they were wearing some form of kit out of an ancient Roman gladiator's manual in the most true sense of the word.

"Magnificent specimens, aren't they?" Rhona was particularly impressed by the chiselled shining coal coloured features of the black American's face. It was totally unmarked.

"The Brit has got a tough fight on his hands, *this time*." Both men wore what looked for all the world like some kind of leather undersized ski suits that were snugly fitted with shiny plastic solid breast plates each containing large heart shaped hole cut outs toward their left side to expose an attack area to the heart. The full light weight plastic extended from the throat down to just above each man's groin that was left unguarded, continuing downwards those skimpy material of the ski suit type outfits had neat fitting plastic guards that covered their upper and lower legs but, the area around the knee caps was completely exposed. The really sinister impact was what was worn full length on the arms and around the upper part of the feet. These two areas were altogether covered in black leather, each filled with bright shining steel studs that now danced and flashed their reflective menace against the bright overhead lights as the men moved about in preparation for the bout. To complete the gladiator's uniform, both men now donned plastic masks fixed with straps to the back of the head. It was only a half mask covering the nose and upper face, but, leaving the jaw completely exposed to the opposing attacker.

"Ladeees and gentlemen! Your attention pa-leese! This fight will be over six rounds of four minutes duration each, ...that is unless, one of the gladiators is hurt or unable to continue!" The tension and exhilaration of anticipated battle was being heightened and so felt by all seated at their finely ornate fare laden tables around the large arena room. They all knew what was about to happen, they were all about to witness the maiming, or more than likely even death that represented barbaric pugilism at its worst. Norman sucked deeply on his wet Churchill Havana cigar while Rhona could see that he was savouring each and every moment of this build-up as he listened to the compère.

"Your referee this evening is, ...George Mellis. Pa-leese give him your warmest welcome!" The burly, well known championship boxing referee entered the ring to thunderous applause. The compère continued his very carefully rehearsed and familiar building up of the crowd, milking their tension for all that it was worth. Norman had been through this so many times that as he concentrated on the two combatants while trying to decide which one would walk away with a truly handsome prize tonight. They had both already been paid handsomely and would each earn more than one hundred thousand pounds sterling, plus expenses for simply turning up for tonight's work. This was the tenth tournament that had been staged so far and both men had already been seen by the audience before tonight's fight. The American twice having fought and McTavish only once. In all of those fights, each time the unfortunate loser had been smashed up so badly that they would remain crippled for life. Norman always made sure that all underground medical expenses were paid for these gladiators because the fighters could not be taken into regular hospitals. During the previous ten bouts, only two fight losers hadn't made it and died due to multiple horrific injuries to their systems but, where Norman was clever, also meant that all money due to the fighters were automatically sent to the direct relatives afterwards with the proviso that nothing was fed to the outside world. Both audience and fighters were always fully aware of the potential consequences that these illegal fights brought with them, but then when men want a large payout for that one last fight, they all realised that risks had to be taken to stage these events. The *sport* of Kixing under Norman was fast developing an elite following, gathering wealthy patrons who were increasingly prepared to pay substantial sums for the luxury of being invited into an inner circle to witness this unusual dinner entertainment. Invariably any extra cash that remained after paying all expenses, was always then split between the two entertainers for their part in proceedings.

"Right. This is it." Rhona felt Norman's hand tighten as the two men were called to the centre of the ring, the crowd stilled to a whisper as the gladiators faced each other and the referee confirmed the few rules that the sport contained. It wasn't that long ago since Norman devised this form of martial art cum boxing by noticing that there were four vulnerable open spots on the human body to attack; the jaw, which could end up smashed; next, the heart with its non protected breast plate being a possible clean death blow position; lower down, the fighter's genitals and lastly, the open knee caps in order to lame the opposition before moving in for a kill. Using both feet and fists covered with sharp studs, the protective plastic guards tended to spread the force of all incoming blows. It was when the open areas were hit squarely, that any *real damage* was done. The genuine art of this competition being to keep the opponent away from the vital regions while searching for an opening without being compromised. It was a carefully constructed rule that all blows to any parts of the back meant automatic disqualification and non-payment of fees. Therefore, fighters in trouble when hurt, would immediately try and turn away or lie down to protect themselves. Punches and kicks were carefully measured to ensure that they all made contact to the front of the body. Rhona tensed, feeling the adrenalin pumping full stream into her every being.

"I'm think I'm going to shout for Spikey. We've got to stick by our own, you know?"

"Then let me give you a present, I'm going to place a bet for you." Norman leaned forwards and tapped some numbers into a small keyboard that was placed on each table, its red light immediately turned green indicating the bet had been accepted. By the end of the evening bets totalling many millions would have been made.

"You're crazy, that's too much." Rhona giggled.

"It's only money and you deserve a treat, if your guy wins you double that fifty grand. Good luck my darling."

When the bell sounded the two were set off like carefully stalking cats, each measuring the others' height, length of reach and punching ability. They both knew that to make one mistake it could be their last as they flicked out arms tentatively trying while attempting to distract their opponent. The American led with a short kick towards his opponent's knee, but moving quickly, Spikey danced to the side and countered with a right hand to the face to catch Brown full on his face protector. The American retreated and gathered himself in case Spikey lunged forward to press home his attack.

"C'mon Spikey!" Tension broken and screams for blood suddenly hit the air. Rhona and the rest of the crowd were suddenly egging on their favourites. Blows rained in from both players and skilfully parried, ridden or blocked until the bell rang for the first two minute break.

"That American is far too quick for McTavish. The yank is going to take him out, just wait and see." Norman had been to so many boxing matches that he had a sixth sense who had the upper hand in the early rounds. He was seldomly incorrect in his judgement as a beautifully bronzed young man wearing the tiniest of piece of material he could've found then entered the ring with sign denoting the next round. It looked as if he had stuck a softball down the front of his briefs and at once, the refined females surrounding the arena became extremely audible by whistling and shouting sometimes obscene suggestions at the parading Adonis. He played up to them by moving his lower body in rotating fashion in what he considered was seductive until he reached the starting point and as he exited the ring, the bell sounded for the second round.

"I'm still going to shout for the British man!" Rhona shouted back over the roar of the crowd.

"I hope you're wrong just this once." As happened in the first round, the two circled, waiting for the other to make the first move or slip up, Spikey darted forward flashing a full blooded kick towards Brown's genitals. The American, balanced on the balls of his feet swayed right taking the blow on his left thigh and aimed a looping punch at the incoming British attacker's jaw. It missed its target by the smallest of margins because Spikey was already on the retreat, stepping back, there was blood pouring from the left side area just below the face guard and where the studs had punctured the soft skin around his cheek. The crowd's hysteria became more frenzied at their sight of first drawn blood, this however, wasn't considered as any sort of real damage by both fighters as they moved around preparing themselves for the next attack.

"See, told you! He's hands are just too fast for McTavish." Rhona smiled as Norman shouted over the noise around them.

"Okay, so you're the expert. But ...that's just a scratch, there's a long way to go yet and my boy has very fast feet."

"Agreed. I don't think he's fast enough though." McTavish feinted with a blow towards the head and Brown swayed backwards to prevent the punch from landing. This left his lower regions protruding and exposed to a knee kick which his opponent delivered with full force. Fortunately for the American he moved just in time to prevent the full blow landing and the knee struck home, Brown dropped to the floor immediately. It was evident from his grimace that the blow had still hurt but, the referee sent the bleeding McTavish to the neutral corner and started counting. Payments to the fighters depended on their performance and if Brown was now counted out he would only receive ten per cent of the purse. He took a deep breath and rubbed violently at his nether regions, the fight resumed with McTavish rushing to try to catch the wounded opponent. Rhona gleefully shook Norman's sleeve.

"See, I told you!" Women and men alike were now standing and cheering encouragement for their respective heroes, although noisy, Rhona could sense the building tension from the surrounding patrons throughout the whole room was like that, of a coiled snake waiting for the right moment to release itself. Unseen, but real tension was there and mounting as McTavish slammed a studded fist towards Brown's chin, but the man was too quick, taking the blow on the side of his face guard. Under the lights Rhona could see where the studs had scarred the mask as they had glanced off the brightly coloured plastic. Brown immediately tried to relieve the pressure of the attack by holding onto his oncoming opponent, the crowd now possibly sensing that the finish could be in sight, screamed abuse as the referee cautiously separated the pair. McTavish feinted again but the black American didn't fall for the trick twice, he was again beginning to move more freely, the restricting ache in his groin mentally forgotten. Rhona saw that Norman's face was wet from perspiration and his eyes now studied the two men closely, not daring to blink in case he missed anything. She also knew how excited he had became, Kixing was more of an aphrodisiac to him than sex could ever be. She leaned close to his ear.

"My boy's got him, he's going to kill the American." Without looking at her, she just caught his words over the screams from around the hall.

"It's not over yet." The bell rang and tension seem to momentarily relax, this time a young girl wearing similar golden briefs and no top entered the ring carrying a sign for round three, it was inevitable that wolf whistles and sexist taunts greeted the topless girl.

"Saved by the bell. Huh Norm?" Norman just gave her a simple knowing smile as the lucid bell rang out for the start of the next round. Both men moved to the centre. McTavish tried to pick up where he had left off by throwing an arcing punch towards Brown's head. The black American was waiting for it as he swayed and shot out a foot straight at the Briton's kneecap. The blow was vicious and true as it hit home, the audience saw pain momentarily etch the man's face as realisation struck fear. The American drove his studded fist hard into the soft flesh to the left side of the breast plate. It struck its target like a hammer blow that could be heard from the back of the hall as the helpless Spikey McTavish started to drop, Brown threw a long punch which seemed to start from the other side of the ring towards the defenceless man's head. The crushing and smashing of the man's jawbone could also be heard right around the room. His body lifted, then dropped like a fully loaded sand bag until it hit the floor. The referee didn't even bother counting and he quickly stepped in to try and release the unconscious man's face guard, the heavy jaw-line was almost at right angles to the rest of his face as blood spilled out in throbbing gushes from distorted aperture. A doctor raced into the ring and took over his main concern wasn't for the ugly twisted mouth, but for the blow to the heart. The man's body was writhing and starting to go into traumatic convulsion, the doctor placed one hand on the man's heart and then thumped down hard with the other to arrest the convulsion. Norman turned and studied some of the faces in the crowd, it pleased him because he could see a look of fascinated horror as the doctor struggled to save McTavish's fast dwindling life. The prone body heaved and then lay absolutely still, after what seemed like an eternity to Norman, the doctor stood up and shook his head sadly. Stretcher bearers entered the ring and the doctor continued trying to revive the fighter with a defibrillator shocking brought into the ring, no matter how hard he tried, nothing or nobody moved, everyone totally captivated and fascinated by the sight of a life being snuffed out so quickly in full view of the baying crowd. Norman secretly knew that this death would increase the opportunity of expanding his underground sport and quite whispering would somehow induct more followers when the stretcher bearers carried the dead contestant's body away. Brown also left the ring after the stretcher had left the arena, there was now a hushed calm that had befallen the large hall, Rhona had absent mindedly noticed that there was absolutely no look of remorse as Brown had lifted the face guard from his head and hurled it into his corner. Nobody cheered most in slight shock never uttered a word, Norman slowly turned to Rhona.

"There you have it, maybe next time, maybe you'll listen to me." He spoke in hushed tones. The compère again entered the ring.

"Thank you one and all for coming tonight, for those of you who are staying on, ...there will be a free bottle of Champagne at each table." Odd cheers went up, breaking the highly-strung moment and suddenly the tension was over. People coughed and laughed nervously as everyone tried to settle once again, Rhona kept her eyes firmly fixed on Norman because his whole body now seemed to be quivering from some form of release. She had seen the same thing happen every time there had been a Kixing fight, it was as though he was having a gigantic orgasm now that his high degree of tension had been fulfilled and liberated. She squeezed his hand as he began to settle.

"You okay?" He took a long breath regaining his composure.

"Yeah. That was something, wasn't it?"

"Uh huh."

"Over-confidence was your man's downfall, he thought he had it over and done with, but he didn't reckon on the American's resilience. Oh well, that's life, I suppose. Want a drink?"

"Let's have one glass. I'm exhausted, I never realised how much energy each Kixing tournament takes out of me." Some of the crowd were starting to drift away amid excited chattering while others stooped at the gravity at seeing a man killed in front of their very eyes. Norman opened the bottle and poured two glasses of Champagne, several people, who were recognised household names passed their table on their way out and thanked Norman for the performance asking to be placed on the next list. A relative of the royal family sauntered across from the next table, shook Norman's hand and handed him an envelope. Norman waited until the group had left before opening the large letter.

"It's a personal invitation to share their box at Ascot, who knows, maybe I'll get a knighthood out of introducing Kixing to the world?" Rhona laughed loudly and took a long sip at her drink.

"Then again, because you're a bachelor and there won't be a Lady Minter, they'll wait until you're married." Norman ran his finger down the side of her face. "If that were the case, I would probably have to marry you so that the problem would be solved."

"Oh no you don't, I'm too old for you and anyway too set in my ways to get married to you or anyone else for that matter. Working with your father, then being your stand-by mistress and the business, has been my happy reward. I don't want anything to complicate that, so you would have to find someone else to fill that role." Norman smiled. Rhona had always been there for him, she was his best friend, sister, mistress and secretary all rolled into one. She was part of him and that would never change, again he gently ran his finger along her hairline then lovingly tugged at a loose hair.

"I know, Come on old lady, let's get you home for your rest." They both laughed at his teasing, he was quick to rise and pulled back her chair as she stood up. Taking her by the arm he guided her between the array of tables stopping now and then to greet someone of extreme importance. Outside, he ushered her into the passenger seat of his Rolls-Royce. On the way home she rested her head on his shoulder, both boss and secretary felt happily contented with their current lives. Neither expected any form of sexual attachment tonight, they had both had more than their necessary amount of fulfilment for one evening.

"THE KIXING"

CHAPTER TEN

Early the following morning Susan showed Mary Young into Norman's office.

"Tea or Coffee?"

"Tea, white and two sugars would be lovely, thank you."

"Please take a seat, I won't be a moment," said Norman who was on the telephone discussing a forthcoming world championship fight with a manager of one of the contenders.

"Don't give me that, we've already agreed terms and you can't up the ante at this late stage. If you try anything as stupid as that, I'll have you in front of the boxing board before your arse can touch ground." He smiled at Mary as he listened to what the manager had to say.

"Right, now you're being sensible just say your boy wins, then for his next fight we can arrange far better terms. Just accept that while he's the challenger he only comes second as far as the world is concerned, it's up to you to make sure he becomes the champ." Norman replaced the receiver.

"Each time the same thing, every fighter suddenly becomes some sort of a Prima Donna. Really when they are outside the ring they can perform better than any actor or ballerina, it makes me sometimes wonder whether it's all worth the hassle putting these fights together."

"Then why do you do it?"

"That's the thing it's all the hype, it's always so exciting to know that everything comes together and the two gladiators finally enter the arena. Believe me, it always gives me a buzz that I couldn't even begin to explain." Susan returned with David following close behind.

"Right. Now let's get down to business." Mary Young handed Norman a thick file that she had spent more than five hours balancing, extracting and compiling the report last night. She wasn't sure that she had managed to find everything, but for the point of discussion this was her best effort in the little time allowed to her. David could see that she was exhausted as he rose and walked to a position so that could jointly study the report, after a few minutes Norman whistled softly. "Jeez. If these figures are correct and I don't doubt whether you may have only have found part of it, it would now seem that your Mr Edwards has spirited away over three or four million from the company."

"That was all that I could find out in the allotted time, you'll also note on the following page that there are some further queries that amount to another two million that is unaccounted for as yet. There wasn't time or means for us so we couldn't check them out last night."

"Have you done anything about Edwards yet?"

"Yes we have, the directors have got a meeting with members of the fraud squad this morning." Norman pointed to the outstanding amount owed to Johnson Interiors. David nodded.

"Thank you for this, believe me I greatly appreciate your efforts last night, these numbers show that the company is in worse shape than expected. I'll need to spend some time going through the figures before deciding whether we can arrange some form of offer. My advice to the directors is to call in the bank and ask them to appoint an administrator immediately. Armed with these figures, they will immediately have the power to retrieve the funds from Edwards. That is, if he hasn't spent it all already." Mary pulled a slight face and wearily pulled herself to her feet, Norman didn't have time or heart to really feel sorry for her now that he had seen everything he wanted to and had been assured by the figures he had seen he was certain that Johnson's were in big trouble. He also realised that his group stood to lose nearly two million and the saving factor in his mind was that armed with this information, he was going to acquire a super little shop fitting company without a struggle.

Ernest Johnson was busily dictating notes to Jean when the call from David came through. " Mr Johnson, your company have held up payment to us for nearly four months and because of this and in requisites of our normal credit terms, I must now ask you to pay everything. According to our records you owe us a little over three quarters of a million." Ernest sucked in hard because he knew full well that the banks were chasing him to reduce his overdraft facility and if he drew a cheque for MH Holdings, it would be rejected by the banks. " Mr Lividsky, I'll have to speak to our accountant and see what can be done to rectify the situation."

"I don't think you understood me very well, we will not accept any excuses and want the amount paid in full today."

"Somehow, I don't think that will be possible, we just don't have those kind of funds sitting around so what I can do is to arrange a part payment and we could come to some arrangement to repay the amount over the next few months. Would that be acceptable to your group?"

"Certainly not, from today, I'm instructing our group to suspend all supplies being made to Johnson's and if I don't receive the total amount by tomorrow morning, I intend to take immediate legal action."

"That's a bit harsh, isn't it?" We've always paid up on due date and because we've hit a slight snag in payments to you, you're not prepared to even be reasonable about the whole matter."

The Kixing

"You should have made arrangements with us beforehand, you didn't and now we're calling in our total debt to be paid in full immediately. Just make sure it's here tomorrow morning or else we have no alternative but to collect it from you or shut you down." The line went dead and Ernest's mind raced at a million miles an hour.

"Shit! What a bastard, Jean, I want you to find out where Christine is. I need to talk to her immediately."

"What's wrong?"

"That call was from MH Holdings, they're demanding that we pay them about three quarters of a million and we just don't have that sort of cash. They're threatening to close us down." Sandy's prophetic words were now coming to conclusion she thought as she made her way to her office. Christine had taken several days off to be with her daughter, it was an unusually warm sunny day when Ernest slid his Porsche in beside her Jaguar. Both mother and daughter were happily romping about in the swimming pool attached to the back of the red bricked, double-storied house. At the back built of glass like a giant conservatory, the indoor pool had a Jacuzzi and a sauna at the end nearest the house while the rest extended outward into the beautifully kept garden at the other.

"Anyone home!" Ernest shouted.

"Who's that?"

"It's only me." Christine wondered why she had even asked the question because it could have been the dustman, postman or rapist with that type of answer. She had immediately recognised her brother's voice but his answer still slightly upset her for that instant of stupidity.

"Why say, *just me,* you've got a name, haven't you?" Both women made their way to the edge of the pool, they were without a stitch of clothing and hadn't been expecting visitors.

"Hello you two nymphs." Ernest walked through the only open glass door and stood at the edge of the pool.

"What would you do if it was a complete stranger?"

"Scream for him to get the hell away from here, I suppose, his is a pleasant surprise, what brings you out here dodging the office for a change? You are supposed to be the one looking after the fort."

"We got to talk, there's big trouble brewing and we will have to get certain things sorted out very quickly."

"Ernest, I'm taking a short break and right now am having my regular morning swim so either you join us or you're going to have to wait until we're finished."

"I rather fancy hopping into the Jacuzzi but believe me, this is really serious, we must talk immediately." While Ernest went off to the changing room to hang up his clothes, Christine's daughter slipped her tall frame from the pool and wrapped a towel around herself.

"I'm going to leave you and uncle Ernie to have your business talks, they don't interest me, I'll be in the study when you guys have finished." Ever since the death of her husband, Christine had quickly returned to her previous carefree normal self having even made it a rule of the house that the family bathed nude because of his intolerance and jealousy and having been always ultra possessive and strict with both wife and daughter that when he died, Christine had quickly reverted to her natural carefree ways and made sure that her daughter was able to immediately relax from his excessive tyranny, it was only when friends were invited that swimming costumes were worn by both women. At first Ernest had shied away from her nature loving ways but soon found his consciousness accepting, then enjoying the freedom that swimming naked had brought to his normally staid behaviour

"Why not come in and have a swim first? Then, I'll join you in the Jacuzzi." Ernest raced to the edge and dived full length into the pool, he had never bothered hiding his nudity from his sister but with his gorgeous niece looking on, he had at first felt slightly embarrassed but that had all changed the more times that they shared the pool together. He swam several lengths before ducking under the warm water and coming up next to his twin.

"That's fantastic. It's cleared a lot of the business cobwebs away."

"Somehow I had the feeling you are really uptight and needed to relax a bit more, come, let's get to the Jacuzzi and you can explain what's bothering you." They entered the small bubbling square fixed at the house end of the swimming pool, it was large enough to hold four adults each seated on the broad tiled step situated under the water. Facing each other, they stretched their bodies across so that their weight was carried by the back of their legs and their shoulders.

"Now, what's all this about?"

"What happened to Peter Edwards the other night?"

"He paid up."

"How though?"

"I don't care how, he did pay up and that's all that matters."

"Chrissie, those thugs kidnapped his bloody child, how can you be associated with people like that?"

"Oh yes. What did that sonofabitch threaten to do to us? The man only understands violence, anyway, I told you to leave it to me. Who I employ to get the job done, doesn't concern you."

"Were they friends of your husband." Ernest had always had difficulty in calling him by name.

"Yes."

"I've never interfered in your life, but tell me something, Are those rumours true that your husband was somehow connected with the Mafia?" She stared long and hard at her twin as if trying to make up her mind about something which she had never been able to discuss with him before. He thought that he knew her every mood but he had never seen that particular look before and it sent a slight chill coursing through his body, now he regretted asking the question so directly and suddenly wished that he had left sleeping dogs lie.

"It's only because we're so close and I love you so dearly that I'm going to answer that question. You and I are as one and so inwardly, you know what the answer is going to be and I feel your every mood, so you know what's happening to me and never exactly said so. I appreciate your never asking or prying into my affairs, but you sensed that your husband was high up in what you term the Mafia, he was, in fact was what you had rightly presumed was called a Godfather, those men that used to call here were seeking his help and being given orders. I never got involved or ever questioned what he was doing but what I did know was that his family made an oath to protect me after he died and that's all they were doing for us the other night. They're always there if I should ever need them."

"Where's that payment now?"

"As you probably know, Edwards was about to do a runner, fortunately and with a stroke of luck on our part we got there just in time and he was made to give up some of the illegal stock bonds and bank drafts that he was about to flee abroad with. The reason the boy was held was for leverage against Edwards and it took almost a full day to have them cashed quietly without raising any flags. That's why the boy was held but I promise you, no harm would have ever have come to him, it was simply a ploy and he was taken to the Park Lane Hilton, treated like the prince he is all day. The funny thing was that he apparently wanted to spend another day living with the two men who were watching him and was very disappointed when they dropped him back at home." Ernest felt some form of relief.

"The reason I had to ask the question after all this time is because now, we have a much bigger problem."

"What is it?"

"MH Holdings are threatening to shut us down if we do not pay back everything we owe them, nearly one million, we don't have it."

"Tell me something, we haven't yet been officially been paid by Powerbuild have we, I know for a fact that Edwards has already left the country and I suspect.., in fact *I know*, that we're still due that debt by his company. If we simply placed almost a million into the firm's account, questions are going to be asked. Somehow this suits me because we'll have to smuggle the funds back into the firm, somehow without anyone except you and me knowing"

"You're right. If that amount was suddenly introduced through one of your accounts the Inland Revenue would be down on us like a shot, MH Holdings have very long tentacles and some really good friends."

"Don't worry, we'll think of something to get those funds into the company. Perhaps an external loan might be a good idea, it would mean we could repay it back to ourselves via our trust fund. I'll get somebody to work on it at the moment."

"We've still got MH Holdings to contend with."

"Don't worry, the money's there in the background just leave it to me and I'll take care of them if they start getting rough." Christine's daughter, now dressed in tennis whites approached them carrying a tray which she placed at the edge of the Jacuzzi. A glass jug filled with orange juice and ice was flanked by two tall glasses.

"Thought you may like something to drink."

"You're a darling."

"Mum, I'm going to the club for a couple of hours, so take your time and if you finish your discussions before I'm back, why not meet me there?"

"Okay. See you later my baby."

"Bye uncle Ernie." Ernest saluted his niece, except for her dark eyes, he couldn't help noticing how much she had begun resembling her mother at the same age, tall, purposeful and full of confidence.

" She's really turning into a beautiful woman."

"Yes, I must agree and when she finishes university next year I doubt that she will want to come into the business, but at the moment she's very much in love."

"Whoa! Who's the lucky man?"

"I haven't met him yet, it's some good looking Adonis from the club, from the way she describes him, he sounds like a bit of a playboy, I just hope she doesn't get hurt, but then again, you can't rule their lives forever, can you?"

"Nope, she's got your head on those shoulders, God help the man that crosses her."

Christine laughingly ran her hand along the inside of her brother's leg until it reached the top of his thigh. Very gently, she playfully pinched the loose skin below his scrotum.

"You say the nicest things." Ernest twitched and yelped at the unexpected move. Christine didn't take her hand away immediately, but let it linger at the top of his leg for some moments, he sensed her sudden change from genuine playfulness to something far more intense.

"The other thing that I stupidly promised Eduardo was that I wouldn't ever betray his love."

"What does that mean?"

"It's too complicated to explain in detail, but it means that I've vowed to keep his memory. I'm married to the family and can never get remarried."

"What?"

"Promises to the family, are promises for life. If I tried anything as silly as taking a lover or a husband after making a vow not to and then, in front of witnesses at his death-bed, means my life would be forfeit if I did."

"That's bloody ridiculous. You mean..."

"Yes, I've vowed to remain celibate for the rest of my life. Oh God, Ernie, what a stupid vow to make."

"How would they know?"

"I just couldn't take the risk, lately, it's been hell. As you know from our young days I have a sex drive that is second to none. Now, it's become my worst enemy." Ernest thought back to the day that they made a pact and changed from children to adults. It had all been her idea because they had both left their mother's womb together and Christine had insisted that they should become adults together. On the morning of their thirteenth birthday she had surprisingly climbed into his bed and coaxed her almost, but not quite reluctant brother to submit to her will and they had both lost the virginities together. She was not a tearaway as far as other males were concerned, but, whenever she could, she and her brother experienced the most wonderful love making sessions openly learning, teaching and experimenting with each other. This practice continued right up until the day Christine married Eduardo, the last time they had made love was on the morning of her marriage, she had come to his bed after midnight and they made non-stop love until the sun rose. Back then, it seemed as if they were losing each other forever and even now, Ernest could still feel the strong sense of being ripped apart with that final act.

"You could trust me, you know?"

"That's something I've been wanting to talk to you about however, I wasn't quite sure how you had feel about it after all this time."

"If you think about it, the only reason we're in business together is because we can't stay apart from each other. Chrissie, I need you and in some strange way *you need me*. Think how you fought your husband on many occasions, he was so jealous of you, he hated me and I'm sure he thought that there was more to us than just a family relationship. That's why I never brought up the subject again, I was scared for your safety."

"You're right, he did dislike you and was very jealous of you and constantly had me watched. The reason for not liking you was he thought you were weak and that's why I distanced myself from you. Believe me, if he ever thought or even suspected that we loved each other as much as we do and then been committing incest, he would have personally killed both of us even if he did not have the slightest proof that we were more than just twins."

Again she ran her hand up between his legs, this time she didn't stop short of his now erect penis. Lovingly, she began to run her fingertips all over, below the turbulent water line, somehow it was like a blind person rediscovering an old friend and needing to feel every tissue, crevice and contour in order to re-establish whether there had been any significant changes to his love toy over the many missing years.

The Kixing

"Ernie, I'm sorry if it seemed that I stopped loving you from the day I got married but I had to distance myself from you for your own protection."

"I understood that perfectly." Ernest began to reciprocate her movements by slowly investigating her most private of places. The two didn't have to say anything to each other as they both lay in the warm bubbling water rediscovering what had been missing out of their lives during these long years.

"Bubbling water," muttered Christine. "It's as if we're starting from inside mother's stomach again." As one being, the slow relaxing environment lifted their sensations until both felt the sudden explosion of love at exactly the same time.

"We don't have too much time, let's make love right here in this warm womb of a place." In that Jacuzzi the two renewed their lifelong understanding. In Christine's mind, she wasn't betraying her vow to Edwardo, this was family and as they splashed in frenzied lovemaking they both somehow knew that they were again renewing their twinning bond that should never have stopped because they had never ever discontinued loving each other.

"THE KIXING"

CHAPTER ELEVEN

It was late morning when Ernest and Sandy were going through the list of payments to be made, trying to ascertain where they could make cuts and who would have to wait, when Jean entered the office.

"There's a Trevor Reece and David Lividsky in the reception wanting to talk to you, they don't have an appointment but insist on seeing you." Ernest felt the hairs at the nape of his neck rise having received threats and pressurised tactics of this kind before and knew that MH Holdings weren't about to be fobbed off with silly excuses. If he didn't talk to them now, then it would have to be later that same day or first thing the next day.

"Sandy you stay for this meeting, I want a witness to everything that's said. Jean, show them in." Inwardly he knew that the company would be safe once Christine was able to transfer the Powerbuild funds into their account but, he couldn't tell anyone about it because of the way it had been obtained. He also knew that the transfer could take time to arrange and that he had to stall MH Holdings for at least a couple of days without giving the any clue as to where the funds were to be coming from and definitely not to let on that he already knew that the funds were available.

"Please come in gentlemen." Ernest walked to the door to meet Trevor, he gave Ernest a pleasant smile but Ernest again took an instant dislike to the surly looking lawyer following behind the tall accountant. Once introductions were complete they sat down to the business in hand, Sandy was immediately wary that the lawyer of such a large organisation should attend this meeting. Normally it would be left to the minnows somewhat like Trevor to handle any financial negotiations with the directors or chairman pulling the strings in the background to conclude acceptable terms. Trevor left the talking to David who came straight to the point.

"Do you admit that you owe us more than three quarters of a million?"

"We've never denied it."

"Right. Then would you please draw a cheque in our favour for the full amount?" "As explained to you yesterday, we have a slight cash flow problem and therefore, cannot give you a cheque for the full amount. However, as also explained, we are quite prepared to give you..." He paused as he mentally calculated his finances. "Let's say, one hundred and fifty thousand today and then six fortnightly post dated cheques for one hundred thousand pounds in order to clear the amount and we are all set to draw up an undertaking agreement to that fact." David had arrived expecting some form of ducking and diving or even having them begging for extra time to pay, but this outright offer to settle caught him by surprise. Ernest was either a very good liar trying to stall them, or else David had underestimated the company strength however he also knew that it wasn't like Trevor to make a mistake, the company was in financial trouble with the collapse of Powerbuild so the man must be bluffing and trying to delay them with his offer. He decided to push them to see how far they would go before revealing all and winked at Trevor, a sign that he was going to keep pressing Ernest.

"Like you, we're not in business for our health, those terms, although a good start are nowhere near the amount we expect to leave here with today. We suggest you come up with at least half, that amounts to at least four hundred thousand now and the balance paid before the end of the month."

"Be reasonable Mr Lividsky, we are going to need a little time to sort out a financial hiccup and we've made the best offer that we possibly can under the circumstances. You should know, we are almost at the limit of our overdraft and if we tried to draw any more than offered, the bank would bounce the cheque."

"How the hell do you expect us to accept that your company has purchased goods for over eight hundred thousand and now, you offer us less than a quarter. That's just not good enough Mr Johnson. MH Holdings has over a hundred subsidiaries and if, as a group, we allowed credit facilities like this to all our customers, we had soon be out of business. How have you managed to survive this long if you run your company in this slap-dash, hit and miss fashion?" The little lawyer knew exactly what he was doing, he was forcefully pushing Ernest into a verbal corner, hoping that he would crack and relate the firm's exact predicament. That would then open the way for Norman to enter discussions within twenty four hours and offer a package which would lead to their taking over the whole company. Like one of Norman Minter's boxers, he could see that he had Ernest against the ropes as he prepared to land his verbal knockout blow. He pressed home his attack.

"Why don't you get out there and collect your debts? If you can't, then it means you're trading illegally and that your firm must be in liquidation. Is that the case?"

"This firm may have a problem with its cash flow but there's no crisis here." David opened his bag and withdrew a legal document and placed it in front of Ernest.

"Then you won't mind signing this form."

"What is it?"

"It only gives us a first call debenture over your debtors and assets, that way, if anything goes seriously wrong with your calculations and the cheques aren't met or honoured, we at least have a guarantee that we'll be able to recover something of the amount owed to us." Ernest was furious with the suggestion at first, but then, he suddenly realised they had been given a way out. Instead of David delivering the knockout blow he had been expecting to come, he had unwittingly opened the way for Ernest to retaliate.

"Mr Lividsky, I don't care for your tone or your insinuation that this company is trading illegally, therefore I want you to leave this office with what I've offered. If you feel it necessary to take legal action, then so be it but, I'm not going to be insulted like this." Ernest rose to indicate that the meeting had come to an end as far as he was concerned.

"Sandy, please give these gentlemen a cheque for a hundred and fifty thousand and six post dated cheques for the balance." David remained seated as Trevor took out his pipe and lit it. They were about to move into the second phase of the meeting.

"Wait a minute," said Trevor, once a plume of smoke rose filled the space between himself and Ernest. " Things are getting a little heated here and nobody's achieving anything." He sucked on the deep bowled pipe again.

"Like you, we're only doing our jobs. You see, Mr Johnson, the only reason we're a bit nervous is that we've heard rumours that your firm is in deep trouble by being caught out by the Powerbuild debacle. If this is the case then the amounts offered to us will not be met, so instead of kidding each other why don't we put our resources together and come up with a plan? From our side, we don't want to find ourselves losing a large chunk of finance from first them and then another bulky lot from your company. You can understand that, can't you?" Ernest leaned back in his chair, realising that Sandy was now squirming under the intense pressure but that he couldn't tell anyone that they had already collected their amount. Because they knew about Powerbuild, he suspected that they knew what the damage was as well and knew he had to stall for time until Christine had managed to inject the funds back into the firm.

"I don't know how you found out, but yes, you're right, we have been placed in an awkward position by Powerbuild however, right now we're trying to make certain financial arrangements and hopefully, will be able to weather this unfortunate mishap type storm."

"Like what?" David snapped.

"I can't discuss details at the moment, but..." He knew that he had to be careful to reassure the lawyer that they meant to repay the debt.

"We feel very confident that we'll shortly be able to raise the necessary finance to get ourselves out of this hole."

"How?" David interjected.

"By raising a loan first or if that fails, by taking on a partner." David smiled inwardly. The words were exactly what he wanted and needed to hear.

"We know that your position has been caused by an unfortunate liquidation and because of your past record with the group we would like you to consider that we could be interested in taking a shareholding within Johnson Interiors." This sudden change surprised Ernest. From being tough and vicious, the lawyer had immediately settled and taken the opportunity to invite his company into negotiations. Ernest laboured the point in his mind for a minute, the only reason he could think of was so that MH Holdings could protect their own interests. His frankness coupled with sudden turnabout was also the way to gain time for himself, inwardly he congratulated himself on his manipulative strategy.

"Let's see what develops over the next few days, until then we wont make any hasty decisions. Sandy get those cheques drawn up.

I'll sign them immediately." While Sandy was out, Trevor extolled the virtues and advantages of a small company belonging to a major conglomerate. The way he presented the benefits of being part of a major group was to carefully envelope the gains that would be derived by the struggling smaller company. Ernest was clearly impressed by the time Sandy returned with the completed seven cheques ready for Ernest's signature. David had worn his serious mask throughout the meeting and only once they had entered their vehicle and moved away did he allow himself the pleasure of a broad smile

"Hook, line and sinker. This one is going to be a doddle, we've got this one hooked now all we have to do is reel the catch in." Both men laughed openly for the first time since leaving their office that morning.

"Come in David, how did it go?" David sat in a chair opposite Norman Minter. "As we thought it might, they gave us a hundred and fifty and six post dated cheques to cover the balance."

"What about the debenture?"

"Nope but then again they openly admitted that they were in trouble and are now trying to raise a loan from somewhere. If that fails they're prepared to negotiate with a partner."

"Pity about the debenture, it would have made things that much easier. Try and find out who they're talking to for a loan. I'll make sure they get rejected. The squeeze is on, it's just a matter of time before they come begging. I doubt whether any of the cheques will be met on time. Also, find out who else owes them money and let's try to stall payments to them. In the next fortnight I want them to come begging to hand the business to us, lock, stock and barrel."

"One thing that concerns me is that with their assets, they may easily find an alternative buyer for the firm. What I'll have to do is to get Paul and Julie to continue their close friendships with the two Johnson employees and find out what's going on from the inside and if possible find out who they are talking to."

"Good thinking, those two really do enjoy their work, don't they?" Both laughed.

"Don't worry. Somehow, we'll keep more and more pressure on Johnsons, I think that you and I should return with some form of supposed proposal early next week."

"Okay, lay it on and let me know what you've organised."

"I don't think Ernest Johnson liked me very much though, perhaps if we arrive bearing gifts he may change his mind." Again both laughed.

"They'll like me though, by the way, what's his sister like."

"I don't know, apparently she's on holiday, but, if the reports are correct she's attractive but is the tough one of the family."

"At least it sounds as if she's not a bimbo type, that's good, I really do like feisty females."

"Far from being a dog's body according to reports apparently she takes no nonsense and also manages all contracts with a hard line while he takes a softer line handling the business's administration."

"Speaking of taking over businesses, have a look at this. It arrived in the morning post, isn't that the law firm where you did your articled training, the name rings a bell?" David took the folder from his chairman, stapled to the front was a letter marked 'Confidential' from the old established law firm, Harper and Marcus. David often shared a meal with Bernard Marcus the senior partner at the firm and the letter went on to say that Martins, one of the country's largest bookmaking firms could be up for sale. David paged through the portfolio and then looked at Norman.

"So?"

"It would be a super acquisition and would slot in nicely with our current promotion investments."

"You're seriously thinking of making a bid? It's not for me to tell you your business, but the fight promotion business is only a hobby for you and for sure, this would be a totally different bag of tricks. Remain within the construction industry, don't rush into uncharted territory, you could get severely burnt if you take something like this on."

"On the one hand I tend to agree with you, it has its underlying risks but on the other hand I feel it could tie in so beautifully and could also be the means of us possibly controlling the fight game as well as other sports. My gut reaction is to at least have a look what's on offer before even condemning it out of hand. I've been thinking of trying to buy a smaller bookmaking outfit for some time."

"I know you have. But *this is not a small outfit*, it's far too large for you to cut your teeth on, here you're talking mega-bucks."

"Get Trevor to investigate the ins and outs of Martins, let's see what comes out in the wash because I can't help wondering why it's come up for sale now. The last set of figures were extraordinarily good and the dividend paid out last year made me think of investing in them. They're represented throughout Europe and are very big in America, I think we've got to look at it because this could be our opening into the States. Once we're in with this, there's nothing to stop us expanding into the construction industry over there as well and I think it could be tailor made for the group's next big push." David knew that determined look and he, just like his father before him got this same look when they were determined to proceed with something of interest to them. Both men would search, counsel and investigate any new venture with the thoroughness of an ant or a bee out searching for food, always knowing what they wanted and how to get their hands on it. David also knew that his warning had already fallen on deaf ears because when the Minter family made up their mind, they generally carried it through no matter what pitfalls may stand in their way. Only on the rare occasion when they had managed to uncover something highly suspicious regarding an intended acquisition would either of them turn away otherwise, once a target had been established, it was odds on that it would end up belonging to the Minter empire.

"I don't want to sound like the eternal pessimist, but I honestly think you should walk away right now and leave this one alone."

"That's a laugh, David *you are the eternal pessimist.* I've never known you to gamble on anything why are all lawyers the same, everything must have a down side to it. I wonder just how far we would have progressed if my father and I listened to the many times that your advice has been to walk away? After all the way this group has grown to the size it has is because we are definitive entrepreneurs and not lawyers or accountants, it's in my blood to take vetted chances."

"It's your company. I've already stated my opposition, we'll just leave it at that."

"David, this won't be a ride by the seat of your pants outfit but there are times when I get a hunch and follow it through and before going in, I aim to take every precaution making sure there are no hidden surprises lurking around in any of the corners of anything I acquire."

"I know, but you've never tackled anything as big or as far away from what you are comfortable as this before."

"Just get Trevor to look at Martins through a very broad microscope, he's to go in and scour the operation with a fine tooth comb."

The Kixing

"How long has he got?"

"You read the letter, there's no stipulated time but I would imagine that they would like some kind of show of interest. I'll get a letter drafted to them asking for more information. I expect that we may have a fortnight and just one thing, I know that you are friends with Bernard Marcus. Do you think he'll tell you whether we're in competition?"

"I doubt it but I'll ask." As David left consult Trevor Reece, Norman thought back to the last fight that he had promoted because it wasn't the first time in his life that he had arranged for a fighter to lose so that he could bet on the winner and make a small fortune. The excitement of being able to make money illegally always put him on a high for several days after a fight. The added incentive of being able to rig the outcome was now like a drug to Norman. However, certain hints, whisperings and questions were travelling through the boxing world, some of the bookmakers taking the large bets from two men working on Norman's behalf weren't pleased when the outright favourite had been knocked out in the third round. They had openly accused the champion of taking a dive and even at an enquiry held in camera by the boxing board of control, it was shown that the boxer was in fact hit on the side of the head and that the bookmaker's claim of rigging was invalid. Now, they had made it clear that they were highly suspicious that someone of high standing in the boxing world was fight rigging, Norman knew that he had to be careful and had secretly decided to make sure of adding to his personal fortune by investing in a bookmaking company which would then lay off his large bets. The offer arriving from out of the blue was exactly what he had been seeking and with majority control of one of the largest firms of bookmakers, he would be able to fix some of the largest fights legitimately by adding to his personal fortune and allowing him to carefully start controlling the international fight scene. If certain black and Jewish promoters could get away with it in America, the main centre of the fight game, then why couldn't he do it in Europe.

The Kixing

For too long, the Americans had held the monopoly of boxing and Norman's aim was to change this.

"Now that I've got the opportunity and possible vehicle to control gambling at my fingertips, I'm not going to be dictated to by those demi-gods of boxing from the States." He felt warmly smug about the whole matter at that moment.

The Kixing

"THE KIXING"

CHAPTER TWELVE

Jean thought back to the previous evening as she busily typed a letter for Ernest, right now she was feeling slightly jaded this morning having had very little sleep because Paul Hunter had spent the night at her flat. She still couldn't believe her luck, not only was he very good looking, but also lovingly attentive to her every need, she thought that he was the finest lover any woman could ever want. A warm glow passed through her body as she considered the way that she had now suddenly allowed herself the luxury of dropping all previous inhibitions and do things to him that a few days ago she had never thought possible. It was as if she had at last managed to shed some dark and heavy mantle that had been weighing her down mentally for so many years and now, he had released her covering releasing her to feel as free as any bird in flight. Last night had provided her zenith when she had soared to new heights, not only had she gone so much further than she had ever thought she could but, also found that she enjoyed her new exploratory inner self. She secretly allowed herself a slightly wicked smile because just like an emerging butterfly, Jean felt as if a different person had emerged from within and it didn't matter if they had spent all night making love, she was now on such a high that no matter what happened at the office today wouldn't change her present mood. Christine Johnson appeared at her door.

"Can't you stay away from this place, I thought you were supposed to be on holiday with your daughter?"

"I am, I've just popped in for a minute to see my brother." She swept into his office and closed the door. That was very unusual, it had to be about the company's present situation Jean thought to herself as she returned to her work.

Ernest rose to meet Christine. She closed the door so that prying office eyes wouldn't be able to hear their discussion or to distinguish the newly found joy between them. It needed time for both of them to readjust to the circumstances that had suddenly come about after so many years of enforced love and sexual abstinence and also because she had secretive and pressing business to discuss with her twin that nobody in the office should be aware of. Like genuine young lovers, the two fell into momentary embrace, it was Christine who quickly separated herself from the tight clinch. She moved to the desk and wrote *'The office was bugged by the family last night, be extra careful what is said between us'*. Ernest couldn't believe what he was reading as Christine gently pushed him towards his chair.

"Ernie, I need to tell you what happened at a meeting yesterday afternoon." Christine's face had taken on her serious business mask. "I went to see someone to talk about the trust fund we discussed so that Powerbuild's payment could quickly be put in place. You can imagine my surprise, when I told them about needing the money to repay MH Holdings, to be informed that we were under siege from that company."

"What are you talking about?"

"Apparently it's the way they operate, they've got us under constant surveillance and there could even be some MH Holdings employees spying in on our operation right at this very moment."

"I don't believe this."

"It's true, you're just going to have to believe me, they already know that we've been caught on the hop by Powerbuild as well as thinking that our company is in dire financial trouble and because of this they envisage that we're weak and won't be able to survive.

Right now, you can believe me but they're busily homing in on us, the thinking being in order to catch us unawares and then easing themselves into the position to make a hostile bid for what they feel is a pressurised and lame company.

"That explains it."

"Explains what?"

"Yesterday, I was paid a visit by two MH employees, an accountant and a nasty little company lawyer called Lividsky. How did you come by this information, anyway?"

"I told you that I was being watched over by the family, they've got eyes and ears everywhere and told me various things that you wouldn't even start to believe, it was like listening to some cruel radio drama." Ernest shook his head slowly in total disbelief.

"Why?"

"Greed, that's the way of their world, it's a feeding chain where big fish swallow little fish, that's what the commercial world is all about. But MH Holdings don't know that the art of surprise no longer rests with them and hopefully we will have enough muscle behind us to tackle them head on."

"What do you mean, we don't have that sort of leverage or power behind us, if MH Holdings are gunning for us, we're as good as being dead in the water."

"That's where you're so wrong Ernie, Powerbuild's money is going to be invested through Willis Investments. All this time you have been led to believe that all they were our sleeping partners simply creaming off profits each year but, they aren't. As you were slightly aware, Willis Investments was Edwardo's contribution to setting up the company and keep a watching brief on my activities but Willis actually belongs to the family and acts as a front for their money laundering operation. Neither of us told you this back then because I didn't want to have to explain and anyway, you wouldn't have agreed to having this degree of involvement had you known what lay behind it."

"What? You and that husband of yours deceived me all those years ago, how long have you known that he was mixed up with the Mafia?"

"From the outset, at the time, if you recall, we needed more funding to start up and it was the only way that I could get Edwardo to agree to me working with you, I had to give up something in return for my freedom. Once you're in the family, there's no way out and that's why I said nothing and now, we have to be extra careful." Christine winked. Ernest immediately picked up on the double edged meaning to her statement.

"I don't believe this is happening to us."

"The next few weeks are going to be hell for both of us, simply remember, we've already got a big brother hiding in the wings and you don't say anything to anybody, understand?"

"I wouldn't, nobody would believe me."

"Anyway, what else was discussed at the meeting yesterday?" Ernest told her everything.

"Right, so they've already made their opening gambit, from now on, only you and I are to know what's going on and you keep playing it along and as if we haven't got any money, let them think that we're squirming and just playing for time. Now Ernie, it is imperative that you keep me informed of their move and countermoves at all times and remember, there's a lot more at stake than you are aware of and so to them, it must seem if we're going through a major financial crisis period."

The Kixing

"Can't we at least reassure some of the employees that everything is fine."

"Most definitely not. It's going to be a strain on the staff and cracks will begin to form but, you mustn't say anything. Be sure of my words because from here on, you cannot trust anybody, that includes those staff that you would hand your life to, because those ones could be plants by MH Holdings. Believe me, if what I was given to understand, MH are highly efficient experts and industrial spying is only a way of life for them and we cannot take any stupid chances to alert them of our plans whatsoever. Now promise me you'll say nothing, not even to Jean, just keep on making everybody think that we are in a really vulnerable situation."

"Okay Chrissie, if that's the way it's got to be, trust me I won't let on to anybody."

"I told our friends that I was going to explain the general plan and tell you what was going on so that some of the things that are going to happen over the next few weeks won't seem too irrational to you." Ernest just nodded slowly his mind too numb to grasp the full reality of what had been discussed during the last few minutes. He desperately wanted to hold his sister and tell her just how miserable he felt, but knew he couldn't even do that.

"Now that I've brought you up to date, I'm off to finish my holiday break. Call me, the moment anything happens." Christine stood up and walked to his side of the desk. She leaned forward and gently kissed him full on the mouth, there was hunger there, but she couldn't allow herself the pleasure of making it seem more than a sisterly reassurance kiss.

"Don't worry little brother, we'll beat this damned conglomerate." She lifted his pen and wrote another message. *'We can be alone this afternoon, why not come around?'* Ernest smiled and nodded his agreement when he walked her to her car and watched in admiration as she drove off at speed. As he turned back to the office he noticed a man leaning against a pole at the corner, the past few minutes had now honed his senses making him acutely aware of anything out of the ordinary. Ernest wondered whether the man could possibly be an innocent bystander or could he be someone working for the family or alternatively for MH Holdings, he questioned himself.

"This is stupid." The man moved away down the road, Ernest surreptitiously knew that with what his sister had revealed, his life was about to take a dramatic turn, for the best he hoped. He also knew he had to get his thoughts together and a little tighter while trying to act out what was to be a very unfamiliar role. With a slight spring of anticipation in his step, he again walked back to his office. Christine hadn't gone straight home but after leaving the office she decided to turn west and then drove straight to a large mansion on the outskirts of Surrey. There were two burly men at the gates who immediately recognised Christine's car and opened the huge steel portals and as she passed by she waved and moved the Jaguar down the winding drive to the partially hidden large white building that nestled deep within the surrounding forested gardens. Top security seemed to flood the place with an occasional glimpse of patrol guards being escorted by dogs, cameras and two lots of fencing, an outer ring and an electric inner one nearer the house. Christine parked the car and the front door opened, coming from the house to greet her was Antonio, the man that had visited Peter Edwards. Because of the dog bite, he now walked with a pronounced limp and it was obvious to Christine that the man was still in great pain.

"Signora, this is a pleasant surprise."

"Hello Antonio. I decided to drop in and talk to you before returning home because I've already been to the office and told my brother what's going on. I also wanted to find out about the other thing you mentioned last night. What's happening?"

The Kixing

"Let's go inside where it's more comfortable and I can sit down, my back hurts when I stand for a long time." He took her hand and kissed it before leading her into the large sitting room. She settled onto a deeply cushioned sofa while he carefully let himself down into a leather chair which she noticed didn't match the rest of the luxurious furniture in the room. The chair had obviously been recently brought in for Antonio and after some small talk and refreshments were served he got straight to the point.

"For a long time, this Norman Minter has been a thorn in our side, but lately he has been getting too greedy and has been stealing from the family. Although he's one of the few independent fight promoters not connected with us and because the Minter family have been there for years, it was considered that it was more of a hobby for them and so, we decided to leave them alone but now, matters have substantially changed and some of the smaller promoters are trying to muscle in on our territory. As you probably know, one of these promoters was shot in London the other day, the police tried to pin the charge on one of his boxers."

"How are you going to stop this meddling?"

"We know that he's been fixing fights by skilfully outbidding us with the fighters and then collects from our bookmaking outlets, we have found that it's of no use trying to take out the boxers because they're only motivated by money. We then tried to expose his activities by arranging a hearing with the boxing board of control but he is slippery like a snake and very clever managing to walk away with his winnings intact. To date, he's cost the family many millions and we were going to have to stop him and if we made a hit on someone like Minter by the traditional ways, then with his wide ranging contacts many questions would be asked and it could bring the spotlight onto our activities. We didn't want that, so we prepared an alternative plan, it was purely coincidental that he should now be making a bid for Johnson Interiors at the same time that we have set the trap for

Norman Minter."

"How've you done that?" The Italian took a loud sip from his cup.

"Greed is the downfall of all men and that includes members of the family. We're going to exploit this mans' greed for riches by taking his company away from him."

"How?"

"We have devised a very clever sting and because of the man's overwhelming greed, we're going to sell Norman Minter one of the family's main bookmaking operations at a very over inflated price. Once he's been to his bankers and comfortably managed to raise enough money to purchase Martins, then we will do to him what he's been doing to us. Not only that, but his construction businesses will all start having trouble and begin to lose money. By the time he realises his mistake, we'll have doubled our losses and be able to repurchase Martins from Minter at a much lower price than he originally paid for it. MH Holdings will be so over extended on their borrowing that they will have to sell Martins and possibly some of their other assets simply to clear their debt. Once they're into this position they won't want Johnson Interiors or any other firm for that matter, the huge shortfall coupled with the amount of interest that they will have to pay back, will create great losses for them. It will take Minter years to recover from this setback and perhaps he'll not be in a position to muddy our betting waters any longer, hopefully he will get out of the fight game and leave it to us."

"That's not enough."

Antonio lit a cigarette and as he filled his lungs with smoke as he mulled over Christine's words.

"Not enough?"

"No because by the time you're finished, we're going to own MH

Holdings, including the construction and promotion sections. We're going to teach this man a lesson he'll never forget. If we let him carry on, he'll live to fight another day and from what I understand, he's very tough and resilient, like any fighter once he has been knocked down he must not be allowed to get back up, I don't want that to happen."

"But Signora, this could use all the resources we have at our disposal."

"Then use them, if you must, you can call in further help from America if you have to. I'm not letting this vulture attack me and my business and then get away with it, anyway we now need to spread the operation throughout Europe and this company will be our new flagship to achieve our objectives."

"But we already have a flagship."

"Betting and gambling still has a certain stigma about it in Europe, this company has perfect breeding and a track record and therefore, will be a far better proposition to hide our activities. If we manage this then we can free ourselves from the hold that America has over us. We'll have come of age all on our own."

"Your husband would be proud of you, God rest his soul." Antonio made the sign of the cross.

"Let's see if Minter takes the bait and falls for the trap first, how long has he got before he must make a bid?"

"There is no set time although we expect him to check out Martins and to make an initial offer within two weeks."

"What if his offer isn't high enough?"

"Initially we don't expect it to be then, we're going to outbid him through one of our other companies this will push him until he squeaks and then we'll let him have Martins."

"Good."

"In the meantime, get the Powerbuild funds into our trust account and then we will treat it as a personal loan from Ernest and myself. MH Holdings have already played their hand, they visited the office and suggested that we allow them to buy us out. It won't be long before Norman Minter arrives clutching a proposal in his hand, I can't wait to see the look on his face when I turn him down."

"Consider it done."

"By the way, are our offices fully bugged?" Antonio leaned over and opened a drawer in the table next to his chair.

"Here are your keys Signora, we have the whole place covered and It won't take us long to discover who is doing what. Within a week, we'll locate everyone connected with MH Holdings even if they're not working directly for that company. Don't worry, it won't take us long to get rid of them."

"No. All your findings must come to me first, it could be to our benefit to give false warnings to these sharks. Let's play them at their own game."

"It is good that you've reverted to your maiden name, if you hadn't then possibly he might have not made the offer."

"Powerful men do not take women seriously enough, we are there to guide the strengths of over inflated men, just look at women like the late Rajiv Gandi's wife. She was offered India's leadership and she declined, back then, she then ran the country from behind the scenes." Antonio just smiled and shook his head. This beautiful woman was clever but also had the nasty sting of a deadly scorpion. Ever since he had met her he couldn't help admiring her regal bearing as she now set about the destruction of MH Holdings. Minter should have known better than to cross Christine, it was going to be his day of devils, kings and clowns.

"Signora, we must be very careful because when Minter finally realises what's happening, he is going to turn very nasty and be something like a caged animal, he'll turn to violence and if he even suspects you or your brother are involved... It could become open warfare and there are sure going to be casualties. It will not be pretty and you two must be kept out of his firing line."

"I know anyway, I must get home." Christine rose and Antonio battled his way out of the leather chair.

"Don't bother walking me to the door."

"It is my honour. I've been hurt far worse than this in the past and survived." He walked her to her car and again took her hand and kissed it as a pure mark of respect. As Christine turned homewards she wondered whether her daughter would have arrived back at the house from the club yet. She made a mental note to find out more about the man who had stolen her daughter's heart and if her daughter's new love was half as beautiful as her own, then she was very happy for her.

The Kixing

"THE KIXING"

CHAPTER THIRTEEN

It was Tuesday morning when Ernest eased his Porsche around the corner nearest to the Johnson Interiors offices, he had a slight turn when realising that the man standing and looking towards the building was also the same one that had been there last week. He slowed down to try and have a good look at him in his rear view mirror, but was too late because the man turned and walked away as he had done before. When Ernest parked the car he made his way to the building and went straight to his sister's office, it was her first day back at the office.

"I'm sure the building is being watched."

"Good morning Chrissie," she said sarcastically.

"Chrissie, didn't you hear what I said? There's a man standing on the corner and he's watching the building."

"Could be that your imagination is running riot. How do you know he's keeping an eye on this building? There could be a thousand reasons for someone standing on a corner."

"It's the same man that was there last week when you drove away, when he noticed that I was looking at him he then turned and walked away. All highly suspicious don't you think? He did exactly the same thing just now when I arrived and now I'm sure he's watching this building. Do you still keep that camera handy? I want to take a picture of him, just in case."

"Don't be silly. It's only natural that ever since I told you what's going on, you're on edge and I strongly suspect your mind is now chasing shadows. Now that you're aware of our friend's intentions, your senses are picking up on anything unusual. The poor man's probably having a smoke break or something and what I had suggested is that you go out and acquire a mirror tied to a handle."

"What for?"

"So that you can look around every corner to see if there's a bogey-man waiting for you?" Christine laughed loudly at her own joke but Ernest didn't think it was that humorous, but he smiled weakly at his sister anyway. Ever since he was a young man Ernest hadn't appreciated anyone scoffing or making fun of him especially when it was about a serious subject instantly he resolved that he would have to somehow prove to his sister that the man just wasn't a figment of his imagination, then he changed the line of conversation.

"How was the rest of your break?"

"We had a fabulous weekend together, I hardly saw her yesterday because she spent most of the day with the new boyfriend. I met him briefly last night before they disappeared to some disco, you should have seen your niece this morning, she was washed out because she apparently got home at six, had two hours sleep and then drove away and back to university. I won't see her for a month now."

"God. Don't you think it's dangerous driving three hundred miles after only two hours sleep."

"The young have this extraordinary capacity to recuperate, especially after a wild night of drink and love making, their staying power never ceases to amaze me but eventually age catches up with all of us, I only wish that I could still be like that."

"What's the new beau like?"

"A dreamboat, that's the only way to describe him. Handsome, charming and fashionable, it would seem that she's chosen well because I didn't like her last one, he was too surly."

"That's nice." Ernest leaned forward and gave her hand a firm squeeze, he had suddenly remembered that the place was bugged and their every word was being listened to. He wondered if he should have openly said anything about the man on the corner as his twin smiled lovingly at her brother holding onto his hand for longer than was necessary.

"Now go and get 'em Ernie. I've got so much work to catch up on." He went to his office stopping at Jean's desk to check the morning mail.

"How are you this morning," he asked.

"A little fed up."

"Why?"

"Oh, nothing. I'm probably feeling a little insecure at the moment."

"Why?"

"It's just that there's a rumour going around that the company's in trouble. Is there any truth in the rumour?" Ernest immediately thought of his sister's words.

"Don't its nothing to worry your pretty head about, we're just going through a normal business hiccup. Up one day, down the next, don't worry we've been through a worse crisis and come out smelling of roses. All company's have good and bad stages. We just happen to be in a bad stage at the moment." To avoid any further questioning Ernest made for the safety of his office. It was late morning when Ernest returned to his sisters' office.

"Trouble."

"What?"

"They're back."

"Who?"

"MH Holdings, this time it's the big guns it's Norman Minter himself no less. He's waiting in reception to see me, what do you think I should do?"

"See him. If you give me a minute to finish this costing then I'll join you. Remember what I said, we plead poverty and let them think that we're in serious trouble."

"We are, at least until those funds come through."

"The funds were placed in our number two account this morning."

"Why into the profit account? Why not straight into our current account?"

"Because you dummy, we don't want to alert anybody that we're not in trouble just yet. Trust me ,we must try to retain that element of surprise for as long as we possibly can. We let them puff, swell and threaten, promise them the earth and give them nothing."

"Let's get our stories straight, what do we tell Minter?"

"Pretend that the funds haven't yet been transferred, that way you'll be telling no lies and once things get going, let me do the talking. I've got a personal bone to settle with mister bloody Minter. I'm going to teach him not to mess with us. It's time somebody pulled him down a peg or two." Ernest just smiled as he left the office. He knew that Minter was in for a bit of a surprise, but at the same time, didn't like the idea of embarrassing such a powerful supplier. It could have nasty repercussions to their business later on.

"Wheel them in Jean. Would you also ask them whether they want something to drink?" Jean disappeared and returned with both men in tow a few minutes later.

"Mr Lividsky, you seem to make a bad habit of just turning up unannounced. I wonder what you would do if I had been out?"

"We leave nothing to chance because this time we already knew that both you and your sister were in before coming across." Ernest was taken somewhat by surprise, all sorts of questions filtered through his head trying to find an explanation. Had they telephoned first? Was somebody from the firm relaying details of their movements? Could it be the man on the corner? He decided to get to the bottom of this.

"How did you know we were in or do you have your own spies watching us?" Ernest said half jokingly.

"We have our ways." Jean arrived and started serving each member of the meeting with refreshments. David didn't wait for niceties and immediately started the proceedings.

"Now, we've been thinking about what you said last week when you stated you may possibly be taking on a new partner and that's why Mr Minter has come along to this meeting because he was interested and so wanted to see your setup in order to gain some type of feeling for the type of outfit that we're looking at partnering with."

"A little presumptuous of Mr Minter, isn't it?" Nobody knew how long Christine had been standing and listening at the doorway. Norman rose as she crossed the room, he was impressed by the way she carried herself as she moved forward and firmly took his hand and introduced herself. If first contact was anything to go on, David had been right, this was someone of higher than normal quality.

"Yes, I suppose it was a little presumptuous especially when a fine business like yours runs into trouble through no fault of its own, we at MH Holdings are interested in helping. From my reports your company up to now has an exemplary and wonderful record with us but this is about business, it's a pity Johnsons is having difficulty and that's why we're here, to try to ease your burden."

"Is that right? How do you mean to help, by offering to purchase our shares?"

"David said that your brother mentioned raising a loan or taking on a partner and we are only offering to throw our hats into the ring should that come about." The onlookers were fascinated by the sparring taking place, it resembled two unequal fighters, one much heavier than his opponent. They were now carefully sizing and measuring each others strength and capabilities before entering battle. Each fighter's supporter knew that their champion would win this fight.

"It was wrong of my brother to even suggest selling shares in this company and as you rightly stated, we've built up a perfectly sound business and we intend keeping it. If you really want to help us, then don't pressurise us by stopping supplies and forcing us to pay you immediately. Yes we are in a financial quandary, but it won't last forever." David smiled, sure that Norman would go for the jugular.

"We don't think you'll survive this period and that is why I'm here, it's only once you have reached the bottom of any deep hole that you find there's very rarely a way out. What we're offering right at this moment, is a kindly helping hand to avoid your slipping further into this terrible financial chasm."

"In other words if I understand you correctly, we are to negotiate on your terms now in order to save ourselves. If we slide any further into the hole, then you're going to be at the forefront hurling rocks down to help bury us.

"You must understand that we're not a charity and have to accept our offer of help or else we'll have no alternative but to take immediate steps to retrieve our money."

"I see. So your offer of help is an..." She paused, "either we comply or you kick us in the teeth. It's tantamount to placing a loaded gun at a man's head when he's already standing on the hangman's scaffold."

"I wouldn't have quite put it like that but David has already prepared a proposal for negotiation. I would like you to look at it and see if it's a fair assessment of the company's share value. We think it is a very good offer, given your present circumstances."

"Tell me something, if all the cheques that were given to David are met, then what?" This sudden deviation argument caught Norman off guard, he respected a clever adversary and Christine wasn't simply trying to turn the conversation, there was a definite purpose to her question. He had to be careful how he phrased his answer as he looked at David to try to create a slight diversion.

"Your first cheque was surprisingly paid in full, however, we're extremely doubtful if any of the others will be honoured." By making this statement David had made sure he put MH Holdings and especially Norman Minter's feeling quite clearly but he also noted that Christine did not seem at all flustered.

"We have always honoured the first of our payments and I repeat the question, what happens if all the cheques are cleared?" With sudden skill, this clever fighter had suddenly confused her opponent and manoeuvred the heavyweight around and against the ropes. It seemed the fight wasn't going to be all one sided because Christine had enough guile to be able to penetrate Norman's defences.

"We would be very relieved."

"Right, let's leave it like that then, we'll be happy to give your proposal due consideration over the next few days. You in the meantime will maintain your position and give us the necessary space, time and opportunity to repay your debt in full. If any of our cheques are not met, we will be happy to sign the agreed proposal. Is that fair comment?" Norman was in a corner and taking a hiding. He knew that their offer would stand up in any law court, but if one amount was not met he would have the upper hand but right at this minute he could do nothing but concede that he had lost the first round. He needed to get back to his corner and rethink his strategy. He had underestimated the Johnson twin's strength and knew that his next attack on them had to be far more forceful.

"Okay, I suppose that'll have to do for the moment. I want your counter proposal in my office by this time next week. Because we are being so lenient, I would prefer to have my stake in this business protected. David tells me that you've refused to sign a first call debenture with us. I would feel much more at ease if I at least had some form of cover." Norman was now hitting out and trying to defend himself at the same time. Christine was fully aware of what he was trying to accomplish.

"The reason we won't sign your debenture is that we already have a debenture over our assets signed with our bank. Therefore, everything will be taken over by them, so any paper signed by us would be irrelevant." Christine was lying through her back teeth and wasn't prepared to give way at this stage.

"Anyway, as Ernest has given you full payment, even be they in the form of post dated cheques and you having accepted them as such and cashed the first payment means acceptance in law of our offer, we have already fulfilled our obligation."

"All your cheques still have to be cashed, any slip ups will spell big trouble for your little company. I will be watching this account very closely now."

"Nobody here doubts that, an agreement was made this morning so let's wait and see what happens. As I said at the outset, this slight blip will be sorted out in time. I must thank you for helping us in this manner, but I wish you would reconsider about supplying us with material, you do realise that if you don't and we get over this period, you will have lost a large account to your competitors."

"When I receive your proposal and your next cheque is cleared, then, I'll review the situation regarding re-implementing supplies."

"That's blackmail and you know it. Therefore, I'll make your decision an easy one, right now, would you kindly inform your subsidiary companies to instruct their representatives not to call on Johnson Interiors any longer. I intend to switch suppliers and even if it means paying a premium to import goods from Europe, I never intend buying from any firm connected to you." Again, a stunned silence. Christine was making the most of her advantage. Both Norman and David had expected the Johnson twin's confidence to be very low and this was supposed to be an easy ride, but now, both men were utterly confused at the way Christine had hammered them. There was no doubt, she was the one giving the pasting. Norman knew that they had to get away to find out what the twins were playing at. It was obvious from her attitude that they had overlooked something. She was far too confident and could be carefully setting them up with an extraordinary bluff.

"That's a harsh decision to make in view of your plight."

"I don't like being bullied, you know we have a problem and yet come into our offices holding an olive branch in one hand and a battering ram in the other. No, we've spent a lot of time, sweat and tears building a fine reputation and I'm not about to surrender this company without some form of fight." Although Norman admired her stance, for the first time he suddenly saw a ray of hope and found himself being happy with her words. She had almost admitted that there was no way out for the company and that her defiant attitude was simply a knee jerk reaction to the ever closing noose being strung up by MH Holdings.

"We don't take kindly to threats and if you persist, it will only make the inevitable negotiations to acquire your company count against you. You're not helping your cause you know? We came here in good faith to offer constructive advice and you have done nothing but block and scorn our attempts."

"Oh no you don't, you're like vultures moving in to see what see what best bits you can strip away. However, this time you've made a mistake, this particular beast is a long way from being dead. Get too close and you may be in for a nasty shock, the seemingly dead animal may sink his teeth into you and end up by stripping *your* bony carcass." Norman and David laughed. They had both seen this sort of retaliation before. It was human nature to fight all the way to the final post. Norman rose.

"We'll see but fair warning though, the longer you leave the commitment to join us, the lower the price for your shareholding." The two men left and once in the car, David revealed his real thoughts.

"A right she-cat, isn't she?"

"I like her, she's got balls alright. David, are you sure you've closed all lines of escape?"

"One can never be a hundred per cent sure. Why?"

"I don't know, it's just a feeling I've got. She's a fighter, but I've met people with similar attributes before. I got the feeling that she still had another card to play. Don't ask me why, somehow there was a little too much confidence in her voice. I think you better double check everything again."

"I'm sure I've missed nothing, but I'll go through everything with a fine toothed comb."

"Get your squad to find out what the office's mood was like after

152

we left. That might give us a clue whether the whole thing was simply a facade or whether those two really have something nasty waiting in the wings. We cannot afford any slip-ups at this point."

"I'll talk to Paul and Julie as soon as we reach the office."

"If, as we suspect they are in deep trouble, I want the financial guillotine to fall as quickly as possible. That really is a nice company and I really want to get my hands on it, I must own it and then I'll tame that one yet. Do you know whether she is married?"

"Widowed several years ago and has a grown up daughter currently at university." Although Norman wouldn't admit it to David, he had found her exciting and stimulatingly fresh. He decided that this wasn't the last time he was going to see or go into battle with her because now he was determined to meet her again, preferably under more relaxed circumstances.

The Kixing

"THE KIXING"

CHAPTER FOURTEEN

Julie was in the shower when Sandy arrived home, she had only just reached the cottage ahead of him by minutes after having been delayed in David's office.

He told her and Paul Hunter that he and the chairman had started pressurising the directors of Johnson Interiors and instructed them to pull out all stops and find out what was being said at the Johnson Interior's office, he also wanted to know whether the Johnson twins were sombre after they had left and especially to try to find out whether the company could be negotiating any possible rescue packages with outsiders. Paul had offered to use his skills to find out directly from Christine Johnson, it was a long time since she had seen David explode when he told Paul to stop being so flippant. She had then raced at breakneck speed to Paul's cottage and, knowing that she had almost no time to spare, quickly ruffled the cushions to make it seem as if she had spent some time lounging about the place.

"Why don't you join me?" She tempted as he made his way into the bathroom.

"I wasn't expecting to see you tonight."

"Don't you just adore most of Andrew Lloyd Webber's musicals?"

"Who doesn't?"

"I've managed to get hold of two front row tickets for *'The Phantom of the Opera'* for this evening. Can I tempt you?"

The Kixing

"Just try to keep me away." It was a stifling hot afternoon and Paul was undressed and in the shower in a trice as Julie slowly started soaping his whole body. Teasingly she carefully skirted around his lower regions, she did not have to guess what his innermost thoughts were, the projecting muscle told her all as her hands moved downwards from his chest to his stomach and just when he thought she was going to reach his nether regions, she quickly progressed onwards down to his muscular legs. She finished at his toes and then made her way around to the back of his calves, then Julie ran her hands up the insides of his slightly parted legs and over his buttocks to finish up at his shoulders.

"Now, you can do exactly the same to me." It took every ounce of will power not to let his hands stray and when he finally completed the given task, Julie suddenly dropped to her knees and took him deep into her mouth. He found himself battling to remain upright as he began to lose strength and felt a familiar explosion developing somewhere in the lower regions that were now under a constant barrage from her soft lips. He desperately wanted to reach out and fondle and touch her, but was unable to because of her prone position well below his midriff. The earlier coolness of the rushing shower seemed to be dissipating as his whole being suddenly seemed to be transformed by her gentle persuasion when the spasm came with unexpected force and he found himself slowly sinking to the floor of the shower because the trembling legs no longer contained enough strength to hold him upright. He sank his head between her legs and reciprocated the favour in return, for some time they made glorious love in the cramped cubicle. She ended up almost upside down and the fine spray of water kept hurtling down into her face, with both legs widely straddled apart against the uprights, one in each corner while Sandy was bent almost double, skilfully balancing on his hands and knees while driving his manhood deep into her soft under flesh. They both reached the climax of man's animistic eternal ritual together then for several moments they lay and waited for the pulsating pleasure to subside before Julie managed to untangle herself only to repeat the whole washing sequence again, this time not omitting to take special care of the area that had given her so much pleasure a few moments ago. They moved from the shower to the bedroom and Paul relaxed on the bed while Julie sat in front of the mirror and started getting herself ready.

"How was your day?"

"Terrible. Arriving home to that very special treatment has been my absolute day's highlight."

"Is the liquidation saga still running?"

"Oh it's being compounded. We're fast going down the drain."

"Why, what's happened now?"

"Do you remember me telling you about those men who visited us last week and demanded that we settle their account?"

"Yes, vaguely," she lied. " They were back again today. I wasn't at the meeting, but both Johnson directors met them and I've never seen Christine Johnson in such a foul mood. She's been away on holiday and after the meeting she ripped my costing apart. What was said at the meeting, I know not, everybody at the firm knows we're in a spot of bother, the office seems to be clouded with a sense of doom. After the meeting adjourned, the whole place felt as if it had been covered by a huge black cloud, there's nothing that I can pinpoint, the light hearted atmosphere that's always been a hallmark at Johnsons just weighed heavily on everybody today."

"So, what're the directors going to do about it?"

"Nothing, by the looks of it."

"Can't they extend the company's overdraft or something?"

"Not unless Christine underwrites the loan. She's quite a wealthy woman in her right but, I think the bank would want her to put up her assets as financial collateral."

"Wouldn't it be worth it to save the business?"

"I don't know whether she would because she's also a very private person and I don't even know if the house belongs to her or whether it's in her daughter's name."

"Couldn't the company take on a rich partner?"

"Those men apparently offered to take over the shareholding of the firm, but then again, after having worked so hard to get it to its present position, I don't think the Johnsons are prepared to give up that easily."

"Perhaps they could be talking to somebody else that you're not aware of."

"No, I don't think so, if they were doing that, I would have had to prepare figures and produce budget forecasts for them. They haven't asked me to do anything like that, no, they're not looking for outside partners just yet."

"Maybe all is well, but they're not telling the staff."

"If you had been in the office today, you wouldn't be talking like that. They're both very worried at the moment and I don't think the company's going to survive. In fact, I'm only one of the staff that is looking around for another position. Got any ideas?"

"You really think that it's that bad?"

"Yes I do." Sandy got off the bed and moved to Julie and placed his arms around her undressed body and very gently took her nipples between each thumb and forefinger.

"I don't think we have time. Let's get dressed and enjoy the evening."

"Tell you what, seeing you're providing the tickets, I'll treat you to a meal afterwards."

"Deal."

"We'll pick up from here when we get back. Okay?" Julie smiled, it wasn't at Sandy, it was because she now had all the information that David had asked for. It was also because she loved her work, it contained all the job satisfaction that she had ever needed.

"Okay." As they waited for David to arrive for the meeting, Paul and Julie exchanged notes of their current assignment.

"It would seem as if Johnson Interiors is ripe and ready to be picked. Paul paints a picture of doom and gloom throughout, the staff's confidence is as low as can be and one was for sure, it was that David would have no option but to take them all out when he reads my report."

"This is the part that I hate, I spent most of the night consoling Jean and now, I'll be glad when this assignment's over."

"Why?"

"Two things. Firstly, Jean is becoming very possessive and I've often wondered why most women fall in love so deeply and unreservedly? Now the thing becomes messy, take last night for instance, because I went out with someone else and didn't turn up as promised on Monday night, she went ape shit yesterday. She didn't know what I had been doing, but carried on all evening about me being unreliable, later on, she cried because she was so pleased to see me. I'll never be able to figure out what makes all women tick. When we went out for drinks she got upset when I made a pass at a gorgeous young thing at the pub. Over the weekend she bitched when I went off to do my parachuting practice, no I don't really enjoy this phase of the operation but I'm glad it's almost over.."

"You said there were two things, what's the second?"

"She's having such a miserable time at work and brings it home with her, it's incredible, she just loves her job and the present troubles are having an adverse affect on her health. The only time she doesn't talk about her job is when we're making love." Paul smiled wickedly at his colleague.

"The only way to shut her up is to continually make love to her."

"You bastard."They both laughed.

"What's yours like in the sack?"

"Mmm. Not bad, on a scale of one to ten, I would rate him an eight and even though Sandy is a true accountant, he expects nothing from me and he's a lot of fun to be with. Very pragmatic though, totally uncomplicated, I could easily continue our friendship for a while when this assignment is finished. Instead of going out with a bang, I might let him down slowly by letting the relationship fizzle out in its own time."

"That's very unlike you."

"I know, but this one's different, he's so cuddly and comfortable to be with. There's no pressure to end this one."

"Careful, you're getting sentimental in your old age and that's not good for our type of profession. Julie just smiled.

"You work your way, I'll work mine." David swept into his office and bustled around collecting some papers from his desk before seating himself at the table.

"Sorry I'm a bit late now, let's have a quick look at your reports." He read through the two handwritten reports.

"Yes well, everything seems to be as we suspected, you're both sure that there's nothing untoward going on at Johnsons?" Both nodded in agreement.

"For safety sake, I think you better continue your assignments going until at least next Tuesday, just in case there are changes." Paul clicked his tongue. David didn't even seem to notice his act of objection.

"We've given them a takeover proposal, but, as you would expect, they're resisting any sort of interference but during this week they'll probably try to obtain a loan or they could begin talking to other outside parties. You know the drill, we need to be on top of it if they do and while we're the only interested party, we won't make a move, but, if they open talks with others, we'll immediately spread rumours of their plight and create a campaign to undermine their credibility, nobody will touch them after we're finished with them."

"Why don't you do that anyway?" Paul enquired.

"At the moment, they're sitting ducks and we're the only ones in the fray. If we get wind of talks with others, then we'll move quickly because we don't want to make things worse than they are if we can help it. When we gain control, it could take a long time to repair any damage and it would mean that we would have to carry them until their credibility is again restored. No, the less damage we inflict now, the less we'll have to repair later on."

"Do you want us to carry on concentrating on Powerbuild?"

"No, they're finished. Their managing director has made his escape taking all the stolen funds with him, we're having to write them off."

"That's some amount you're writing off."

"Now you can see how imperative it is for you two to keep us up to date. If we manage to gain control of Johnsons, then it'll offset the massive loss made by Powerbuild. At least that way we'll come out of this debacle with something worthwhile."

"Then let's get to it, that is, if you're finished with us?"

"I want a daily update meeting with you two so let's make it at this time each morning. Is that all right for you?" Both nodded as they collected their papers and left the office. David went through the reports for a second time, had he missed anything and just like Norman, he had an uneasy feeling in his bones that Christine Johnson still had another ace to play. In all the takeovers that he had been involved in, the pattern always had the same hallmarks but there was something a little different about this one, he couldn't quite place his finger on it, but he would, given time. Norman and Trevor Reece were quietly mulling over some of the initial findings made by the accounts department and Trevor had a bulky report stating each and every shareholder's stake in Martins the Bookmakers resting on his lap.

"So you see, the majority of the shares are owned by Sibling Investments. Having checked, if you gain control of just four of the shareholder's shares, then you'll have more than fifty per cent of the company."

"How did you arrive at those figures?"

"So far, we've managed to check the backgrounds of most of the shareholders. It's a nasty little web of domination, almost all of the Martins' shares are held by the directors of Sibling Investments either directly, or through some of their nominee companies. Over several years they've managed to slowly acquire total control of Martins."

"What about the balance sheet?"

"Nothing adverse has flagged up so far, the company is well run and seems to make above average profits for this industry, what I like about it is that it is that it is a cash cow type of outfit. The price per share has increased steadily over the last four years and they've acquired some smaller firms which all seem to be well organised."

"So why are they selling such a cosy business?"

"As far as I can see, this group of investors have done well out of the company. No great shakes, just a comfortable return on their capital. Someone hinted at something which could explain why they want to get out of Martins and leads me to think that funds are required for a major takeover somewhere else."

"Cashing in to purchase something larger or more profitable you think?"

"It's a possibility. We can't find any other reason for them getting out of Martins this way other than they could be contravening the stock exchange monopoly's law."

"How are they doing that?"

"The main shareholding is being held, in effect, by only one group of investors who would have trouble dumping a big block like that onto the open market. Questions would be asked and the share price could fall dramatically. These boys are clever, they're staying away from prying eyes on the stock exchange for their next takeover by offering full control of Martins and selling these nominee companies to specific interested parties as a block. If the shares were cashed in on the open market through more than ten different sources the price would definitely plunge. If they reveal that it is a single company holding all these shares, then Sibling Investments could be prosecuted by the stock exchange for not declaring its total interest in Martins. If you should decide to purchase these nominee companies as a block, that would put you in breach of the Stock Exchange rules as well."

"We're looking at something illegal then?"

"Technically, yes we could be. However, the whole operation is so well camouflaged that it would be the devil's own job to prove any form of collusion between each of the nominees. They've covered their tracks extremely well and the answer is to make a bid for the main control and let them carry on holding the minority shareholding. That way you effectively own and run the company and as funds become available, you slowly acquire more shares, that way, nobody will interfere with you."

"If they've been so careful, then how come it's only taken you a matter of days to uncover whole setup." Trevor tapped his nose to demonstrate that he was in the know.

"Even I couldn't prove it in a court of law and though I know what could be going on, proving that Sibling Investments are instrumental in creating the construction of this web of nominees, would be totally impossible no matter what resources were thrown at it."

"Then, for God's sake, don't even whisper your findings to David. What you've just told me, remains a secret between you and me and if David should in any way suspect that we intend purchasing an illegal operation, he would immediately be on to me to pull out. I don't need that in my life just now."

"Done."

"I can see why Sibling haven't placed the shares on the open market and have covertly come to us through a law firm, what is your gut reaction regarding the price?"

"It depends on how many players end up in the bidding, I would think this prospectus has been sent to... er, maybe half a dozen interested parties. My feeling is that Sibling will be looking for something slightly better than the current market value for this single block."

"You do realise, we're talking of well in excess of a hundred million for the whole shebang."

"I'm just the messenger, don't blame me. I think you should pass on this one, it's far too large for us to handle. As a group, we do not have those sorts of funds available to play in this league. You would have to go to the financial institutions and borrow very heavily and right now, we're really cash positive, but if you take this on, MH Holdings will be heavily over geared. That's not a healthiest state of affairs to jump into, but, you're the boss and so it's your decision to make."

"Umm, well keep checking. With all those profits currently being generated by Martins we could always break up the company and dispose of some of the assets and repay a large chunk of those borrowings."

"You would still be too highly geared for my liking, because I think we're possibly one of the most professional conglomerates within the construction and associated fields but, taking on this and placing ourselves under massive financial strain is suicidal madness."

"Mind you, on the plus side, it would also almost double our size." Trevor suddenly wondered whether he should possibly prefabricate stories about Sibling Investments having a downside to it. Perhaps this would deter Norman from rushing into something which up until recently, had simply been his passionate hobby. Inwardly he knew he wouldn't be able to dissuade his thinking and he wasn't a liar by nature and inwardly he knew that his exceptionally astute chairman would know immediately. He lit his pipe for the umpteenth time as he rose to leave the office.

"Trevor, I'm still just looking. I'll take these reports home and study them more carefully." Trevor pulled his tall frame from the chair and moved to the door before stopping and turning to his employer.

The Kixing

"Norman we will be over extended and could find ourselves in difficulty. Realistically, that would also mean that if we go this route and it does not work out we could even lose the corporation. We need to be a little more prudent and spend time examining all aspects of this acquisition. I am not very happy about it, even if you seem to think that it would benefit the group as a whole, we have always involved ourselves in the area of construction and now going into the betting business seems at the very outside, more than a risky bet. Let's not rush this, take it steadily, I will go into the background thoroughly to check out Martins standing, directors trading record and everything that is normally associated with a take over deal. The other thing that worries me is that their headquarters are not based here or even in Europe, there are just too many unwanted variables to contend with. Don't rush into this, if you miss the cut-off date then so be it. It is your decision and I am not preaching to you, I simply have a feeling that something is not quite right and that we must follow it up?"

"Trevor, I have been in the construction field and fight field for many years and really, I do value your opinion but you are now somehow treating me as you would a child Now get out of here ...Dad." Both men laughed as Trevor just shook his head and made his way back to his own office.

"THE KIXING"

CHAPTER FIFTEEN

By the following week things were starting to happen, the bank had already called Sandy and asked for him to arrange a meeting with the company's directors to discuss the company overdraft. Sandy was now under pressure and worried about how to pay the company's suppliers without encroaching even further on their already limited facility but when he approached Ernest about the meeting, the man had nearly gone berserk while Christine on the other hand remained quite calm.

"They probably just want to discuss an extension, it is possible that we may have to hock our homes to the bank." said Ernest as he and Christine were shown into the bank manager's office by a spotty faced youth, the grey haired bank manager rose to greet them.

"Ernest, Christine, it's been some time since we last met. How are you both?" Ernest was the last to be seated.

"What's all this about, Brian?"

"New brooms up at head office, they're insisting that we evaluate our customer's overdraft facilities and try to reduce them and I'm pretty certain that someone there has in fact highlighted your account and now they're insisting that I cut it back. If it were left to me, you know very well that I have no qualms at extending it but then again I'm only the manager and have to listen to them." Christine could feel her blood starting to boil.

"C'mon Brian, we've been one of your best customers for the last ten years and you've never had to call on us for anything. Our account has been as clean as a whistle since the day it was opened, so why this sudden concern?"

"I promise you Christine, this is none of my doing and you're right, I've never had any reason to question the running of your business before. Yesterday, we were unexpectedly paid a visit by two inspectors from our head office, they immediately homed in on several accounts, but come to think of it, yours was the one that seemed to attract them most and now I've been ordered to try and reduce your facility by as much as fifty per cent."

"What? How the hell do you expect us to operate under those conditions?" Ernest blurted. "I know you're somewhat extended at the moment and if it were purely my choice, I would gladly double your overdraft facility. But, it's not my decision because those at the head office tend to be my masters and I must comply with their commands, I have no other choice." Christine looked across at her stunned brother and then turned back to the slightly lumpish bank manager.

"How much time have we got to achieve this miraculous act?"

"They want you to do it almost immediately. I'm sorry."

"We can't." Ernest said simply. Christine's mind was racing as she quickly summed up all the possibilities open to the company.

"Brian, will you do us a very large favour?"

"What?"

"Stall your head office colleagues for forty eight hours. Tell them that you haven't been able to contact us or something like that."

"Why?"

"I think I know who's behind this. We're being squeezed into a tight corner by a large corporation who wants to take over the company. If my assumption is correct, they've somehow managed to bring pressure to bear on your head office in an attempt to force Ernest and myself to sell."

"Impossible," Brian studied her face for some time and realised that she was serious.

"You really think so? I'm not sure that our bank would be cajoled into such measures by anyone, no matter who they are or how big they are." Christine watched his every reaction carefully, she could see that he wasn't sure what she had revealed and after several minutes she had made up her mind to place her trust in the man.

"Then ask yourself the question, why would two inspectors come in and pick on the account of one of your best clients to reduce their facility when you've never had cause to doubt our capability? You said that you had gladly increase our facility if push came to shove. No Brian, we're being squeezed and we need that forty eight hour period to rectify the position."

"How do you propose to do that?"

"One, by collecting all outstanding debts, that will bring our overdraft down to the levels you require but we need as much time as possible to achieve that. Two, and this one remains between us two, nobody, but nobody outside this room must know what I'm about to propose, is that a deal?" The man's position could be on the line if he agreed to anything unlawful or underhanded.

"Christine, tell me exactly what's going on and then I'll consider your request." "No. First of all, if we're going to get out of this mess, then you must give us your word that nothing will be repeated outside these four walls because nothing I'm about to tell you is illegal."

"That's fair. I promise nothing will go further if you've not doing anything underhanded."

"What we're about to tell you is not a fairy tale, even Ernest doesn't know the full facts. Should what I tell you, ever leak out I'll know where it comes from." Christine told the grey headed bank manager everything that had happened during the course of the last few weeks. Ernest occasionally contributed to the discussion and also asked questions when he didn't understand something and by the time Brian had heard all, he knew where his loyalties lay and he had decided to try to help the Johnsons in every way possible.

"That's pure piracy on their part, what you're about to ask must not be unlawful, as a banker I wouldn't be able to condone any irregularities. Now, how can I help you beat these thugs?"

"By utilising our number two account because only we three know about the funds lodged there. With the extra million deposited last week we have just enough to cover your requirements. If we transfer the whole amount from our deposit to Johnson's current account, we then show all our cards to the opposition and I'm sure that your head office will be pushed even further and will insist that we reduce the amount even further and then, we'll really be in trouble. Getting the funds into the account without alerting anybody is going to be the problem."

"Not really. If as you say, you can collect the outstanding monies and reduce the present overdraft amount, that will immediately take the heat off your account. In the meantime, you must change the name of your number two account so that it won't be linked to Johnson Interiors."

"How will that help?"

"If head office come back and try to reduce the overdraft even further, I'll have grounds to be able to argue on your behalf at the highest levels. At least that way, we'll stall them for some time and meanwhile, unbeknown to my superiors, I'll make the necessary arrangements to have the disguised second account issued with as large an overdraft facility as is possible. That way, we are simply transferring your existing facility from the current account to another account, so in fact, you shouldn't be any worse off than you are now." Ernest breathed a sigh of relief.

"How do we pay our debts from the hidden account without anybody smelling a rat?"

"Easy. I'll arrange for you to open a trust account elsewhere in your personal names and every so often, you'll be able to transfer funds from your secret account through your trust account and back to Johnsons. That way, whoever is putting the boot in, will think that you are both propping up a failing business with personal money. It's called the bankers kite flying operation, now you see it, now you don't, but believe me it's there."

"Brilliant, then if they then try to expose the trust account, they'll have to come out into the open. That way, we'll collect the evidence required to take them to court."

"If, the bank is allowing this type of underhanded practice, you'll pretty quickly be able to put a stop to it. Banks don't like adverse publicity, it undermines customers confidence."

"How can we ever thank you for this? At least with your help, we can survive the initial onslaught giving us enough time to hit back at these bastards."

"You must reduce your overdraft within forty eight hours, that is the prime requisite. If what you've told me is correct, then, I'm sure you've got a job on your hands. They've got to the banks, so they could have enough clout to persuade your clients to hold back payments to you."

"Don't worry about that Brian, this is outright war, I have plenty of hidden ammunition that I haven't even considered using yet."

"Be careful Christine. I've seen some of these big boys in action and when they're gunning for somebody, they can be very rough. It doesn't matter who gets hurt." Christine stood up and just smiled at the grey headed banker. She made her way towards the door.

"I owe you one for coming down on our side, we won't forget your help and by the time we're through this sticky patch, you'll become one of your bank's shining stars."

"How do you work that one out?"

"Sit back and watch." Brian took Ernest's outstretched hand and shook it warmly. He could see that the whole affair was way over Ernest's head and the man had a sort of dazed look something like that of a fish out of water.

"I wouldn't like to be on the wrong side of her when she really gets cross. Anyway, keep a brotherly eye on her, these big boys don't play around."

"I've seen her operate in tight spots before and I'll stand in her corner any day. This tigress fights dirtier than anybody I know." Brian walked them to the door and then returned to his desk. He immediately called a friend at another bank and arranged for the joint personal account to be set up in the twin's name. Inwardly, he was only slightly worried about the circumstances, but knew that his position was well covered if the balloon suddenly went up. He had clearly pinned his colours to the mast by helping them and now all he could do was wait to see what casualties emerged. He desperately wanted the small company to win their battle of survival, but somehow the large conglomerates always seemed to have the muscle to beat down all in their paths.

"How did it go?" Sandy sat down opposite Ernest as Christine went and placed her bag in her office. On her way to Ernest's office she asked Jean to rustle up sandwiches and tea. Her brother was busily explaining what the bank wanted from them. When he had finished he turned to Christine.

"Anything else?"

"No... Now Sandy, how's the debt collection going?"

"Not very well. It would seem that everyone is in the same boat as us. I've never known money to be so short and I've probably heard every excuse possible to delay payment."

"So, what are you doing about it?"

"I've managed to get a few of them to commit some of the money which I've arranged to collect this afternoon. Better something, than nothing. I'll just have to keep bashing away trying to get them to pay in dribs and drabs."

"That's not good enough. Sandy, I want four copies of all outstanding amounts."

"Why?"

"I have a friend in the debt collection business and if we can't get these companies to pay up immediately, maybe then these professionals will have better luck at it."

"I doubt it because most of these long-winded customers would prefer it for us to take them to court, that way, they are able to drag their feet for a year or more before paying up." The twins knew that Sandy was working as hard as he could. Christine recalled the friendly bankers prophetic words. Maybe MH Holdings had already got to some of their clients.

"We'll see. As Ernest explained earlier, the situation with our bankers is becoming chronic, we need to use every means at our disposal to try and collect outstanding amounts within the next few days." Jean entered the office and could not help overhearing

Christine's words. She looked directly at Ernest and wondered if he hadn't lied to her about being able to rescue the business.

Once Jean had finished and left the office, Christine turned to her brother.

"Ernie, please give me Minter's proposal, I did promise that we would let them have it back sometime this week. I'm going to hand it back at their offices this afternoon."

"What?"

"If those people can just pitch up on our doorstep unannounced, there's no reason for me to make an appointment to see the great Norman Minter."

"What I really meant was, what are you going to offer them?"

"I haven't quite worked that out yet, I was thinking of making a counter offer that would stall them while they're mulling it over and will also give us a couple of days grace to collect our debts. That way, when they come storming back, we'll have a better picture of our financial position." Ernest took a pink folder from his drawer and pushed it across his desk, this was the first time that Christine had even bothered to look at Minter's proposal. Her eyes quickly scanned the pages until she found the price that Minter was prepared to pay for the business.

"This is the last straw, how can they insult us like this? Haven't they got any respect? Their offer doesn't really make any sort of provision for payment to us. What it is, is an offer to take over the business and rescue it by injecting capital into the firm to compensate for the shortfall. I'm going to give them a piece of my mind.

"But..."

"No buts. I'm not lying down and dying for Minter or anybody else."

Christine lifted her cup and finished her iced tea in one gulp then rose and without another word left the office. Sandy and Ernest sat staring at each other for several minutes.

"Boy, is she steamed?" Sandy finally said. It was more a way of getting the conversation going again than an informed statement.

"You don't know the half of it and somehow, my sister's going to find a way to make Minter pay for this indignation."

"He holds all the cards. It would seem that he's got us exactly where he wants us, it's just a matter of time before she capitulates."

"Don't be so cocksure. Nothing is ever final until the fat lady sings."

"Huh?"

"You don't know Christine like I do, just when you think you've won, she'll find a way to move the goalposts and turn certain loss into a resounding win. She just never gives up."

"I know, but..."

"Only time will show you how right I am." Sandy didn't say anything because he thought that the forlorn man was grabbing at fresh air in the hope that his sister would find some miracle cure for the ailing company.

"Sandy, get those reports done for Chrissie as soon as possible." Sandy smiled weakly at his employer. He stopped at Jean's desk and shook his head.

"Not good, I'm afraid." Right after lunch, Christine left the building and drove to MH Holdings. The receptionist informed her that Norman Minter wasn't in the building. She asked to see David Lividsky, within minutes, she was ushered into his office.

"I promised to return your proposal this week, your terms were totally unacceptable. If I didn't know better, I would have thought that it was someone playing a joke on our company. So, to be polite to Norman Minter, what I've done is to write you a letter with a counter offer and I think you're going to need time to digest my proposal."

"Do you want to give me a broad outline of what you've proposed?" Christine thought about it for a moment.

"No, we are still in the same position. MH Holdings have technically been paid everything owed and I have you to thank for that. If you hadn't have accepted our post dated payments then it would be a different matter. If we don't fulfil our obligations then perhaps we will talk again. Right now, we're both losing business because you're not supplying us with material and we're having to establish a complete range of new suppliers. However, you can tell Minter that that's the way it'll remain until we default on a payment." David paged through the letter.

"I can tell you now, you're upsetting MH Holdings, Norman Minter is not a man to forget this." Christine sprang to her feet.

"Norman Minter is like a bloody spoilt child and if he doesn't get his own way, he kicks and screams for attention. If that doesn't work then he makes these veiled threats through you, just who the hell do you people think you are, God?"

"Johnson Interiors is a small cog in the wheel of business. MH Holdings almost controls the construction industry here. When Norman Minter wants something, he generally gets it."

"Well, he's in for a nasty shock then, isn't he? Johnson Interiors is a family business and that's the way it's going to stay. Just you tell him that." Christine spun on her heel and left the meeting without another word. She roared out of the parking area heading south-east for awhile, suddenly on a whim she called out the number on the receiver of her car-phone to call her brother.

176

The Kixing

"Ernie, just finished the meeting with David Lividsky, it was as expected. We need to discuss the matter further, so I'm heading home, get in your car and meet me there." She had chosen her words carefully in case Antonio's men were listening in. She had no intention of talking to her brother and by the sound of his reply he had understood what she had implied. She turned north and headed home knowing that today could be the company's turning point. Her thoughts were now for Ernest who was at a very low ebb and needed to be held and loved so that his confusion wasn't so great.

The Kixing

"THE KIXING"

CHAPTER SIXTEEN

It was an early morning meeting at MH Holdings, when all the directors, as well as David and Rhona, Norman's secretary, were all seated around the long table in the chairman's office. Norman headed the meeting and was ensconced at the far end of the table in his customary position regally seated in the imposing chair with the black eagle looming large behind him. Rhona had completed the reading of the minutes of their last director's meeting which had been confirmed and signed by Norman as chairman on that occasion.

"Now, onto new business, you've all had a copy of the report of Powerbuild's liquidation and how it's affected us. To balance the loss incurred, we are now attempting a to gain possession of Johnson Interiors, a relatively small but, very sound and potentially lucrative shop fitting company. We should have control of them within the next eight weeks, they are also an unfortunate result of Powerbuild's demise and their profitability during the next fiscal year will help to offset the two million lost to us from the crash. I've been to that firm's headquarters and really like what I've seen and I feel that this company will be an extremely healthy acquisition. Although we're countering a certain amount of resistance, David and his team are currently poised to takeover the company for us." Most of the directors were friends and associates of Norman's father and were happy to let their young charge get on with the running of this empire without raising any pointed questions. Norman preferred it this way, he could push through just about anything without too much argument because most of these older people seated around the table were more than happy to simply collect their director's fees whereas, younger members had the tendency to question him.

The Kixing

Norman continued his brief of the conglomerate's achievements during the last quarter expounding that business was good and MH Holdings was extremely healthy and growing very steadily.

"Gentlemen, I've decided the time has come for MH Holdings to start diversifying its activities and move into an alternative field." Members at the table shuffled and reacted differently in anticipation. MH Holdings had been run along the same lines for almost three generations and the word *'change'* wasn't going to be accepted very easily but Norman pressed on.

"As you know, my father set up a fine boxing promotion company, which to date I might add, has always contributed more than its fair share to the holding company. I've continued to expand its activities and now, it's one of the largest of its kind in Europe. The promotion business has reached its pinnacle here and if we want to expand further, we have to enter the competitive and highly money-grabbing American fight market." Norman had carefully thought out how to pitch his intended move to the board as he could see them all begin visibly relaxing as they realised that the change was no more than an extension of the company's existing progress. But, Norman knew that he still had the difficult task of convincing the older board members that what he was about to attempt was definitely in the firm's long term interests.

"In order to achieve this step, we are going to need to takeover a company which already has its roots set down firmly in that part of the world. Should we try to go in from scratch, the present promotion companies will simply be able to freeze us out. We need an already established base from which to operate and then, once that is achieved and the company will be seen as a properly legalised American conglomerate and we'll use it to start purchasing into the construction industry. That way, we kill two birds in one stroke and by obtaining the majority shareholding in what is basically a British company we'll have a network extending through America and therefore, allowed full powers to operate there. We'll also have offices in all main centres to start acquiring smaller companies in our related fields." Norman took a sip of water. He wanted to see the reaction of his older board members before continuing. They were all relaxed and Norman knew that he had achieved his goal.

"Right, we have been offered just such an opportunity and the company in question is Martins PLC, the bookmaking operation. You'll shortly all be issued with trading results over the last four years and you'll see that the company is strong and has achieved a steady growth pattern. You'll also note how powerfully Martins is placed throughout the entire international area and what's more enticing, will become the ideal launch pad for MH Holdings to gain a secure foothold in Northern America." Rhona issued a copy of the minutes to each person. The room fell quiet as everybody studied the trading figures of the company, finally once when everybody had read their reports, Norman poised himself for the question which he knew was going to be uppermost in their minds. It was Larry Margoles, Norman's Jewish uncle by marriage and former company accountant that asked the all important question.

"This my boy, is not small potatoes so please explain just how do you intend funding such an operation?"

"Two ways, by borrowing the capital and then, you'll notice that I've marked several companies that we'll sell off to reduce the borrowings. By the time I've finished carving up the dead wood we should have a very nice company." Larry wasn't convinced.

"What happens if you don't manage to sell those companies and of course you realise that MH Holdings will then be so highly geared during this initial period that if anything goes wrong, we are in the hands of the bankers then."

"I know what you're saying, this company has always dictated its own terms and never put itself on the line. For the first time we will become reliant on outsiders for a loan. This is modern day business practice, we must take a short term risk and in a few months we will be back in full control and will have more than trebled in size. We will also be firmly entrenched in the very lucrative American marketplace. Isn't it worth the slight risk?" He sat back and waited but nobody was really in a position to argue, the whole thing seemed to make practical sense.

"Just a small point of warning for you to be careful my boy. I know you have done a tremendous job with the company since your father died, may God rest his soul, but this, it's a helluva leap forward in one jump."

"Believe me Larry, I've had this checked out from top to bottom, we've missed nothing. Martins is a very upright firm without any faults and we'll monopolise the gambling industry in Europe as well as becoming one of the three largest in the States."

"Well, if you think you can do it without harming MH Holdings, then you have my blessing." The other board members, now led by Larry as their spokesman, all nodded in agreement. Norman quietly breathed a sigh of relief because he had thought that his colleagues would have given him a rougher ride. He had been awake almost all night preparing for confrontation and instead, they had agreed without a whimper. The sudden relief was a bit of an anti-climax as he realised that they were all so happy with their lot in MH Holdings that they had just accepted his word as law.

"It's agreed then, I'll enter negotiations and make the necessary offer in writing for Martins PLC, right away. Who knows, maybe by the time we next meet, this firm will be one of the world's top hundred privately owned companies." He could see that his enthusiasm was beginning to spread to everybody, except David Lividsky.

"That's all the business for this quarter, are there any further questions before we bring this meeting to a close?" Everyone seemed content so the meeting was brought to a close. Standing practice was to retire to a local Chinese restaurant and have lunch but for the first time since Norman could remember, David excused himself from the ritual saying that he had too much work to catch up on. Norman knew that this wasn't a valid reason and thought it must be because he hadn't been consulted about Martins. Norman was sure that David would have opposed his move from the outset and that was why he had sprung it at the board meeting and received the full backing. Now, this was David's way of showing his disapproval, he made sure that afternoon David was summoned to Norman's office.

"Okay David, let's have it. What's bugging you?"

"I've already told you, I think you're going in over your head on this Martins takeover."

"You heard them in there today, it was a unanimous decision. Nobody thought it was a wrong move."

"It was what wasn't said that slightly bothers me and anyway, those old farts would agree with you no matter what you said. They follow with blind allegiance, when you say *'jump'* those old men would become superstars and do triple somersaults to please you but I'm not as gullible and say what I think."

"David, we've been friends for a very long time and I've never misled you besides which, you're the finest counsellor any businessman could wish for, and I really value your opinion. Because of your advice, I've been extra cautious on this one. I've had people checking inside and out and nobody's found anything that could harm us."

"Martins could be a gold mine for all I care but what worries me, is that you're going to borrow more than we can afford to repay without problems, we see that scenario regularly, take Johnson as a perfect example. Like a fat man standing on a weighing machine, his weight may be too much and once one of the springs gives way, the rest follow and the whole thing ends up in a heap. We are continually picking up on others misfortunes, now you're about to place MH Holdings in a situation where it could, I'm not saying it will, but it could, find itself at the mercy of the banks so its your personal decision and I don't have to like it."

"Fair comment. The fact is, we're going to make the offer. Please accept the fact that it's going to happen and help me with the takeover."

"All right, but only if you record my opposition to the project in a memo."

"I'll get Rhona to type it immediately."

"Right, now how can I help?" Norman handed one of the two pink files from his desk. It contained copies of everything that Trevor Reece had unearthed on Martins PLC. " Double check everything and you'll find my proposal to the lawyers at the back. We also need to set up a meeting with them to discuss the whole matter so what I need you to do is to try and find out what, if any opposing bids have been received."

"Before we see them officially, I'll call Bernard Marcus straight away and arrange a lunch. I don't know whether he'll assist our cause, but I'll try to gain an inside advantage anyway."

"Good man. One last thing, I see from your morning report that you had a meeting with Christine Johnson and they've made a ridiculous counter offer. What are we doing about it?"

"Their bank has already been instructed to reduce their current overdraft by half and if they were in trouble before then, this step will simply compound their problems even further. We've managed to obtain a list of all outstanding amounts owed to Johnsons and dropped words in the necessary ears to prolong payments as long as possible. It would seem that the trap is quickly tightening and there's no possible route of escape. Another week or two should see them come begging."

"Great!" David punched the air.

"It's going to give me pleasure to see Christine Johnson come down off her high horse."

"Get Rhona to type the memo and I'll get stuck into Martins." Norman quickly dictated the letter which was quickly typed and within minutes returned for Norman's signature.

"Happy now."

"I'm a lawyer Norman, I always cover my backside, no matter what the circumstances. I just hope my fears aren't well founded." Norman simply shook his head. This was the first time that he had ever seen David so passionate about anything businesswise.

"You're just an old woman and we'll see who has the last laugh." David waved the file as he walked to the door.

"I hope you're right." After having had lunch with Bernard Marcus, David immediately reported his conversation to Norman.

"It gets worse, after several glasses of wine I managed to convince Bernard to open up and there are going to be three bidders for Martins."

"Who are the others?"

"That's the one thing he wouldn't give away. He's a very ethical individual but what he did let slip, was that one of them is American?"

The Kixing

"Shit! It's probably the black or Jewish promoters. If they get their hands on Martins then that will give them control of the European scene. We can't have that. Can your friend be coaxed in any way?"

"Not by traditional methods but, because of our long standing friendship, he's prepared to do me a small favour."

"What?"

"He won't reveal who the bids are from until Martins has been sold, although, he wants us to have the company and for it to remain British. By later this afternoon or by tomorrow morning, he's going to let me know if we're even in the running."

"Did you indicate how much we're prepared to offer?"

"Not exactly, I said that MH Holdings was thinking of offering just below market price for the shares."

"What did he say to that?"

"Not a lot. His gut reaction was that we were pitching our price a little too low."

"You see David, now, maybe you'll believe when I tell you that you're not a businessman, your lawyer friend immediately saw through your disguise. When you pitch an offer, it's got to make the buyer think you're serious, but then again it mustn't be too high or for that matter, too low. Your suggested bluff was too low. From now on let me handle the negotiations. All I need to know is how we stand and it's a pity you can't find out who the other players are."

"I was just sounding him out."

"If you think about it, why should they sell to us at below market price? All they have to do is to slowly filter the shares into the market and they'll get their price. No David, they're going to want a higher price than par for the complete block." Rhona came into the office.

186

"Sorry to butt in. David, there's a call for you from a Bernard Marcus and Susan says you told here to patch it through here."

"Right." Rhona turned and went through to her office.

"Now we'll know the worst." Norman handed David the receiver and lifted a second earpiece in order to listen to the discussion.

"Hi Bernie, what've you got for me?"

"Firstly let me thank you for a superb lunch. Next, I think you could be out of the running if you forward your bid. The yanks have indicated that their offer is going to be substantially higher than yours. The third party have fallen away because their offer was in line with yours. The Americans must want Martins pretty badly to come straight in with this type of bid."

"How much higher?"

"Are you sitting down? About fifty per cent higher?" David glanced across at Norman. The big man's features gave nothing away. " A hundred and fifty million is their indicated opening bid. There is no way that our client would even consider your offer, they had be stupid if they did. I don't think you're even close enough for us to try and influence a decision."

"That's fine Bernie, at least we know where we stand. I'll talk to Norman Minter and get back to you and at this moment I doubt whether we'll be increasing our offer. From the figures that I've seen, Martins isn't worth a hundred and fifty million. At a hundred million it was a nice buy, but that price is too steep for us."

"So you won't be making an offer then?" Norman held up his hand to indicate that he needed to talk to David.

"Just a second Bernie, I have another urgent call to attend to but don't go away." David pushed a button so that Bernard Marcus was placed on hold and couldn't hear them.

"Stall for time, tell him that you'll have to discuss it with me and that we'll get back to him by no later than midday tomorrow with our answer."

"You're crazy. I had bad vibes about this deal before, but now, this is planned suicide. How can you even consider it?"

"THE KIXING"

CHAPTER SEVENTEEN

"I felt, ...that you were making a mistake earlier, but this, its suicide. There's no logic in acquiring Martins at this over-inflated price." Trevor Reece and David Lividsky were seated at the long board room table. Norman was magisterially seated between them in his spread winged eagle chair at the head.

"I'm fully aware that monetaristically, it may not seem to be the most brilliant move that I've made during my career because there's no initial advantage to be gained from the sale. It's the long-term benefits that I'm looking for."

"Yes but..."

"Wait! ...Let me first finish what I was saying." Trevor went for his matches and attempted to light his forever extinguishing pipe.

"I know that we need our borrowings to increase substantially and as you are aware, the consortium of banks have agreed to back us on this one. Any shortfall will come out of our own reserves and that's the reason we're going for Martins, its that acquisition opens up several fronts to us that in the past, have been closed to this company. America is a gigantic market and the time has come for us to begin expanding our activities."

"But, you don't have to go this route, there are many other avenues."

"Granted, but this way, we also acquire top status in the boxing promotion and bookmaking business. If you look at it coldly, chances to kill several birds and all that, ...we must not miss this opportunity.

The Kixing

There will never be another opportunity like it. In order to build a company like Martins will take many, many years, it's not just a matter of money, it's also reputation; client credibility; status and many other things that go into this large cooking pot of commerce to make a large firm so successful." Trevor tapped out the ash from the large pipe into a large circular glass ashtray. He started filling it while Norman continued.

"Now, I know that both you and Dave are opposed to this decision, but, I'm going ahead. It's not often that we disagree about any of my requests, but this time I feel very strongly that this will turn out to be the best takeover yet." David shuffled the papers in front of him.

"Norman, both Trevor and I know that you have the board's blessing, the bank's are prepared to back you and it's your company to do with as you see fit. God forbid we run into trouble somewhere down the line, there just will not be enough latitude for us to escape. Over-gearing of companies is the main recipe for failure. Until now, this firm has always been self sufficient... building, expanding; building and expanding again and *that* formula has worked extremely well over a long period. Not only are you entering untried fields, but you're doing it without sufficient backup resources and the omens cannot be good." Trevor lit his pipe and exhaled a large grey plume of smoke.

"Now I must play the devil's advocate, by purchasing Martins, you're getting this firm into *very* deep water and from hereon in it's sink or swim time." Norman waited until Trevor was quite finished.

"Right, now that we've all aired our grievances, can we get down to the business in hand? I take it, that although you disagree with me, you'll back me all the way once we acquire Martins?" Both men nodded in agreement.

"David, I want you and Trevor to draw up the offer along the lines discussed with Bernard Marcus yesterday. Then, once I've signed it, you must meet him and explain that this is going to be our final bid. If the Americans improve their offer, we are not going to follow them, they can have it."

"You've gone *this* far, why won't you be prepared to go further?"

"Logistics... I'll have to start selling assets in order to simply make a bid and that won't be worthwhile."

"Okay, I'll call Bernard and set up another lunch date. He can pay today." Norman and Trevor smiled. David stood up and gathered his papers together.

"C'mon Trevor, we've got a lot to do before lunchtime." Norman started to rise. "By the way, I expect to see both of you at Saturday night's championship fight. It should be a cracker."

"I wouldn't miss it for the world, I reckon he'll keep his world title though," Trevor replied.

"Take my tip. If you're betting on the fight, go for the challenger, I think you'll find that we have a new champion." David followed Trevor from the room.

"Are you going on Saturday?"

"Oh yes, I wouldn't waste a ringside seat at today's prices." David entered the *'Park on the Inn'* hotel where he had arranged to meet Bernard Marcus for lunch. He made his way to the restaurant and found his short companion already seated and waiting for him.

"I ordered a Bloody Mary for you, I hope you don't mind?"

"No, that's fine." They both studied the menu before David settled for steak, which is what he always had. Bernard, very rotund and showing definite signs of 'the good life', went for a couple of crayfish. He also ordered a bottle of wine to go with their meal.

The Kixing

"Now that the important matter of food has been taken care of, what do you have for me?" David took a large brown envelope from his briefcase and pushed it across the table. Bernard, without even looking at its contents placed it in a file.

"I'll read it later, just give me the outline."

"MH Holdings is bettering the American's office by one hundred thousand."

"Impressive."

"Listen Bernard, we are making a one time offer and Norman isn't prepared to get into a haggling match. If the yanks improve their offer, we're not going to make a second bid because this is our first and last, it's up to you now to see that Martins accept it." Bernard pulled his mouth into a ball shape.

"That may not be so easy."

"How long have we known each other? Twenty five, thirty years? You know me well enough by now to know that I don't go back on what I say. As it is, Martins is getting a superb deal which is *way* over-valued compared to their real asset value. I don't care what the Americans think or do, there's just no more money in the coffers for us to be able to increase our bid. We've gone as far as we can." The wine steward arrived and opened the bottle next to Bernard. He took a large sip, swirled it around in his mouth and then swallowed.

"That's good." The penguin suited man despatched wine into two glasses and left without saying anything. Bernard lifted the glass towards David.

"Cheers." They clinked glasses and both took long sips of the rich puce coloured liquid. Bernard picked up his fork and with his napkin, vigorously rubbed the implement as if to clean it in anticipation of the grand dish about to arrive.

The Kixing

"David my boy, I understand, leave it with me, I'll sort something out. Don't worry."

"I *know* you will. Two waiters arrived, one carrying two plates with their orders, the other with a piping hot platter covered with an assortment of vegetables. David noticed that Bernard's fat jowls seemed to puff up as his eyes took in the array of elegantly arranged regalement being placed before him. As far back as he could remember, Bernard had always been a greedy individual. Back at the office, David asked his secretary Susan to get hold of Paul Hunter and Julie and ask them to attend the now delayed daily meeting. She found them and very soon, all four were assembled at David's long board room table.

"I'm sorry we had to cancel the meeting this morning but something quite important came up anyway, that's enough said, we're all here now. Anything to report?" Paul took the lead.

"From my end, reports are that staff morale at Johnsons is dwindling daily. Jean is becoming a real pain in the arse, she does nothing but complain about the company. She was fun at first but her jealousy and little girl lost is now getting me down." David looked at Paul's written notes.

"Julie?"

"Much the same as far as Johnsons are concerned, Sandy's already thinking of looking for somewhere else, mind you, he seems happy enough in himself. I like him, he's fun to be with." Paul gave her a wry smile.

"Still in love then?"

"You mind your own business, the way I handle things and the way you handle yours are somewhat different. He's a very nice gentleman to be around." Over the last week David had watched the two snipe at each other. Julie was content with her lot, but Paul was having his emotions tested and was very uncomfortable.

"Right you two, you're finished with Johnsons, I think that we've learnt almost everything we need to know."

"Yes!" Paul punched the air with a closed fist. David smiled.

"Now, now. That doesn't mean you won't be back. Paul, I don't want you rushing in and shutting all routes back to Johnsons. In the meantime we will keep the telephone tapping going just in case anything develops."

"But..."

"I'm sure you'll find a way of putting your contact on hold for awhile. Just don't go and slam the door, keep it slightly ajar. Butter her up somehow, we're not finished with Johnsons until we own them. Okay?"

"I suppose I could lie through my teeth and tell Jean that I'm going back to the Middle East."

"That's more like it. Jean what are you going to do?"

"Oh I'm happy to keep my relationship going with Sandy. That way at least, if Paul does something stupid, we still have a positive pipeline into Johnsons."

"Good idea. All right Paul, that way if you are unable to get out neatly and it starts becoming messy, then you'll have to ensure that you are able to get out cleanly."

"This women is so jealous that I would prefer getting away altogether. Thanks Julie, I owe you one."

"Just remember your words." David placed the notes in the now thick pink folder. Your next assignment is to try to get into Martins, the bookmaking company. What I'm about to say remains within these four walls, all right? We've made an offer for them and I want all the inside knowledge you can group together." Paul whistled.

"The old man's reaching for the skies this time because Martins's is a really *big outfit*."

"Exactly, try to get in as high as you can, here are some details." David pushed two files across the table.

"We're not going to use the entire team on this one, it would serve no purpose, because the offer's been made already leaving us little alternative for us to just keep a watching brief from within." Julie looked up from the opened file.

"That's unusual."

"What is?"

"Mr Minter always investigates an intended marker so why hasn't it been done so, this time?" David shrugged.

"He's the owner and he's decided to go in without an investigation, anyway there wasn't time to carry out our normal investigation and he needed to make the call, the decision is all his, believe me, I certainly am not a happy bunny."

"Just wondering, that's all because I believe it's always been company policy to have a thorough search, but then again, I suppose he's the boss so, he makes the rules."

"Quite right, now good luck with the new venture, keep me well posted." As they left the office, Paul once again punched the air.

"Today's the day, tonight's the night, we shot the stork so I'm *alright!*"

"That's what I like about you Paul, you're so consistent, you are just a macho pig, your entire existence simply always remains between your legs. You're coarse, do you know that?"

"Oh, ho, ho. Look who's talking."

"I enjoy my work because each new chase means everything, it's exciting, to me the sexual side is simply an added bonus. I love working on the limit knowing that I could be found out at any minute. That's my reason, but yours is all down to screwing, isn't it?"

"Yeah! I love it."

"That's the difference between us, its all about me, me, me and you've done nothing but carp on about your assignment this last week. You treat everything as a toy for Paul Hunter, not as a job of work. I get on with it, no matter what straw I've drawn because I'm a true professional and you're just a clown."

"You're a professional all right and a highly paid one at that."

"You see, that's what I mean, to you everything's only a game, nothing's ever treated seriously and mark my words, one day you're going to caught out and then, well, you'll regret your flippancy. Remember my words because one day your disrespect will let you down."

"Yeah, yeah." The two parted as Julie reached her office as Paul continued down the passage and stopped to talk to a new girl that had started work that day. David in the meantime answered his telephone.

"Hello Bernard, what's happening?"

"Uh... bad news. The sellers have told me to go to the Americans again and tell them that they've been outbid, what if they come back with a higher bid, you know David, I really want your group to gain control."

"Bernard. I told you that we will not raise our offer and I thought I made that abundantly clear, we want Martins, do what you have to, but we're not raising our offer. Now stop messing about, the next time I hear from you is when you tell me that our offer has been accepted. Do you understand?"

"But..."

"No buts Bernard. That's the position. Okay?"

"I'll see what can be done."

"Not good enough. Make sure we get Martins before you next talk to me." The line went dead. David was furious as he walked to Norman's office.

"Sit down and tell me how it went."

"Bernard Marcus and the sellers are playing silly buggers with us." Norman leaned forward, his face now etched concern.

"Why? What's going down?"

"I've just given Bernard Marcus a rocket. The sellers want him to tell the Americans that we've beaten their bid. They're matching both sides against the middle. I've told him this is our final offer and to sell Martins to the other side if they come in with a higher bid."

"What! Who the hell gave you the authority to stop the bidding?"

"You did, your exact words were that there was no money in the kitty and I took you at your word. I'm calling both your.and, the American's bluff. Let's call a halt to this nonsense right here and now. I know Bernard very well, if we keep pushing upwards he'll get the others to do the same. His fees will gather momentum as well, no Norman, nip it in the bud right here."

"This is the first time I've seen you feel so strongly about anything. You've never done this before."

"This time is different, you're doing things from the heart and outside the box, everything else has gone out of the window for instance where is the strict format we've always adhered to? Consider for a moment, no investigation, the place could be rotten to the core. Large borrowing, stretching ourselves to the limit. Paying an over the market price, this whole thing is so unlike you, nothing balances."

"Whew! That bad, is it?"

"Yes."

"Then I suggest we do something about it, let's just wait and see whether they accept our bid. We can't pull out now that we've made the offer in writing and if the Americans improve their stake then we simply withdraw from the running. I'll honour your decision, only, ...because your argument suddenly makes a great deal of sense. David almost did a double-take, this was the very first time that he had ever seen Norman back down.

"Now what's happening with Johnsons?"

"Not a lot, depression, doom and gloom among the staff prevails. In fact, I've started pulling Paul and Julie away from that project. I thought it may be an idea to try and get them busy around Martins, just in case we end up with protracted negotiations."

"Good thinking. By the way has Johnsons next payment cleared?"

"It's not due to be presented until tomorrow. Somehow, I have the feeling that it won't be met." Both men laughed.

"It's wonderful to be able to wield so much power and one last thing, would you cast your eagle eye over this." Norman pushed some contract notes across his desk. David lifted it and scanned the first lines.

"Cocksure, aren't you?" It contained the outline details of a proposed contract to be drawn up to acquire Johnson Interiors. David fanned through the notes to see what the offer price would be. All Norman Minter was prepared to offer was to invest one million in order to save the business from collapse.

"Nothing for the shareholders?"

"If the business goes under, they are going to have to repay the bank and this way they walk away owing nothing. We invest a million, put the firm on a steady footing and... voila, everybody's happy. I've offered to retain them in their present positions at their current salaries, what's simpler?"

"Power my friend, you said it yourself."

"I know, beautiful, isn't it?" Norman laughed loudly. David returned to his office to look at the notes in more detail.

The Kixing

"THE KIXING"

CHAPTER EIGHTEEN

"I wonder what this is all about?"

"Brian only said he needed to see us urgently. He wouldn't expand on the telephone." Christine and Ernest were shown into the bank manager's large office.

"Ah, Christine, so glad you could make it so quickly. We have a problem, how are you Ernest?" It was clear to Ernest that Brian considered Christine the main spokesperson.

"What now?"

"Head office are piling on the pressure as I thought they might."

"How?"

"Look at this, it's ludicrous."

Brian pushed a memo to Christine. Ernest leaned towards her in order to be able to read the slip of paper and saw that it stated that in view of the bank inspector's visit, several overdraft accounts were to be reduced by two thirds with immediate affect. There were six names shown, one of them being Johnson Interiors, which Ernest realised instantly was the only company account.

"Jeez, they could've at least been a little more subtle about it, couldn't they?"

Christine handed the letter back to Brian.

"I thought you should see the letter, this is so blatant that it's a joke. Really, I'm a little more that just infuriated, at first I was going to resign or at least have it out with my head office. But now, thinking things through, it would not serve your purpose any good if I raised objections it would probably be far better to surreptitiously go about this quietly as we are doing right now."

"May I have a copy of that memo?"

"Why Christine?"

"At the end of all this, I'm going to confront your head office."

"That will lose me my job."

"Don't worry Brian, I promise not to use it without your full approval."

"I'll tell you what, I'll copy it and keep it at home together with other notes from the inspectors, I don't agree with these banking practices so let's see if we can somehow build up some sort of case against those heading the the whole out. Just remember that it's not that I don't trust you two to keep the matter strictly private, but feel that I would prefer to control matters in my own way. That way, my job will remain safe."

"I understand, but this is simply a word of warning, these are dangerous people and so each letter copied must be taken far away from the bank's premises."

"Why?"

"If your head office should ever find out about the shuffling of accounts, you could lose more than your job, at first you will be sent home without being allowed to remove anything further from the bank and next either the police or banking inspectors or worse will turn up at your premises, All the proof you have must be away from here and your house because what you're doing means you're taking a massive risk by helping us the way you are."

"A few days ago I wouldn't have believed that *our bank* could operate in this way, times are changing but still it simply shouldn't be allowed. I'll make copies and take them home with me and then hide them somewhere safely, possibly at my brother's house."

"Good. Now, ...there's a large cheque going to be presented by MH Holdings today and it must be honoured."

"I understand." Brian fiddled about in one of his drawers then extracted a bank form and pushed it across the desk.

"Here, sign this, has your new trust account been opened yet?

"Oh yes, I arranged it with a very close bank manager friend of mine."

"Oh yes. One very large payment from our lawyers offices have already been made into that account."

"Superb. Then I want you to transfer more than enough to cover the amount paid out into your secondary account." Both Christine and Ernest signed the transfer.

"This will allow me to utilise your second overdraft here."

"How?"

"Simple, with one payment from your newly opened second account to your trust account, we reduce Johnsons overdraft by increasing your borrowing facility on that second account. It's something like a pair of scales, we take the overdraft out of one side and place it in the other, the whole thing is out of kilter. So what do we do? We simply move the money from the unbalanced side back to the other side via your trust account. It balances until you move money from the outside trust fund to the second account to repay the temporary loan. Again, it's out of balance, the second account has far more money than your current account and nobody knows the difference."

The Kixing

"Sleight of hand, it's like a bloody magician."

"Nope, it's more like Chinese whispers."

Brian tapped his nose.

"In our world it's generally known as account kiting, I've been with the bank long enough to see all the tricks. Head office will never even know what's happened, they'll be furious if ever they found out what's happening but you must place funds from the trust account into Johnson's account to cover both the payment and the reduction of your facility. It must be done today, okay?"

"Will do."

"It would be far healthier if you did it by bank transfer and do not make a cheque deposit, it could be risky. Meanwhile I'm sending funds from your second account to your trust fund today. What you'll have to do, is go straight to the bank, sign a form like this instructing the bank to send the funds to Johnsons account. I'll take care of the rest."

"Again, how can we thank you Brian?"

"You can't, or rathere don't need to because I simply like to see fair play, that's all. We've been friends for a long time, and I can't condone my head office's actions."

Christine and Ernest rose.

"Just one word of warning, you must carry out my instructions to the letter for this to work without any slip ups because one blundered interchange could cause our chain reaction to fall flat."

Christine smiled and extended her hand.

"That's a small request, we'll do everything right on cue."

"Good and remember, we're not quite out of the woods yet, but at least the tide's been stemmed for the moment." The twins headed straight towards the bank where their trust account was held. After completing the paperwork Ernest returned and eased his Porsche into his reserved parking spot behind the Johnson Interiors office block. Walking towards the entrance he grabbed at his sister's sleeve.

"There he is again." He pointed to the man standing at the corner.

"Who?"

"You remember, I told you the building was being watched. That's him." The man suddenly spun on his heel and walked away behind some buildings and out of sight.

"You're sure it's the same man?"

"Positive. That's the third time I've seen him, he always stands on that corner and wears the same suit. I couldn't be mistaken, let's call the police."

"To tell them what? There's a man standing on the corner, no, it deserves something more than that to call them in. Okay Ernie, don't panic, just leave it with me."

"What are you going to do?"

"Speak to a friend of mine, let's see why the grubby man is keeping an eye on our building, that is, if he is. C'mon now, I've got a lot to do."

Christine stopped at the reception desk and asked Lynne whether there had been any messages for them while they were out. Ernest went to his office and. Jean followed him in.

"Here are your messages, nothing really important and Sandy would like a meeting with you as soon as possible.

"There's no time like the present." As Jean turned to leave, Christine walked into the office.

"The nerve of that man."

"Who?"

"Mr Bloody Minter, that's who."

"Why?"

"He's requesting my presence for lunch today."

"Hey!"

"Yup."

"Why?"

"How do I know? I suspect he's going to talk about another proposal for the company, his little lawyer wasn't happy with me the other day when I returned their unsigned offer. His timing is immaculate, today's the day for the first cheque to be paid. Minter's probably already had our account checked and found we don't have funds to cover the cheque."

Sandy knocked on the door.

"Come in Sandy. What can I do for you?"

"The post dated cheque, we don't have sufficient funds to covert."

Jean winked at Ernest.

"We were just discussing the matter and we've just come from meeting with an investor who's made the company a loan to cover today's cheque."

"What about the rest of the amount?"

"We'll have to wait and see, discussions are proceeding, perhaps we'll have a new partner in the company, perhaps not. I've just got to make a call to an idiot."

Christine waved the paper in her hand so that Ernest knew who she was calling, she then made her way to her office.

"Whew!" Ernest could see the obvious sheer relief etched right across Sandy's face.

"Thank God for that. I nearly called in sick today because I've been dreading coming into the office all week. What, with no real incomings on the horizon and this large cheque being presented today, I was expecting it to be a nightmare day."

"See how wrong you can be? I warned you that Christine would fight with her every fibre to save the business."

"How did she do it?"

Ernest suddenly became guarded, he had got used to the idea of having the offices bugged and it was an automatic reaction to think out his every word lately.

"I'm not sure." Ernest simply shrugged his shoulders.

"But you were with her at the meeting, weren't you?"

"Yes. I don't yet know who our kindly benefactor is, it was all done through a firm of lawyers."

"When will we receive the money?"

" Hopefully, today."

"Great!"

"Another thing you ought to know, the bank has cut our original overdraft to a third of its previous amount."

"What? How can they do that?"

"They just have, we received notification of this fact earlier this morning."

"Christ! How the hell are we supposed to operate on that basis? Things are tight enough as it is."

"Let's see what happens during the next few weeks, at the moment we're really down, but then again, a long way from being out for the count. Keep your pecker up, we'll come through in the end."

"I don't share your confidence although you were right about Christine, *this time*, but we still owe MH Holdings a lot of money. Given time we could possibly repay it. The short interval payments don't give us enough breathing space."

"Take my advice, just keep the faith and we'll win out in the end."

Christine returned to Ernest's office, her features now bore some kind of resemblance to that of thunder.

"That man infuriates me, do you know what he had the audacity to say?"

"No."

"He knew."

"What?"

"That we didn't have sufficient funds to cover the cheque what I want to know is how the hell did he get hold of that private information? I'll tell you how, the senior bankers told him, that's who. That man has tentacles spread everywhere."

"No? Who are we talking about?" Christine pushed on without taking notice of Sandy's question.

"Oh yes, that bastard has got some sort of a pipeline straight into our account and he is aware of our position and knows to the nth degree what this company is worth."

"So what did he want?"

"With all the charm of a spitting cobra, he told me that he wanted to discuss the sale of the business to him, he then calmly informed me to the penny, just how much we have in our account and that their cheque would not be met."

Ernest smiled at his twin.

"Then?"

"I told him to go to blazes and that today had not ended yet."

"What was his reply?"

"Icy, I think he was expecting me to lie down and die and by the sounds of his voice he was not a happy person. He again threatened to take the business from under us."

"So?"

"Ernie, that man brings out the worst in me, I did something that I've never ever done before."

"What's that?"

"I swore at him then slammed the phone down, I know that it doesn't help our cause but it gave me great pleasure. Who the hell does he think he is?"

Ernest raised his eyebrows and chuckled softly.

"God ...maybe?"

"God or not, nobody, but nobody, treats me this way and shortly he's going to rue the day he ever tangled with Christine Johnson."

Later that day, Jean and Sandy left the office to have a quick drink together at the Monk's Head pub, Sandy was both elated not to have had a company cheque bounce leaving him free for a while from the struggle of keeping on balancing the company's accounts. Jean had heard some of the goings on in the office and had accompanied Sandy for the sole reason of obtaining the complete low down of what was `really happening. By the time she left for home she had had enough and inwardly determined to find herself another position. No sooner had she reached her flat than there was a knock at the door, it was Paul Hunter and she threw her arms about his neck.

"You're just what I need right now." He tried to ease her arms apart.

"I'm tired. It's been one hell of a day."

"What's the matter, you never cuddle any more? Why do you push me away. I love you Paul and it's been a real stinker at Johnson today. I've decided to leave Johnsons, the strain has become too much."

Paul's ears suddenly pricked up at the news as he slumped down onto the long settee.

"Tell me more."

"Today was the last straw because the company's running on a prayer and promise. Somehow they *just managed* to pay an outstanding cheque today. If they hadn't paid it, we probably would have the bailiffs knocking at the door by tomorrow."

Jean sat down right against Paul and to his irritation, started running her hand through his hair. Her news came as a new twist, rather than suffer her demanding attentions, Paul instantly decided to get her into bed immediately to start letting their relationship come to an end, he kissed her and she responded immediately.

"You're such a stallion, we never really talk, do we?"

"What do you mean?"

"We don't, when we're not making love, we're eating. If we're not doing either of those, we're arguing and you storm out. It's not like it was at first, please tell me something, am I too possessive?"

Paul pulled his lips over his teeth in a simulated broad grin.

"Frankly yes, you simply keep crowding me with questions about my movements and don't believe me when I tell you anything. You haven't given me the benefit of the doubt, not even once."

"I'm sorry, I don't mean it, it's just that I love you and the office is just such a pain, I'm so scared and simply needed something to hang on to, unfortunately you became my only foil. I'm sorry, please forgive me."

"Jean, you're becoming stifling, if you're not picking an argument, you're moaning about your work. There's no fun to compensate for your darkening moods."

"All right! I'll tell you what, tonight let's try to change all that, let's go somewhere and get drunk or something and we don't mention the office or my problems."

"It's not that, I love to hear what's been happening at the office, that's only normal, but it's you that's the problem. Everything seems to revolve around on how badly you are being treated and I can't take it any more."

"If I promise faithfully to shut up can we try and start afresh?" Paul sat quietly for a moment considering her request, he knew that he had led her into the ideal situation to enable him to walk away, but now, he wanted to know more about Johnsons. Perhaps he could achieve both goals by the end of the evening.

"Okay. How about a drink first?"

"Anything you say my lord and master." Jean bowed low and walked backwards in mock servile attitude. Paul smiled wryly.

"When you're finished that, ...my servant, I want you to come and do the dance of the seven veils in front of me." He mocked in return.

"Oh master, I do not possess seven veils."

"Then the outfit you are wearing will have to do."

"As you insist, O' master. Thy will be done." Jean returned with a whisky, water and ice. She placed it on the table next to his chair and placed a DVD in the stereo and as the music filled the room she began dancing slowly while acting out the part of a stripper. Paul finished his drink just as she had removed everything except her very small briefs.

"You've got a sensational body my slave."

"You like, then come and get." She teased moving slowly and seductively. This was a different woman and he had now been titillated enough to begin responding as she moved slowly and seductively in the direction of the bedroom.

"No slave, not in there. Here!"

Paul pointed to the floor in front of him.

"If the master wants his slave, he too, must remove his clothes."

Paul stripped quickly and stood in the middle of the room with his arms folded across his chest in lordly fashion. Jean moved around him very slowly.

"The master is excited, yes?" The charade broke down at that moment, neither could keep up the act of their straight laced appearance as both howled with laughter. Paul grabbed her and pulled her straight down to the grey carpeted floor.

"That's more like the Jean I know."

He immediately entered her and they made raw love where they were until Paul finally rolled over onto his back, totally exhausted. After a short time Jean sat up and slowly ran her fingernail across his stomach in a scratching motion.

"You're a fantastic lover. I'm sorry about my caustic comment earlier, let me tell you, I just love you making love to me."

"You see, it's so much more fun when we're happy and fooling around."

"I know and from now on, I'm a changed woman and I'll even continue being your slave O' master mine."

Both laughed.

"Do you want me to rustle up something here or would you prefer going out for something. I'll pay this time."

"I think we go out and have something special."

"Why?"

"Well... I was going to tell you later, but there's no use putting it off. I have to return to the Middle East for a while."

"No... You must stay."

"It's only for a short time, I'll be back and then we can work something out."

"I'm not going to argue... I'm not going to argue. There O' master, I can do it if I put my mind to it."

"You see, it's not that hard, come here."

He pulled her on top of him and holding her head steady made her look straight into his face. Slowly he moved his lower body into position until he felt himself against her. He hesitated, wanting it to happen slowly, before allowing himself to move inside her, her eyes closed momentarily as she gasped loudly.

"Look at me!" Paul ordered in his sternest tone to underline his authority. "Right now, we're quits and starting all over from scratch, now, you were saying something about Johnsons just being able to make some payment. What happened?"

Making slow love, she battled to focus and simultaneously recall the day's events and what she had learnt at the office. Paul skilfully measured his movements until she had related all she could tell him. Suddenly both of them couldn't talk anymore as they both climaxed simultaneously but much later and after a shower, they set off for the restaurant.

"THE KIXING"

CHAPTER NINETEEN

On Saturday, Norman was extremely busy all day although he was like a mother hen hustling her chickens here, there and everywhere. It was the day of the much awaited and talked about world championship fight between the local man, Stephen Blair and the South American world champion Ramoz Caetano. The weigh-in had already taken place and both men had come in within ounces of the middleweight button weight of one hundred and fifty four pounds. There had been the obligatory nasty words and staring at each other for the all important media circus pictures. Now, it was down to hard graft making sure that the last minute mechanics were all correctly in place, and working, seating arrangements, dressing rooms, ringside doctor, correct gloves etc. had to be checked and double-checked to make sure that all was in order for the big night. Television pictures of the fight were due to be beamed across the globe and cameramen, lighting specialists and crews were going through their final checks to guarantee no slip-ups. Norman was in his temporary office screaming into the telephone.

"How the hell did they forget the bell? I need someone up here immediately to connect the bloody thing. Did they expect to wave a flag between rounds? I want that bell fixed and working within twenty minutes or I'll have your heart on a spit, now, get your backside in gear!" He slammed the phone down with such force that for a moment he thought he had busted it again he lifted the receiver and checked for dialling tone.

"Bloody cretins! Have to do everything myself."

"Easy, you'll bust a blood vessel Norm." Rhona Steel as always, acted as Norman's 'man Friday'. For years, she had acted as both Norman's, and his late father's chief assistant and bottle-washer and it had always been the same before every fight she had to take notes, type up long check-lists and arrange contracts among other things for both men. She loved this part of her work, everything she did now had become second nature to her as she busily hustled around.

"Don't you just love this?"

"What?"

"Look out there, right now it's nothing but a large empty hall with a few workmen pottering around checking all the working parts all you have to do is go down and quietly stand in the ring and listen to the atmosphere, the whole place is silent yet it echoes, somehow it feels as if the entire hall is a long slumbering giant that in a few hours, will awaken and rise with urgency. Then the whole place will throb with passionate expectancy for within this heart of the giant, two fighters in the ring will bring it all to life and its blood will boil at fever pitch for a few hours. Then the hall empties and once again, this giant settles down to sleep once more. It's the most fantastic feeling in the world."

"Rhona... wherever did you get that romantic streak from? You know something, you can still surprise me sometimes. That description was one of the most amazing things I've ever heard, perhaps it's a women's view; I've always simply looked at it as a place where two skilful men dissect each other's weaknesses in combat and now this explanation has just blown me away."

"Oh no, its because you're a man and thinking only about the fight while I'm talking about the place and the atmosphere generated by a great occasion."

"Yes I suppose the end result is all that counts as far as I'm concerned."

The Kixing

"That's just your nature Norm, you become too involved with the fight itself and miss the more special moments, all men do. By the way, Harry Peters called about ten minutes ago and said that he was coming around straight away."

"Damn! I wonder what's gone wrong now?"

"He didn't say. Do you think he could be having problems laying off your bets."

"I hope not. This fight has cost me more in back-handers than any of the others put together, I stand to make a packet today."

"Do you mind me asking how much you've asked Harry Peters to lay off through other bookmakers this time?"

"Not at all. One million."

"I just don't know why you do it?"

"What? Promote boxing or bet so heavily?"

"You know what I mean. Fight rigging, you don't do it with the Kixing matches, so why here?"

"It adds spice to my life because conventional boxing doesn't have the edge of Kixing, so this is my way of creating an edge."

"How? Doesn't this type of fight give you the same sort of buzz?"

"By placing my promoter's licence on the line and if I ever get caught rigging fights, which is a distinct possibility, then I automatically lose my hobby. That's one of the reasons why I first thought of illegal fights, you know me too well, I just can't live without excitement."

"So what you are telling me is that it's not the fight, but the behind doors risk taking that gets you going."

"Let's just call it *'the supreme challenge'* shall we?" Norman's feature extended into a huge grin that almost covered the full width of his face.

"I'll never understand you Minter men, you're never been content with your lot, are you?"

"Goals Rhona, they're meant for achievers in life. If you don't have any, the excitement disappears and you become an ordinary mortal, there has to be an edge to our lives. Why, I've even seen you become excited at a fight and so the question is why do you enjoy these bouts so much, huh?"

"With me it's nothing more than animistic instinct, I love it when highly trained gladiators who're both finely honed to perfection, try to beat each other into oblivion. It's always been the same for most humans since eternity somehow something violent stirs in here." She pointed to her head.

"Nothing else? It's not a turn-on or a way to get your kicks."

"Oh yes... fighting churns each emotion differently because with me. there are times when I *wish* that I was male. I would love to be down there, the centre of attention pounding someone's head to a pulp. Sex, as an example, is a powerful emotion but, could never, never give me *that* wild sensation, for many years I have needed boxing like a drug addict needs heroin." Norman shook his head because this was the first time he had seen this totally different side to her makeup.

"You never cease to amaze me, sometimes you are such a demure, restrained lady turns out to be amatorious at the sight of blood and here I am just thinking you liked the fight game, how wrong could I be?"

"There you go, men and women think differently. Oh well, haven't got all day to sit around and chat, there's still a too much to do."

Rhona collected her file and left the office and Norman busily viewed her progress as she made her way across the large hall to the see the television producer. Later, Norman saw Harry Peters, a short man with an extremely large nose who never seemed to be without his lucky hat, picking his way between loose chairs and several busy workmen. He saw Norman and waved his arm fiercely.

"Norman, wait!" His voice seemed to echo right around the large hall and he moved very quickly for one with such short legs, Norman idly reflected to himself.

"How's it going Harry?" The question was a rhetorical one.

"Not too good I'm afraid. I've only got three big ones laid off so far."

"Harry. The odds are shortening by the minute. I want the million all put away."

"But, Norman. I've tried everyone I know. I must have at least fifty runners spreading the bets among the bookies in this town. After last time, the word went out and they're all very nervous because it cost them dearly when the challenger won, if it happens again, they'll go mental."

"Right, what about the Americans, can't we lay off something over there?"

"My son, Billy, is already working them, but then again, so are many of the regular bookmakers here."

"What are the odds now?"

"Two to one the champ and three to one the challenger, it's now fallen from fives to three since your bets were placed."

"Keep trying."

"I think you should back off and be happy with what we've got so far."

"Why?"

"That's what I came over to tell you that there's whispering in the market and the *'big boys'* were pissed off last time, the word on the street is they're trying to find out who's sourcing the large bets."

"So?"

"Please Norman, ...these guys are not your friendly corner shop owner, they break heads."

"Listen Harry, you owe me big time and so I'm calling you. I want this one to go down. I promise that this is the last."

"I've already been paid a visit and I had to lie like hell to save my skin... and yours, if they ever found out..." Harry drew a finger across the line of his throat.

"Right. Stop laying off here and Europe and concentrate getting the rest into the States. Okay?"

"You're not listening, are you? These boys control gambling worldwide and don't take kindly to losing heavily, they're looking for us. It doesn't matter whether the bets are laid off in Hong Kong or Texas, *these guys control* the betting market and you have hurt them. Very likely right now, they're probably ordering the challenger to take a dive."

"No ways, both boys are safely hidden away for the next few hours."

"Don't be too sure, these people have eyes and ears everywhere. Norman I'm shit scared, let's stop while we're ahead." The big man grabbed Harry by the lapel of his jacket and almost lifted him off the ground.

"Don't cross me Harry, if you're scared now, you'll be petrified when I'm finished with you. Now bugger off and get it done, I don't want to hear differently, for your continued healthy living, you better understand my meaning?" Harry arranged bets for Norman's Kixing matches and knew that death meant nothing to the big man.

"Yes, sure Norman, I'll work on it. Don't say you weren't warned though." Harry moved like lightening when Norman released his jacket, he was up the stairs and out of the hall as fast as his short legs could carry him. Norman returned to the temporary office, Rhona was now seated at the long trestle table going over her check list for a final time. She raised her eyebrows.

"Harry being a bad boy?"

"You saw? He's messing me about."

"Careful Norm, he moves in a very troubled world."

"Don't worry, I can take care of Harry and his cronies."

"Well, that's the lot, as far as I can make out everything is now in place."

"What about the bell? Is it fixed?"

"Long time ago, didn't you hear them testing it?"

"No. Okay pack up, let's go, I'll drop you off at home and collect you again at six o'clock."

"Good, I need a shower, just look at me." Dust and grime had collected on her hands, face and clothes. She was a far cry from her normal self and didn't look like the motherly figure that he was used to seeing each day.

"Ladeees and gentlemen, we now come to the main bout of the evening!" Great cheers filled the hall, the noise was almost overwhelming, the place was packed to capacity with almost thirty seven thousand fight hungry boxing fans come to see the local boy attempt to secure the world crown. It seemed to the outsiders that about a third of those fans were gathered inside the ring. The fighters hadn't yet appeared and the stewards had their work cut out with an almost impossible task of ushering bystanders and fans from the ring.

"What a fantastic atmosphere!" Trevor shouted in Norman's ear. Norman always reserved the front three rows on one side of the ring for preferred staff and clients. He turned and could see that further along the same row that Paul and Jean were seated with Sandy and Julie. Norman had made sure that there were four tickets held back for them. Curiosity to see the deliverers of Johnsons to MH Holdings had got the better of him. He had intended asking Christine to join his party, but after being sworn at, decided that it wouldn't be such a clever move. He turned to Rhona.

"I was expecting a message. Did Harry call you?"

"No. He left a strange message at the door though."

"What?"

"Here." Norman read the message. It informed him that another hundred thousand had been laid off in America and that Harry was quietly confident that the final amount would be put to bed before the fight started. It finished with the strange message. *'May God bless you, the hyenas are already on your trail,'* Yours truly, Harry.

"What hyenas does he mean?"

"Oh nothing. It's just a little joke between us." Rhona knew him to well, he had suddenly become excited and started perspiring freely. Something in the Harry's cryptic note had caused this surge of excitement. That *edge* that he had talked about made him react this way and she knew it.

The Kixing

"Pull the other one Norm." The crescendo in the large hall suddenly lifted as the challenger, surrounded by helpers started pushing his way through the crowd towards the ring. Norman simply gave her a broad grin. The covered fighter entered the ring and immediately stripped off the shining gown with his name in silver letters on the back. As had become her usual custom, Rhona secretly slipped her hand into Norman's.

"I saw his last fight on television and he's such a clinical finisher."

"Have you bet on him?"

"Yes, ten pounds for the underdog."

"Not this time, he's going to win tonight."

"There you are, you spoilt it for me. It's no fun knowing beforehand."

"If you're betting heavily, it is." She pushed his hand with hers.

"You wicked man." The noise level catapulted as the South American champion entered the hall. Like the challenger, he and his helpers struggled to the ring. Once in and stripped and strutted around the ring, arms high in the air. At his corner, he lifted his huge champion's belt and paraded around the ring for all to admire. Rhona felt sorry for the proud man, because of Norman's warning she suspected that his belt was going to be handed to the challenger before the night was out.

"Ladeees and gentlemen..." The announcer proceeded to introduce the fighters. Further along the row Jean was terrified as she clung tightly to Paul's jacket. During some of the preliminary bouts she had had to excuse herself and go to the toilets once there, she had been physically sick. This was her first real experience of the violent world of pugilism and as far as she was concerned, this wasn't an art, it was two wild animals trying to rip each other to pieces. She had seen it on television but never thought it would be as bloodthirsty as when sitting only feet from the two men. The surrounding crowd bayed for blood, nothing less was acceptable. Paul had become furious with her.

"How can you three stomach or condone *this*? It's barbaric."

"I told you to shut up, if you don't like it, then go home. Stop trying to spoil a good evening for the rest of us because if I had known you were going to be squeamish, I had have brought someone else."

"Like who?" Jean retorted.

"Anyone, rather than you."

"But this seems to be nothing but organised violence, I have a right to my opinion, haven't I?"

"Yes, but we don't all have to suffer with you." Sandy had offered to take Jean home but she had declined. Paul made a nasty comment about Sandy to Julie. The night wasn't going at all well for him and Jean. Julie and Sandy were comfortable with each other and this seemed to antagonise Paul even further. When Julie pulled him down a peg or two, he had nobody but Jean to take his frustrations out on.

"Jean, you've done nothing but moan all evening. Do you get some sort of twisted pleasure in making other people's lives a misery?"

"That's unfair."

"Unfair is it? Not as unfair as us splitting up tonight. I can't stand this any longer." Jean was about to say something, but stopped short. Her mouth moved and she suddenly found the words she was seeking.

"You bastard!" The noise lifted as the two boxers met in the middle of the ring while the referee, George Mellis, gave them both his curt instruction. They returned to their corners and the bell sounded, the fight was on. For the first round the two pried, parried and tested each other's defences. The fight still had eleven rounds to go. Julie leaned towards Sandy.

"I want to see another knockout, it's so exciting." Sandy kissed her upturned forehead.

"Apparently there are two separate fights going on, one out here..." he pointed towards Paul, "and one in the ring." Julie giggled. The second round started and the same pattern developed. The South American followed the back peddling local man. Again, not many blows were exchanged and the crowd roared its disapproval.

"The last two fights had much more action, his could be boring." Paul was becoming upset. He had hoped for at least some blood and guts. Jean was disgusted and showed her animosity by sulking.

"Maybe it'll become a little more bloody later on."

"Oh, keep your sarcasm to yourself." The whole fight continued in the same mould, Caetano chasing, Blair running. In the seventh round Caetano caught his opponent and with the only good blow of the fight had floored the Briton. Getting to his feet he hung onto to incoming fighter so spoiling the champion's chances to finish the fight. The crowd were incensed and booed continuously. Caetano was trying to make a fight of it but his opponent simply kept running. At the end of the final round, coins, cold drink cans and other missiles rained into the ring. Norman waited until their anger had abated before climbing between the ropes to congratulate both contestants. He quickly returned to his seat.

"Ladeees and gentlemen, if you pal-eeze! There is a unanimous decision." Everyone had agreed that it was the worst fight they had ever seen.

The Kixing

"Judge Peters scores the fight 115 to 113, judge Rowlands scores 116 to 112, and judge Kim scores 118 to 114."

"Predictable," Paul whispered to Julie.

"The winner and new world champion is ...Stephen Blair!" The hall went silent for a split second as if everybody thought they hadn't heard the announcer correctly. Blair jumped in the air to show his delight and suddenly all hell broke loose in the hall.

"Fix! Fix!" The calls were chanted as more debris was hurled into the ring. Ushers hurried the two fighters away to protect them from the blackening mood of the crowd. Standby police moved into the hall to try to control the crowd before things became too nasty. Norman indicated to his friends and employees to head for the nearest door.

"C'mon, let's get out of here!" They dragged themselves through the nasty crowd to the door and out into the fresh air. Norman quickly gathered them together.

"Go to the 'Pièce de Résistance'club off Park Lane, I've booked a room and there's a buffet and drinks waiting for us." The party broke up, as Norman and Jean walked in the direction his car a man with a limp came towards them. His hand moved to his inside jacket pocket. A large crowd of young people came racing from behind Norman shouting about the fight being rigged. The jostling group slowed to a walk just as Norman passed by the limping man. Norman hardly noticed him as he reached his car and he and Rhona drove off to the club. The limping man climbed into a car driven by a chauffer and moved off behind Norman's vehicle.

The Kixing

The Kixing

"THE KIXING"

CHAPTER TWENTY

"Bernard, what's the news?" Susan told David that Bernard seemed agitated and had called three times that morning.

"They've accepted your offer and yesterday I started putting the draft agreement together and it's being typed up right now so when can we get together to finalise the papers?"

"Let's see," David flicked through his diary, "I'm relatively free this afternoon... why don't you email the papers to me when they're typed up?"

"All right, that will give you time to look at them before we meet, let's say three o'clock then, okay?"

"See you then."

Trevor entered and placed a file on Norman's desk then sat down while the boss perused the paperwork.

"Honest opinion, do you think this is a clever move?" Trevor said with a hint of doubt.

"Sure, it would also almost double our size." Trevor suddenly wondered whether he should possibly prefabricate stories about Sibling Investments having a downside to it. Perhaps this would deter Norman from rushing into something that up until recently, had simply been his passionate hobby. Inwardly he knew he wouldn't be able to change his chairman's mind as well as he wasn't a liar by nature and his exceptionally astute chairman would know immediately should he try anything funny. He lit his pipe for the umpteenth time as he rose to leave the office.

"Trevor, at this moment I'm still just looking and I'll take these reports home and study them more carefully." Trevor pulled his tall frame from the chair and moved to the door before stopping and turning to his employer.

"Norman, if anything goes wrong and you're going to be somewhat highly over-borrowed. You could even find yourself losing three generations of profitable company building so I trust that you realise that it's something like marrying someone of different class or culture, it doesn't matter how much parents warn their children that they're courting trouble because love is blind and they'll simply disregard that advice and go ahead just to prove the parents were wrong. Then, it's only later when the young lovers have settled down and have had time in bed together, that they realise their mistake and the whole affair ends up in a mess. This time I'm playing the role of the parent by acting as your conscience."

"Then I'll have to remember your prophetic words Dad." Both men laughed as Trevor just shook his head and made his way back to his own office. David opened the file and inserted a line across the pages from three to six. He estimated that their negotiations could only take at least three hours to inspect and agree the fine print of the contract. David called Rhona and checked that Norman was free for a meeting. David then made his way to Norman's office.

"Morning David, How was your weekend."

"Good, but it was a terrible fight though. Disastrous decision."

"Well, you can't expect a classic every time."

"The result was a travesty because there was no way that Caetano lost that fight, it was a real hometown decision and that type of thing should be referred to the boxing board, it's not going to do your intended promotion business any favours, is it?"

"I only stage the fights, I don't judge them." Norman beamed broadly. According to his reckoning he had made nearly two million from his large bet through Harry's hard graft.

"Don't worry David, I've come out of this one smelling of roses, I even made money out of it."

"Oh well, as long as the group has profited by the fight then I suppose that's good." David never really showed any great emotion and over the many years, Norman had tried to come to terms with this matter-of-fact attitude, with little success.

"Anyway, why the sudden urgency for a meeting?"

"It's about the Martins bid, the offer's now been accepted." Norman sprang from his chair as if it had suddenly contained a thousand volts of electric current passing through it.

"Yes!" The big man just about leaped across his large desk to race around and grabbed David's hand, almost shaking it from its sockets.

"That's great work David, now we're really going places. I better notify the bank immediately so that they can get their end tied up with the rest of the financing consortium."

"I'm expecting Bernard's proposal contract by email this morning, I'll let you have a copy on arrival and then we'll go over the contract this afternoon, so if you want any points altered, please try and let me know as soon as possible."

Antonio led the way through to the large lounge,

"You need to sit, that limp of yours seems much worse."

"Yes, yes, I'll do that, but first things first, please first be seated."

Christine could see that his temporary leather chair was still in its original position.

"Is it very painful?"

"It's not really the pain and it's because my main leg muscle was damaged but, with a little exercise, it is now healing quite well. The doctor says it will be a few more weeks before I can walk properly again."

"That's good. Now about our friend Minter, how are we doing?"

"Great, he has taken the bait, hook, line and bloody sinker. As we thought, he's a very greedy person."

"It would seem that he is somewhat over confident as well."

"My thinking is it would probably be far better to kill him right now."

"No Antonio! I want this man to see what it's like to suffer and killing him would be too fast as well as being too good for him."

"You know that we could do it very slowly."

"Oh no. I want it to be done in stages, the pressure has to build and build until he's in a corner with nowhere to run. I want any death that he suffers to be of his own making."

"I feel that America wants his death to occur immediately because of what he has done to them."

"America? What do they have to do with Minter?"

"We suspect he took us for about three mill betting on Saturday's big fight."

"How?"

"By fixing that fight, there was no way that that idiot won that championship and they are sure that the judges were paid off by Minter."

"How strong are your contacts within the boxing commission?"

"Mine personally are not very good but the family have a very powerful say on both British and American boards. Why?"

"You have got to get onto them immediately to announce an enquiry into Saturday's fight. That way, all bets will probably be suspended."

"It may be too late to prevent that."

"That doesn't matter because the spotlight will immediately fall on Minter. This my old friend is much better than your original plan because if he's about to purchase a bookmaking business and is then exposed as having been involved in fight rigging, that business will suffer badly."

"So, how will that help us?"

"Don't you see, once he's paid for the bookmaking business, we play him at his own game, it will be a quick sale and then with business falling off, they will take on almost any bet, that way we'll then make the bets and fix the fights. That way, the company will come back to us in weeks rather than months. He'll be finished as a businessman, and all through his own greed."

"Yes, I see although, I think we should wait until we've been paid for the bookmaking business."

"You're probably right, do it that way. Now, you wanted to discuss Johnsons with me."

"Yes, first thing is that two of your employees are unknowingly giving information to Minter."

"What? How?"

"Your accountant Sandy Martin is one of them and the other is Jean, your brother's secretary. I don't think it's directly down to them because they really don't know what's going on."

"I don't believe it."

"Both of them are presently dating employees of Minter and fortunately both you and your brother haven't told them everything. We've listened in to their telephone calls and they were both at the fight on Saturday. We already know that they've been able to tell Minter very little."

"I'll kill them both!"

"No, Signora. It would be far wiser to use them in order to feed false information to Minter and that way, you can control what Minter hears." Christine thought about his suggestion for a minute.

"You're right Antonio."

"The two staff don't know they're being used in this manner, so we must use that ignorance as much as we can to your advantage. Minter employs professional industrial spies whose duty it is to try and find out what is happening from within. Their whole organisation is all very cleverly instituted." Christine stroked at a loose strand of hair.

"Yes, but several members of my staff are already seeking alternative employment elsewhere."

"I know, here, this is a list of them. If you don't want to lose these people you must somehow lift their morale." Antonio handed the list to Christine. She shook her head in amazement.

"We've been so busy fending off Minter that we never gave a thought to our staff. Maybe it will turn out to be a good thing. I'll start rectifying the matter immediately without Minter getting wind of it. Thanks Antonio"

"The last matter is the man your brother saw watching the building, I've got someone keeping an eye open for him, but we haven't been able to find him. Is your brother sure this person wasn't just some passer-by?"

"I don't think so, he's seen him about three times."

"Okay, we keep looking because this unknown man worries me, I don't like loose ends."

"Anything else?"

"Not really, I'll inform America of our new plan, I don't think they'll object if we kill this man your way, er, very slowly.

"Well if that's all, I'm going to have lunch with my daughter." Antonio's eyes lit up and a smile crossed his face.

"How is she? I thought she was supposed to be back at the university?"

"She is, it's just that she's just having a long weekend and goes back tomorrow."

"Ah, bella. How our children grow up so quickly and she is so beautiful, just like you. Her father, rest his soul would be so very proud of her." The limping man escorted Christine to her car, kissed her hand and made his way back to the house as the Jaguar moved up the long drive. He had a lot to do today. Christine headed west for the meeting with her daughter.

"No thanks poppit, that was terrific lunch and I've had an elegant sufficiency, Honestly I couldn't eat another thing." Christine finished the last fork full of salad.

The Kixing

"I would love a cup of coffee though." They had had a game of tennis before lunch at the club, this was one of the most ostentatious of its kind in the country. Built on a still operating small aerodrome left by the air force after the war, the club had over many years expanded greatly to encompass a fine double golf course, tennis and squash courts, an Olympic indoor swimming pool with an attached gymnasium and a large clubhouse that had originally been the officers mess. Members of the 'Flying Club' now tended to be drawn from the extremely wealthy moneyed population and most of them treated the place as a restful holiday sports farm.

"Shall we stay here or take our coffee in the main lounge."

"Here is best because I can't stay too long, some of us have work to do you know?" Christine's daughter laughed, her dark eyes glistening mischievously. Christine's first thought was that it must be the amount of wine they had shared together.

"I really enjoyed your company because we tend to be more like sisters than mother and daughter."

"I'm so glad you feel that way, tell you what, at the end of this year, why don't we take a few weeks off and go on a skiing holiday. How does that sound?"

"Marvellous. You can be my sister and we'll find you a young ski instructor or even a toy boy."

"Don't be so naughty." The waitress took their order and returned almost immediately with two coffees.

"Really mom, you could easily pass for someone... let's say fifteen years your junior, those young guys will be falling all over you." Both giggled.

"Talking about that, how are you and your latest love getting on?"

"Fabulous, I was with him yesterday and I'm seeing him again tonight. Being at university is going to be a bit of a wrench for us."

"Do me a favour? Don't drive all the way to university tonight, it is better if you come home, especially as late as you did last time. You know that I worry about you?" The look in her daughter's eyes teased Christine.

"Just remember you were young once, weren't you?"

"You're lucky your father isn't around any more otherwise you would have to have an escort until the man married you if he was still alive."

"That's so old fashioned but tell me something, why don't you ever use your married name?"

"It's a very long story and I will explain all one day but for now all you need to know is that your father was well known and a bit of a tartar that scared people. I simply felt at that time that it would be far better for all concerned if I reverted to my unmarried name and that's all I'm telling you. Anyway I must leave, I'll be at home because I've got a lot of paperwork to catch up on."

"I wish you didn't have to leave."

"I must and once again thanks for the lunch, I won't have to eat for a week now."

"Get away with you, you're still so slim."

"It's because I live on a perpetual diet. Bye, poppit." Christine kissed her daughter on both cheeks and made her way to the car park. As she moved away she couldn't help but notice an old Mercedes pulling out behind her. The only reason the car had caught her attention was that it was very dented and old, almost antique in appearance. Lined up against newer vehicles parked in the area, it stood out from the crowd like a grey spotted carbuncle.

"Probably just one of the staff," she muttered softly to herself. She reached the main road and checked her rear view mirror and saw that the grey Mercedes was following at about a hundred yards distance. Christine gunned her Jaguar onto the motorway and headed in the direction of Heathrow airport, she took the slip road that would take her home then glanced into the mirror again.

"What the..." The grey vehicle's blinking indicator showed that it was about to follow her.

"Could be he lives in the area, let's see." Christine put her foot down and accelerated up to the roundabout then circled and swung the Jaguar back onto the motorway now travelling in the opposite direction before the Mercedes could reach the roundabout. She managed to slide the car away down the slip road and was certain that he couldn't have seen her car from its oncoming position. For ten minutes she travelled East coming off at the next interchange and taking the long way home, by now she felt a certain pleasure with her astute observation and handling of the situation. As she turned into the road where she lived, she saw the Mercedes parked almost outside her house.

"Jesus!" She slammed at the brakes and threw the car into reverse hoping that the driver of the other car hadn't seen yet her arrival. Around the corner she raced the car along the road, turning left and right at each corner in case whoever was following her, had seen her and was now trying to catch up. Panic was the order of the day, 'get away', her only thought and when she was absolutely certain that the grey monstrosity wasn't following, she finally pulled into the kerb. Christine threw her head against the headrest and took a deep breath.

"Who? ...Minter, there's nobody else." She grabbed for her car telephone and dialled a number.

"C'mon, c'mon. Hello Antonio, I've got myself into some trouble."

"What?"

"There's someone following me in an old grey Mercedes. I think it's one of Minter's people. I lost them but now they're parked outside my house." She was surprised when she heard him chuckle.

"Antonio, what's so damned funny?"

"It's Mario he works for us. He called in, a few minutes ago and told me he had lost you."

"Why didn't you tell me you had somebody following me? It's not funny."

"Signora, it is my job to look after you and I'm very glad to see you're aware of your surroundings."

"I couldn't help missing that car, it's a mess."

"For two reasons we use that particular car, if anybody tries to follow you, they too, will see the vehicle and possibly be scared off and believe me that contrary to its looks, that old bus is armour-plated, terrifically powerful and very fast. It's all for your own protection, we don't want anything happening that we can't control."

"Next time, tell me these things."

"Si Signora."

"Okay, 'bye Antonio." The line went dead and again Christine drove home but this time she waved at the two men in the old car and they acknowledged her greeting. Once inside the house, she called her brother.

"Ernie, I'm doing some work at home, be a darling and pop in on your way home, there're a couple of things we've got to discuss."

"Like?"

"I'll tell you later but right now it's imperative that you just keep your mouth tightly shut because our office has more ears than first suspected."

"In principle, that's fine. You simply have to check the finer details." Norman was seated at the head of the long table having checked through the emailed outlined contract from Bernard. He was quite happy with what he had so far found in the documentation.

"I'm inserting a protection clause that if we find anything unlawful in Martins, we have the right to reclaim our investment, plus interest and I'm sure that Bernard will squeal about it but, we need to protect ourselves."

"David, don't go upsetting the whole thing by inserting your usual gamut of get out clauses, I want this deal through within two days and by your adding all your normal legal paraphernalia, we're going to end up negotiating for a couple of weeks. No please leave it alone this one time because it's better to leave the thing as is. We've got nothing to fear, Martins is a respected name."

"I must protect the company from all eventualities."

"David, David. I know you're only doing your job the best way you know how. Search that document for anything untoward but don't go changing the thing as you usually do. I simply want this deal wrapped up by no later than Wednesday." Norman could see that he had upset the little lawyer.

"We're moving into this with our eyes open, don't worry so."

"You're the boss and I've never liked this deal from the outset. There are just too many ponderables to consider for my liking but I'll talk to Bernard and see how far we can move in a hurry."

"Remember, this must not be a lengthy negotiation. Open and shut, that's what we want." David retreated to his own office in unhappy frame of mood.

The Kixing

"THE KIXING"

CHAPTER TWENTY ONE

What?"

"A bank transfer from some trust account and it looks like they either have a financial backer or else... I'm not sure, but they could have more hidden up their sleeves than we were aware of." Norman looked like he was just about to have an apoplexy as the dark threading veins in his neck suddenly protruded like a rich oil pipeline about to burst its seams.

"That cunning bitch! She's been leading us a merry dance all this time, it's no wonder she seemed so confident the other day. Well, my girl, two people can play the same game." He rose from behind the desk and stared through the large aluminium glazed window, looking down to the grass bank he could see a mother Muscovy Duck leading her six ducklings around, instructing them in life's ways and their search for food while in the river, the beautifully incandescently green headed drake swam around in circles near the bank. Norman turned away from the tranquil scene and slowly paced towards his desk.

"David, we've got to find out more about the donor account and need to know whether there is an actual benefactor and if so, who it is or, whether the finance is a one off loan to Johnsons to stave off our threat and give them time to somehow recover."

"This time it is not your normal commercial high street bank advance and I don't think we won't have many contacts that we are able to call on."

"How so?"

"It's come via a Swiss account, namely The Union Bank of Switzerland who won't be very forthcoming with much information."

"Damn!"

"We still have a track to the inside of Johnsons through Paul and Julie, perhaps they could find out what's going on. It's our only chance."

"Get those two to earn their fat salaries and I don't care how they get the information, I want it. I'm not going to be made to look like a bloody fool by Christine Johnson. Somehow she's behind this sudden turn around, I just know it."

"Right, I'll get Paul and Julie onto it immediately."

"How long have we got until their next payment is due?"

"Two weeks."

"We've got to shut down that financial lifeline source somehow?"

"Agreed."

"Tell Trevor Reece to do some deep ferreting among his diplomatic contacts to see what he can come up with and then also get every available body working on any personnel at the U.B.S., somehow we have to stop the Johnson's wriggling out of trouble. Throw every resource we can muster up at this matter. Can't you think of any other way to halt their progress? What about their suppliers or workman? C'mon David, it's time to get your clever mind on it, I don't want to lose my bet with you, you know?" David opened his pink folder and started searching through the many pages for anything that he had possibly missed.

"My gut reaction is that I think we should now start concentrating on Ernest Johnson because if there could be a weak link to their chain, it's somehow got to be through him."

The Kixing

"You know that they're twins, aren't they? That means they are two peas in the pod and that means it's going to be very difficult to prise them apart in two weeks."

"No, I didn't know that but I do agree with you, but what if, well, if he could be made to divulge their source of funds. The weakness could be that he's divorced and lives alone, we might be able to exploit that position somehow. We should have concentrated on it before?"

"Good thinking, who have you got in mind to get into him?"

"Hmm, possibly Julie might fit the bill, she has a way of making most men relax in her company."

"Get on to it, we only have a fortnight to act, no stone is to be left unturned, we have to crack this nut, I leave that up to you and your team. In the meantime I will also lean on a couple of big banking hitters to see if they are able to come up with anything."

"Right."

"Now what is the present status with Martins and are the papers ready yet?"

"Not quite but by this afternoon, all going well. ...Bernard Marcus and I have agreed the terms and his office emailed the contract last night. Everything seems to be in order, have you already finalised the finance package?"

"Don't worry about that because from my side, everything's already in place."

"Right then, so signing can take place this afternoon when Bernard arrives. I really do wish we had more time to carry out due diligence."

"Don't you worry about Martins, concentrate all your energies to get us moving in on Johnsons. Remember that when in doubt use a hammer, the bigger the doubt the bigger the hammer so in this case you need to use the biggest hammer you can come up with and if you feel your team have to do it, hurt Ernest Johnson if you must, but get those results somehow David. I really do need that company on board as soon as possible." David returned to his office to organise the meeting with his soldiers.

"No, definitely not because I can't take any more of her whinging any more,.iIt's over and done with, can't Julie somehow get her little hands on that information?" David was chairing the daily meeting with his soldiers and Paul protested vehemently when David informed him that he was required to extend his acquaintance with Jean.

"No! There is nothing more to say, if you remember I warned you that you needed to at least leave the door open just in case we needed further information from her side. How could you have been so bloody stupid? Now it's up to you to put that right somehow and either you do it, or we find someone else and, there are many out there capable of stepping in and you try to find another job."

"But we said Julie would continue..."

"Enough! You get back in there somehow, we need to know how, or who, is supplying these funds to Johnson Interiors." Crest fallen, Paul dropped his head so that nobody at the table would see that inside, he was seething by them all knowing that he had to force himself to return back to start up the unwanted relationship all over again.

"Okay... I'll try." Paul muttered/

"You better not only try Paul. You do it because she's Ernest Johnson's personal secretary and If anybody has an inside track to his operation it's her, she could be the key and can tell us where the funds have come from. He's our main target from today, if we are going to crack this Johnsons nut; it's somehow got to be through Ernest Johnson, I have a feeling he could be their weak link." Paul looked up and saw that Julie had a self satisfied smug look on her face, this fuelled anger only served to heighten the animosity between them at that moment because he knew that he was trapped with nowhere else to find such admirable working conditions with all expenses paid in a job he excelled at.

"Julie, you're to work a little harder on your man, being Johnson's accountant, he must have a clear inkling as to what's happening and where this extra money is coming from."

"Will do." David organised the rest of the team to stir trouble within the shop fitting company and once he had finished the meeting he intimated that Julie should remain seated and the others should leave, David gave her specific instructions to try to get at Ernest and when finally alone he called Johnsons.

"I see your first payment has been met and that's very good however, if you now have the resources, then we want the rest paid immediately and I must also warn you that we now intend taking out an immediate injunction against your company to freeze all Johnson's banking accounts." David heard Ernest gasp.

"You can't! We have an agreement and we are holding up our side of the deal."

"Just wait and see if we can't."

"You're being unfair to us I don't think any court in the land would agree with you."

"Unfair... unfair, all we want is the money you owe us."

"You've been paid a quarter of a million and it's been on time all as promised. Having said that, we'll also meet the other payments as well."

"Not if you've got an injunction against you, you won't. There's still a half a million outstanding and we want it right now."

"No you don't, you simply want our business at a knock down price. Pull the plug on us and you'll get nothing, let us work this one through this unfortunate set of circumstances and you get repaid."

"If Johnson collapses, we'll get the business for nothing, anyway."

"You're nothing but bone picking vultures."

"Full payment in seven days or we carry out our threat Mr Johnson. Do you understand?"

"Impossible. You're going to have a fight on your hands."

"Not us, you're the one with the fight because we're not the ones that are struggling, you are." David heard the line go dead.

"Chrissie, get in here immediately!" Ernest shouted into his office intercom. A minute later she shut the door seeing nothing but agitation written across her brother's features.

"What's happened?" Ernest related what MH Holdings were about to do, Christine tugged at her hair as she listened and then weighed up the prospect.

"Right, we still have time on our side, so we must move quickly, maybe we can divert their attention away from us." She lifted the receiver and called Antonio.

"Minter's applying huge pressure on us to pay the full amount. Have you spoken to the board yet? We can't leave this situation to stew for much longer."

"The transfer of Martins shares are going to be signed later today and tou can be sure that this acquisition will be in all media by the morning because it is big news."

248

"So how does that help us?"

"Well, coincidentally on purpose, the boxing board will also be in session later tonight and I do believe they will then make their announcement of a fight fix in a couple of days time. One and one will soon add up to two, fight fixing plus acquiring one of the largest bookmaking businesses equals a conflict of interest."

"That's so clever."

"By the way, the Americans liked your plan and are taking things even further."

"How?"

"As you know, we control almost all bookmaking activities worldwide and now they are all going to insist that all payouts are to be returned with the pending proviso of an investigation meaning that all bets laid on that fight are off. That way, they'll also be able to eventually reveal to the world that there was a tie-up between Minter and the fight outcome."

"Self gain, I love it. We will have that bastard on the back foot, I wonder how he will like the added pressure."

"I must warn you that it could take time to break down the trail back to Minter though."

"Still, that announcement to retract payments alone, will give the man a very large headache."

"Signora, the trap is closing quite nicely and it's simply a matter of timing now."

"Thanks Antonio, that's all I needed to know, speak to you again tomorrow." The line went dead then Christine took her brother's hand and stroked it very gently.

"Now that is what I can tell you, was a really good call to make. Don't lose your trust in me and these associates that I have, everything's going to be all right in the long run."

"But how?"

"Trust me and do not panic, I still want you to carry out what we discussed yesterday, now get both Sandy and Jean in here and then feed them that information to send back to Minter. I would just love to be a fly on his wall tomorrow morning."

Arriving home, Jean slipped her key into the lock of her front door and a sudden movement along the passageway caught her eye. Her insides melted as Paul moved from his temporary seat on the window ledge along the darkened aisle, e carried an enormous bouquet of flowers in one arm and a magnum of Champagne in the free hand.

"What's all this, I thought you said you were through with me?"

"It's a peace offering to apologise for my behaviour the other night. Things have not being going well and I took it out on you, I'm so sorry, I didn't really mean all those horrible taunts aimed at you. If you want me to leave, I'll understand." They both stood still staring at each other like two prize fighters, Paul hoping that he hadn't blown it, Jean wondering how not to show her true feelings.

"Come inside, we don't want my neighbours listening about to our most intimate discussions." She let him into the flat while trying to act as cool as she could, Jean closed the door and then leaned against it waiting for his explanation.

"Why take it out on me? What have I ever done to you to warrant that sort of abuse? You went out of your way to belittle me in front of everyone." For the second time today, Paul bore his 'hang-dog' look because inwardly, his brain was scheming and plotting every move to regain back her confidence in him and he was acutely aware that his livelihood depended on it.

"I really am so sorry, there was no excuse for my behaviour on Saturday, but there was something that I never told you, the fact of the matter is that I was given the results of my test and it's confirmed that I have a small cancerous growth in my duodenum. If they don't cut it out soon it could then spread throughout my body. That's why I was so raggedy, it's no excuse, I know."

"No." Jean put her hand to her mouth and all fighting and animosity instantly forgotten.

"Why didn't you tell me, I would have understood, of course I would have. You poor, poor man." Her motherly instinct automatically came to the fore as she led him to the settee.

"Cancer? That's horrible."

"It scares people witless, it does me." Inwardly he was battling to keep a straight face because like magic his story had worked, she had been suckered into his little boy lost routine.

"Can I get you a drink?"

"Yes, that would be lovely."

"Only if you promise never to keep any more secrets like that from me. Now tell me, how serious is it?"

"Quite bad, its only one cyst at the moment and they're going to have to operate shortly. Let's hope that's all, they'll only know once they open me up relieve me of that and carry out a biopsy. Only then will we know the full facts."

"You poor man." Jean handed him a drink and took a large sip of her own before sitting down.

"We made a pact to be good to each other and unfortunately, that broke down and now we know why. I'm happy to pick it up where we left off on Friday and let's pretend that Saturday never even existed."

"You're wonderful." Paul leaned across and gently kissed her on the cheek, she immediately responded by placing her hand on the back of his head and pulling him off balance so that he ended up on top of her.

"That little bump isn't going to affect your libido, is it?"

"Knowing that that bump as you put it, could somehow put an end to our love making will only enhance my ambition to grab everything life has to offer from now on. That includes you, very strange isn't it?"

"Not really but wait, you lie back and let this nurse treat you back to health, my way." He stretched out and allowed Jean to remove his clothes knowing that he had time to settle into the matter of Johnson's business venture but, that was for much later. Right now, all that mattered was that his job was secure and he was having fun so he had brought himself back onto track.

When Sandy arrived at the cottage he saw that Julie was wearing one of his white shirts and was now busily cooking up some form of grand meal in the kitchen.

"Hi babe!" He called from the lounge.

" You're home early."

"Had a really good day today. I'm just going to have a shower, the traffic was murderous on the way back home. Want to join me?"

"Love to, but I've already had two showers today and if I leave this now, it'll be ruined. You go ahead, I'm making something extra special for us tonight."

"Don't give me that, every night is special with you. As a matter of interest, do you really like cooking or is it something you just do because you have to?"

"I've never really been domesticated, it's just that I have fallen in love with this kitchen, I can ter things out and believe it or not, am also quite partial to its owner."

"Lovely girl, I won't be long." Sandy moved through to the bedroom noticing that sometime during the afternoon, Julie had thoughtfully acquired and placed several little fancy potpourri jars and candles around the room. The scented aroma struck his nostrils immediately he entered the room.

"The hand of a beautiful lady has been at work I, I should have met you years ago!"

"What?"

"You, what's the occasion? The little knick-knacks, that's what, I feel as if this cottage is no longer a house and its fast becoming a home. Before now, I've always hated coming here but nowadays, I can't wait to get home to you."

"Get away with you, go and have your shower and cool down."

"When you're around, not even ice water could calm my ardour." Sandy stripped down and had his shower and when he arrived back into the lounge a tall drink was on the table awaiting him.

"Cheers. This is exactly what I mean, you spoil me rotten, I love it."

"Right, that's finished, we can eat whenever you're ready." Julie entered the lounge. Sandy couldn't help just staring at her because today she somehow looked so young and slightly boyish with his shirt being far too large across the shoulders and almost reaching down to her knees. He whistled softly, she had this habit of being dressed differently every time he arrived home.

"God that's so destructive and sexy."

"What?"

"The way you wear my shirt, it's about ten sizes too large, but on you, it just looks so magnificent."

"Thank you kind sir," she said, curtsying politely. Julie sat on the footrest at his feet and started massaging his toes.

"Tell me about your wonderful day."

"This is the first time I can see a possible light at the end of the tunnel and now I think I'm going to hang in there for a while longer."

"Oh?"

"I had a long talk to Ernest today and he's managed to convince me that the firm is going to make it."

"That's nice and just how does he see you making it through this period, is it because of the new benefactor that paid your cheque?"

"Well sort of and from what I understand the Johnson twins have been secretly negotiating with some major foreign investor. Apparently the company is major player in the investment market and because our shortfall is nearly a million left by Powerbuild debacle I understand that this is pocket money to these investing deep pockets."

"So who they? C'mon you must at least have some kind of idea."

"The whole deal is being transacted in secret by some lawyer, my bosses haven't yet said who it is but my guess is that it has to be Arab money and they wouldn't have given us the loan unless they're quite sure that some kind of merger with them was going ahead."

"Why?"

"Don't really know but today Ernest let slip that the investor already has many interests in over four hundred companies outside his own country. By any standards that's big and my personal assumption is that it can only come from oil revenue."

"What makes you so sure that it's oil money?"

"I'm not too sure, but my calculation is as follows, let's presume that each of their interests amount to only one million or more, you can imagine, that would be the vicinity of maybe half a billion alone meaning that type of investment must come from the Arabs, nobody bar the Russians or Chinese generally invests that heavily."

"What about... say European bankers or even American institutions? They could have those sorts of funds available couldn't they?"

"Yes, but I don't think so, this is Arabic funds, in fact I'm sure of it."

"I'm intrigued, this is like some sort of a thriller. Tell you what, why don't you become a detective and find out for sure. You could ask Ernest directly, he sounds like he is a reasonable person and will possibly tell you."

"I've tried that, but apparently it's Christine that is doing all the negotiation and she wouldn't give anything away. Mind you, come to think of it she was really in a good mood today."

"Oh?"

"It's funny how things work out, both of them were like different people. Probably because a tremendous burden has been lifted from the company. This morning, I even heard Christine humming a tune and I haven't heard her do that for over a month."

"I'm glad and fascinated at the same time, I would love to know who's behind this transformation, go on and find out for me because I'm dying to know." She could see that she had aroused Sandy's curiosity level.

"I tell you what, I'll go into the office a little earlier tomorrow and If nobody's around, I'll do a little snooping and have a look through her papers to see if she's written anything down. Okay?" He was almost whispering like a child with a secret to hide.

"Great idea, but please don't get caught. Micky Spillane and partner limited, that's our new role." Sandy giggled nervously as Julie took Sandy's big toe in her mouth and bit down gently. He laughed and tried to pull his foot away and found he couldn't without either hurting her mouth or alternately tearing the large digit from its socket. The mood changed rapidly as he relaxed and she slid her hand up his leg and into his shorts. Instead of what was expected she began to roll one of his testicles between her thumb and forefinger, she looked directly into his eyes and even though it was gentle, there was a distinct and dangerous look that made him scared to move. As quickly as it had begun the frightening moment was over as she released him and headed for the kitchen. It was some sort of warning as if she was just letting him know she could hurt him, he was suddenly confused, she periodically did this type of thing as if to show she was in charge.

"Food's ready!" she shouted.

"I love you so much that it frightens me sometimes."

"That's why I let you know in my own way that he difference between pain and pleasure is the amount of pressure applied. I could have hurt you and you could have hurt me, but we didn't because we trust each other." Sandy smiled and rose from his comfortable chair as Julie returned laden with two plates.

The Kixing

The Kixing

"THE KIXING"

CHAPTER TWENTY TWO

"At least we at least know who the opposition might be." David chaired the daily meeting of the 'soldiers'.

"Trevor, I know it's still in the early stages yet, but anything to report on the Union Bank of Switzerland front?" Trevor Reece shook his head.

"No. I finding that it's useless approaching them without an account name, can't you at least give me more information even an account name and number would help."

"I should have that name today sometime., we already know that it's a trust company of some sort and that can hide any number of a multitude of sins."

"Right, as soon as you talk to your man Julie, I want you try to wheedle an update immediately and we may have to reconvene this meeting when we know exactly who our target is." David collected the individual reports together and handed them to Susan to file.

"A job well done, keep it up gang, we can't afford to slacken our vigilance because the clock's still running. If you can, please remember to keep us informed of all your movements during the day so that if we have to call a snap meeting, we will be able to contact you. That's all." David pushed his chair backwards indicating the meeting was at an end. Leaving the office Paul walked alongside Julie.

"So you managed to get back together with Jean then?"

"Yeah, it's my body she wants, lay them and then leave them, that's my motto."

"You're not only a prick, but a sexist prick."

"I know. Can I help it if Mother Nature dealt me the cruel blow of making me irresistible to all women? They love my body so that makes me their male whore. When you analyse it, there's really no difference between you and me, except that is, for our individual plumbing."

"You're a bloody idiot Paul!" Julie almost choked on her words.

"Yeah, yeah, you must admit that I'm a beautiful idiot though. Well, I've got nothing to do today until the whining Jean gets home to partake of this idiot's body once again so I think I'll head off and practice some free falling."

"You'll be at the Flying Club then if we need to contact you?"

"Uh-huh because I need to get in as many jumps as humanly possible and the British parachuting championships are only three weeks away."

"Leave a message with Raymond, the club barman, he'll immediately get word to me and I'll come a-running."

"Okay, will do." Paul broke off and stopped at the telephonists cubicle to also inform her of his movements during the day. Paul had made two jumps and was busily refolding and packing his parachute on the long table inside a small building adjoining the airfield when the door opened and his pilot entered.

"Almost ready for your next leap?"

"Yes, just let me double check the lines again, don't want any of them them snagging up, do we?"

"Of course, take your time, by the way has that ever happened to you? Snagged lines?"

"Just once. I nearly shit myself that time, everything I had learnt went out of my head and I almost froze but somehow, I managed to cut away my main 'chute and release the emergency. To this day I don't even remember doing it."

"Jeez! It must have been scary?"

"Not really but the landing was the hard part, it was like falling from twenty feet onto solid concrete. Nope, I don't want to go through that experience ever again and that's why I always pack my own equipment." The man lifted Paul's emergency pack fitted with the altimeter and shook it up and down as if weighing the thing.

"Listen, would you do me a big favour?"

"What?"

"I've got two mates who've never been up in a small plane before and they're always on to me to take them up and I always said I would, once things were a little quieter. You know what the weekends are like? Seeing it's only us using the airfield today, I thought this might be an opportune moment to ask you if you mind the company."

"So?"

"Yup, they are here today and it would be an extra bonus if they could be inside the plane with a skydiver leaping out but then again, my plane is yours today, you're paying for the time, so the decision has to be yours."

"Sure no problem, bring them along." The pilot turned around and placed the emergency parachute on the floor below the table as a small plane started revving up its noisy engine right outside the building. The pilot then stood up just as Paul completed the final folds to his main parachute canopy.

"Thanks, I'll just call them and we can be off." Paul finished pulling the canopy lines together on top of the carefully folded multi-coloured nylon and placed the lot onto a canvas spread. He closed the ends of the canvas around the parachute and fitted all the release toggles into their correct positions then pulled on the harness and snapped the buckles until everything was secure before skirting the table. He picked up his packed emergency parachute from under the table and clipped it into position. The extra load roar of a revving engine denoted that the pilot was now ready. Paul turned and quickly collected his helmet and headed for the door.

"This is Paul Hunter." The two burly men were already fastened into their seats at the back of the Cessna, they greeted Paul as he boarded the small plane and took the front seat next to the pilot.

"Paul, meet John and Robert."

"First time in a small plane?" John seated on the right answered for both of them.

"Yeah, great isn't it, first time ever. "

"Don't worry, it's not as bad as everyone thinks."

"Yeah?" The engine increased its tempo as the pilot revved it and then moved the plane slowly across the well cut grass strip to the end of the runway. The pilot swung the Cessna into the oncoming light breeze, pulled a large knob on the dashboard and the small plane roared down the runway and up into the early afternoon sky.

"There's not much wind today, it's been easy to hit the target!" Paul shouted over the roar of the engines.

"Get ready! We're almost over the airstrip!" Paul slid out of his seat and moved to the back to open the wide door in preparation. Wind rushed into the cabin and the small plane bucked slightly as the engine revs dropped. Without Paul's knowledge during this fast readjustment of flight, John stealthily leaned forward and using a pair of steel cutters neatly snipped the thin steel wire leading from his 'pull-ring' to the six release toggles. The blades cut through both inner and outer cables like butter and Paul didn't hear or feel anything as the man leaned back into his seat.

"Right, ten seconds!" The pilot screamed. Holding onto the handle of the door, Paul manoeuvred himself neatly onto the footrest situated a little below the wing. His whole body was now being buffeted by the rushing wind on the outside the small plane and his full weight now rested on the small plate.

"See you down there!" Paul screamed.

"Right, go!" Paul let go and for a momentary second almost seemed to fly next to the plane as the wind drag of the aeroplane pulled at his body, then the suction effect let go and he disappeared from sight behind the small aircraft.

"Get the door closed!" John leaned forward and with his foot gave the sliding door a hefty heave. It slammed shut.

"Quickly, get us down to the ground!" John shouted and the pilot banked steeply towards the airstrip. Below their position, Paul relaxed into the familiar pattern of a skydiver. He spread out his body, arms and legs wide open, head down watching the dizzily spinning altimeter signalling the fast approaching ground. He quickly checked around the sky and then placed his right hand inside the chrome pull-ring. As the meter on his chest reached the required height he gave the ring a solid tug.

"Christ, malfunction!" The chrome ring still clasped firmly in his hand seemed to glow like some sort of circular death mask, he instantly let it drop and quickly rechecked the altimeter again.

"Thank God the main hasn't released and I don't have to cut away first." Paul grabbed at the red emergency parachute handle mounted on his chest and gave it a hard sideways yank.

"Oh God. No!" He screamed as it too came away in his hand. His body plummeted closer and closer towards the fast approaching ground below. He frantically inserted his fingers under a loose flap and managed to get his finger hooked around what was left of the steel strand holding the release toggles of his emergency parachute. He pulled at it with all the strength his adrenalin filled body could muster. The wire cut deeply as he almost tore off his finger, then suddenly as if by magic, the red material ballooned out across his chest. He rotated around in order to allow the life saving material to rise high above him, it shot open and he felt the air brake pull hard at his body. He had not been concentrating on anything below so it came too late for him to do anything as his body slammed hard into overhead electricity wires strung between huge criss-cross pylons. Paul died almost instantly from the impact which nearly cut him in half and many thousands of volts passing through the tangled mess. His parachute became entangled in the wires and his body hung limply in its harness.

"Quickly, let's get out of here, you know exactly what to say and do, we were invited here by him and you give them misleading descriptions. Understand?" The pilot nodded and waved them away as two men walked away from the small Cessna straight towards the parking area. They drove away at speed and once they were clear of the airfield the pilot stopped feigning throwing up as two airfield men arrived in a battered Landrover and collected him.

"What happened for God's sake?"

"Don't know, he just seem to drop and drop and unfortunately didn't stand a chance hitting those wires. Did you call the police?"

"Yes we have.". The Landrover made its way in the general direction indicated by the pilot, then the group caught sight of Paul.

Hanging there like some sort of Monday morning's washing on a line.

"Jeez!" The driver stopped the Landrover, they instinctively knew that there was nothing they could do to help him.

"David, it's terrible news." He could see that Susan was shocked.

"What?"

"Paul Hunter's dead."

"Hey? What? How?"

"Skydiving apparently his parachute failed to open properly and he became entangled in high voltage electric cables."

"Oh... shit." Susan slumped into a chair and held her hand over her mouth drawing a large breath from between her fingers.

"When you told me to call the meeting I couldn't find him in the building and Julie told me to call his club. I called and spoke to the barman who said he would pass on the message but now a policeman has just called and told me that David had a parachuting accident and that he's dead. He asked me about David's family and I told him to contact personnel."

"Accident? The man was an expert parachutist, I wonder what happened?"

"The policeman didn't say."

"Well, that leaves an inconvenient hole in our team. Sue, get hold of that company that employed Paul for us and tell them we need another man of similar stature and temperament to fill the vacancy. Unfortunately life must go on and I suppose also... er, that we better offer to bear the costs of the funeral. I know its not nice, but will you see to it then try to reach that policeman and make sure the media don't know that he worked for us. Okay?"

"Uh huh." Susan dragged her deflated body out of the chair.

"Just one other thing before you go, tell Julie to come here and please don't say anything about Paul."

"Right." After a few minutes had passed Julie made her appearance.

"You wanted to see me?"

"Yes Julie, sit down, I've got some grave news." Julie seated herself opposite David.

"Paul died in a parachuting accident this afternoon."

"No!"

"I'm sorry but you're on your own now and our only link into Johnsons accounts section."

"I feel terrible because I was so nasty to him before he left. It's a true saying that, words have wings, right now I wish I hadn't been so beastly."

"No time for recriminations now, he's dead and there's nothing we can do about it."

"I know, but I feel terrible about it." She wiped at her cheeks. "Believe me or not, I actually forecast that something would happen to him because he was becoming reckless."

"That's usually known as Déjà Vu."

"I better call Jean."

"No don't, she will have to find out in the due course of time, it'll probably be on the news this evening or in the papers tomorrow. The reason is that we don't want her making any connection between Paul and MH Holdings. Right now we're working on it to try and keep our name out of the media."

"What I'll do then is tell Sandy that I heard it on the radio, he can break the bad news to her then."

"Much better plan."

"This is so terrible."

"Talking of Sandy, have you spoken to him yet?"

"I was on the telephone to him when Susan told me you wanted to talk to me."

"Anything interesting."

"The only reference he found to any money movement was a bank form with both Christine and Ernest's signature allowing their bank to transfer funds on verbal request from either of them. It was dated last Friday but, that doesn't help us find the name of the trust account."

"Which bank was the transfer for?"

"The bank is where they maintain their company account."

"No funds, ...and yet, they sign a transfer form, maybe they're expecting more large incoming amounts, ...I wonder?"

"It's got Sandy confused, he's keeping at it, but unless he finds something more he can't help us and we have to find out through Union Bank of Switzerland."

"Yes, I suppose so. Okay, good girl, keep him hard at it."

"Will do." Julie still somewhat shaken by events went to the tiny cubicle she called her office and called Sandy to tell him of Paul

The Kixing

Hunter's tragic demise.

Sandy leaned back in his chair and whistled through his teeth.

"Ohhh, hell. I suppose I better get it over and done with before she hears from someone else." Sandy went through to Christine's office.

"Can I talk to you for a minute?"

"Sure, what's up?"

"Delicate subject because Jean met this bloke a couple of weeks ago and they've been having a most tempestuous on and off relationship."

"And?"

"Well, apparently I believe he held back from telling her everything about himself because he initially said he was here from the Middle East on business, but at the same time didn't tell her his hobby was parachuting."

"So?"

"Jean is crazy about the man and he's now been involved in a fatal accident and there are reports that was killed this afternoon. Would you help me break it gently to her?"

"How tragic, of course I will, let's get her in here in a minute but first, some details, what was his name?"

"Paul Hunter." Christine's knuckles tightened noticeably.

"Who? Are you sure?"

"His name was Paul Hunter."

"Do you know this person?"

"Yes. I've met him twice."

"Describe him."

"Tall, handsome, blonde, a real smoothie."

"I also knew of him."

"How?"

"He's been dating someone I know."

"Really?"

"Yes. It's obvious that his charms have seduced more than one woman at a time." Sandy noted that his employer's sun tan had visibly changed from a light brown to an almost greyish hue.

"Where did she meet him?"

"At the Monk's Head, he took Jean and I and a girl called Julie to the Gasworks, it's a small restaurant. Things just seemed to develop between Jean and him from there on in. Mind you I saw a nasty side tp him last week at that boxing match that I told you about."

"I see."

"Listen Sandy, don't say anything about his antics to anyone."

"Right."

"Let's get it over with, call Jean in." Sandy disappeared and Christine banged a fist lightly against her head several times before moving to the front of her desk and leaning back against it, seating her buttocks against the edge.

"Oh, what webs we weave." Jean appeared at the door with Sandy close behind.

"Sit down, both of you."

The Kixing

"Jean you've got to be brave."

"Why? What?" Her surprise was complete then becoming wary, it was as if she had suddenly expected to be given her walking papers.

"There's no other way to break the terrible news to you." Jean had been expecting the firm to close for some time and now thought this was it.

"I'm not stupid you know, I've listened to doom and gloom reposts in this office for over a month. Somehow, I was hoping we would pull through this bad patch, but I suppose we haven't made it and you're trying to tell me in a nice round about way that I'm now redundant?" Christine let her finish before taking the big step of telling her the truth.

"No it's nothing like that and your job is still safe. We've managed to weather that storm but my news is far worse so gather yourself together for a shock at what I have to tell you."

"What is it?"

"Paul Hunter, the man you were seeing was killed in a parachuting accident today?"

"You lie!" Jean screamed. "He can't have, he doesn't know anything about parachuting, he would have told me about it." Sandy placed his arm around the distraught girl's shoulder.

"It's true Jean, he's dead."

"Nooo!" Sandy cradled the sobbing Jean in his arms.

"There, there, let it all out." She cried uncontrollably for several minutes. Christine handed her a continuous stream of tissues. Jean finally took in a deep stuttering breath and blew her nose. The worst part of her shock was over, now she still had to come to terms with her own sudden emptiness.

The Kixing

"I'm so sorry Jean, there's never any easy way to break news of a tragedy, it's a shock to anyone's system. Have you got anyone to go home to or where you can be among friends, I just don't want you going home and suffering on your own tonight."

"No there's nobody close by."

"Right, then you are staying with me at my place tonight."

"No, I'll be alright."

"No, you're coming with me because now is the time you need to talk and get his memory out of your system. Collect your things and let's go."

"I would prefer to work."

"Don't worry, you'll be kept busy at my place, you and I can cook for both of us and we'll find something to do this evening. The main impact of this is yet to hit you, you'll need someone close by to lean on. Believe me, I know and I'll be that special friend for the next few days." What Christine was really saying was that she too now needed someone to share her pain with.

"Thanks."

"Get yourself together, I'll be ready in a few minutes, I've got a personal call to make." Jean and Sandy left Christine on her own, she lifted the receiver and dialled a number, now she had to suffer the repetition of the last few minutes all over again except this time it was on the telephone without being to do it face to face. Within, she hurt for both victims of Paul's devastatingly untimely loss.

The Kixing

"THE KIXING"

CHAPTER TWENTY THREE

"I don't believe this, why have they waited for five days before saying anything?" Norman, David and Trevor Reece were gathered at his boardroom table. An announcement was made jointly by both the British and American boxing boards that an enquiry was being carried out into the Caetano verses Blair world championship fight. David noted that Norman's tenseness showed through as his fingers drummed on the top of his desk

"The Americans are behind this." He pointed at the emailed communiqué.

"They've waited until we've taken over Martins before making their move and I think it's sour grapes because we outbid them, in fact I'm sure it's their doing." Norman had had a telephone call from Harry saying that all major bets paid out were being recalled until the enquiry had taken place on Thursday.

"I told you that the fight decision seemed out of order, have you seen the papers lately? They're scathing about the outcome and because maybe huge public outcry and pressure has been so great, that they've had to take the unusual step of being seen to hold an investigation." Trevor offered in his matter of factly style, taking the large pipe from his mouth. "As David pointed out, they'll probably drag out any enquiry and then let it die a natural death once things have moved on. They might even insist on a rematch and leave it at that."

"Maybe, but I suspect there's more to this." Norman said.

"Like what?"

The Kixing

"Something else is happening, I can feel it in my bones. Yesterday Paul Hunter gets killed under very questionable circumstances because even the police seem to suspect foul play and then, our new acquisition gets hit by an enquiry. This is creeping attack and no gentlemen, I think that someone's gunning for us."

"Aren't you being just a little paranoid?"

"I don't think so. Think of it this way, once we target any company, they generally don't know anything is happening until it's too late, usually the signs are there but strange events are dismissed until the takeover is complete. Likewise, there are more than tell-tale signs here, someone or somebody has begun stalking us and I want to know who it is." For about a minute there was silence as all three minds considered Norman's claim. It was David that broke the stillness.

"Why kill Paul Hunter if we're being targeted? He had nothing to do with the running of the company, it just doesn't make sense."

"Agreed and on its own, I wouldn't have given it a second thought, but this email makes me absolutely sure that we're under attack. Put the word out, we need to know if any strange coincidences start showing up anywhere within our group. We're supposed to be the experts on takeovers and that should mean we should be able to pick up on any signs while still in the early stages. It may be nothing, but personally I don't think so, let's find out, shall we?"

"What will happen if the fight is deemed to have been 'fixed'?"

"That's what's worrying me, Michael Lyndon, the chairman of Martins called this morning and stated that they had already paid out over twenty eight million and were going to start trying to recall the money, but he doesn't feel confident. Twenty four hours after taking on Martins, we could be losing a bomb. I've spoken to all the members of the British board and dropped a word in their ears, let's hope it helps. Word is, it's the Americans doing most of the screaming and that's why I think the boxing mafia over there, is somehow attempting to undermine our position."

"They'll be watching your American companies likes hawks then." Trevor observed.

"If they're that powerful, I suspect they'll place all sorts of trading restrictions on us if we try to get a foothold in the construction industry. Now maybe, you can understand why David and I were so dead set against the merger."

"Possibly, but it's too late to try and push the Genie back into the bottle. Minter's have faced more hostile opposition and come through so let's first get to grips with the problem at hand. Now, is there any other bad news that can help to brighten my day?"

"Just that we haven't yet managed to make any significant in-roads into the Johnsons Swiss account or the transfer yet, although it seems like we might have come up with the name of their benefactor." Norman scribbled something in his diary.

"I should have all that information for you today, David?" Trevor said.

"Nothing much more to report, except it would seem that Johnsons could be expecting to settle all debts shortly."

"What? How do you know that?"

"Both Johnsons have signed a transfer of funds form with their bank and that would suggest that they're expecting another large incoming payment to be made shortly."

"Damn!" Norman pushed the intercom button. "Rhona, get Muggeridge at the bank on the line." Norman started drumming the desk once again and the call was not long in coming.

"What can you tell me about the matter discussed yesterday?" He again scribbled into the diary.

"Nothing about who's behind the trust account?" He paused. "No I didn't think so, those Swiss gnomes are very secretive about their accounts because they have to be. Oh well, not much but I suppose this will give us something to go on in the meantime, please call me if you find out anything more. ...Yes, 'bye." Norman replaced the receiver.

"Trevor, the name of the trust is *'Jay & Jay Trust Account'*. I wonder, ...could that stand for Johnson and Johnson but anyway, it is a new account and has substantial cash funds lodged. Apparently U.B.S. wouldn't give any more information than that, it looks like we're not going to be able to reach the head of this particular snake, any thoughts about another way of bringing them down? By substantial, it would seem as if they have enough funds to cover their shortfall. I think I'm going to have to pay you our bet David. They've slipped the noose and escaped. Pity, I would love to have them on board."

"What do you want us to do about Johnsons then?"

"Let it go in the meantime, hopefully there'll be another time let's keep a watching brief and see what pans out. For now we must concentrate our efforts on getting settled into the States. Right, that's it for the moment, not a great meeting, more doom than gloom." Trevor and David left the crestfallen Norman and As Trevor turned towards his office he summed up the situation.

"Well, things happen in threes, hopefully that's our quota for the day."

It was late morning when Christine knocked softly on the door of one of her house's spare bedrooms before pushing open the door,

Jean was awake but Christine could see from the dark lining under her eyes that she had not slept very well

"Tea?"

"Um, lovely." Christine had awoken early, made a telephone call and then busily beavered away in her study. It was only when she heard a toilet flush upstairs that she made tea and placing the tray with two cups, teapot and various rolls, croissants and toast.

"I haven't had tea from a teapot in years. I normally use tea-bags straight into the cup."

"My father use to rise at five o'clock every morning and brew up and I've simply picked up his bad habit. I prefer tea made this way when I'm home, I suppose it's just that it tastes stronger and somewhat different."

"I can't remember the taste, so it'll be like a new experience for me."

"I thought it best to leave you to sleep as late as you could."

"Look at the time, I'm sorry."

"Goodness sakes, there's nothing to be sorry about, maybe because we were chatting until nearly two this morning had something to do with it? Did you sleep well?"

"Not really, in fact I couldn't get to sleep until the sun was already well into the sky. I expect that's the reason for me oversleeping."

"At least you have slept, when my father, then later, my husband died, I didn't sleep for several days. My mind was so filled with uncertainty because death of someone close does something strange to one's mind process, women are especially affected, somehow it makes us all recall those good times shared. We tend to forget the bad things that happened and start feeling a sort of deep sorrow for ourselves and what we are going to miss. Usually we are in fact simply mourning for ourselves and not for the dead person."

"You're right, we become selfish in our own interest, don't we?"

"In the main, yes, you're right our mental systems are designed to cope and look after ourselves and sorrow forms part of that process. Hope you like strong tea?" Christine poured two teas, placing one on the bedside table for Jean then placed a knife and napkin on a plate.

"What would you like?"

"Hmm, they all look so good, the last time I was served breakfast in bed was when I was in hospital four years ago. I quite often sit in bed and watch television and have a snack or indeed, sometimes have my dinner in bed. Just laziness I suppose."

"I'll let you into a secret, I do the same."

"Those croissants look good, could I have a couple of those?" Christine placed two on the plate and added a dollop of butter to the plate before handing it to Jean.

"Jam or Marmalade?"

"Neither, I prefer warm croissants with butter on its own, by the way, I don't think I could ever thank you enough for your hospitality and friendly shoulder to cry on. I did go on a bit last night, didn't I? It was probably all the lovely wine, I don't drink as a rule."

"We both did. I felt as if he could almost be one of the Johnson employees," she lied,

"You told him everything, didn't you? I wonder what he must have thought of the company?"

"He never really passed an opinion one way or another, he just seemed to ask many questions and was a good listener but never

ever offered any sort of comment in fact, I used him as my personal sounding board. "

"Oh well, no harm done, he must have just thought we were all an incompetent. bunch"

"No, I don't think so, on the evening before his death, I told him about our mysterious benefactor and he was so pleased for us. He was very interested and asked all sorts of questions."

"Did he now? I wonder why?"

"I don't know really, he was always delving deeply into my work but told me very little about his."

"Interesting, more tea?"

"Yes please."

"I've got one further bit of bad news concerning Paul and it's better you hear it from me than read it in the newspapers or hear it on the radio." Jean visibly tensed.

"What? It can't get very much worse."

"The police suspect foul play, they think he could have been murdered." Jean's reaction surprised Christine.

"You know Christine, I've now come to terms with Paul's death and I wasn't mourning his demise until five this morning, I was logically summarising what was, a short and stormy relationship with Paul. Does that shock you?"

"Not really. After all, it's only after any break-up that one can then see things in their true and proper light, it is part of the recovery process."

"Exactly, Paul really didn't want me in his life, really he was simply using me, don't you think? I suspect our whole relationship was based on a pack of lies, although with he's looks he could have had any woman he chose to." Christine knew this was the moment. She handed Jean a cup of tea.

"Jean, Paul didn't fly in from the Middle East, he worked as an industrial spy for MH Holdings. You're right, he was using you to gain company secrets which were fed back to his head office."

"What? That doesn't really surprise as much as it might have yesterday, how did you know this was happening?"

"We've only recently found out that you and Sandy are both being used."

"Of course, Julie was introduced by Paul. Oh what a fool I was?"

"No. These people are professionals but not a word to Sandy though, we're feeding him false information which must be causing havoc at the MH offices." "Poor Sandy. He really likes here and they make a really handsome couple."

"What's she like?"

"Really nice. The other night she stood up for me when Paul was in one of his foul moods. If I didn't know any better, I had have sworn she was very much in love with Sandy. She has that sort of glow that women in love seem to radiate."

"Maybe she is in love with him, how ironic it would be, the hunter caught in her own trap, still, we must use her."

"I agree and if I can help in any way, just ask."

"Go to Paul's funeral and try and gain evidence that Minter or MH Holdings was in fact, employing Paul because if it ever comes to a real showdown, we're going to need the proof."

"All right. That breakfast was just the thing to start my morning, are we going to the office?"

"Not today. I'm going for a swim in a few minutes, why not join me?"

"I can't, I don't have anything to wear."

"You don't need anything, there's a standing rule here, we always swim in the buff. Only when children or complete strangers come to visit my daughter does the order change."

"I've never swum without clothes, I would be too embarrassed."

"Nonsense, you came into this world naked and I think you'll enjoy it once you've tried it. Coming?"

"Oh what the hell, let's be daring, you only live once." Christine packed everything onto the tray and went to the kitchen, then through to the swimming pool, stripped off and dived into the clear water. Surfacing, she swam several lengths before coming to rest on one of the underwater stairs. Jean was now standing next to the pool and had stripped to her briefs.

"Come on, it's lovely!" Hesitatingly Jean turned her back towards Christine and removed the white panties before hurriedly slipping over the edge and into the pool. She struck out immediately and came to rest at the other end of the pool.

"You're right, it's beautifully warm!" Jean shouted across the pool.

"Don't shout, come here." Jean swum slowly until she reached the step.

"After my swim, I always enjoy time in a sauna and then jump into the Jacuzzi, it's a really vitalising way to start the day."

"No wonder you're in such fine trim, I really do wish I could do this every day."

"Tell you what Jean, why don't you spend a few nights here? It'll do you a power of good and I could use the company."

"I'll have to go home and get some clothes for the office."

"No problem, together we can work out and understand what all you told Paul and try and dream up different ways to fool Minter."

"That would be lovely and yes, I accept. Thanks." By that afternoon, the news that the Boxing Boards in Britain and America were holding an enquiry on the fight had spread throughout the world media. Speculation of fight manipulation was rife as the afternoon papers reached the streets of London. Calls were pouring into Norman Minter to get his opinion from media all over the world.

"Hell Rhona, I told you to stop all calls, make some excuse, tell them I'm in conference, or something."

"I suggest that you take this one, it's from Roy Bradley."

"Okay, put him through." He lifted his receiver.

"Roy! Long time, how're Liz and the kids?"

"They're all well Norman. Listen, I know the world and its mother must be at your doorstep and I'm the last person you want to talk to right at this moment, but something's come up on the wire that you should know about."

"What?"

"The 'American Tribune' have accused the promoters of the Caetano/Blair fight of being the main instigators behind, er, ...what they call the *Fixed Fight of the Decade*. They're not accusing you by name, but, it's quite clear who they mean."

"I'll sue the bastards for every penny."

"Because of our long standing relationship and knowing you

wouldn't get involved in anything this stupid, I'm going to do something about it. Norman, give me some names so I can redirect attention away from you. Like them, I'll make accusations that'll have the press running around like chickens without heads."

"Right! Michael Ruscon, the chairman of the British Boxing Board, and Gary Michelhoff, the president of the American board, they are the ones behind this, but I have no proof you understand?"

"Of course. I love it. My leader page heading will read something like *'Boxing Boards Bamboozle Bets'*, for sure that'll get tongues wagging, I'll wager."

"I can just see it now. The holders of the enquiry having to defend their own position. Roy, I owe you one for this."

"I'll bear that in mind, you can buy me a drink at the amateur championships at Wembley on Friday. You will be there, won't you?"

"Oh yes. I'll see you there. Thanks again."

"Lovely man and no need for gratitude, wild speculation, it's simply our way of stirring things up to get at the eventual truth. I suspect that's how the Americans are testing the water." Norman breathed a huge sigh as he replaced his receiver. Rhona put her head around the door.

"Norm, There's a call from Muggeridge at the bank, do you want to take it?"

"Yes." He lifted his receiver again.

"Norman, the shit has hit the fan here."

"Why?"

"Apparently this furore being created is playing havoc with Martins's shares in the market and there are even rumours that your company has lost heavily and will take a huge hiding. Can you throw any light on the matter?"

"Yes, it's only a temporary blip, our people are attempting to rectify the situation as we speak."

"That's not good enough, you've only had Martins a few days and it's already in a great deal of trouble and now the consortium are becoming twitchy and are not going to be happy. We must try to stop the run on the market otherwise the company will soon need further substantial funds injected into it."

"Don't panic, it's only a short term blip, it'll probably all be over in a matter of days."

"Days? In hours, the financing package could be wiped off the market. They're not too worried here, they're bloody petrified because your losses appear to be quite substantial. Heads are going to roll if this carefully balanced deal falls down so early in the dealings and we'll be carrying your loss, I suggest you start looking at increased collateral in case we here, have to suggest a refinancing package."

"Collateral?"

"Yes. Maybe you will have to contribute a large percentage of that new marina complex."

"You're mad. We've only just finished the project."

"Don't get mad at me, being the messenger I'm only making a suggestion. Anyway, we're trying everything we know to stem the tide from this end. I'll keep you informed." Norman replaced the receiver and placed his head in his hands and thought through what had been the blackest day of his career history.

"It's those blasted Americans." He said softly. "What next?"

The Kixing

The Kixing

"THE KIXING"

CHAPTER TWENTY FOUR

"Umm, this is so comfortable and it's really good to have someone to talk to in the evenings. I'm now very glad you asked me to stay for a few days, it's as if an enormous pressure build up has been released.

Christine and Jean had just completed supper and both had settled into reading. Christine was relaxing with Thomas Kenealy's novel, 'Shindler's Ark' for the second time around, while Jean busily paged through a large pile of 'Country Life' magazines. Christine looked over the top of her book at Jean stretched out full length on the autumn coloured sofa.

"It's amazing how one misses female company, when my husband was still alive, we used to sit here for hours without saying anything because the mere fact that he was there, was contentment enough."

Jean yawned and lifted her arms and the black and gold kaftan spread out like a bird's wings in flight.

"I suppose that's why I allowed myself to get into a mess with Paul, I missed company in the evenings us humans are funny you know? We crave the need to be with others and will do anything to hold onto a potential partner, just look at your lifestyle, you've got everything, looks, money, why don't you simply get married again?"

"Never met the right person I suppose." Christine lied.

"What about companionship, don't you miss having, er, ...how can I put it? Some sort of relationship."

287

"You mean sex?"

"Well, yes." Christine giggled loudly.

"Occasionally."

"Paul was a wonderful lover, in fact, it was the only thing he could do well." Christine immediately turned back to her book.

"I don't want to know about it."

"I'm sorry, did I embarrass you?"

"It's not that. Shall we drop the subject?"

"I just thought..." The front door bell rang. Christine moved quickly to relieve continuing the unwanted subject. It was Antonio.

"Signora, we must talk."

"Come in, but keep quiet for the moment, I have a visitor." She put her fingers to her lips.

"Visitor?" Antonio seemed perplexed and irritated at once.

"Yes, its Jean, my brother's secretary, she's staying here for a few days."

"Oh!" He suddenly relaxed and smiled.

"We'll talk in my husband's study." She guided him past the lounge door into the book lined room.

"Just a moment, I'll tell her that I have business to take care of, can I get you something to drink?"

"No thank you, but tell me something, how come my men didn't know this woman was here?"

"I don't know, she came home from work with me."

"I'll have a word with them later. This is not good enough." Christine disappeared and told Jean, returning a few minutes later and closing the door.

"Now, it's obviously something important that brings you out here tonight?"

"Si Signora." Antonio waited until Christine sat down on the leather couch before seating himself, he placed his walking stick across his knees.

"It was us that sent Paul Hunter to meet his maker."

"Yes, I suspected as much. But, why?"

"We were going to let you use him to feed information back to Minter, then something else came up."

"What?"

"Signora, ...this is difficult. Why don't you control your daughter."

"Why? What do mean, control her?"

"We found out that she has been sleeping with that pig of a man and if your husband was alive today, none of this would have been necessary."

"What are you saying?"

"Paul Hunter, he has been meeting your daughter at the club and then taking her home and spending nights with her. I don't know how long it's been going on, but it has."

"I didn't know?"

"He has defiled your daughter and we all took the oath and promised your husband to look after you and the bambino when he died. Tracy-Anne is a beautiful lady now, but that bastard has been screwing her. We could not allow that, he had to die."

"I understand but hy didn't you just tell me first? I would've sorted it out, now we've lost one of the main pipelines back to Minter. You Italians haven't thought things all the way through, and seem to only control your emotions with your hearts, not your minds."

"Not Italian, Sicilian. You still have your accountant to pass on information, don't you?"

"Fortunately for you, yes, we still have more than one way to deal with Minter."

"What about your daughter? Will you tell her?"

"Don't worry about Tracy, I've already taken care of that and she's very strong, in fact she's a lot stronger than I am. I explained that he was just using her. Unluckily for him, I don't think that he ever connected Tracy-Anne with me because I use my maiden name, I only met him fleetingly and my surname was never mentioned."

"We've been to his home and checked it, there was nothing of interest there."

"Good. Now what about Minter? How're things going?"

"He's under pressure. Mr Minter is a very slippery customer, he also has friends in high places and they're all trying to help protect him."

"I know, but we'll just have to keep working at it."

"It would be better if we took him out."

"No. We want him to suffer."

"What if he slips out of the trap, he could then become very nasty."

"With who?"

"With anyone he suspects that could be plotting against him. Signora, he's not a very nice person, especially now that he has been backed into a financial corner."

"We go for him all the way."

"It would be far better if he met with an unfortunate accident."

"There you go again Antonio, you must think things through, the police already know that Paul Hunter was murdered. If Minter suddenly died, that would bring them into play. Our family will be jeopardised, we don't want any unnecessary attention."

"Yes, you may be right."

"I am right."

"Okay then, but if he seems to be slipping out of the trap, we must react."

"This time, talk to me before going ahead."

"Si Signora."

"Antonio, keep an eye on Minter, if he gets desperate he may do something stupid. I suggest you get someone to follow him and keep tabs on his every move."

"We are already doing that."

"Any news on the man that was watching the building?"

"Nothing. Believe me that guy still worries me."

"All right, I suppose that's all and thank you for protecting Tracy-Anne's interests. I'll have to speak to her when she comes home from university and although she's her own young lady now, she has never been told the truth about her father. I think the time has come to tell her all so that at least that way, she'll know what sort of life she's expected to live."

"She doesn't know?"

"No. It was better to let her grow up first, it's going to be hard enough for her to come to terms with my activities without having had them forced onto her as a child. My idea was that i should explain all when we went on holiday in December."

"Si, I agree let her become a proper woman first because there will be many difficult times that lie ahead for young Tracy."

Antonio heaved himself off the wine coloured couch, his limp was still visible but had improved substantially since Christine had last seen him. She walked him to the door and when his car pulled away she returned to Jean in the lounge who was still stretched out reading her way through the pile of magazines.

"Okay, that's my family business taken care of, what say to a cup of coffee and a liqueur."

"It'll hit the spot admirably."

"I feel weary, I think I'm going for a swim. Join me?"

"Tell you what, let's have the swim and have our coffee and liqueur in the sauna."

"Good idea, that'll make us both sleep very well."

"I'll prepare the coffee, you bring the liqueur and we'll meet in the pool."

Christine smiled, what she hadn't said to Jean was, that whenever she discussed what she referred to as 'family' business, always ended up making her feel somewhat dirty. Even after all these years, she had still not come to terms with her own role.

"Look at this! It's a bloody outrage." Norman threw a letter from the lead bank of the consortium across his desk at David.

"Pure panic, that's what I call it. They're prepared to cough up and take their interest payments, but at the first sign of a minor problem, what do they do? Scream and shout like little children. No spines, that's what I reckon."

"This is not a little problem Norman, its mega-money you can understand that they are a little nervous. What're you going to do about it?

"Nothing, what can I do?"

"Well, I agree that we haven't got that sort of funding available to us at the moment, the problem is that they want us to provide extra collateral for our share of the deal, otherwise they're pulling out."

"I know that, where do they expect me to find instant funds?"

"The trouble is that they know all about the costs and profits from the new marina project and they probably expect us to put it up as collateral."

"Oh, no. I'm not going to let them get their hands on that, if they want Martins, that's fine, but the marina, no ways."

"As I see it, there could be another way out of this."

"How?"

"Cut your losses, sell off Martins at the best price you can get and undertake to repay the banks the balance over a period. I'm sure they'll go for that."

"What? Lose a fortune, just for buying Martins, we've only just acquired it, we would been working for ten years to repay the debt."

"Better that, than letting this Martins deal drag us under and we made a big mistake, so what? We can still get out of it even if there is a loss."

"Definitely not, the two boxing boards are now under pressure, didn't you see the papers this morning, they're being accused of rigging the fight."

"I know, but what, if, they can prove they had nothing to do with it. The spotlight is going to fall on you again and the media will be baying to find a scapegoat and you may just be it. Martins' shares will plummet even further and you'll struggle to offload it. I implore you get out while we're still afloat, leaving it would mean that MH Holdings could be doomed to take a massive dive. No Norman, staying with Martins just doesn't make commercial sense."

"I realise now that I should've listened to you and Trevor. This however is only a temporary setback but don't let it worry you, I'll deal with the banks. They're not getting their money grabbing hands on any part of MH Holdings."

"Soon, you may have no choice."

"I'll have a choice alright, I'll make these buggers eat their words, just see if I don't."

"Okay, you're the chief and know best."

David flicked his head to one side to show his annoyance that Norman was being pig-headed but he could not permit his pride to accept that he had made a really costly mistake.

"Just in case and with your agreement, I'm going to have lunch with Bernard Marcus."

"Why?"

"Well, if things don't work out too well, we'll need to get out quickly and there were several bidders for Martins at the outset. Perhaps we can test the water and find out whether they could still be interested."

"Good idea, not that I think anything is going to happen simply because I haven't lost my nerve like the rest of you."

"Of course, but it's wise to lay the ground in any case."

"Right. Now, anything else to report."

"Nothing much, except that we've found out that Paul's girlfriend in Johnsons is staying at Christine Johnson's house."

"How did you find that out?"

"Julie told me. She got the information from her accountant."

"You know, I wouldn't be surprised if Christine Johnson had something to do with all this maybe we underestimated her because it would seem she could have friends in some very high places."

"Coincidence, that's all."

"I don't think so, possibly she found out about Paul, and had him killed, I think it all fits and proving it will be difficult."

"No don't say that, no, our problem is of our own making as we just moved forward too fast, and now we're in trouble."

"Are you saying it's my fault, no David, my guess is that somebody's behind this attack on us and I get this feeling that she's somehow got something to do with it. Well, she'll learn not to fool with me."

"Why? What are you going to do?"

"I not sure yet, but I give you my word, she and her powerful friends won't touch MH Holdings. God! I love this company, nobody's going to lay a finger on it. Mark my words." David just shook his head.

"I can't fathom your reasoning."

"Don't try to. I just have this gut feeling and believe me, I'm very seldomly mistaken."

The sun had set when Ernest finished his day, tomorrow was the beginning of the weekend, he felt tired having gone through a topsy turvy few days but things were going well once again and he had been able to throw himself full length into his work once again. Jean and Christine were walking out of the door and he wondered how long it would be before he and his twin could have some time alone together.

"Chrissie, a quick word if you don't mind."

"Certainly. Jean, you go to the car, I'll be there soon. Here, the keys, catch." She tossed the bunch of keys to Jean and then moved around behind the seated Ernest and laid her hands on his shoulders before starting to rub his neck very gently while reading the note he was scribbling onto a pad. It asked when they could meet.

"Jean is good company, I'll be sad when she leaves at the weekend, but it's been fun."

"Yes, she seems to have got over the problem in an inordinately short time.

Ernest smiled and nodded his head and wrote the word 'Sunday' on his pad. She smiled.

"I'm taking her home on tomorrow evening so why don't you come and have brunch with me on Sunday. We've still got a lot to that must be discussed."

"That's sounds good to me."

"Only if you haven't got one of your girlfriends around for the weekend."

They both laughed. Christine had added that piece of information for whoever was listening to all conversations in the office.

"I've got nothing arranged and even if I did have, I would have brought the girlfriend with me."

"Anyway, Jean's waiting, what did you want?"

"I received two cheques today, they'll bring down our overdraft."

"Good. I'll see you tomorrow. Take care."

She leaned forward and kissed his ear knowing it was his sensitive spot. He pulled back and laughingly pointed a finger at her.

"Night. Drive carefully."

Ernest heard the front door bang as his sister left, he then spent a further half and hour dictating letters and before walking through the factory. This was a longstanding ritual when he was in the building by himself, loving this time looking around and blessing the day that they had set up their business.

"It's all ours," he said aloud.

At the back of the building he looked through the window to the dimly lit company parking area, his Porsche was not the only vehicle parked in the large open yard. Quite often, local people would use it to park their cars at night and this always upset Paul.

"Damn!" Paul made his way to the front finding a piece of paper he scribbled a message to the owner of the large old Vauxhall. He opened the door and then made his way towards the car before noticing that the old vehicle's engine was running. Wary, he stopped in the middle of the parking area, not quite sure what to do when the vehicle suddenly lurched into life and straight towards Ernest.

"Jee-sus!"

His quick reacting senses somehow knew this was for real, spinning quickly he raced back towards the lit up building knowing full well that whoever was at the wheel would be able to see him clearly against the lighted backdrop. Ernest turned to see the car now with its headlights on was fast bearing down on him. His brain was travelling at lightning speed as he suddenly shot to his left, but too late. The driver was expert and swerved violently, swinging the backend around and catching Ernest against the hip sending him sprawling onto the hard asphalt and the roughened surface tearing at his clothes and skin.

"Shit!"

He rolled and came to his feet still trying to run, there was definitely something very wrong, his right leg just wouldn't take his weight. The Vauxhall crunched into the building and seemed to stall before the driver turned the motor over, meanwhile a panic stricken Ernest dragged his frame along the ground towards the open door and possible safety. Suddenly he heard the motor take, splutter and die, the driver turned the motor again and this time it roared to life.

"Oh, God, I'm dead."

As the vehicle wrenched itself free from the building Ernest shut his eyes and kept hauling himself along the ground. Suddenly he heard a second sound and opened his eyes to see what was happening, there was suddenly another pair of lights bearing down on him.

"Shit!" The prone man screamed. He was helpless on the ground as he watched the lights heading straight towards him, suddenly the lights swerved left and the car stopped within a hair's breadth of his body. He could not see what happened next, except that the Vauxhall came racing past the back of car which had come to rest. It shot straight towards the far side gate and into the road with a shower of sparks as it bounced and landed, swerving out of control hit a car on the opposite side of the road, bounced into the middle and screamed away into the distance. Someone got out of the car next to him and Ernest thought this last moment was upon him.

"Let him go!"

The voice came from inside the car.

"Are you okay?"

Ernest looked up, he couldn't see the man's face.

"No, it's my leg, I think it's broken."

"Right, we get you to hospital immediately."

"No wait. I've got to lock the place."

"Tell me what to do, I'll do it."

"My keys are in my office, it's the one..."

"I know which is your office. Just try to relax."

The man was gone.

For what seemed like an eternity he lay there and in the stillness of the night, he heard the man's echoing footsteps racing through the factory and then the back door slammed shut. The one inside the car got out and between them they eased Ernest into the backseat.

"Thank you."

"Try to relax. I turned on the alarm, everything at the factory is safe."

Ernest knew immediately that these two saviours were somehow connected to Christine and that now he was safe. He lay back on the seat and could see that one of them was making a call on his mobile phone. He heard the man talking in Italian and then his whole body jolted and screamed in pain at each slightest bump. He tried to hang on, but couldn't, he passed out.

"THE KIXING"

CHAPTER TWENTY FIVE

Antonio limped to the door that he had left only twenty four hours ago. He pushed the front doorbell and waited until Christine appeared.

"Antonio, can't you stay away from me," she joked.

"Signora, can we talk?"

"Yes, come in." She ushered him to the study, left him and returned as she had done on the previous evening. He, again waited until she was seated before sitting down himself.

"We were lucky this evening, we managed to prevent someone from killing your brother." Christine sucked in a rush of breath that felt like a red hot molten lava being poured into her throat. Confusion crossed her face.

"Ernest, ...what? Where?"

"Steady Signora, he's at the hospital, I'll take you there, but first, we must talk."

"What happened?"

"In the car park, somebody tried to run him down but fortunately for him, the men assigned to follow you and your brother were close enough to stop him being killed. We were just very lucky, this time."

"Do you know who did it?"

"We think it's Minter's men but you must not worry, I'll find out soon enough. We've found out who the man watching the building is, it could have been him. The whole family are out looking for him and the car at the moment, don't worry we'll find them and then we'll have the answers."

"So, Ernest's all right?"

"Not quite, they think his leg is broken."

"I must go to him, it was his right leg, wasn't it?"

"Si, how do you know?"

"Driving home this evening, I had what I thought was a violent cramp in my right thigh, followed by a panic attack because I was at the wheel of my car. The pain is still a dull ache and hasn't gone completely I think was me experiencing something my brother was actually going through, and I didn't even recognise it."

"This man must be stopped immediately, we were lucky this time, your brother could be dead now."

"No! If Minter is behind this attack on my brother, then as I said before he must suffer slowly. I'm going to relish him being taken apart bit by slow bit until he's completely ruined. His world must be shattered as he has done to others."

"I think you are flirting with danger."

"That's my decision, my plan goes ahead. Is Ernest still protected by the men?"

"Si."

"Right, then let's go, I'll just get changed." Christine composed herself and went to the lounge, Jean looked up and smiled as Christine entered the room.

"Jean, I'm going to have to go out for a while but please wait up for me, I'll tell you all about it when I get back."

"Why? What's wrong?"

"Not now dear. I've got to rush." Christine knew that if she said anything, Jean would then want to accompany them and she needed to talk to Antonio alone to find out in more detail what had happened and he wanted to do that in the car.

Norman Minter was seated in the front row ringside seat directly behind the judge's table watching the British amateur championships, most fights through the weights having gone according to schedule. One upset had occurred in the welterweight division when an almost unknown fighter had stopped the reigning champion with his first haymaker punch. The crowd were still buzzing with excitement at this new British find and there were still five fights left to go ranging from light-middleweight to super-heavyweight as Norman turned to his trusted companion.

"Enjoying yourself?"

"Uh huh. I was just looking across the room. Harry's here, did you see him?"

"No, where?"

"There." She pointed across the ring and Norman saw the little man's hat first.

"I need to urgently have a word with him so don't go away." Norman made his way around the ring and approached Harry, who was deep in conversation with a young man. From what Norman could see of the man, it had to be Harry's much talked about son. He was short and stout with all the attributes of his father, the two were so deeply engrossed in their discussion that Harry didn't see Norman until he was almost standing next to them.

"Norman! How good to see you again." Norman knew the man was lying through his teeth mainly because he looked like a frightened hare with shifty eyes seeking a way to run to safety.

"You haven't contacted me Harry. What's going on?" Harry stood up.

"You haven't met Billy, my son. Billy, say hello to Mr Minter." The young man nodded.

"We must talk Norman, come let's go somewhere quiet. Billy, don't let anyone take my seat." They made their way to an exit area.

"Right Harry, now what's happening about the money you owe me?"

"I'm sorry, but I didn't want to contact you because I think the big boys are having me watched."

"Bullshit. Where's my money?"

"Honestly Norman, I've been staying away on purpose as I have heard on the grapevine that the boys are trying to follow the pipeline to who is placing these large bets. I'm having to make them think that I'm just one player of a bunch of players. They're watching me very carefully to see how my payments break down. So what I'm doing at the moment is laundering the funds and then when I've lost them in among others, do not panic because I will pay you. Yesterday, I received a call from America, they want the money back pending the outcome of the enquiry. I told them to piss off because I had already paid out for the fight and there would be little chance of retrieving funds."

"Don't talk crap. I want my money, do you understand?"

The Kixing

"Norman, Norman." Harry held his finger to his lips. "Listen to me carefully, these people play for keeps I simply ask that we do it my way and all will okay. If I rush things and they find out who laid the bet, you're dead, come on Norman you have to trust me on this, have I ever let you down?"

"You had better not this time, or else you're dead meat."

"I'm caught between you and them. ...Oi you! I'm the only one to lose in this deal, but never again."

"Right. You've got until Wednesday."

"Sure, I'll get the money to you by then." The two men walked back into the hall and as Harry turned to head towards his seat he grabbed at Norman's arm.

"Remember my words, these boys play for keeps and if they suspect you're involved, they'll kill you as sure as we're standing here."

"Yeah, yeah, Harry. Just make sure it's no later than Wednesday." Norman reached his seat as the next fight was about to start. Rhona took his hand, it was wet.

"Norm? What's happening?"

"Nothing much, Harry's just messing me about." She knew there was more to his excitement. The bell rang for the first round as she turned to watch the two young fighters face each other. The rest of the fights went according to expectation and at the end of the evening Norman was asked to present a trophy for the best fight of the evening. People filed out ahead of them into the narrow street. Norman and Rhona discussed the new welterweight find as they left the front of the building.

"He's going to go far, I like him a lot and believe me that when he turns professional he'll only need about two years to head straight for the world title. Mark my words, he's that good." Norman was the first to notice the masked man that appeared from somewhere out of the crowd, the tall person wore a zipped up anorak and balaclava that hid his features. The figure moved quickly and reached the couple.

"You bastard!" He shouted and it was then that Norman saw his leather glove holding a gun and it was being raised and now pointed directly towards his chest. He knew he had but a split second to move before flame poured from the small round orifice pointed at him. Norman tried to dive to his left, but it all happened so quickly and then he felt his body being thrown backwards and sideward at the same time. People screamed and dived for cover while others stopped, not quite knowing what had happened.

"Norman!" He heard Rhona's scream as he hit ground but all he could feel was the searing heat within his stomach area that sudden excruciating pain automatically informed him that the gunman hadn't missed his target.

"Norman!"Rhona saw the flash and then watched as the hooded figure turned and raced back into the crowd, she hadn't realised she had screamed and then again as she turned to see her escort curled up on the ground much like the position taken by a baby in it's mother's womb.

"Get an ambulance, he's been shot!" She screamed.

"Lie still, don't move, we'll get you to hospital. Where does it hurt?" She slipped her hand to the front of the prone man and felt the warmness of his blood. Involuntarily, she pulled her hand back in horror and then remembered that Norman always carried a large white silk handkerchief in the top pocket of his tuxedo.

"Norman listen, we must stop the bleeding." Her hand searched to find the handkerchief then she pushed him onto his back and pushed the white silk into the bleeding hole as hard as she could. She held it tightly for what seemed an eternity.

"There, there, hang on and don't worry, we'll have you fixed up in no time." The sound of running feet brought two ambulance men with a stretcher. The white silk looked peculiarly like blotting paper soaking up ink as red blotches were now steadily spreading from the centre towards the outer white edges.

"We'll take over now." Rhona moved to comfort the shot man, a background ambulance siren wailed loudly in the confined street as red and blue lights flashed and bounced around the walls of the adjoining buildings.

"Norm, can you hear me?" His twisted features as he nodded his head.

"I'm going to take your keys from your pocket. I'll take the Rolls and leave it at my place then I'll see you back at the hospital, okay?" She found the keys as the two men placed him onto the stretcher. As she rose she felt a tight grip on her arm turning, she faced a young policeman.

"A gunman, he went that way."

"What was he wearing?"

"Grey balaclava, blue anorak and tall, that's all I saw because it all happened so quickly." The police called in to his base via a small shoulder microphone.

"I'll need your name." Rhona gave the man her details and the policeman let her go while he searched for further witnesses. Several people that she knew, offered assistance but Rhona declined just wanting to get back to the hospital as soon as possible. As Norman was lifted into the ambulance she asked one of the helpers which hospital Norman was being taken to.

"Rhona!" Norman shouted before they closed the doors.

"Go in," The man helped her into the ambulance.

"Yes."

"It's important that you get hold of David Lividsky and make sure that Harry pays me before Wednesday."

"Shush! You're not to worry, I'll sort out everything.

"In the light of the ambulance she could see that his face was almost devoid of any colour. She kissed him gently on the forehead.

"See you at the hospital." Rhona quickly made her way to the underground garage to find Norman's Rolls-Royce, once inside the vehicle where she used his car phone to call David and relate what had happened. She then drove home, changed into something comfortable and used her own car to get back to the hospital. She knew that it was going to be a long night. When she arrived, she found out that Norman was already in the operating theatre and was shown to the waiting room. David arrived about ten minutes later.

"I've contacted the Chief-of-Police, he's a friend of Norman's and with his input he'll probably get things moving very quickly hopefully we'll get the bugger before morning's over.

"David sat down and took Rhona's hand for the first time she found herself shaking almost uncontrollably.

Back home Christine lifted the morning paper that was always delivered to her door both she and Jean had just finished having orange juice followed by a boiled egg and toast. She had amusingly noticed that Jean still cut her toast into 'soldiers' and dipped them into the egg this was some form of sign of insecurity, she thought to herself. Since Jean had arrived on the scene, they had both taken to lounging in comfortable adjustable canvas chairs reading the papers each morning before having a swim.

"Good God!" Jean swung her feet over the side and leaned towards Christine.

"Read this." Christine recognised Norman Minter's photograph instantly, the headlines stood out on the page *'Well Known Boxing Promoter Been Shot'*. As she read the account of the report, her mind went straight to Antonio, how dare he take matters into his own hands when she had expressly asked for Minter to suffer. She searched the page and found that Minter was still critical, but comfortable.

"They've given nothing away. Isn't it coincidental that Minter is in the same hospital as Ernest." She thought back to the previous night's events, after having made sure that Ernest was alive and comfortable, she had had a word with the doctor who told her that her brother had been lucky. He had sustained a broken leg and was going to have a badly bruised hip and most of his pain now, would be from the area where several small chips of stone had embedded themselves under his skin. Christine had told Jean that Ernest was hit by a car, but hadn't elaborated about the so-called accident being a possible murder attempt.

"I don't blame whoever tried to kill him, tyrants like that shouldn't be allowed to mess up other people's lives as he has. I'm glad." Christine noted a slight hint of hate creeping into her companion's voice.

"I'm just going to call the hospital and find out how Ernest's doing."

"Send him my love and tell him I'll see him this afternoon." Christine went to the study and shut the door and called Antonio. When he came to the phone she could hear that she had wakened him.

"I thought I asked you to leave Minter to suffer."

"I did." She heard the surprise in his voice.

"He's been shot."

"I heard. None of us did it."

"You're sure?"

"Very sure. He has many activities and many enemies out there, believe me, we're not the only ones that want to see him dead. You mustn't forget he's taken over many companies in his lifetime, someone could easily have a grudge and done our job for us."

"I have your word that it wasn't the family?"

"My honour of your late husband." She somehow knew that he would not lie to her and suspected he really was speaking the truth.

"Right, anything else?"

"Yes. We found the man."

"And?"

"He was there to watch your movements for Minter at least that is what he said, and I believe him, because I personally, ...well let's say, have spoken to him. He definitely doesn't know who tried to kill your brother."

"Okay, then keep looking, we've got to find out who's out to kill us." Christine called the hospital and was told that Ernest had had a restful night and was comfortable. She asked about Norman Minter and the call was put through to another ward. The sister asked who was calling and a male's voice came on the line asking the same question. She realised her mistake and replaced the receiver, the media would soon reveal whether Minter had lived or died and she didn't want to become embroiled or come under any sort of scrutiny, especially if the voice belonged to a policeman.

She returned to the poolside to report to Jean that all was well.

"He's had a good night and they'll probably send him home today."

"That's great."

"Well, when you go home, I'll have another guest here for a while I think that Ernest should spend a few days here."

"Your home seems to be becoming a home for wayward strays, isn't it?"

"I suppose so. You coming in?"

"This will be my last chance to swim freely, you couldn't keep me away from that water, even if you tried." Both dropped their dressing gowns and plunged into the clear water.

At the hospital David and Rhona had spent almost all night in the waiting room while two detectives had questioned her for almost an hour. Norman had pulled through the worst stage and had had the offending projectile removed from his stomach.

"Want breakfast?"

"Yes, but I think we better stay around here until we know whether he's going to make it safely."

"Let me talk to them, again." David made his way through the wards until he reached Norman's private room. There had been a detective there at five o'clock, when David had last visited the room and now he was gone. Even the old battleaxe of a night sister was no longer hovering around the passageway. David wondered whether he should try and find her, then decided against it and he pushed open the door. The ward was empty and the bed still unmade, he quickly checked the cupboard and the small locker, everything was gone. He raced back to Rhona.

"C'mon, he's gone, let's find out why." The two raced through the hospital corridors until David found a nurse coming in the opposite direction.

"Can you tell me about the patient in room 206?"

"No."

"He was there at five and now he's gone, get somebody of authority up here immediately."

"Calm down, there must be an explanation."

"Don't tell me to calm down young lady, someone tried to murder him last night, perhaps you think he decided that he had had enough and walked out of this bloody hospital?"

"No, that's not what I mean, there must be an explanation, and perhaps he's simply been moved. Come with me." The trio marched through the long passageways until they reached an office.

"Wait here. What's the patient's name?

"Minter, Norman Minter." The young nurse disappeared and soon returned.

"Come!" The little band moved off along another long passage. She stopped outside a room without a window in the door.

"After you." She opened the door. Norman was asleep, pipes into the stomach looked like twin transparent veins extending from his nose and a drip-feed bottle had another clear vein leading into his arm.

"He was in an intensive care ward. They had moved him to this private ward this morning, now that he's out of danger."

"Thank God!" Rhona moaned.

"Thank you. May we stay with him?"

The Kixing

"Oh yes but let him carry on sleeping, he needs all his strength now." She left the two with the sleeping Norman. David suddenly felt drained, for several minutes he had thought Norman had been whisked away by his killer. He had seen it happen in a film. He took Rhona's hand, it was still shaking uncontrollably.

The Kixing

"THE KIXING"

CHAPTER TWENTY SIX

"How's that?" Christine readjusted the large leather footrest for Ernest after he had been discharged on Sunday and she had collected him from the hospital and taken him straight to her house. During the rest of Sunday and after much protestation from Ernest when Christine insisted that he remain in bed all day, he had decided this morning that the time had come for him to try to do things on his own. It was now Monday and Christine knew that she would have to run things at the office. She had arranged with her daily help to feed the invalid at lunchtime.

"The leg's fine, stop fussing so, you're like an old woman, come to think of it you remind me so much of mom when you get into a mood like this."

"Just making sure that's all. Is there anything you need from your place? I can collect them on my way home."

"Just a few pairs of trousers, make sure they're older ones because they need to be cut along the leg, a shirt or two and some underwear will be fine. Oh and also my toothbrush and electric razor from the bathroom."

"Right. Anything else?"

"A hug and kiss before you leave." Christine giggled and tousled his hair. She then disappeared and Ernest picked up the morning paper and began reading the full account of Norman Minter with interest.

"I wish I knew who shot Minter!" He shouted because he wasn't quite sure where his sister's whereabouts in her large house. She returned having changed from dressing gown which she had slipped on after her morning swim.

"Why?"

"I would pin a bloody medal on whoever did that because the man's a bloody hero."

"Who says it was a man."

"Well... Women don't generally do those sorts of things, do they?"

"I couldn't really say."

"Did you see what the papers said? They reckon the attempted killer could be a fanatical boxing fan or a gambler that lost a packet and people like Minter shouldn't be allowed to retain their promoter's licence."

"He won't, if I have anything to do with it, I'm just going to rearrange my face, if you need anything, ask Maria, she'll be here all day. She has instructions not to let you out of that chair."

"What if I need a pee? Will she help me then?" Christine giggled loudly as she swept through the large double doors, it didn't take her very long because she didn't wear much makeup as a rule.

"There you are all the cracks plastered and ready to face the day, anything you want me to do at the office?"

"Stop fussing so, come and give me a kiss." She moved to his side and leaned over to give him a sisterly kiss but he threw his arms about her and pulled her off balance onto the arm of the large chair.

"A proper kiss is what I need."

"Stop it! You're going to crease my dress." Ernest's mouth met the protesting words. Christine stopped struggling and relaxed as they held the position for a short time before she pulled herself away from him.

"Well, you seem to be on the mend and back to your old tricks, must be off now, are you comfortable?"

"Stop mothering me, the only pain is on my stomach where I scraped myself, these remaining tiny stone chips are playing havoc, more so than my broken leg."

"I'll give you a bed bath when I get home." Christine let out her infectious giggle once again.

"Promises, promises, now be off with you, some of us have to work while I stay home." As she left the house she noticed that there were four men in the battered grey Mercedes. Two got out and returned to a car parked behind it and as she reached the corner she saw the Mercedes pull away from the curb and start following her.

"At least they're earning their pay." Christine muttered.

Later that morning, David sat at the imposing board table together with the rest of the directors. Due to Norman's hospitalization, they had decided to call an extraordinary board meeting. The special chair at the head of the table remained vacant, nobody had the gumption to presume that with its rightful incapacitated occupant in hospital, that anyone could take over the chairman's place.

"Gentlemen, I suggest we appoint David Lividsky to the board as an interim measure until Norman is fit enough to resume duties." Larry Margoles had taken it on himself to act as spokesman.

"All in favour raise your hands. Good, we're all in agreement then. David, because we're all sleeping partners and old men, we think someone should take over the day to day running of MH Holdings. You've just been appointed into that position." Rhona, taking notes, looked up from her pad and winked at David.

"Thank you, I'm seeing Norman this morning and will explain what has been decided by you all, I called the hospital this morning and his condition is satisfactory, but they say he'll be there until they're certain that his lung has healed properly. Apparently they're still worried about the damaged lung filling with fluid."

"How long will he be in hospital?"

"Nobody's committing themselves but the best estimate seems to be between two and three weeks. He needs time to recuperate and in all, he'll probably be out of action for about two months."

"What are we going to do about these scandalous accusations in the media?" David pulled his mouth, his role as legal advisor had been changed and he suddenly now had to make positive management decisions which would affect the livelihood of the thousands of employees.

"I'll look into the matter and see whether we have any legal recourse but what worries me more than anything is what these insinuations are doing to our new acquisition's share-price."

"Why?" David explained about the letter from the banks and his discussion and alternatives that he had laid out to Norman.

"In conclusion, my feeling is that we would be wiser to cut our losses." David waited as various members at the table talked through the Martins saga and what, if anything, should be done to correct the matter.

"I suggest that you decide what you think is in MH Holdings best interest and draft a memo to that effect. Rhona will type it and then once you've signed the memo, I'll deliver it to Norman." The elderly directors were clearly worried with the situation and the thought of losing the new marina complex to the banks was not being greeted with any enthusiasm.

The Kixing

"David, would you and Rhona excuse us for a moment because we have to consider this latest turn of events, but need to discuss it between ourselves." David and Rhona retired to her office.

"That wasn't nice, I would call it back stabbing." He looked somewhat perplexed. " No, because the simple truth is more like the words we should use. Norman's not being left out of any decisions, I am only a temporary stand-in and believe me, I want what is best for the company and you saw the letter Norman wrote confirming my objection to this Martins deal."

"Yes, but my personal feeling is that while he's in hospital and unable to defend his stance, your actions are beginning to smack of deception."

"Rhona, I'm only placing all the facts before the board and once they've decided what to do, then Norman will still have his say. Remember that he still controls this company and will always have the final word. I must not be seen to be anything but above board with everyone and please feel free if you like, why not come to the hospital with me to talk to Norman?"

"I spent most of Sunday there, but yes, I would like that. You're right, I was totally out of order." A buzz on Rhona's intercom summoned them back to the table. Larry Margoles asked Rhona to take a memo.

"We have discussed the matter and think the best course of action is that MH Holdings should try to get out of this Martins deal as cleanly as possible." He dictated a letter for Norman to that effect. Having completed their meeting after Rhona had typed and copied the letter for each director, and they had all left, David sat down at the table with Rhona again.

"I didn't want to alarm them but Norman's in really big trouble because the American boxing mafia are upset with losing Martins to him. They're extremely powerful and will use every dirty trick in the book to break him and that's the only reason why I'm doing what I'm doing. Do you understand?" Rhona put her hand on top of his.

"I know that. I knew something was going on, but he wouldn't tell me what it was, that man is so very secretive and obsessive sometimes."

By lunchtime, Christine had completed her inspection of the major sites and then discussed the accounts with Sandy, making sure she included a surprise tit-bit for possible transfer to MH Holdings. She crossed the car park and could still see the tire marks where the Vauxhall had swerved and hit Ernest. She climbed into her Jaguar made a quick call then headed for the large white house on the outskirts of town.

"I came as soon as I could." Antonio had had the swivel chair removed from the lounge, he sat alongside Christine on the couch.

"Minter was shot by the brother of a boxer who fought for him."

"That doesn't make sense, why should a boxer's brother shoot Minter? Anyway, how do you know?"

"Two of our men were following Minter, remember?"

"Yes."

"When he was shot, one of them followed the man and we picked him up yesterday, purely to find out why he had done it. I was also worried when you accused me of arranging the shooting so needed proof."

"Why did he try to kill Minter?"

"It seems like our Mr Minter is being a naughty boy and holding illegal fights in private."

"So?"

"These aren't your usual boxing matches, they're called Kixing tournaments, something like Thai boxing but apparently far, far more malicious and deadly."

"There's nothing wrong with that, is there?"

"Not unless the losers are killed, there isn't."

"Hey?"

"Yes, the fighters are dressed like gladiators with sharp spikes on their hands and feet. This Kixing sounds like it is a mixture of bare-knuckle fighting, roller-ball and pit-bull terrier fights all rolled into one."

"No wonder it's kept quiet."

"The man that shot Minter was also the trainer of a very good boxer and when he found out what had happened, he went mad and tried to kill Minter."

"How do we find out about these fights. We need proof."

"Apparently these Kixing matches are only attended by his extremely wealthy client society and it goes right up to the top of the political and financial world. You can bet, nobody's going to admit having ever witnessed a man or even many men being killed this way."

"Are you telling me that there's been more than one fight? We must find out how many there've been and their venues. This little venture of his is going to let us off the hook this time because we've got Minter in another trap even if he tries anything else."

"I'll try to find out but can't promise immediate results, but if we search for missing boxers, the trail will lead us somewhere, I'm sure."

"What are you going to do with the brother?"

"Let him go, I suppose, he told us all and he can't help us any more."

"You can't do that."

"Why?"

"You're not thinking this one through, are you? What if he falls into the police's hands and he tells them about Minter and these, er, ...what did you call them? Kicking tournaments?"

"Kixing, a mix of boxing and kicking."

"The police will arrest Minter and we won't be able to humiliate him or, for that matter, kill him. It'll be too quick, no Antonio, see if you can buy this man off and if not, offer him a position in the family, possibly training some of our young fighters. He must not be allowed out there while this is ongoing, try to make him hate Minter even more than he does at present, tell him that we'll keep him safe and when the time is right, he can enjoy seeing Minter crucified."

"I'm glad we're on the same side."

"I've decided that the ultimate disrespect we can offer Mr Minter is to take over his business, that way his indignity will then be complete, it'll send him over the top, we won't have to kill him, he'll do that for himself."

"Oh, ho. I like it like a coup, while he's down and injured. He'll never know what's hit him and right now Minter is on a downward roller-coaster ride from which he'll never survive."

"Now, I must return to work." David knocked on the door of room 206. Norman still looked terribly weak and the assortment of tubes protruding from various parts of his horizontal frame didn't add to the bleak picture. Rhona leaned over the bed and gave him a peck on the cheek.

"How're you feeling today?"

"Bloody awful."

"At least you're feeling something, a few inches to the left and you wouldn't be feeling anything."

"I know, the doctor told me that if you hadn't stemmed the bleeding so quickly, I would possibly have met up with St Peter. Have they found out anything yet?"

"No, not yet."

"So, tell me, what's been happening in that big world out there?"

"Larry Margoles called an extraordinary board meeting this morning."

"Panicking a bit early, is he?"

"Darned right, he still thinks that you're going to die on us." Norman coughed and spluttered as he tried in vain not to laugh.

"Ow! That hurts."

"In their haste and wisdom they have decided to make David a provisional director until your return."

"David, why did they do that?"

"Somebody has to make the day to day decisions and they must have presumed that I fitted the bill."

"Sensible. It's better than having Larry nosing around or trying to run the place, he's just too old and doddery and will muck up the place in a matter of days." David stepped forward.

"Norman, things are becoming worse as far as Martins is concerned even the board raised it and I managed to outline the possible options open to us. They discussed it among themselves and wrote a memo for me to deliver." David opened a file and produced the letter. Norman read it through twice.

"Very clever of you all, because the time to depose a leader of anything is when he's away from the seat of power. I'm not even cold and the vultures are already starting to circle."

"Norman, the banks are screaming."

"Let them shout as loudly as they want to, I will not be dictated to. You all seem to forget that I own a sixty five per cent holding in the firm and what I say, goes. Just because I'm on my back doesn't mean I don't know what's going on because I've also read the newspapers and as I told you the other day, those bastards are not laying a finger on my business. Is that understood?"

"Quite clear. I told you that I would be speaking to Bernard Marcus after he called me this morning and said that even with this thing hanging over our head, he thought he could interest one of the other parties."

"And recover the full amount paid, I suppose?"

"Not quite, he thinks he'll have to bid them up because the price currently being offered currently is only about sixty per cent of what we paid for Martins."

"What? We would lose a cock-eyed fortune on that basis, no David, I would rather sit it out."

"We could do that and given enough time, possibly manage to

repay the banks over an extended period."

"If Bernard can't come up with a much better offer, then forget it, I'm not losing that sort of investment for anybody so let's just drop the subject. What else has been happening?"

"Nothing much really. I heard that Ernest Johnson fell and broke his leg over the weekend."

"Oh? How is he?"

"Fine, I think but he's already back home, so it couldn't have been too serious."

"Back home?"

"Yes. It seems he slipped and fell and broke his leg and will probably be off work for a few days."

"Damn! He should have been killed." Rhona was quite taken aback at this sudden outburst.

"What's the matter?"

"It's nothing, he should have broken his bloody neck, not his leg. That reminds me Rhona, would you contact Harry for me. I would like to see him here, today." Rhona scribbled in her pad.

"Anything else?"

"No, that's it. Go back to that deteriorating group of mindless imbeciles calling themselves directors and be sure to pass on my message. No sale; no loss and no more decisions without my consent. If any of you try this stunt again, I'll have you horse whipped over a barrel. Now, I need my beauty sleep." Rhona kissed him on the cheek and they left.

"He's being so stubborn because defeat isn't something in his vocabulary."

"Tell me about it but believe me it's becoming really serious, I just hope he holds his nerve when the going gets really rough, because it's going to turn into a boardroom bloodbath. Thank God, I'm only the messenger." They reached David's car and were soon back at the office. David made the call.

"Hello Larry, just been to the hospital and Norman was furious, there's no way he's going to entertain any idea of selling Martins. He maintains that we have to sit it out and he's currently calling everybody he knows."

"Calling in his favours at this stage? I'll tell you something David, if I was thirty years younger, I would probably back him right to the hilt but I'm an old man and I've seen many things in my life. Norman's father and grandfather wouldn't ever have gone out on a limb like this."

"He's the boss and these are his orders."

"I'm not happy about his decision but never the less, will go and talk to him this evening and ask him to reconsider this foolish move."

"Will you pass his message on to the rest or do you want me to put it in writing to all concerned?"

"Better cover your arse. I'll tell the others but send the memo to them anyway." David rang off and quickly dictated the letter to the board. He then called Bernard.

"He didn't go for it, see if you can squeeze them a little further."

"No ways, he's lucky to have been made this offer if it were my decision, I wouldn't give more that fifty per cent."

"Speak to them Bernard, at this moment we're only the go-betweens now." David walked through to Trevor's office.

"Get me an up-to-date valuation and costs on the marina project as quickly as you can."

"This evening be okay?"

"Fine, I'll be in my office all day."

The Kixing

"THE KIXING"

CHAPTER TWENTY SEVEN

Christine helped her brother from the makeshift bedroom she had set up in the ground floor study where she had temporarily installed a bed, a television from her daughter's room and a set of drawers in the comfortable room in order that Ernest could move about without having to climb stairs.

"Don't worry, when you're ready to make your way upstairs, you'll tell me because for the moment it'll be easier for you to move to the lounge and kitchen."

"I know, but I feel so useless, it's being trussed up like a turkey that makes me feel utterly helpless." They reached the lounge.

"First, a promise is a promise I think that you need a bath and aren't ready to face the upstairs bathrooms for that just yet." Ernest noticed the smiling gleam in her eyes.

"What?"

"I'm going to give you that bed-bath, can you lie down on the floor?"

"Oh Chrissie, stop fussing, I've done perfectly well on my own today."

"You're never going to receive an opportunity like this again so relax and enjoy it, you'll have tremendous fun." She giggled loudly and disappeared to find the instruments of torture to be used on her brother.

"Any further developments on the Minter front!" he shouted after her as he gently eased himself off his bed and onto the floor before rolling over to lie on his still painful stomach. Ernest gingerly then raised himself onto his elbows in an attempt to watch the news on the muted television.

"Chrissie, come here quickly!"

"What is it?"

"Turn it up, there's something about Minter on the news." She lifted the hand held control and pushed the green button and the news-reader's voice flooded across the quiet room.

"Norman Minter is still in hospital and so was unavailable for comment but we're sure that this particular story will run and run." The screen went blank as she switched off the television.

"I wonder what all that was about? Well we will probably discover all when the ten o'clock news comes around."

"It would have been something to do with boxing because they showed two fighters before Minter's picture came up."

"Now, you're going to have to lift your body so that I can slip these towels under you."

"Yes sir, at once sir." He carefully raised his body and Christine could see the pain etched on his features hurriedly adjusted two large beach towels underneath him before he flopped down once again.

"Now, we somehow have to manage relieving you of that gown." He pulled his arms to the back so that Christine could remove the robe. She dipped a flannel into the warm water and then applied soap to it she, began tenderly washing his back. Ernest relaxed when he felt the warm cloth moving very lovingly across his prostrate body.

"Umm, that's terrific."

"Guess what? I've got hold of a super present for you."

"Where?"

"Just a moment, I'll get it." Christine moved away across the room, she collected something and returned.

"Here. It's called a Mediscratch."

"Mediscratch?" Ernest studied the thing for a moment. All it was, was a long piece of thin flat plastic with a handle at one end and completely smooth on one side and had a series of small raised bumps on the other face.

" What's it for?"

"Brilliantly simple, isn't it?"

"Yes. But what's it for? You're going to thank me in time; a clever somebody dreamed up this invention and patented the one thing everybody donning a plaster really would need. Here let me show you how it works." Christine took the Mediscratch and slowly pushed it into the top of Ernest's plaster.

"You see, before long you skin will flake and is going to itch terribly and this is a medical scratcher and it's completely safe." Ernest burst out laughing.

"How do you think of these things? Where had you find it? It's fantastic." Christine handed the thing back to her brother and continued washing the back of his body before giving his backside a fairly swift smack when she had completed that task.

"Right young sir, now onto your front." He rolled over with great difficulty mainly due to the stony chips still embedded under at skin and also as he yet still hadn't mastered the encased leg that hindered all free movement. Seated now, he tried out the new plaything by pushing it deep down into the plaster his face contortions showed her that his leg was still very tender.

"Can't it break off in there?"

"Apparently not."

"It's a fabulous present, thanks."

"My pleasure, now lie back and relax." She fondly pushed her hand against his chest then took a step back while allowing her eyes to scan her brother's body in all its glory stretched out before her. It was still firm and except for the covering of white to his leg, the large gauze patch covering his stomach where he had hit the ground and his downy shaved hair below the wound, his body looked in good shape, she thought to herself as she again soaped the flannel again.

"Christine, just take it easy around my hip, it's still extremely painful."

"Shut up and leave it to me remember that you're the patient and at this moment I'm the nurse, all you have to do is lie back, trust me and enjoy." Ernest closed his eyes and allowed the warm hands to move across his body. Her doting cleaning process in small circulars movements continued from forehead and moved downwards. Only once she reached his stomach, did he suddenly feel a stirring and warmth starting to rise from within. Christine could see the result developing and with wicked pleasure began slowly teasing him by running her hands from his pubic hairline and around his risen manhood to the inside of his thighs and back again several times before continuing down the inside of his right leg to the top of his plaster. She then concentrated on his left leg until all was left except his right toe that extended from the white cast. She finished scrubbing his toes while at the same time carefully removed excess white chips of plaster that had remained behind. She could see that his passion had declined to normal once more.

"Almost finished, did you enjoy that?" Ernest kept his eyes closed but she could tell that he was now drifting somewhere between utter pleasure and sublime delight due the sensation of her gentle fingers working magically all around his body.

"Wonderful. You have such an astonishing touch, you should use it more often."

"Good, only now there's\one more small area left for me to wash and then I'm through."

"What a pity, you could keep washing me like this all night, it's so relaxing."

"We'll see." Christine placed the two bowls to the side and moved to his good left side.

"Thought I would wash this part a little differently." Ernest felt her mouth close over his almost deflated penis, is entire body suddenly awoke and now alive.

"Uhhh. Not fair" Christine slowly but deliberately lowered her lips until they contained his full but rapidly hardening length. His gasp told her everything as she moved her restricted tongue in a licking movement as far up and down as she could before then moving upwards to concentrate of his tip very slowly . Her eyes never left her brother's reactions and at his crucial point, she then released him and studied the proud muscle that was now rigid and firm.

"Now, that's a wash I would love that all night long."

"I thought you might, you're not to ill for me to continue then?

"You cannot stop now, that would be inhuman." Christine smiled at him then continued the treatment for a short time, she could feel his emotion building second by glorious second and for another teasing moment she stopped at the crucial moment.

"Having fun?" Christine whispered.

"Please nurse, finish the bath?"

"Only if you relax."

"I promise but it's not easy." She continued the slow movements until his body started heaving and then quickened the pace before he suddenly let forth an almighty grunt, he was unable to hold back and simply could not hold back any longer. Christine felt the vibration arriving and stayed with him until his thundering explosion broke through and only then slowed her rhythm to a tender licking. When all tremors had died down she took hold of the flannel, dipped it into the still warm water and washed his dying member.

"Christ! That was absolutely fantastic you've never done that to me before."

"I loved it, but do not think I am going to wash you that way every night." She continued to tend him until he's fully relaxed and wound down.

"Now, would you like a brandy to finish your bath?"

"Hmm, love one." Christine collected all the paraphernalia and returned them to

the kitchen, returning she helped her twin into his gown and onto the couch. Christine pushed the button on the control of the television. The news was just starting as he poured two brandies into snifters and swirled the alcohol around the balloon shaped glasses.

"Come and sit down." She sat in a large chair after handing her twin his drink. They watched as events worldwide were related by the news-readers.and it was close to the end when the female announcer turned to the subject that they were waiting for. Ernest leaned forward to gain a better viewing position over the arm of the couch.

"There have been dramatic developments in the world of boxing. Following the amazing scenes at the Caetano-Blair world title fight, accusations of *'fight-rigging'* have been circulating the globe and the two main Boxing Boards of Control in Britain and America jointly announced an official enquiry is going to be held. This is the result of what is seen as an unprecedented and usual move, I fhink it is mainly because of intense media pressure piling up against them that has forced their hand and now they have decided to move against that fight outcome. The chairmen of both boards have tonight resigned from their posts until the enquiry has been completed. Michael Ruscon of the British Board of Boxing claimed the step was taken only in order for them to allow the enquiry to proceed unhindered. Norman Minter, the promoter of the fight is still in hospital after being shot by an unknown gunman, his condition is said to be comfortable." The news switched to sport and Christine pushed down the mute button. Ernest shrugged his shoulders.

"Was that good or bad news?"

"It means that Minter's friends have achieved their objective and by insinuating that the boxing boards are involved, the world's media have a governmentally appointed body to tackle this matter, it's far more newsworthy. If it was true, it would be far more sensational than simply pinning down the blame onto some little insignificant boxing promoter. By getting himself shot, Minter has attracted the sympathy vote, he's being very clever, but we're only just at the beginning, there's a long way to go yet."

"I take it, that that meant its bad news then?"

"Someone told me he was slippery and now he'll play the sympathy vote for all it's worth and those two retiring officials are simply the scapegoats for the moment. The enquiry could die a natural death if allowed to proceed for too long, that's what generally happens."

"Do you think he'll come back at Johnson Interiors?"

"Not for the moment, he's got his hands too full at the moment to even worry about us." Ernest breathed a sigh of relief.

"Ernie, I'm just going to make a quick call because its now that the next part of our plan must go ahead." She went to his makeshift room and called Antonio.

"Did you see the news?"

"Si. It's not too good for us."

"Don't worry, he's not off the hook yet.

"Oh no? The two men are being blamed for the fight outcome and even if the boards don't find them guilty, the whole world will just think it's a cover-up."

"That's what's so good about it, we can use it to our benefit."

"I don't see how."

"You will, get hold of that friendly editor of that American paper and make certain that he runs a story that Minter's in league with the two men because he's just acquired a majority holding in Martins the bookmakers and that he is the bag-man for the two Boxing Boards."

"Jesus! That will implicate some of our friends on those boards, our cousins over there won't be very happy. Signora, we cannot do that."

"All right, I'll tell you what we do instead, just get the paper to tie the three men together and forget about the boards. Tell everybody what's going to be done."

"Si, that could work well, I wish I had your brain because I thought we had been beaten by this Minter trick and somehow I now think you could even turn defeat into victory."

"Anything else?"

"MH Holdings are making enquiries about selling Martins back to the market and our group offered to take it off their hands at nearly half what they paid for it."

"As soon as this report breaks, your people must adjust your offer down by another twenty per cent because then there will be nobody left in the market that will touch anything from Minter. The financing banks will be crawling all over him for repayment and now he won't be able to even touch boxing for some time. I wouldn't like to be in his shoes by tomorrow."

"I agree, you women are supposed to be the gentle creatures, but you, you're beautifully coloured, just like a snake. You seem to be relaxing quietly, but all the time you're being very dangerous and now Minter's fallen into the trap and you're going to finish him off in your own time. No matter what move he makes, you have several tricks up your sleeve to respond with, he's dead but only he doesn't yet realise it."

"Don't be so damned Italian and just remember, we've got a war on our hands. It was him that started it but now let's see if he's got the stomach to carry it through."

"I'll talk to you tomorrow Signora please sleep well... Oh, by the way, how is your brother?"

"He's well and very relaxed but exhausted at the moment." Christine cupped the instrument and giggled softly to herself. If Antonio ever found out about her and her brother, Ernest would be dead.

"That's good. I hope he recovers and starts walking again soon because the leg is a very sensitive area. Ask me, I know."

"Talk to you tomorrow. Bye Antonio." She heard the line click and burst out laughing loudly as she walked back to the lounge, she couldn't help humming a tune. She was very pleased with herself and the things she was achieving right then.

. Sandy and Julie had just arrived back at the cottage and were watching the news as well. Julie didn't say much while the article about Minter came onto the screen

"That man is a damned vulture because he's the cause of all our troubles lately, thank God, we're out of the financial hole and able to trade normally again."

"Him? I wonder who could hate him enough to be so desperate?"

"Every company boss where he's ever taken their company from them with his devious ways. It's a pity whoever it was didn't quite do a better job of it."

"My goodness Sandy. I never knew you could be so bitter."

"Oh yes and I have this feeling that somehow it was him that indirectly engineered Paul's death."

"Hey?"

"You heard what I said, he even employed Paul as an industrial spy."

"What are you talking about? I've never heard such nonsense."

"It's not often that I get cross and blow my top but I was talking to Jean today and without knowing it, she let it all slip." Sandy looked hard and long at Julie.

"Now that two and two add up to four, you were introduced to us by Paul and I want to know whether you are also working for Minter and possibly been leading me on or know more than you're letting on."

"What do you mean?"

"I've never called you at this so-called temporary workplace of yours, you've always called me. Would you like to give me your office telephone number right now?"

"Sure, why not?" Julie had a direct line to the outside world in case of just such an incident and rattled off the number, her senses now, fully alert.

"I'm sorry to so pedantic, but I've got to be sure. Julie, since meeting you, I've allowed myself the luxury of becoming besotted by you but I just don't intend getting hurt."

"I fully understand your thought process because you did tell me about the girlfriend who got killed, it's taken a long time for you to let go of her or that memory. I'm going to do something I've never done before, that is, explain myself to you. This is a one time offer, I'll tell you about my relationship with Paul because I never ever want this hanging over us."

"You don't have to, I'm sure that I can trust you."

"No you don't." He watched her carefully. She was having difficulty coming to

terms with what she wanted to say and possibly, she was now mentally arranging events.

"Yes, I worked with Paul and I also work for MH Holdings." Sandy's mouth dropped open as if his bottom teeth had suddenly acquired lead weights.

"This, or rather you, were to be my first assignment and I never even contemplated on my becoming so emotionally involved with you so that when my feelings for you unexpectedly changed, I then offered to resign. They wouldn't hear of it and told me to stop being silly and I have tried as hard as I could to forget what I'm doing because somehow I knew that one day, I might have had have to walk away from you."

"How could you?"

"I'm giving up my job at MH Holdings because it's not really my line of work, at first. I thought it would be, but, it's not and I'm only sorry you found out when you did because it would have been so much easier to live the lie and if you hadn't taxed me about it."

"Tell me something? How much of what I told you went back to Minter?"

"Everything and to tell you the truth, I was so pleased when your company worked through this terrible cloud hanging over it. I take my hat off to your directors. Do you know? Johnson Interiors is the first and only company to escape Norman Minter's clutches. That says something, doesn't it?" She sat back and watched his every move. She had gambled, his metal jury were deliberating and now she awaited the decision and her sentence. Sandy jumped up.

"No! I don't believe it. One half of me wants to tell you to get the fuck out of my life while the other half wants to kill you."

"Look at it this way, at first, I wasn't going to tell you anything and was simply going to walk away and never see you again. All I can say is sorry, but when you confronted me and I intended lying through my teeth but then something in here snapped," She placed her hand on her heart, "I just couldn't do it to you and if anything, somewhere beyond all this treachery I'm now hoping for a fresh start because I simply don't want to live a lie. Can you understand that?"

"I suppose so, you do realise that I'm going to have to reveal all to the Johnsons about you and that could mean your going to prison?" Julie had always looked after number one as she drew in a large breath preparing to play her only trump card that would hopefully pull her free of any interrogation and the mess she had become embroiled in.

"Yes, I do understand and if you tell me that you forgive my deceit I'll simply leave quietly and never enter your life again. Sandy, I'm truly sorry this fiasco didn't pan out the way I had first expected it to because I wasn't expecting to fall in love with you."

"Oh, no, you don't! You cannot simply say sorry then just walk out of my life like that, if you really mean what you say then we have work this out responsibly together. We're going forward from here, trust is going to be hard to come by but I'm as much to blame for this mess as you are, we're both victims."

"How so?"

"I dived in headlong and now you've gone a long way to restore my confidence by telling me all. Had I found out later that would have been me, finished. It must have been as difficult for you to tell me, as it was for me to listen to. Today is the first day of our new relationship so it's truth from now on, deal?"

"Deal now I'm truly exhausted, telling you about my dishonesty was probably the hardest thing I've ever had to do in my life."

"Tomorrow we should go and explain everything to Christine and she'll probably go ape." The two went to bed and Julie snuggled into the crook of Sandy's arm. He listened to her gentle breathing as he lay awake wondering whether he would have a job by this time tomorrow.

The Kixing

The Kixing

"THE KIXING"

CHAPTER TWENTY EIGHT

"It looks as if the shares have stabilised and could even be rising, could it possibly be the case that Norman was right and the slump would only be a minor hiccup? By the way, how's he doing?" David was speaking to the lead banker about Martins.

"We believe that he's out of danger and well on the way to recovery though it's going to take time for a full recovery."

"In a telephone conference this morning we decided to take a 'wait and see' type approach. Everybody received a big fright when the shares started tumbling like that.

"What you should really be saying is that you guys panicked and came on too strongly to Norman and now that the market has again settled and potentially turned itself around, you're worried at what Norman's going to say and do. Well, if the truth be told, I expect he'll be as relieved as you."

"No, it's not that but we did put our money where our mouth is and this particular buyout was right on the limit being far higher than we would've normally allowed. The financial gearing just wasn't right, so when Martins started losing ground like that, like any banker we might have needed a massive refinancing package to be put in place, we simply wanted to know whether Minter was in or out."

"In other words, we had to come up with some form of collateral for our share of any new package so that your backside was covered. You bankers make me laugh, when things seem to be against you, you'll always find someone to kick out at but when a deal is going well, you're always first in line to start creaming the fat that you don't

343

care about the bad days. How do you fellows sleep at night?"

"That's totally unfair, we put financial packages together and most of the time, make money for all shareholders concerned but sometimes we are liable to hitch ourselves to a bad one and then it does it cost?"

"You mean heads roll? So when the signs are not positive, it's every man for himself, is that what you're telling me? Bugger the rest, you bankers only take care of number one?"

"Well don't you do the same thing when the chips are down?"

"I suppose that the world is full of financial sharks so what do you want me to tell Norman?"

"That things are now picking up again and at this moment we're not going to press him for assurances."

"So if things go wrong again, you'll happily back the venture and not demand collateral? You're in this one all the way to the hilt?"

"Don't twist my words Mr Lividsky, you know what I mean?" It wasn't often that David felt this livid. The voice was so condescending, yet David sensed fear in the man's voice.

"I most certainly do and should Martins now prove to be the livewire that Norman expects it to be, you want your share of it and if it turns and slides, then you're going to bail out unless Minter coughs up for the loss. Nice babies but I'll pass on the message to him. I'm sure he'll be relieved to know he's got your people's firm support and backing is up behind him."

"It's not what you think?"

"No, I bet it isn't, you and your banking cohorts have helped to create a house of cards that could collapse around this company's ears. Now you tell me, what the hell am I supposed to think?"

"I can see it's no use talking to you, please give Norman my regards and tell him the pressure is off, he'll understand." David replaced the receiver and banged his fist on the desk.

"Jerk!" Trevor Reece smiled and dragged on his large pipe.

"Bankers, they're all the same, they only get into a ring if their opponent is securely tied up and gagged then they have this way of convincing everybody that it was a fair fight. There are never any winners against the bankers, they are even more crooked than our chairman and that's saying a lot."

"I hoped Norman would have more sense than to get into bed with these hyenas, I get the feeling that they'll strip him to the bone if Martins doesn't come up trumps."

"Speak to me about it, its my job to deal with them every day and fortunately, up until now, we've always managed to stay out of their clutches. This is a different ballgame though." David watched fascinated as Trevor drew on the large pipe and skilfully exhaled one perfect grey smoke-ring and continued to produce smaller ones which passed neatly through the quickly breaking up outer circle of the large ring.

"That, is what it's about, some smaller items manage to pass through the system while it holds perfect formation but when it loses its symmetry, chaos prevails and the smaller ones trying to make it through, just disappear into oblivion in among the rest of the pandemonium."

"Much like the small companies we take over?"

"Exactly, that's why I didn't say anything the other day when Norman suggested that something or somebody is stalking us. I feel as if we're in for a rough baptism shortly. Norman's right, don't ask me why, I simply feel as if something's going on behind our backs."

"Ghosts, that's what and now you're all simply chasing shadows."

"I don't think so."

"Anyway Larry Margoles and company will be here shortly, I had better be on time for the meeting." David collected his file from Susan and made his way to Norman's office. Rhona pulled him to one side.

"Thought I would give you the heads up because there is trouble brewing, Roy Bradley's been on the line saying that the Americans are playing foul."

"Why?"

"Read this, he emailed it through a few minutes ago, you mustn't tell the board about this or they'll go mad." David read the email which implied that Norman was laundering funds for the two heads of the boxing boards.

"Oh-oh, this is not good. I better get to the hospital and show it to Norman."

"What about the board meeting?"

"Norman's the only one that can react with authority, I'll talk to them." He entered Norman's office and seeing everybody already seated, began the meeting.

"Gentlemen. I'm afraid we're going to have to cut this short, something important has come up which needs my urgent attention."

"David, we've discussed the matter and are going to back Norman's decision all the way."

"I see, he will be pleased because the banks have let me know that they feel the same way, I seem to be the only odd man out." Larry smiled at his companions. They had all seen the Martins' shares reversing their recent downward trend.

"However, hold on tight, we're not quite through these rapids yet, these Americans are out for blood and I don't think they'll give up easily. Now, I wish I could sit and go through all the figures and happenings of the last few days, but, I can't. If you want to, we can reschedule today's meeting in two days time. Sorry to mess you about, but it is important and I must act immediately." David said.

"What's so important that you have to cancel a board meeting at this late stage?"

"Something I need to discuss with Norman, I can't explain right now, it's got to come from him, those are my orders. If he gives me the go-ahead, I'll call you immediately. Don't worry, it's not as serious as you think it's just that Norman and me have to act quickly on something that's come up."

"Withholding information from the board is not a way to run a business."

"I suggest you accompany me to the hospital and tell that to Norman, I can't work for a number of people at the same time and therefore, something as important as this should first be discussed with Norman." Larry Margoles didn't like the idea of questioning his nephew so he simply waved his hand to dismiss David.

"I'll call you later Larry." David left the room knowing he had incurred a certain amount of hostility from the board members because of his off-handed handling of the matter. Time was of the essence and he needed to get to the hospital quickly.

"David! This is a pleasant surprise, I'm becoming bored just lying here, I need to be active and even your esteemed company is very welcome." The tubes in Norman's nose had been earlier removed and so he now looked half human once again. The drip to his arm was still in place.

"How're things going with you?"

"As you can see, they've got rid of some of the pipe work and the doctors seem pleased with my recovery and to top that I even had my first decent meal this morning, although they mashed everything, makes me feel like a baby once again. I feel as if I'm reliving some kind of childhood."

"That's good, you are getting you sense of humour back again, you are going to need it."

"You didn't come here to enquire about my health, did you? What's wrong?"

"No I didn't, I received a call from the bank this morning, they're easing off." Norman grinned knowingly.

"I told them it was only a blip and that we would be back on course before long."

"Don't count your chickens... Read this." He handed the patient a copy of the email.

"Shit! They don't let up, do they? How the hell did they find out about Martins? Somebody's feeding them the inside information, I told you, they're after us."

"Norman, this is a serious allegation and the media's going to have a field day tying the whole thing together. It looks like a very juicy story from their point of view. We have time, let's get out of this before the thing breaks onto the street."

"No ways."

"If the shares drop again, which believe me they most certainly will, the bank is going to come down hard on us and they could possibly bankrupt you."

"You think so?"

"I know so, this news when it breaks will cause absolute chaos. You've got two options open to you as I see it, you sell or you resign from Martins immediately so that you're not seen to have any interest within the bookmaking industry. Either way you're going to be branded as the fall guy and will have to carry the can and pay for the shortfall."

"Call Marcus and sell our shares within Martins immediately. you do it from here now so that when the story breaks I can hold my hand on my heart and say that I no longer have anything to do with bookmaking." David called Bernard Marcus.

"Bernard confirm a bid for Martins immediately and call me back at this number." He gave the lawyer Norman's bedside number, David pulled up a chair as they waited. The telephone rang.

"Yes Bernard. What? How much? They're crazy, try the others and I'll call you back in a moment." He replaced the receiver.

"They already know, the price has dropped to nearly forty per cent of the original price. We've lost the gamble."

"No we haven't, I'll show you." David called Roy Bradley at the newspaper.

"Roy. Thanks for the warning, would you please do me another favour? Print a front page story that I only acquired Martins late last week and that I'm attempting to sell off the gambling side to retain only the leisure activities. I'm currently in negotiations with a European buyer and make sure you stress the word *European*. Deny, deny and deny again, that I needed Martins for their bookmaking activities, that's your lead story and the reason for someone taking a shot at me because I outbid the Americans and then told them I was breaking up Martins. Roy get this out immediately, we've got to beat the Yanks by admitting that I purchased Martins. Get it on the 'Media Hotline' immediately so that the television and the other papers run the story, its got go viral. Better still, I'll get our friend, the Chief of Police to confirm that they are following up leads in that direction."

"Quite finished Norman."

"Yes."

"You're asking me to purge myself?"

"Not at all, I'm telling you to find the truth."

"And what you've told me, is really the truth?"

"It is, check with the Chief of Police."

"That's another favour you owe me, it's a great angle, so I'll run it. If I find that you have been involved, I'll hang you out to dry, believe me."

"Thanks Roy." Norman called his friend in the police and gave him a story about an American dealer who had tried to outbid him and phoned several times threatening him.

"The newspapers are way ahead of you on this so you better tell them you have been following it up." He replaced the receiver and turned to David.

"You and Rhona heard the threats, didn't you?"

"Norman, now you're really playing with fire."

"I'm gambling for my life and the banks will go mad, but when they see what is really going to happen, I'll then become their blue eyed boy. Clever, isn't it? No boxing mafia bastard is going to drive me into the ground. Phone Bernard and tell him to tell his client to stuff their offer. David immediately called.

"Bernard, the deal's off, now tell your client, we're not giving Martins away. Watch this space, the fun's about to begin and war's been declared. Norman thinks you've suckered him and now he's going to fight."

"I'll let them know immediately." David looked at Norman enquiringly. Norman shook his head to indicate that he need say nothing more. David put down the instrument.

"That was good, I think you could've put the wind up that friend of yours, let them know who's taking the lead. Any bets, Bernard will be back within hours with a decent offer."

"Let's hope your plan works. It's going to be a trying day. Larry Margoles, Muggeridge and the rest are going to have apoplexy if they find out what has taken place."

"That's your problem. I'm ill and you're going to have to face a baptism of fire, let alone thunderbolts on you own."

"Well, I better get back and alert the troops and also the bank Gods in that case." David made tracks, leaving Norman to contact some more multi-millionaire financial friends to call in outstanding favours.

"That's the whole story, it's up to you now." Sitting opposite Christine and explaining the story were Sandy and Julie, they held hands like two naughty children having been caught out and were now awaiting their punishment. Christine weighed up everything that had been said without saying anything for some time and although she knew of Julie's involvement, this admittance out of the blue had come as a total surprise.

"I should be mad and call in the police, your story is like a tale from a book, I just don't believe we could have been duped this way."

Christine decided not to let on that she knew or tell Jean anything of value in case she was trying to find out more than she already knew.

"What to do? It is only right that I should want revenge, but against that, you could've kept quiet and I wouldn't be any the wiser about the whole saga and I have to commend you for that at least. Have you told me everything?"

"I think so, I'm going to hand in my notice today."

"Julie, stay on for a while, let's play Minter and company at their own game. Would you do me that favour?"

"I don't really like this type of life. I would rather not."

"A couple of weeks is all I'm asking for."

"I deliberately set out to harm you and probably did but now that you've outsmarted MH Holdings, I don't think they'll be very interested in you in fact, we were given new assignments the day Paul Hunter was killed. But that too, is on hold for the moment."

"Oh? And why is that."

"It's a company that the group has recently acquired, called Martins, you know, the bookmakers and we were told we were to infiltrate Martins and ferret about. Highly unusual that one, apparently, it's the first time that Norman Minter's acquired a company without investigating it first and I suppose he just wants to check the workings from the inside, he trusts nobody."

"I see ...tell me something? Do you know anything about boxing matches held in private because I've heard several rumours about Minter organising such bouts." Christine hoped this question would test Julie's new found truthfulness.

"No, I don't know anything about private boxing matches." Christine was disappointed

"Although, there is a rumour in the office that Minter does occasionally put on fights between gladiators and it's supposedly very bloody but its just a rumour so if he is doing this, it's been kept very quiet."

"What do you mean ...gladiators?"

"I can't tell you much but when a friend of mine found out I worked for Minter, he told me that he had been to one of these bouts, he simply said that it was very bloody and that a fighter had died."

"Can you find out more?"

"I don't know, this friend and I don't move in the same circles, he's very wealthy but I'll see what I can find out."

"Whoa! Don't just go barging in because if Minter is still arranging illegal fights in private, nobody will want to openly admit they have attended. You've got to be very subtle about your enquiries." Christine suddenly turned to Sandy.

"Sandy, we'll say nothing more about what's been going on here, now why don't you leave Julie with me for a little while? You've got your job to see to and as soon as we're finished up here, why don't you take her out for lunch?" She waited until he had left the room before rising and closing the door.

"Now you listen to me, I don't care how you do it, use pillow talk if you have to, but I need information about these illegal fights. You scratch my back and I'll make sure you stay out of prison for your part in this."

"But..."

"No buts, I want to know everything about these fights, where they've been held, names of people attending and most importantly, Minter's involvement. You get that for me and nothing less and I promise, your name will never be mentioned then you and Sandy can get on with your lives, so the quicker you get down to it, the sooner you can get out of this mess." Julie shook her head knowingly, she had played her card by opening her mouth a little too wide and now Christine had her trapped in a vice. She had no alternative but to try and find out about the Kixing tournaments. The only problem was that it had been Rhona that had told her about these supposed bouts that someone else was holding. At the time, Julie had only suspected that it could be Norman Minter until Christine had now confirmed her thoughts. Somewhere in Rhona's files she knew she would find carefully documented lists, times and venues. The only problem was that only Rhona had a key to her inner sanctum and its files meaning that this was going to be the problem.

"I'll do what I can, give me a little while and I'll find out what these fights are about."

"THE KIXING"

CHAPTER TWENTY NINE

"There's pandemonium out there, how are you going to get away tonight?" David, Trevor and Susan were standing at one of the windows looking down upon the entrance below where a pack of photographers and newsmen had begun to encamp at the build's entrance. From the minute that the newspapers hit the streets, wild speculation of Norman's collusion in the fight-rigging scam had become rife. The media wolves wanted a tempting story and the best place to find it other than at the hospital, was from someone at these offices.

"It's not me they're after but, as my being the present company spokesman, I suppose I'll have to face them sooner or later so let's prepare our version of a statement to hand to our friends from the press." Trevor was actually seeking shelter in David's office. Trevor's telephone hadn't stopped since the story broke and he didn't have much of a clue what all the fuss was about so had rushed into David's office to find out. Everyone without exception leaving their building was being hounded, questioned and hassled by the inquisitive pack below. Trevor flopped down into one of the two chairs facing David's desk.

"Right at the moment this attention is just what we don't need."

"I know, but what can we do? It's happened and that's all that matters for now we must simply try to stem the flow. Susan, get your pad and let's draft something for them." It didn't take David long to come up with a statement declaring that the company was in no way involved in the fight and that its acquisition of Martins was to obtain the very healthy and more lucrative leisure industry division within that group and that the company's sole intention was that the bookmaking division was going to be sold off and that MH Holdings was currently negotiating its sale to a European Group.

"I didn't realise we were going to sell off the bookmaking side, that's the most productive division within Martins."

"Norman's orders, it's no good if it is under such severe pressure. Trevor, you know nothing as far as the press is concerned and that also goes for everybody else that works here. Please make sure that the message is understood by all employees before they leave the building, we do not need any speculative guesses flying around as it will simply inflame matters."

"Will do." Susan handed David the short statement which he read through carefully before signing.

"Get about fifty copies run off and I'll take them down to that baying bunch myself." A few minutes later David was standing in front of the group.

"Ladies and gentlemen, as you know Mr Norman Minter is still recovering in hospital and therefore, the company has produced a statement for the press." He handed the batch of copied statements to a fair haired reporter.

"Please hand them around, if you need any more copies, I'll gladly organise for them." There was an instant scramble as everybody raced towards the young man in order to secure one of the pieces of paper.

"What does Norman Minter say to the accusation that he's involved with the Boxing Board to orchestrate championship fights for his underlying company profit position?"

"I cannot answer for Mr Minter, but think that statement clearly explains our position." There was a cacophony of questions that pursued David, who chose not tot answer as he returned to the building. When David reached the safety of his office he took a call from Muggeridge the banker.

"Have you spoken to Norman yet?"

"Yes, directly after I spoke to you and I told him what you said."

"Was it his idea all along to break up Martins?"

"No, it was simply a move to take the heat out of the present situation."

"Do you know what he's done? Investors are scrambling to get out of this Martins debacle again and as we speak, the price is plummeting all over once again. Is he a complete idiot to issue a statement like that?" David heard the man sigh.

"I think we'll have to have a meeting as quickly as possible and fortunately, since the last fiasco, the banks taking over the main responsibility have now also become the main investors, so the downward fall is being seen as a short term thing. But we're bankers, not businessmen and don't want to be saddled with the full burden of Martins' shares. That statement from Minter has only helped to alienate any remaining shareholders and now we the banks, own slightly more than half of the shares and therefore, need a meeting with you to settle this matter once and for all."

"When do you suggest?"

"Can we make it tomorrow morning? I think the MH Holding board of directors should come to a decision and I must also warn you that the bank intends cutting its losses and distancing itself by selling off its stake in this humiliating experience and unless that is, Minter can come up with something to prevent our losses from increasing."

"Like offering the marina as security, I suppose?"

The Kixing

"That would help."

"Pencil in a meeting at these offices for eleven and I'll talk to Norman before that to see whether he can offer you anything. Okay?"

"Good, we look forward to meeting you tomorrow." David replaced the receiver realising that possibly this was now turning out to be the painful baptism of fire that Norman had earlier referred to. Susan poked her head around the door.

"Norman's on the line."

"Just give me a half a minute for me to gather my thoughts then put him through." The telephone on his desk rang.

"Norman, sorry but that was Muggeridge on the line."

"Whining and howling, I suppose."

"Not really, but warning that they've had enough and want to pull out of the deal."

"Why? We've got the thing to steady itself."

"The statement about breaking up Martins has not met with their approval."

"Their approval? It's our bloody company now, we can do what we want to."

"Not entirely accurate, behind our backs it would seem as if they have quietly been purchasing the shares and now own a larger block of shares than you do. That means they can dictate company policy and they intend to do just that which means that we will have to take up their shares at inflated prices or alternatively they intend selling Martins and taking the loss."

"They can't."

"They can and will and you'll be landed with owing them for the financial shortfall. In order to steady the marketplace it would seem like we've all taken more than a fifty per cent loss due to this fall in share price and it could become even worse."

"So what does Muggeridge want?"

"That somehow, for you to take up the full compliment of shares."

"Christ! The only way to do that is the marina project, we'll be into Martins for over three hundred and fifty million. That's ridiculous."

"What do I tell them? They've insisted on a meeting here tomorrow morning."

"Try to stall them David, the various holding companies used by the American shareholders have already begun offloading their blocks of shares in order to force the price down and all that has happened is that our so-called friends at the banks became greedy and in the interim have picked them up instead. Ask the bank for some form of leeway to offload some of the shares, that way, we'll be able to reduce our input."

"The banks aren't stupid, they've already taken a hiding and I don't think they'll fall for that."

"David, just do it! We need time to weather this storm and the share price will rise again."

"I think you're simply enlarging the hole you've dug for the company."

"Maybe, or maybe not, we'll have to wait and see. Don't lose your nerve because first we've got to get the bank to agree to our request and next we have to stabilise the investor trust. Anything else happening?"

"The news has broken and reporters are camping on our doorstep,

I gave them a statement, shall I read it to you?"

"Yes." David read out the lines as written. "That's very good, perhaps next time fob them off with the old trick of stalling for time by saying that we cannot add anything because of the impending enquiry then perhaps they'll go away and concentrate on the Boxing Boards. I think we've come through this almost unscathed."

"Hopefully."

"Call me tomorrow once you've completed your meeting with Muggeridge."

"Sleep well Norman."

"Minter's almost neutralised our key move at one fell stroke, I told you that he was slippery. What happens now?" Antonio had seen the television report and immediately called by Christine. She had gone to his fortified house straight from the office.

"It presents a problem but not an insurmountable one. Let's wait a couple of days and see what transpires."

"You're always so very calm, by the way how is your daughter taking the news of Hunter's death."

"As I thought she would, she's strong and when she found out what he was up to, she's simply dismissed him as a wasted part of her life."

"Have you told her about your husband?"

"Not yet, but I will, when the time is right and when we meet up because there are some things that need to be said face to face and not on the telephone. I would have preferred to leave it until the end of the year but with all this going on something might come out, it's better that I talk to her alone at the first opportunity so don't worry and leave that to me."

"Si, I agree and your brother, how is he now?"

"Grumbling a lot, although he should be grateful he's got something to moan about in fact at the moment he's just like a big baby. I think he's getting bored sitting around all day."

"I know how he feels."

"Now Minter, what else is happening?"

"I don't like this report of him splitting the business and selling off pieces because we need it back as one entire entity, not broken up. We've waited until the market price started dropping and then sold off blocks of shares at a very good and profitable price and right now, we've also managed to sell everything we own well above their true market value. It's been an absolute killing and as agreed, your family gets half of that profit and that, makes you an extremely wealthy woman in your own right. But Signora, the American family wants the business back and intact, not split up."

"Who's acquired the balance of the shares, is it Minter?"

"Oh no, so far its all gone to the large institutions, my guess is that it is probably those that are backing him. We have manipulated the marketplace and forced the price down quite low so far, Minter must be hurting and must owe the banks a fortune by now."

"He carries a fair bit of financial clout does our Norman Minter. They'll simply restructure this debt, somehow we must cause more panic to try to get the institutions to sell Martins shares to one of our other companies. Antonio, this is so much fun, its like a huge financial chess game and at present by us outthinking them, we're making millions for buying and selling our own business. This is not a battle for the streets, its a struggle of wits, win that and we automatically own the streets without any bloodshed."

"If he breaks it up, it won't be."

"I know, so we must continue to prevent that somehow. I tell you what, offer to buy all the shares at their current market price as I see the picture, we'll have already made roughly a hundred and fifty million out of Minter to date and if they take the bait, Minter will then have lost that money to us and will have to repay it to the bank, he'll be in so much financial trouble that we can make our move on him."

"What about the Boxing Boards?"

"Keep up the pressure until we get Martins back under our control. I've still have a few more cards to play because Minter won't slip away that easily."

"The banks will scream if we come back with an offer just after we've sold our shares, there'll be some sort of an enquiry."

"I know, this time I want us to make the offer in the name of *'Jay and Jay Trust'*."

"But Signora, that way, he'll soon know you're involved."

"Exactly so, like an octopus, we've carefully wound our tentacles around the man and now he cannot escape now, so we start tightening out grip very slowly to strangle him. It's time for us to reveal ourselves and for him to know who's placed him in this trap. He'll kick and scream, he may even try putting up a last minute fight, but Mr Norman Minter's as good as dead."

"It's very dangerous for you to show your hand."

"Possibly but he must learn to suffer the errors of his ways."

"I know he's devious but, he's also a very dangerous person to cross and I'm sure he was behind your brother's so-called accident. When he finds out, you too, are going to be in terrible danger."

"That's where you street fighting knowledge will have to come in, if his people try anything funny, then we'll get them, won't we?"

"No Signora, this is very bad thinking, we can protect you and your brother only so far, we may not be able to stop these people in time to prevent your death."

"Then, so be it, but we've got to clean up the system, if the family are to build up and stand on their own in Britain. By taking out one of the main pillars of society this way, we will have posted our intention to the rest of the world. Do you understand? Our people are all out there just watching and waiting, if we fail, then they'll have no respect for us." Antonio rubbed his knee.

"Si, I understand and I'm going to place more people around you and your brother just to make sure."

"Make sure they're discreet, we don't want to chase Minter's men away and now my old advisor, I must leave you. I've got an ailing brother to feed."

Several people were gathered around Norman's bed and there was almost a party air, someone had slipped a bottle of Champagne into the ward while others had sneaked crystal glasses into his private room.

"Cheers, this is more like living." Norman raised his glass to his friends. Rhona was seated on the end of his bed because this was the first day that he had been allowed more than two people visiting him at any one time. The nurse hovered around for a few minutes and then left and now the group were able to relax into party mood and enjoy themselves.

"Here's hoping you'll soon be out of this dreadful place," said one of the young ladies, lifting her glass in salute.

"I am slowly coming around to enjoying myself because it's the first time I've managed a rest in years." A light titter passed around the room and a little later it was the strict nurse that finally broke up the party mood by insisting that Norman needed his rest. The group decided that a meal was in order and left the room, leaving only Rhona to talk to Norman.

"Did you see David on the television this evening? I think he equipped himself quite well."

"Yes he did."

"What's the matter? I know you too well, you've been a little down all evening."

"What are you and Harry up to? He's been in to see you several times over the last twenty four hours."

"How the hell do you know that?"

"I've got my methods, is it about the money he owes you?"

"What money?"

"C'mon Norm, I'm not as green as you may think, you have been fight rigging, again, haven't you?"

"How dare you pry into my business? I will not be questioned like this,. Harry simply welshed on something he was supposed to do for me and now I'm just making sure it gets done correctly, this time."

"Norman, I've always thought you were as clever as your father, but now, I have my doubts. Why do it? ...For kicks?"

"Just leave it alone will you?"

"I've always been there for your family and it pains me to see the vultures gathering, you aren't safe from those around you. It's now that you aren't at the helm that the sharpened knives have come out."

"I know they are, okay, I'll come clean, this time. Yes you're right and Harry does owe me a lot of money, but, not for fight rigging. I didn't have anything to do with the decision."

"Norm, don't treat me like an idiot, I'm not a fool. You fixed the Cataeno-Blair fight somehow, I just know you did. You've got nothing to fear, I won't say anything because it's not my business. What riles me most is that you don't trust me."

"I just didn't want to involve you and I trust you with my life, I'm sorry you feel that way."

"David is subtly levering his way into favour with the other directors but he's also scared of the overall consequences and liable to work against you if it comes to a showdown with this Martins business. I'll keep an eye on them and let you know what's going on tomorrow and meanwhile, I suggest you and Harry stop meeting so regularly. If I can find out so easily, others may put two and two together and come up with the same answer that I have."

"Thanks Rhona. I know I'm difficult sometimes, I often don't know what motivates my actions."

"Greed and power. There's nothing wrong with that, like your father and your grandfather before him, you Minter's all simply enjoy the power game. Personally, I think you've harmed yourself this time and according to David, the banks are going to possibly take away that power and you're not going to be able to stop them. You've lost favour with the class system, but saying that, you're still one of them unless you can use your wealth of contacts to wriggle out of this tight situation."

"Let's wait and see." Norman yawned. "I'm just so tired, it's been a long day and I've managed to counteract the American's threat for the moment. I just hope the banks support me tomorrow. If we can keep the Americans at bay for a while longer, we'll end up having a company so strong that we'll be able to fight them on their own turf. If we fail, well, let's wait and see. It's a pity I'm so hamstrung at the moment and can't be out there personally conducting operations and giving them hell. I feel so useless in here."

"Don't panic, I'll be your eyes and ears out there, is there anything you want done at the moment?"

"Yes. Call Harry and tell him to get on with what we arranged and not to visit me here again. I'll call him and also, check that he's paid the rest of my money into the secret account."

"What money? What job?"

"It's just a little item he's been getting done for me and nothing to do with gambling. Promise."

"Okay then, anything else."

"Don't let David or the board do anything without my say so." Rhona leaned forward and kissed his forehead.

"Consider it done, now you relax and get yourself better. You're strong mentally but your body still needs its rest." On her way out, she met the short man coming into the hospital and stopped him refusing to allow him to go up to Norman's room.

"He's tired out and gave me specific instruction to tell you that you're to go ahead with the arrangements and not to visit the hospital again. Norman will call you." The man stared at her incredulously.

"He told you that?"

"Of course, I'm his personal assistant so why wouldn't he?"

"I dunno, it just never struck me that he would tell anyone about it. You're sure he doesn't want to see me?"

"Harry, go ahead and just do it, have you transferred his funds yet?"

"Yes, the last of it was deposited this afternoon although I did keep back enough to cover my expenses as agreed with Norman."

"Don't play games with him, that's all I can say because he's about as mad as a hornet at the moment and if you carry on messing him about, you're going to rue the day you were born."

"It's not my fault." Harry threw his hands apart in helpless gesture.

"Maybe not, but he's pretty irate."

"I'll get the job done properly this time. I promise." Harry spun around and with a wave of his hand walked quickly through the hospital entrance leaving Rhona to sort out a few details with the front desk.

The Kixing

"THE KIXING"

CHAPTER THIRTY

Christine eased her Jaguar onto the dual highway from the entrance ramp, making sure to keep the car at a constant speed so that the grey Mercedes would be able to catch up to her without problem. Ernest was seated alongside her, after insisting that he was well and now fed up sitting around at home all day with nothing to do. He needed to go into the office today and after much protestation, Christine agreed. She thought that the continuous flow of main stream traffic might hinder her shadow's entry onto the highway and Antonio's few words about her life being in possible danger was mentally being taken very seriously. She looked into her rear-view mirror trying and pick out the vehicle but there were three cars now behind her, the only older vehicle that she noticed was an old battered Vauxhall but, try as she might, could not pick out the old Mercedes.

"Probably the new shift." She muttered quietly, more to herself than at her brother.

"I wish Antonio would tell me when he makes these sudden changes." Christine gently moved the Jaguar into the central lane and kept an eye as the older car followed that mirrored her movement.

"Yes, it's my tail." Her mind now settled as she slowly accelerated, occasionally making certain that her follower was able to maintain pace and for several miles the two moved as if tied together by some unseen magical cord. When Christine slowed due of the density of traffic, the Vauxhall followed suit and as she sped up, the old car moved accordingly, never varying the distance between them. She had become so aware of the pattern that it had almost become second nature by not making any sudden movements or lane changes without first giving her followers fair warning of her intentions.

"It's not like you to drive so carefully."

"I know but I don't want to lose some friends who're following us."

"Following us? Who?"

"Both of us are being watched by some friends of mine, it was them that saved you the other night and it wouldn't help our cause to lose them in this traffic."

"No, I don't suppose it would. Thank God they were there the other night, otherwise I wouldn't be sitting here now. I owe them my life." Christine slipped across into the inside lane and indicated that she was about to leave the highway to save time by taking the backstreets to her office. The old Vauxhall followed suit and without hesitation she exited using the narrowing rise of the road to let the Jaguar run to a stop at an overhead roundabout. Turning left, she moved her car along a narrow suburban road noting that there were still two cars between her and her shadow. Waiting its opportunity, the Vauxhall moved quickly past one of the vehicles and Christine could see that it was trying to overtake the next car to move in behind her.

"Different drivers, different methods, I suppose."

"What?"

"Usually my normal tail follows at a discreet distance, this one is making sure he stays close behind." Ernest started to turn and have a look.

"No don't, we won't let them think we know we're being followed, it'll probably only dent their male egos." The procession moved along

370

the ever narrowing road until it reached an intersection where Christine turned right and was still being followed by three vehicles. With a sudden movement, the Vauxhall moved past the following car and started closing on her, the car now free of the other two behind her suddenly injected pace noticeably, so that it was only yards from the back of her car. Instead of being able to pull into the gap, or falling back to its original position, the Vauxhall kept moving until it was almost level with her Jaguar.

"What's the idiot doing?" Ernest spun in his seat and saw the two men in the other car.

"Get the hell out of here!" He shouted.

"Put your foot down." Without waiting to argue, she instantly gunned her car to move well ahead of the Vauxhall which had been caught by surprise by the sudden acceleration. There was now enough of a gap between Christine and the next car for the Vauxhall to slip into, but it didn't. The driver stayed out on the wrong side of the road and tried to accelerate in order to catch up with the Jaguar.

"These men are idiots." Christine spun her Jaguar left into a narrow side street. The Vauxhall, now, nearly on two wheels entered the road behind her and Christine noticed two more cars doing the same thing.

"Something's not right." Having clear passage ahead, she put her foot to the floorboards weaved and the car through the narrow twists of a typical London backstreet. Ernest turned to see if he could see what was going on.

"Ohhh, shit."

"What?"

"It is them."

"Who? What are you talking about?"

"I think that that's the car that tried to run me down!"

"What?"

"Yes, I'm sure it is. Don't let it catch up to us because they're probably armed." Christine was approaching an intersection and was in two minds mainly because there were three cars in her wake with nowhere to overtake. If she slowed, the Vauxhall would be upon her in seconds and God knew what would happen then but she had a good idea and that made up her mind in an instant. As she reached the narrow intersection, she slowed just enough for her following to come racing up from behind, then Christine gunned the car, hoping the driver would think she was going straight across. Her plan worked, the vehicle was going too fast when she swung the steering wheel hard to the left at the last second her Jaguar missing a parked car by a mere hair's breadth. The following driver instantly realised his mistake and that he wasn't going to make the turn successfully and Braked into a skid that brought it to a halt across the intersection.

"Got you!" Christine screamed joyfully as she accelerated down the road.

"Now, let's see if you can catch me." Ernest looked across at his twin and saw something that made him panic slightly for instead of the expected fear etched on her face, there was a look of sheer delight and triumph at what had just been achieved, he understood that his sister was now actually enjoying herself.

"Be careful!" Ernest spun around just in time to see that one of the chasing vehicles had rocketed straight into the Vauxhall pushing it sideways across the intersection. There was a loud crunch as the impact between the two cars and a third non participating parked vehicle happened very quickly.

"It's okay! They've crashed." Christine looked into the mirror at the fast disappearing chaos she was leaving behind it was then that the third car in the following line suddenly swung into view, she instantly knew that it was now heading after her. Again, she put her foot to the floor and raced down the road as fast as she could manage the powerful Jag. At the first intersection she swung left, at the next, right before her follower had even appeared in her rear view mirror. Christine followed the zigzag pattern for several roads until she was sure she had lost her tail, only then did she ease off and again made her way in the direction of the Johnson Interior's office. On route, she called Antonio.

"Where the hell is my backup?"

"Hey? They should be with you."

"They're not, somebody has just tried to run us off the road and my brother is sure it's the same people that tried to kill him the other night."

"Signora, where are you?"

"On my way to the office, thankfully two of them crashed, there were three cars following me. I've lost the third and I'm not sure whether to go to the office or not, they may be waiting for us.

"Find a safe place like a parking garage and wait there, don't go to the office yet. I'll find out what the hell is going on and will call you straight back. Wherever they are, I'll get one of our men to meet you at the office when you arrive. Don't worry Signora." Christine pulled into a vacant parking spot in a multi car park.

"Got a cigarette?" She asked.

"You haven't smoked for year, stuff it, I need one as well." Both twins hardly smoked at all but now Christine noticed that her brother's hands were both shaking as he attempted to light up two cigarettes at once.

The Kixing

"Don't worry, we're safe for the moment and troop reinforcements are on their way."

"It's like a m-most terrible nightmare and what the hell do they want from me? Who are they? What have I ever done to them?"

"It's not only you, its both of us that they want out of the way." The car phone whined its loud pitched scream, Christine pushed a button on the steering wheel and Antonio's voice filled the vehicle.

"Good news Signora, we now have your brother's attempted killer under wraps, that was them trying to run you off the road."

"Oh, great, so where were your men right now?"

"I don't know if you saw two other cars, those were supposed to be your guards but they were caught off balance when those bastards made their move. Well, one of our people smashed into them and they're on their way here with the two pigs now, I will give them my personal attention but as for our other car, it reports that it lost you. My man says you're wasted running a business, instead you should become one of our drivers." Christine heard Antonio's relieved chuckle.

"They're making their way to your office right now."

"Where was the Mercedes?"

"It stayed outside your house. keeping an eye on everything, we don't want any nasty surprises."

"I certainly had one this morning. Antonio, you must inform me when you make these sudden changes to the plan, my brother and I could have been killed today."

"Si, Signora. I'm sorry, but at least we now know you're aware of things going on around you and not a screaming, hysterical female like most women would have been under similar circumstances."

"Antonio, you're an old sexist, anyway, I'm heading for the office now, make sure that we don't have any more cock-ups like this one in future."

"Amen to that." Ernest interjected.

"Si Signora, I did not realise you were open speaker, How are you Ernest? I'll call you both as soon as we find out what this is all about and whether Minter's involved."

"Oh there's no doubt of that." Christine started the Jaguar and drove at a sedate speed to the office where she dropped her brother at the front door before moving around to the back of the building and parking the car in its usual space. As she locked up, she examined all the other cars and everything seemed to be in order, she patted the Jaguar lovingly.

"Good girl, you and me, we'll show them." She walked through the factory and called out to her contracts foreman to join her in her in the office. It was as if nothing out of the ordinary had happened that morning.

Larry Margoles followed David and the three officials from the bank into Norman's office. Rhona took up her position beside David as the rest of the board of MH Holdings found seats at the massive table while Norman's seat was again left unattended.

"Right gentlemen, as you know, Mr Muggeridge and his associates are here to discuss Martins. Apparently and if I understand it correctly, they are now at least equal shareholders of Martins. Is that correct?" Muggeridge a tall thin framed man, nodded his head.

"Because of last week's fight and the accusations hurled at us, present shareholders have abandoned their holdings which, in order to keep the price at a stable level, the banks have bought up. The consortium want to float the shares onto the market and are willing to take the loss just to get out of Martins. Have I read the situation correctly, so far?" Again Muggeridge nodded. It was Larry that spoke up for the first time.

"What happens to us then?"

"I've spoken to Norman and he wants to stay aboard because he feels that everything will settle down and the shares will once again move up. However, against that if the institutions are seen to bail out, nobody's going to want to invest, no matter how good the company is. Right now, we're caught with one foot on the wrong side of the financial river and if, like the bank, we start selling, we take a thunderous loss which will take us years to recover from. On the other hand, should we hold on to Martins, two things are going to happen." His attentive audience hung onto his every word. "First, if we leave the bank's shares to find their own market level, they may plummet substantially, thus compounding our financial problem. In other words, we could find ourselves being liquidated if they fell low enough. On the other hand, if we take up the shares ourselves, we would have to find the necessary capital to purchase those shares that the banks have already acquired." The room remained quiet as each member calculated the ramifications of what had just been suggested.

"What does Norman suggest?"

"He doesn't, not until I've reported back what this meeting has to say about it." Muggeridge spoke for the first time.

"Gentlemen, we don't want to throw away money, nor do we want to put MH Holdings under this sort of excessive pressure but, you must understand, we've got protect our client's position and hindsight tells us we've made a grave mistake. There's no use holding onto a bad investment, we're not speculators we've received orders to get out as cleanly as possible. Now, we're looking to you to come up with some proposals in order to get out of this and need positive suggestions that we can take away with us." The board was dumbfounded all looking towards Larry, hoping that he had come up with an idea.

"What you're saying is that we're onto a hiding no matter which way we go?"

"In effect yes, unless you find a way to acquire the Martins' shares from us." The telephone on Norman's desk rang and David tried to ignore its interruption until Rhona finally answered it.

"David, it's Bernard Marcus."

"Tell him I'll call him back." She passed on the message.

"He says he needs to talk to you urgently it has something to do with Martins." As one body, everybody at the table suddenly took an interest in the telephone.

"I'll take it on your line." David excused the delay and went to Rhona's office. Almost five minutes went by before he returned.

"That call possibly opens a third option to us and I'll first have to discuss it with Norman, but roughly speaking, it could be that that call could solve all our problems."

"How?" It was a much relieved Muggeridge that asked the question.

"Basically, someone is prepared to purchase all the shares above market value. I can't reveal any more just yet until I've discussed it with Norman. I'm sorry to do this to you again but, could we postpone this meeting until this afternoon. Why don't you go and have lunch? We'll pick up the tab, and we can reconvene at, let's say, three o'clock."

"It's in all of our interests, so why not wait and see?" Muggeridge tried to add a little relief to the surroundings as David began collecting his files together.

"Larry, a word before you leave please." When the others had left the room, David turned to Larry.

"Try to get them soaked, we're going to need all the advantages we can muster. Maybe, if they're not altogether in this matter, we could gain extra concessions that they would not normally give away."

"I understand, was that call simply a ploy, or was it for real?"

"That was real all right, we're not off the hook by a long way, but it could change the entire perspective of our loss. Go on now and please remember to try to give us an extra edge somehow, these blokes are not playing, they can sink us tomorrow if they really wanted to." Neither said anything when David joined Rhona as she walked along the long corridor to Norman's private ward. David pushed open the door for her to enter first.

"Hello Norm, how're you today?" "This is a lovely surprise and don't you two have a company to run?"

"David's suspended the board meeting to talk to you and I thought I had come along for the ride, and ...to fluff up your pillows."

"Playing truant? Oh well, no harm done, it's almost lunch time anyway so tell me, what's up?" David opened his file and extracted a hand written sheet for reference.

"You're not going to like this but it's a possible solution to our problems though."

"Uh, uh, here comes trouble, all right let's have it."

"Bernard Marcus called. Now get this, Jay and Jay Trust have made an offer for the entire Martins setup at about sixty per cent of its original purchase price and their offer stands for twenty four hours only."

"Hey? I told you that bitch was behind this. No ways even if she offered one hundred per cent!"

"Don't knock it out of hand, there are merits." The full realisation of what had been said struck Norman and he shut his eyes and leaned back into his several layers of pillows.

"What merits do you mean? They've well and truly stitched me up this time, haven't they?"

"They probably don't even know you're involved."

"Don't be so naive David, of course they know and somehow they have tricked us into thinking they were simply a small company, when all the time they were heavily backed. That bitch is probably laughing up her sleeve right at this moment, but, not for much longer. I'll show her who has the last laugh."

"What do you mean?'

"Nothing... okay, what's their deal?" David outlined the full offer as Bernard had conveyed it to him and left out nothing.

"Sell. Make the bank an offer which will restructure our debt over fifteen years. You were right in the first place, I should've left this deal alone when I had the chance to walk away and you warned me but now its too late to do that, you were worried that it stank to high heaven. Jesus, that's over a hundred and forty million we've lost in a little over a fortnight, my reputation as a fight promoter is in question, I could lose my boxing licence, and someone's trying to kill me. What more can go wrong?" Rhona took hold of Norman's hand, it was ice cold.

"Do you want me to try to force the price up, I could possibly get the banks to hold off selling when they see Bernard's offer."

"The offer is only valid for twenty four hours and if you can't get the banks to commit themselves to long term backing, don't waste the chance. That is probably the best deal we're going to get without putting the entire marina in jeopardy." David nodded.

"Rhona, get hold of Harry urgently and tell him to hold off on that thing we discussed last night. Tell him that I'll contact him when the time is right, but for now, he is to hang fire."

"Do you want me to stay with you today Norm? I can call him from your phone."

"No. I need to be left alone to think this one through. Shit,! All those long years of hard work gone up in smoke in two weeks and now, we'll have to start from the beginning again." David and Rhona left Norman to reflect on his ill fortunes and headed straight back to the office. It was going to be tough sorting this one out with the banks unless Larry had done his job properly, Rhona was the only one to say anything on their way back to the office.

"Although he didn't show it this matter has knocked him sideways. You can't but feel sorry for him and I hope he doesn't try anything stupid." David simply nodded in agreement.

"THE KIXING"

CHAPTER THIRTY ONE

"Jean, would you mind dropping Ernest off at my house on your way home? There are a few things that need doing urgently and I must attend to them." Christine was in Ernest's office when she posed the question.

"No, not at all, it'll be my pleasure." Once Jean had left the office, Ernest turned on his sister.

"Are you mad, or what?"

"Why?"

"It was only this morning that people were trying to kill us and now, you go jaunting off around the sites on your own, I feel that's being very irresponsible, don't you think?"

"Not really, I have heard that those men are safely out of the way and anyway, as you have already witnessed, I can take care of myself."

"Be careful Chrissie, it only takes one slip and you could end up dead."

"I will, but don't worry little brother." With that, she swept out of the office and through the factory to the back door and before leaving the safety of the building, she cast a careful look around the car park finding nothing seemed out of the ordinary. She couldn't see any sign of her protectors at that moment, but this didn't worry her unduly and she walked across towards her car.

"Christine!" She spun around, nerves suddenly stretching every fibre in her body although it was only Jim, the foreman. She breathed a sigh of relief as the burly man raced across to her. He simply wanted instructions about one of the contracts and she spoke to him as they walked to her car.

"Night then."

"Night Jim, see you in the morning." Christine pulled out of the car park and searched her mirror for any sign of her followers, there weren't any. This began to worry her once again so she called Antonio.

"Where is my tail?"

"They should be there." His voice portrayed a slight touch of anxiety, that is when she saw them, the Mercedes pulled out of a side street behind her.

"It's okay, they're here now."

"That's good, I'll see you in a short while." Her eyes continually searched the surrounding areas as she made her way towards the large white house. Even if she didn't admit it outwardly, this morning's fiasco had slightly frightened her and only once she was inside the large house she found that there was quiet relief within her body.

"Signora, we now know the full story, these bunglers have decided to tell us everything."

"Who were they?"

"Just some small time crooks, they run a little betting shop and we became interested in them because it was from there, that Minter laid his bets on the fights that he fixed. The old man named Harry, runs the place together with his son, Billy and they were beginning to expand and move away from their normal activities and thought that with Minter's backing, they had entered the big time. Billy was in the car when it crashed this morning, he's been very kind and doesn't like any form of our ...let's say persuasion. He told us everything we wanted to know."

"All right, so what did he tell you?" Antonio explained the complete story of the fight and how Minter had laid off his large bets as he spoke he also milked the story for all its worth. Then he began the story of how Minter, from his bed, had paid the father ten per cent of his winnings as a desperate measure to have the Johnson twins kidnapped so that he could then gain control of their business.

"So, it had nothing to do with our attack on him?"

"It would seem not and I think we should dispose of Norman Minter right away. Even though he's in hospital, as you can see, he's still extremely dangerous."

"No because by now, he knows exactly who's behind his failure and if he wanted to kill me before, he is now going to have second thoughts. He's embarrassment is almost complete so relax, he'll worry us no longer, no Antonio, you leave Norman Minter to me."

"Si but, we can't watch over you for twenty four hours every day. It just wouldn't be safe."

"I know just a few more days and then Mario and company can go home and take a well earned rest."

"Hey?"

"I told you, the whole saga is almost at an end, Minter's on the verge of folding."

"Yes I would agree, last night I had a call telling me they were prepared to sell Martins back to us at the agreed price. We've made over one hundred and forty million on the deal and half of that really belongs to you. You're a very wealthy woman, what do you want me to do with the money?"

"Ah, don't do anything with any of the profits we've made just yet because we're going to use it for the good of the family. I've just got to work out some of the finer details and only then, I'll let you know what to do with it."

"Another venture Signora?"

"Not another, shall we just say ...it's a continuing one." She patted Antonio's knee in friendly gesture. He walked her to her car and Christine noted for the first time today that he had abandoned his walking stick. Unconsciously she kept checking the mirror as she drove straight to her house. Her daughter's car was parked under the lean-to at the side of the garage, this made her smile at a pleasant surprise because she wasn't due until the weekend Christine thought, as she moved her car in beside Ernest's Porsche in the garage.

"Hello the house!" she called, as she closed the door and placed her bag against the wall.

"We're out here!" She made her way to the swimming pool. Ernest, Jean and Tracy-Anne were comfortably seated in the lounging canvas chairs. She could see from Jean's hair that she had been in for a swim and her daughter's hair was also damp. For the first time ever, she suddenly felt the little green monster of jealousy creeping into her system. Iced tentacles touched about every sinew as she slowly walked towards the trio.

"Had a swim, Jean?"

"The water's lovely, I hope you don't mind?"

"Why should I mind?" She lied. "Tracy-Anne suggested it and even let me borrow one of her swimming costumes." Jean winked at Christine and smiled as if the two of them had a secret between them. Christine laughed. It was partly from sheer relief, but, she wasn't quite sure why she should be upset.

The Kixing

"There's something I must tell you two, you're very lucky I wasn't here, you all know that the rule of the house is that everyone swims nude." Everybody laughed.

"Yeah! Yeah!" Ernest taunted playfully. "I cannot swim with my plaster on, so I'll give marks out of ten." Again they laughed and the heavy atmosphere was again relaxed when Christine dragged another chair to the poolside.

"Will you stay for dinner Jean?"

"Love to." Tracy-Anne had not been her jovial self all through dinner and only once Jean had left, Christine called her daughter aside and asked her what was wrong and why she was at home.

"There's something been worrying me ever since Paul's death and I couldn't do anything constructive with my life until certain questions were answered so, I decided to meet them head on and that's why I'm here, you and need to talk it through with you."

"That sounds ominous."

"To me it is serious and once uncle Ernie's gone to bed, why not let's go upstairs and talk, all night, if we have to."

"What about?"

"Something doesn't ring true about Paul's death, did you have anything to do with his dying?"

"What do you mean, have anything to do with it?"

"Exactly what I mean, I'm not stupid and I've known for years that my father was somehow involved in some kind of underworld activity. So I ask again, did you arrange for Paul's death? That's all I want to know."

"Ahh, so that's it and Tracy my darling, I think it's definitely the time that we had that talk." Christine placed her arm around her daughter's shoulder.

"Come, we'll talk this through, but, I want Ernest to hear what I have to say as well this is family business and never to be mentioned to any outsider." Christine turned off the television and sat next to her daughter.

"Ernest, it's time to reveal my true self to both of you because Tracy has just posed the question to me whether I had anything to do with Paul Hunter's death. The answer is a definitive no, well, not directly. I've never arranged for anyone to be killed, there are far more subtler ways of dealing with terrible and crooked people." She hesitated while waiting to see what their reaction was. Nothing, so she took her courage in hand and proceeded into what she knew was going to be the difficult part.

"Let's go back to my marriage, I went into it a little blind, although sensing that something wasn't quite right so never asked the right questions and only afterwards found out that your father was what the outside world call a... *'Godfather'.*" She was looking straight at her daughter.

"Godfather? Mafia Godfather?" Tracy-Anne said.

"Anyway, after many fights, he agreed to tell me everything, and he did. There was always one proviso in that we tried our level best to always keep you protected form this side of our life, it was extremely difficult to maintain. When he died, the family was in total disarray and were battling among themselves because they did not have an immediate replacement for him but he had seen that his ideals would come apart so before he died he had arranged that I become a sort of *'Godmother'* to the family until I was happy with his successor. That has been my role for the last few years. I have a person in mind that was able to succeed your father, but it would still take a while before I will hand over your father's legacy completely."

"Why?"

"The men of the family are steeped in tradition, it also takes time for thought patterns to change. There are those who still glorify the old ways of blood, and then there's a new high-tech breed, which is what we need, who work by stealth in the background and could only use killing as an extreme measure or last resort. Changing times mean that people of this family are sophisticated businessmen and not thugs and it's now more about business and honour. Lately, I've tended to guide things only when it needs a final decision, or when one of our senior people stray away from the new family ideals."

"Y-you're mafia, that's what you're saying, isn't it?" Tracy-Anne's outburst was surrounded by disbelief.

"Yes my darling and you too, are part of part of the family. Let's say that it's your destination."

"What? Never."

"I spoke about honour and there's a very strict code among the family and although I've tried to protect you, in the family's eyes you broke the code and as a result, Paul died."

"M-me, cause Paul's death? How? No, no, don't push it back on me, that's evil." Surprise in her voice shot out of the door as Tracy-Anne's defensive streak came into play.

"You must believe that I did not order Paul's death but when you started sleeping with him, the family were busily investigating something else that he was up to and incidentally, it was totally unconnected with you. A promise to protect all of us had been made to your father on his death-bed by several associates and that very promise, was upheld to the letter of the law by the family without my knowledge. I only learnt of it after it was done. I suppose that if they had told me about it beforehand, I would have objected violently and they wouldn't have done what they did. It's this old fashioned thinking, I know but, it is combined with their code of honour that made them take matters into their own hands."

"Shit! This cannot be for real we're not living in medieval times. Tell me what happened." Christine told her daughter everything she knew, about Norman Minter trying to take over Johnson Interiors, right up to what had happened at Antonio's house.

"Your past and unfortunately you present are inexorably tied to my duties as were your fathers' to mine. You are going to have to live with that knowledge whether you like it or not. I'll try to keep you away from it, but, I can't promise that I can. Do you understand?"

"Me, a crook's daughter? What do your parents do? Oh, nothing really, they just extort, pimp and kill people, no big deal. I can accept most things, but this, it's revolting. This makes me sick and ashamed!" She raced from the room before anyone could say anything. Ernest sat totally dumbfounded, he had always suspected that Christine's husband was mafia, but his twin being in the role of Godmother, never.

"Well Ernie, what do you think of your big sister now?"

"Shattered. Shall I go to Tracy?"

"No don't, rather let her go away and ponder about it on her own for a while. It's a huge amount to take in that your gentle mom suddenly now turns out to be allied to gangsters. She needs quite a lot of time to think it through." After a few minutes later they heard the front door slam as Tracy-Anne stormed out of the house, got into her car and drove away.

"Why?"

"Why what?"

"Did you become involved with the... family?"

"Because relationships are a partnership and as hard as I fought against my husband for my independence and to be your partner in business, so I remained committed to him and all he stood for. When I enter a partnership, it's for life, maybe it has something to do with being one of a twin. I'm now totally given over to you, both in business and relationship. After much thought, all we've done is to complete the partnership which we first began as children. Our commitment to each other has always been there, even if it was interrupted for marriages and children. I'll never break this partnership again."

"I wouldn't dare." Ernest retorted sarcastically Christine smiled. She knew that for all his attempts to make light of the matter, he was hurting, confused and afraid.

"I'm worried about Tracy so why don't you go after her Christine?"

"Tracy's a tough nut, in some ways, she's just like me, she's like an erupting volcano. There will be fire, thunder and explosions before any settling down period. She's a fully grown beautiful woman and only needs time to work it out in her own mind will do. This could take days, weeks or even months, but eventually, she'll come to terms with her position in life. I just hope I'm not underestimating her mental strength or her reasoning. Do you know that Tracy asked to change her name to Johnson by deed poll?"

"No I didn't. That's great but tell me, will this mean that the Cicirelo surname will finally be dead and buried?"

"If, as I suspect, she forgives me, she'll probably insist on it in the near future."

"Thank goodness, the Johnson name will live on."

"Oh, now there is far more than that." Christine said calmly

"What does that mean?"

"That there is no contamination in her Johnson genes, it lives on inside her because she's your daughter?"

"What? You're kidding... how?"

"That last night before I got married and came to your room. You remember that night, right? Well I was purposely unprotected."

"Are you certain?"

"Positive, I've known ever since the moment she was born and my doctor verified via DNA test that it wasn't my husband's baby and you needn't worry because I swore him to silence."

"Why haven't you told me this before?"

"I couldn't because you could have inadvertently done something stupid that would upset the finely balanced apple cart. Honour would have meant your instant death and if anyone ever found out or yet even still finds out, I just couldn't have lived with that on my conscience. We can't even tell Tracy-Anne the real truth, that would break her and the existing relationship between us forever."

"Anyway, I now know that she our daughter, ...that's enough for me." Christine reached over and gave him a loving squeeze on his arm.

"I realise that it must always remain discreet but now we know that she is our daughter and that will always remain our secretive bond." She could see that her bombshell revelation had shaken Ernest to his very core. His head nodded as it swam trying with difficulty, to sort out one astounding fact from another.

"This whole evening has been a total shock to my system and far more devastating than my accident." He certainly knew that this very knowledge wasn't going to heal as easily, as would his broken limb.

At the hospital David sat on the chair while Rhona on the end of Norman's bed relating recent events back at the office.

"Oh sweet Jesus. I'm ruined."

"All Harry told me was, now let me get it straight, something about his son Billy being taken away by somebody that worked for the Johnson woman. What did he mean by that? What were you two up to? Whatever it was Harry now fears that he will never see his alive again, he is incredibly afraid and talking about going to the police and even the media." Norman didn't answer as the nightmare scenario unfolded, terror like he had never known before, seeped throughout his whole system like some deadly creeping virus.

"Norman? Why the Johnson woman? What's really going on?"

"Nothing to concern yourself with but in a desperate and stupid move we tried something to gain leverage and like Martins, it has now ended up in a large pile of the brown stuff. I can't tell you about it, you'll find out soon enough. Well, at least we've offloaded Martins, that's a relief, thank God for small mercies."

"Yes, but at what cost?" David, who had been intently listening to the account of Rhona's cryptic telephone call to Harry wanted to report what happened at the meeting and then be off.

"I know, over a hundred and forty million and it's going to take us years to repay that but I think we can do it."

"Muggeridge wasn't that bad this afternoon, he even gave in to a lot of difficult concessions."

"More like drunk is the way I saw it," interrupted Rhona.

"They were all three sheets in the wind and that way nobody even put forward an argument to your suggestions." David grinned wryly.

"Be that as it may, we've got twenty years to repay and the interest rates are set well below the norm. It's business as usual." Norman leaned forward. For the first time since the night of his shooting, he was now free of drip-feed pipes.

"Not quite as usual, David, I've decided to take a long rest and you're going to be the man at the helm for a while."

"Where are you going?"

"Away, I'm not quite sure where just at this moment." Rhona touched her employer's face.

"You see, somebody has to shoot you to make you take a holiday. David, for years, I've been trying to make him take a break but he would not listen."

"This may not be a holiday, as it is, you're coming with me Rhona."

"What are you talking about?"

"Wait and see." The room fell quiet for a minute. It was David that broke the

uneasy silence.

"What about Martins? Do I get the share certificates signed or will you want to do that?"

"You're the boss for the moment, you do it."

"Anything else?"

"Yes. I don't want to hear anything about work, please have an announcement made that Norman Minter is retiring from the fight promotion business as well. Try and sell that part of MH Holdings. If you can't, then shut it down. It's just another loss and only money so who cares at this stage." It was Rhona's turn to be upset.

"You can't do that!"

"Just watch me."

"But Norman, I love the sport."

"So? With luck and provided I'm still alive, we'll obtain ringside seats to all the main matches and not have the headaches that go with the fight promotion business. Anyway, I'll still retain an interest in my privately arranged fights." For the first time since they had entered he smiled knowingly at Rhona. David stood up.

"Well, if that's all for today, I'm tired and have a business to run tomorrow so I'm off. After he had left Rhona looked deeply into Norman's face.

"What's going on between you and Christine Johnson?"

"Alright, you have a right to know, but not a word to anyone. Promise?"

"Promise."

"I tried to get Harry to kidnap her and those bungling idiots failed."

"But, why?"

"To try to put pressure on her brother to sell Johnsons to me but to our cost we found out that she's the strong one of that pair. When I found out it was them that made the offer for Martins, I simply panicked, but it was too late. Maybe the police will come knocking at my door, who knows? I just hope Billy hasn't said anything about my involvement because the Johnsons could then pull out of the deal if they found out I was behind it."

"That was stupid."

"I know."

"Do you want me to talk to them on your behalf?"

"No, leave it be. If I go to prison, I go to prison and that's all there is to it." Rhona leaned forward and kissed him ever so gently.

"Don't worry, I still love you."

"If I get away with this, I was serious about you and me taking a long holiday."

"I'll be there." She rested her head on his shoulder, making sure not to put pressure on his affected stomach area.

"THE KIXING"

CHAPTER THIRTY TWO

It was nearly ten o'clock before Christine left her office, wary from a long day at work she automatically checked to make sure that her followers were still there and felt a slight warmth ounce of comfort as she picked out the old grey Mercedes pulling out behind her. It didn't take long to reach her destination and as she walked through the main doors and went in search of her objective Christine unconsciously brushed back her hair before entering the room, she knew she looked good today because she had made that little extra effort this morning. With one final deep breath, she pushed open the door and entered to see it's occupant staring unbelievably at her for a second before quite realising who this visitor really was.

"Hello Mr Minter, may I join you?"

"You, who let you in?"

"Nobody, I just walked straight in, you're in a private ward and now off the danger list. I don't think staff now really cares how many visitors you have during the day." Without waiting any longer for him to answer, she drew up the steel framed chair to his bedside and sat down placing a large box of Swiss chocolates on his side table. From his expression, she knew her entry had staggered him because she was probably the last person he had ever expected to see visiting him.

"Beware, Greeks bearing..." He stopped short for a moment. "You've come to gloat, haven't you?"

"Not at all. I've come to have a serious talk and you're going to listen without being flippant or argumentative."

The Kixing

"What if I call a nurse and tell her you're disturbing me?"

"Oh, stop being so childish, it doesn't become you and both of us know full well that you won't really do that. Okay, so you're just highly embarrassed by my presence and I can understand your position for under the same circumstances, I probably wouldn't act any differently." She watched his reaction carefully and could almost see the gear wheels of his mind ticking over trying to decide how best to handle this untimely awkward situation.

"It was you who had me shot, wasn't it?"

"Now. Just why would I do that?"

"To get me out of the way so that you could achieve that magnificent sleight of hand that has cost me a lot of heartache, and money, I might add that I must congratulate you, it was a tremendous piece of work."

"Grow up, I fully realise that you are embarrassed by my presence here, I can also understand your position, because if the boot was on the other foot and it was me in that bed, I probably wouldn't act any differently." She again watched the reactions of her truly beaten foe and again could almost hear the gear wheels of his mind ticking over at a million miles an hour as he tried to fathom her reason for appearing at his bedside or how best to handle this embarrassing state of affairs.

"Have you come to triumph or is there something more sinister about to take place?"

"Why would you even presume that our accomplishment is cause to take any pride in your position, remember it was your greed that started this conflict and now you are the loser. I take no pride in that, it was war, I now need you to surrender gracefully."

"What about Billy are they going to find him drowned in a river or something as equally macabre." She sat and gazed at Norman for a long time, her silence as if playing the role of a cat waiting to strip the mouse to shreds.

"So it was your doing then?

"I'm truly sorry, I tried to stop them you weren't meant to be harmed, just kidnapped."

"That mister Norman Minter was an extremely stupid move on your part and I've had to hold back a large pack of bloodthirsty men that wanted to simply kill you from outset of this calamity. Like Billy, you're very lucky that you aren't six foot in the ground today." His colour went from pale to grey, he knew that he had nowhere to run to because the hunted had now become the hunter.

"What can I say? My actions were those of a desperate man. Call them my death throes but I had always achieved my objective and this time I felt so helpless, I knew, don't ask me how, that somehow you were connected with my downfall."

"If you had not attacked me, you would still be the top dog of your industry." She waited as he searched for words.

"You're correct because I was like a blind man being led by the hand, inwardly I knew where I was heading, but didn't know why I couldn't let go when I realised I was being led towards a cliff top. It was a bad business decision even, greed clouded my vision I suppose." There, he had admitted his downfall and that was what she had wanted to hear from his own lips, his humility was complete, now she could begin the building process.

"It always the same, a bit of power and we think we are gods? As for you, you have lost your empire but that said, I've also come to offer you a business proposal and I know you'll accept because you have no other choice open to you in this matter."

"Oh, oh, here it comes. The shrouded sledgehammer."

"We want full control of MH Holdings."

"Are you nuts? You walk in here as bold as can be, then inform me that you're going to remove my livelihood, it's not on."

"I said nothing about taking away your livelihood, what I said was that we wanted control of your business. As I see it, you have very little alternative and so, you come along gracefully or, we simply remove your business from you even if you do shout and scream."

"Look, I've already lost a fortune, isn't that enough for you? I know that we can survive this catastrophe and even repay that huge loss over a period and to me it doesn't matter any more. What else can you do to me?"

"You will be surprised at what I can still do to you how does having you put away for life sound?"

"Put away? For what, Billy didn't even touch you, did he?"

"No he didn't you would go away for murder."

"What murder? I haven't killed anyone. Is this just another of your carefully planned setups?"

"You say that so glibly, there are quite a few of murders that I'm sure you'll recognise." She drew a folded sheet of paper from her pocket and handed it to him. He immediately recognised the list of dead and maimed men who had taken part in his Kixing tournaments. Julie had been as good as her word and managed to get into Rhona's files and copy the evidence for Christine.

"Where did you get this?" Inwardly he knew that it could only have come from Rhona's files, but he knew that she would never have betrayed him.

"Ah, that would be telling and like you, we have our ways to conduct espionage. You'll notice that the list is pretty comprehensive, dates, venues and of course, the dead men's names. Now, the papers or the police would love to see that catalogue of events together with the comprehensive guest lists that we also have, don't you think?"

"It's a pity that marksman didn't make a better job of shooting me, it would have been quicker than this suffocation. You are thorough, I'll give you that."

"The man that shot you is in our care and happy with his life, at present. He still hates you and you don't want him loose on the streets, do you? No Norman, you won't refuse my alternative suggestion." Norman felt like one his floored boxers knowing at that moment that his attractive foe was just to powerful and now had him at her mercy and that she could do anything she wanted. Christine waited until he had picked himself up mentally, he capitulated awaiting her death blow.

"So, there's nothing more to say or do?"

"Not quite, we both gave each other a good run for our money but in the end, you were simply outclassed, outgunned and outflanked in all departments, believe me, it was a good fight while it lasted."

"I thought you said you weren't going to gloat. C'mon, do your worst."

"I'm not gloating and as I said before, I'm here to offer you a proposal that now I'm sure you reconsider and won't reject out of hand when you have heard what I have to say."

"All right, I'll climb down off my high horse and shut up, so tell me what you have in mind, I have no alternatives left open and incidentally as you can see, I'm not going nowhere."

"Right, first a little history, your grandfather came to this country and started the business, didn't he?"

"Yes?"

"His name wasn't Minter then, but was Guiseppe Minetti before he cleverly had it changed to John Minter after he had been here for several years."

"How did..."

"Never mind about how, that means you're originally of Sicilian ancestry and that will never change and its time for your family to return to its roots mister Minetti. Have you heard of the La Cosa Nostra."

"Of course, who hasn't?"

"Well, that's what you've been up against all along, you were bound to lose the battle because we are an international group and much larger than MH Holdings."

"Jee-sus and I thought I was the Goliath! I suppose you were right, I'm very lucky to be alive, but I thought La Cosa Nostra was an all man's organisation."

"Times and thinking change but the core values remain, now let me tell you my role in all this." She explained the story that she had told to her brother and daughter the previous evening.

"The Mafia? Godmother? Unbelievable."

"So you see, it is my responsibility to make sure that the family grows stronger throughout Europe and we now need versatile leaders with the right background and especially, the correct circle of friends and contacts. You already have these attributes in abundance."

"How does that affect me?"

"Right now, the institutions wouldn't touch you with a barge-pole, however, if you somehow managed to repay the debt immediately, everybody would come flocking back to you. We have the money you lost and are prepared to place it back into MH Holdings immediately if you are prepared to sell the family that large percentage of your shares we will of course leave you with a small amount. Only you and I ever need to know about it, you build the company with our backing and it'll grow even more quickly."

"Just like that?"

"Not quite," she smiled. "What I'm offering you is the chance to prove yourself and reclaim your heritage and to possibly become the head of a family in time. It'll mean far wider reaching power and responsibilities although it will be on a different scale and be almost like running your own company. You've shown you're not scared of making harsh decisions and also demonstrated your skill at avoiding being driven to suicide. I really thought you might do that once confronted with all the facts yesterday."

"Very clever of you, your group could not imagine what it was like to suddenly realise there were no openings to escape through."

"I do know what that feeling is like and don't forget, you tried to do it to us, but, that's now in the past and you've come through the test. I want you to get well and then resume your post and build powerful contacts. You'll have an assistant who will guide you through an initial period until you understand the rules of the family. With your family background, I don't think it'll take long."

"I want to go away for a while."

"Yes, do that, first let the dust settle and then come back refreshed, there's much to do. My suggestion is that you take a break on a lakeside in Italy and while you're away, I would recommend that you learn to speak Italian."

"I already do, my father always insisted on it."

"Excellent, my feelings that you are the correct man for the family is proving to be growing by leaps and bounds."

"Just to think, when I first met you, you simply struck me as being a beautiful tigress. If the truth be known, I rather fancied you then but if only I had only known then, what I know now, I should have walked away." Christine felt a slight warmth spreading through her face.

"My late husband was a far thinking man and in the new order of things, woman have a very definite role to play and those that take us for granted, do so at their own peril. Norman, you and others have also got to learn to change your thinking patterns as far as women and us gentler sex are concerned." For the first time she saw his boyish grin. No longer was she the predator and he the victim, his light hearted smile revealed the relief of escape as well as the new beginning.

"Me a mafia? I wouldn't have believed it ever possible, do you know what the word means?"

" I do have a fair idea but what is your interpretation?"

"Mafia means *'Swank'* and the word La Cosa Nostra means *'Our Affair'*, that just about sums up you and I, doesn't it?"

"I suppose it does to a certain ring to it, and be careful the family will know and mark my words, keep an eye on you, to make sure you fit the bill. Only you and I will know what's on offer because you've got a long road ahead to prove yourself to them and *I know* you'll come through with flying colours, but betray my confidence and that'll destroy my honour and you'll wish you hadn't been born." Her voice took on a sudden chill that Norman hadn't been expecting and he knew that he had overstepped the mark with a suggestive remark and like a lioness, she was making sure he knew who was Chief and who the Indian were with her warning.

"I understand fully and from now on you can count on me."

"Good." She rose and placed her hand on his forearm.

"I'm so glad we had this little talk and that you've accepted your heritage, before long a family emissary will start conducting and helping you to adapt to your new role."

"Aren't you going to give me the name of this person?"

"No, not yet but trust me, I'll make sure you get on well though." She left Norman and made her way home to have lunch with Ernest who had decided to remain at the house and that he had overdone everything by returning to work the day before also, he was still in semi-shock from the announcement that his twin was actively involved in extortion and protection rackets.

"How are things going at the office?" The two sat next to the pool having cold meats and salads, she was desperately trying to get things back into their natural rhythm once again and after last night's bombshell to her own family.

"Well its good, the business is again running itself and Sandy's always there if anything goes awry. Relax Ernie, everything's fine." Suddenly and without warning, Tracy-Anne was there, they hadn't heard her car and she just appeared at the doorway. Christine wanted to rush to her, but held back.

"Are you going to join us for lunch?" Her daughter disappeared and then, as if there had been nothing wrong, reappeared, plate in hand. As she selected items for her meal from the dishes on the outdoor table, she spoke to her mother.

"I've now thought the whole through and trust me, I really feel that I don't want to become involved with crooks and thieves, its just not me, even if you say it's my destiny. Would you object very much if I changed my surname from Cicirelo to Johnson?"

"No my darling, not at all."

"Uncle Ernie?"

"I would be overjoyed, but my girl you, like me, are bound up with your mom's background and it will always be our duty to remain in the distance and lend her our moral support." Tracy-Anne sat down.

"Of course we do and now, seeing it's our truth time, I think we better get everything out into the open so that we can all get on with our lives. When I say truth, I really mean everything out on the table, okay?" Christine knew her daughter's character and also realised that something major was about to descend on them.

"Okay, so what is bothering you?"

"You two, that day when uncle Ernie visited and we were swimming, remember? I forgot my racket and came back here to fetch it and although you two didn't see me, I saw you two going at it." She smiled weakly.

"What?" Christine glanced at Ernest, his face was an absolute picture of despair.

"This has been difficult to say, the least... er, a little complicated." Ernest's teeth were almost rattling audibly but Christine remained calm.

"Then you know we're lovers. I promise you this, that was the first time since I married your father and Ernest was my first lover since he died and although I loved your father very much and never ever betrayed his trust, we decided to get together because I can never marry anyone again."

"Why not?"

The Kixing

"I made a promise made to your father."

"I understand your needs and I'm grown up enough to accept these situations, even if they are of a family nature, it still does not bother me although, it's going on everywhere but will take me sometime to come to terms with your incestuous affair. I also know it was not the only time because the other day I saw you giving him a... let's just say an oral bath. Somehow, it hasn't bothered me because I've always known about it, just seeing the way you act around with each other, its a inwardly woman suspicious thing because... well with me at least, I was comfortable with that thought and it even felt right. I'm not explaining myself very well, am I? As long as both of you now agree to keep your relationship private and not to flaunt it, I'm very happy for you both."

"Thank you my darling. I was going to tell you anyway but last night wasn't the right time."

"One last question and then we drop the whole subject, Right? Am I going to always watched over, no matter where I go and what I do?"

"No, not at all but one thing though, please be a little more discreet, you never know where and what might be seen by the family members. They promised your father solemnly that they would always keep watch over us and they will do that because the family tentacles reach into all forms of society and so you never can tell just who could be watching us and so all I'm asking is for you to be aware of just who you are and what you get up to." Enough said, Christine reached out and lovingly took Ernest's and her daughter's hands, giving them each a gentle squeeze. "

"You know, we feel like a complete family again and believe me I'll go back to university a very much wiser person but, knowing that I have a mother, and ...well, er, what can I call uncle Ernie from now on? Maybe, er, my second father and that we are all a really happy, tight knit family. Don't worry you two, somehow we'll all work this through with no problems." They all laughed, Ernest relaxed for the first time since Christine had arrived home, it was as if a major weight had at last been instantly lifted from all their consciousness.

"I suppose then that you better just call me Ernie, the milkman. I won't be seen even though, I'll always be there to provide a necessary backup service for this wonderful household."

"I would've put it slightly differently, but we both know what you mean." Christine teased.

"It's going to be strange having a man around us again, tell you what, why don't you sell up that large place of yours and move in here with mom, really I won't mind if you do."

"Now, now, let's take one step at a time." Christine finished her coffee and rose.

"Must fly, some of us must work and there's still one last piece of the puzzle to put in place. Bye you two, see you tonight, why don't we go out and celebrate now that this is all behind us and we have managed to sort out everything between ourselves." Late that afternoon she sat on the couch talking to Antonio having had explained her meeting with Norman Minter and what had been said.

"We need him and his conglomerate as a front to our activities as well as his also having the correct credentials that will take the family into areas we wouldn't even dream of. It's the old story, if you're not a member of the *'old boy'* club, then no matter what you do, you're never going to gain admittance and he will bring that to our family."

"Signora, this was an outstanding coup on your part and I understand now, why you just didn't want him just killed off. We've reclaimed a brother back into the fold and taken a major stride to cut ourselves free from America." His admiration for her had grown considerably over the last months. There was a gentle knock at the door and one of Antonio's men walked in and indicated something to him.

"Si, si, you can show him in." Christine turned and watched the doorway as the man stepped aside to reveal the visitor. Antonio walked towards the door and greeting the short man warmly with a bear hug, led him into the centre of the large room. The man stepped forward, gently took Christine's hand and kissed it.

"It's so good to see you once again."

"David Lividsky, yes its a pleasure because both you and you friend Bernard Marcus, did a very good job of work for the family and we are indebted to you. However, you've still got your work cut out, because it's now, you've still got to teach Norman Minter the ways of our people and help him through his initiation stages."

"He has agreed to everything then? I'm very surprised" The little lawyer grinned broadly.

"Surprised? David he had no other choice. What with our family and your Jewish community working in harmony, he was always bound to lose out?"

"I'm pleased we're now both on the same side and I agree, he'll become a great asset to the family, don't you think?"

"It's been an exciting adventure and a very profitable venture, let us hope this is the first of many." She laughed and nodded at her two associates.

FINIS

"FRANK GRAVES"

Copyright Frank Graves © 2000

All Rights Reserved

The Kixing

Frank Graves

ABOUT THE AUTHOR

Frank Graves is an author and film producer raised in South Africa and is the great grandson of Sir Thomas Maclear named as one of the foremost royal astronomers at the Cape of Good Hope. He is also distantly related to Robert Graves the renowned writer and poet who was a large inspiration for Frank to eventually take up writing. Robert Graves encouraged Frank to start writing with several correspondence letters and stories while still a boy at school.

His first published work was published in 1989 was a fictional political thriller named African Chess (Now revamped, updated and republished in March 2014). African Chess was loosely based on his South African upbringing and the then apartheid system in place before Nelson Mandela's release from prison or his death.

His next major work published by Marshall Cavendish in 1992 was an epic 832 page "The Ancestral Trail" was 'split' into two halves of 26 issues each, making a total of 52 issues in total, all contained consecutive page and issue numbers. The first half, published fortnightly throughout 1993, takes place within a mythological 'Ancestral World' that describes a boy's struggle to restore good to these worlds. After the initial international run that sold over 30 million copies worldwide, the second half of that series was then created and was published in 1994 and took place in the totally different 'Cyber Dimension' all about the same boy's attempt to find a way back to his own world. Graves has now updated and re-written the full "Ancestral Trail Trilogy" in the form of three major novels. In January 2014, the first section covering a journey through an 'Ancient World' within "The Ancestral Trail Trilogy" named "Long Ago & Far Away" in a 450 page novel was published. The second continuing section of the trilogy covers a 'Cyber World' will be published by mid-year 2014 and the third section of the trilogy, covering our 'Modern World' will be published before the end of 2014.

African Chess by Frank Graves is a newly updated and revamped conspiracy, adventure thriller originally published in 1990. Recent events in South Africa such as Nelson Mandela's Death, Oscar Pistorius's Trial, Shrien Dewani's Extradition for Murder, 16,259 Murders in 2012/13 and Epidemic Corruption have all helped to heighten attention and draw in a lot of focus on that country.

African Chess - The Story - Michael and Robert born at exactly same time and place at a remote hotel in one of South Africa's most beautiful regions are treated as equals until they grow up. Robert demands equality and falls foul of the dreaded South African police when he joins the African National Congress (ANC) as a freedom fighter. Both flee to England to escape and at Oxford Robert finds more racism. When the security chief Dirk tries to kill them, Robert is helped by his white brother Michael and beautiful cousin Sharon. Their family business empire gives him certain protection. He learns to wheel and deal on London's commodity markets and uses this financial strength to fight back at the apartheid system. African Chess is relentless suspense, with move upon counter move until final checkmate.

The Culling novel is his third published work during 2014 and the story is that Western Governments use scientific evidence that within a few years, their world faces disaster from uncontrolled population explosion; especially by burgeoning third-world countries probably creating extra desert regions to ruin the industrialised world. No government could openly admit that it intends killing tens of millions of unwanted people worldwide. A number of major international conglomerates collectively called "The Affiliation" are enlisted to conceal this man-made earthquake programme without any awkward questions being raised... It is a human survival war!

The Kixing is his fourth publicarion in 2014

Using hardened trained human fighters with lightweight gladiatorial designer armour, these very private illegal bouts are always held amid sumptuous black-tie dinner events especially laid on for the extremely rich and titled. In every vicious contest, the loser always being smashed to a pulp, critically maimed or better still and mercifully ...killed in full view of the sophisticated audience and is known as "THE KIXING". The reason for protection of this sport is the massive illegal gambling side with ensuing high stakes. There are never any other winners in commerce or sport when the conglomerate chairman promotes his beloved Kixing fights.

A major conglomerate attempts a hostile take-over of a small family company using dirty methods including professional and underhanded industrial espionage methods. However, the large group meets their match as the owners of the small firm that is Mafia connected resists the attempt. The chairman of the major group is also a well known boxing promoter, who when acquiring a bookmaking business using similar type tactics creates his own total undoing of his business empire.

(See the website at http://www.theancestraltrail.com for further detail on each New Book and the YouTube Video promotions)

The Kixing

www.ingramcontent.com/pod-product-compliance
Lightning Source LLC
Chambersburg PA
CBHW080838250626
47161CB00009B/3107